BOUND BY TIES DEEPER THAN BLOOD AND MARRIAGE

ELIZABETH SAVAGE—Her children had realized her bold dream of wealth and power. Would that dream now shatter, destroying them all in the process?

BEN SAVAGE—Her eldest son, he had given his life to build Midwestern Steel. Now not even the threat of death could shake him from power.

PAULINE SAVAGE—As Ben was driven to work, she was driven to pleasure, seeking the oblivion that would make her forget forbidden passion.

JAMES SAVAGE—Ben's son. He had disappointed his father, been denied his love. Now he would turn to others and bring scandal on the Savage name.

EVAN SAVAGE—Ben's brother. Love had sustained him until Ben destroyed that love. Now only revenge from beyond the grave could settle the score.

DYER SAVAGE—His plan to unseat his uncle Ben was perfect and his allies powerful. He was driven by the fanatical force of his own secret hatred.

TORN APART BY ...
FAMILY PASSIONS

Also by Shelley Katz

ALLIGATOR
THE LUCIFER CHILD
THE SHADOW PRESIDENT

FAMILY PASSIONS

Shelley Katz

A DELL BOOK

To my grandmother

Published by
Dell Publishing Co., Inc.
1 Dag Hammarskjold Plaza
New York, New York 10017

Copyright © 1983 by Shelley Katz

All rights reserved. No part of this book may be reproduced
or transmitted in any form or by any means, electronic or
mechanical, including photocopying, recording or by any
information storage and retrieval system, without the written
permission of the Publisher, except where permitted by law.

Dell ® TM 681510, Dell Publishing Co., Inc.

ISBN: 0-440-12482-4

Printed in the United States of America
First printing—November 1983

PROLOGUE

THE BEGINNING
Wales, 1919

The fierce mountains stood out against the quickly darkening sky, hulking giants in a timeless watch over the river. Rising from out of the valley, roughhewn menhirs startled the blue-black sky with primitive grayness.

Nobody knew what these ten-foot standing stones meant anymore. Perhaps they were symbols of Druid dieties whose names were long lost in the passage of four thousand years. Perhaps they were only old road signs or markers. There were many legends attached to these stones, myths that confused the old Druid dieties with King Arthur and the fruitless search for the Holy Grail. In the quickly falling darkness, these legends seemed to take on new forms and shapes, and suddenly the dim past that reached back to the time when pigs were just beginning to be domesticated became sharp and real.

Everything was as it had been then. There was no reminder in those ancient hills of a present filled with soot-gray men who mined the coalpits feeding the great steel mills of England. Here it was quiet. Only the brutal call of birds as they fell into the river in pursuit of fish disturbed the evening. And except for a stir among the damp green grass where Elizabeth Gwynne sat, nothing moved.

Elizabeth Gwynne was a monumental woman, rawboned, ugly, with a strong carved face and piercing blue eyes. She stood close to six feet tall, which gave her a kind of primitive timelessness like the hills she sat in, though she was no more than twenty-five.

Sitting very still, the setting sun glinting off her coal-black hair and carved features, there was a kind of magnificence to Elizabeth, perhaps even a beauty. But among the small, dark Welsh people she stood out as strange and ugly. They called her cawr, the giant. Elizabeth seemed not to care. She was the schoolteacher, at once respected and feared, and she walked through the streets of the village erect and proud, her roughhewn face staring straight ahead, her intelligent eyes always moving, taking in everything.

But inside the monumental woman there was a tightening in her chest, a heavy emptiness that had started this spring and, now that summer was upon her, was squeezing so sharply she found herself almost crying out in distress. She was loveless. She was childless. And she would always be so.

As she sat looking at her thick red hands and her square heavy body, the intense loneliness of the hills called out to her, deeply, disturbingly, awakening longings and dreams she had never felt before.

The summer night was hot. Already stars were beginning to gleam. Already twenty-five summers had passed. Yet still she remained, living her quiet life among the village children, teaching them things they did not want to know and would never use in the deep dark coalpits. Loveless. Childless. And it would always be so.

As Elizabeth watched the evening sky, she became aware of the sound of voices, far off but coming closer. Though she could not hear the words, she could tell the musical lilting voices belonged to the coal miners returning to the little pubs at the outskirts of the village, where they could drink the gray soot from their throats and, at least temporarily, from their souls. The singing voices reverberated against the black *bres*, setting up an echo that resounded through the valley. It was a lonely sound, and it made the large, ugly Elizabeth feel even more isolated and barren.

The silhouettes of the men were covered in moonlight, silvery, almost glowing. Their voices were drawing near, and the music sounded ghostly; the ancient Celtic words, fiercely passionate. There were five men, and Elizabeth could see them more clearly now. She knew all of them by sight except for a small, muscular, dark-haired man. He was almost a boy really; Elizabeth felt sure he couldn't be more than nineteen. His eyes were quick and dark with an intelligence not yet dimmed by his work in the mines.

As they passed below her, Elizabeth couldn't take her eyes from the young man. His voice was soft and beautiful, his gait muscular and athletic. She sat watching, disturbed by thoughts unclear yet riveting. The loneliness grew, the longing shuddered through her body. And suddenly she knew if there was ever to be a way out for her, it must come now while the summer heat was on the hills and the moonlight tipped the valley with silver, now while she was still young and alive, before the deathly emptiness set in forever and she became one of the lost.

Quickly she stood, rising out of the darkness, tall and strong. The sight of her, a dark shape in an even darker landscape, startled the men and their song faded.

Then one of the men laughed loudly. "Fach, it's Miss Elizabeth, the schoolteacher. Proper frighted me you did, coming out of the hills like that. I thought to myself I was seeing a cawr."

Elizabeth didn't answer, for indeed she did look like a giant. She stood there, large and magnificent, as roughhewn as the thrusting menhirs. Then rapidly she started down the hill. The thick green scrub plants tore at her stockings and shoes, making her take in breath sharply. But still she moved forward to the men, until she had joined them on the path.

Once again the men began to walk, undisturbed by Elizabeth's silence. People were often quiet in the hills of Wales, quiet and thoughtful, except in the hazy lighted pubs where the talk was constant and loud to keep off the Welsh winter chills and also the solitude.

Elizabeth was no longer aware of what she was doing. All she could feel was the intense emptiness inside of her and the disturbing strength of the young man with the intelligent eyes who was walking so close to her. She reached out her hand in the darkness and caught his. She could feel the young man startle in surprise, but she had turned from the sight of him, and her eyes were on the hills and the quickly appearing lights of the village. Still the young man said nothing. Elizabeth held his hand in hers, feeling the warmth and the humanity, almost breathtaking in its newness, and she knew that in a few moments the time would be lost.

Her voice came out of the darkness, soft yet urgent. "I would have you."

If the other men heard her, they said nothing, but the young man had heard. She felt his hand quiver, a shock went through his body, and a moment later he dropped back from the rest. She too slowed her pace, allowing the men to continue singing into the night.

These were the only words that Elizabeth said. She neither asked the young man's name nor did she want then to know it. Something else was important now. The rest would come in time.

She found herself leading him back to the grassy place on the hill from where she'd watched him only minutes before. It was as if something greater had possessed her. She could feel the heat of his hand spreading through her, until her whole body was electrified by it. There was a name for this heat, and Elizabeth knew it and understood it. But words had no more meaning than names, and she found to her surprise that she wasn't really thinking at all. Only acting instinctively.

The grass was wet. Slowly Elizabeth dropped to her knees. In the moonlight she could see just how beautiful he was, and the sight of him stunned her. Her hands found the tie of her skirt and she loosened it, staring at the young boy in mute wonder. She supposed she might lose her job as a schoolteacher, and jobs were hard to find in the coal country of Wales, but even this could not stop her now. The heat was rising in her, full and strong, and she leaned back into the damp soft grass and stared into the darkness. The young man stood over her, undoing his belt, and she turned her head away, unable to bear the sight of the strong muscular boy who stood so manfully over her, his silhouette blocking out the moon.

Then slowly he lowered himself onto her. Elizabeth's body caught fire; everything was alight. She felt his body pressing against her, and she shivered from the force and the wonder.

Suddenly the whole world seemed red and glowing. There was a terrible tearing pain as the young man forced his hardness into the center of her. She shuddered, invaded; the pressure was astounding. She couldn't fight it; her body was caught, motionless, in the aching pain.

Then gradually the pain receded, and the longing forced her body to his. Urgent warm ripples spread through her, widening and deepening, until her body was thrilling with it. Hunger drove her, pressing at her thighs and breasts, connecting them with an invisible cord of heat, building, until there was only her urgent thrusting body and the glistening strength of the boy above her. She was out of time, out of space, somewhere in the darkness of fear and animal exultation.

Then suddenly he was crying out, sharply, piercing the night. And then there was silence.

Elizabeth lay back, looking at the stars. It was intensely quiet. The young man lay next to her, but she no longer noticed him.

Everything was concentrated inward for Elizabeth. After the frenzied coupling, there was a peace, as if she could feel what was going on inside of her. As if in that moment of serenity, she knew she would have this child, that she would have this man, and all the half-formed hopes and dreams that had so suddenly been born in her this summer would be realized.

BOOK ONE

MIDLAND, OHIO
Summer, 1980

ONE

Every light in the house was burning, glinting off servants' quarters and gardens, illuminating rosebushes and hedges, leaving a steamy haze of light in the black summer night. A steady stream of cars rounded the long treelined driveway, and people poured out, a crazy-quilt procession of men and women in elegant evening attire, steelworkers in shabby attempts to modernize Sunday clothes, even two nuns, looking unashamedly awed.

Inside the house was the same unsorted confusion. Built at a time when a passion for the classical swept over the Midwest as rapidly as Dutch Elm disease, the house was a schizophrenia of authentic Greek statues, phony Roman frescoes, and tacky antiqued French chandeliers. A mob of people pressed through the rooms, shoving their furs or threadbare coats at cloakroom attendants, piling plates high at the thirty-foot buffet or heading for the roped-off dance floor in the living room where a ten-piece orchestra played to themselves and a few gray-haired protégés of the Arthur Murray school.

James Savage had timed his appearance to be just late enough to aggravate his father, without causing any permanent damage, but the knot of cars in the driveway wasn't moving, and he tapped nervously on the steering wheel of his Mercedes, his tall elegant body slouched over the leather seats like a sulky adolescent's. Though James was thirty-two, there was much of the adolescent about him, the same crazy shifting moods, the same glittering anger and need, especially when it came to his father. It was just one of the things he hated about himself.

Finally James caught the eye of Henry, a tall, loose-jointed black man who was as close to a family retainer as anyone in the North could manage. He was playing head parking attendant, jumping from car to car, revving the motors as he swung them away from the house and onto the treelined streets. As soon as he saw James, he came running and opened the car door.

"Don't worry, Mr. James. I'll take the car from here. Traffic's jammed up tighter than a reverend's asshole."

He chuckled to himself and helped James out of the car, then slid into the driver's seat, keeping the door open, one foot hanging out while he inched the car forward toward the house. But instead of walking to the house, James followed along by the side of the car, staring out at the phony Greek mansion with its white stucco porticoes and long statue-lined lawns. He lit a cigarette and watched the smoke pour lazily from his mouth. He was stalling for time.

"Everyone here?" he asked Henry after a while.

Henry nodded. "I reckon there isn't a person in Ohio who hasn't made an appearance. There's even a rumor that the governor might show up."

"No. I was talking about the family."

"Sure. The works. Your grandma, Aunt Pauline, Aunt Angela, Cousin Dyer. You know."

"Yeah, I know. Another command performance."

Henry smiled. It was an amiable black smile, the way it used to look in the fifties, reassuring, almost enveloping with goodwill and love toward white folks.

"Your father was looking for you earlier. He seemed kind of worried you weren't going to make it."

James laughed. "For my own father's sixtieth birthday? Why, I wouldn't miss it for the world."

Henry was still smiling at James amiably, but there was something behind his eyes that made James wonder what he was thinking. Henry had been with them since the beginning. He had seen so much. What had he thought of them all those years? The idea surprised James. After a while you got so used to servants it didn't occur to you that they might have thoughts.

"He really did seem worried about you showing up, you know."

"I'll bet. I can just imagine him going around saying, 'Where's my son? I need him here next to me.'" James imitated Ben's booming voice, then he laughed. "But you know as well as I, it's all an act. Dad knows I'll show. I always do. Maybe that's part of the problem."

James didn't even try to disguise the bitterness in his voice. He realized he was pushing Henry, trying to crack the amiable Stepin Fetchit manner, but he didn't understand why.

Henry was no longer smiling; his eyes were guarded. "It's quite a bash inside. He's got two bands, one for the older folks in the living room and a rock band in the basement. And you should see the dining room! He's got the biggest spread ever. This has to be the best party Mr. Savage ever threw."

"He's had enough practice."

"Yes, sir, Mr. Savage sure does love his parties." Henry's voice was getting blacker by the minute.

James's face was serious, torn with lines. "Have you ever wondered why he has all these parties?"

"Wondered?"

James pressed. "Yes, wondered, wondered."

While Henry's expression still didn't change, James felt sure he understood what he meant. Poor old Henry, he probably saw and knew everything. He was just a good survivor. That was undoubtedly why his father kept him around all those years. Ben was a man who respected survivors, being one himself.

"Do you think he does it to show off how rich he's become? Like all his millions for charities and benefits. I mean, Henry, you don't honestly think he gives a good god damn about crippled children or failing kidneys or anything besides Ben Savage, do you?"

The blank look was gone from Henry's face, and he seemed concerned. "Mr. James, you been drinking?"

"Sober as a judge. Just speaking the truth."

"I like your dad," Henry said softly. "I guess I almost love him. It's not just my job either. Though I'm not averse to eating. In fact, I've grown real fond of it over the years."

James interrupted. "You really do love my dad, don't you?"

Henry was turned away from James, watching the lighted house through the windshield. "Mr. Savage is the greatest man I'm ever likely to know."

James stomped out his cigarette. "You're right. He is a great man."

This was said with no sarcasm, and it was that which arrested Henry. He turned back from the windshield, but James was already gone, striding purposefully, almost angrily across the lawn, just as Henry remembered him when he was a little boy.

Elizabeth Savage sat on a stiff-backed chair in the corner of her son's crowded living room watching the parade of people. Even at eighty-six years old, riddled with arthritis and most probably cancer, she was a magnificent woman, as rawboned and primitive as the

Welsh hills she came from. Over the years her features had gained distinction; the old-lady clothing draped across her strong but stringy body gave her ugliness a power and force. Her once-round face was now elongated by gravity, and great folds of flesh hung from her cheeks like a basset hound's. But her eyes were still young, sardonic and alert, full of a cold appraisal that her family had learned to fear and respect.

Most of her family was clustered around her, like a stilted photograph, but as she stared out at the room, it was of the dead ones and the past she was thinking, the birth of her two sons and daughter, the death of her husband and one of her sons, the emigration, the poverty, the struggle to wealth, all the sadness and fear, pain, and delight, the memories of over sixty years since that night out on the hill, that night when everything had begun.

Her eyes rested on her grandson Dyer, but her mind was on the past. Nevertheless, Dyer mistook her glance for a question, and with his answer, he roused her back to today.

"If you're wondering where James is, so are we all."

Dyer was a real Savage, tall and thickset with clever blue eyes that were always in motion, more like his uncle Ben than his father, Evan. Elizabeth paused, thinking, then forced herself to stop. She supposed it was just that he was more like her. Yet despite the resemblance, Elizabeth didn't like Dyer, didn't trust him, though she knew in many ways it was Dyer who loved her best.

It was Angela, Dyer's mother, who answered. She sat off to the side of the group, a hard, erect little woman who wore her twenty-three year mourning like a badge. "You'd think James would come to his own father's sixtieth birthday party." She sounded pleased.

"Did you check the bar?" Dyer asked snidely. "If he isn't there, he hasn't arrived."

"Be here he will," Elizabeth snapped. "An important day it is for him too. For in every father's birth is the birth of his son."

Pauline, Elizabeth's daughter, snickered nastily. "Does that mean on your birthday, you always think of me?"

Pauline's taut, angry face was turned to her mother; her overdieted body poised as if to pounce. Elizabeth turned away out of disgust but also out of guilt.

"Of course, child," she answered slowly.

Pauline laughed. "I'll bet." Her eyes scanned the room, then finally rested on a burly young man in an ill-fitting suit. "Well, I'll

Family Passions 19

tell you something. I'm not thinking about you on my birthday. My mind is on more immediate things."

Dyer teased. "And what are they, Aunt Pauline?" He regarded his aunt's rebellion with a fascination born of disgust.

Pauline smirked but didn't answer. Finally she said, "Maybe James won't show. Maybe he's out on the town with one of his pretty friends." She said it with relish.

Elizabeth flinched but didn't pick it up. "I hope he's all right," she said softly.

Dyer laughed. "All right? James? He hasn't been all right in years."

Elizabeth turned away. It was a hell of a family, she thought to herself. A daughter who was a nymphomaniac and two grandsons, one whom she didn't respect but loved, the other whom she didn't love but respected. For in the end that was how she divided them. There were those she respected and those she didn't. With a stab in her heart she thought of her dead husband, Wynn, sitting by the fire, sipping tea, bent double by cares. She'd loved Wynn but she hadn't respected him. Well, there it was and she'd thought it and it was true. She had loved Wynn with the devotion of a mother rather than a wife. She had suffered at the withering of him; she had felt the terrible pangs of guilt that it had been she who had forced him from Wales to America and the exchange of one hard life for another. Every cough had shot through her like a knife. But no, she hadn't respected him; he wasn't a survivor. And her son Evan had been the same, and James too. In the end, there was only Ben—Ben who had been conceived that night in the hills. Ben who had started it all.

Once again Elizabeth's mind had drifted to the past. But Pauline was watching her now, and she tried to stop her mind from working in its old-lady round. She wondered if she hadn't gotten to the point of talking to herself. She saw them all, all the old ones, walking down the streets with their shopping, lips moving, chattering away to people who were long dead or who had long ago stopped caring. There but for the grace of money she went. But she knew it was the grace of Ben. It was Ben who had arranged her life the past forty years, Ben who had saved her, just as she had been saved all those years ago in the hills of Wales by Wynn.

Pauline whispered to Dyer, "Well, now, isn't this fun? Don't you just love family reunions? I do."

"Yeah, it's real fun," Dyer answered sourly. "I haven't had such a good time since Ben's Christmas party."

"You mean the one where Ben invited a fifty-voice choir to sing carols, and James got so drunk he pushed over the buffet?"

Dyer leaned to her. "I was remembering it more as the one where you took off with a twenty-one-year-old welder."

"Now, isn't that funny? I don't remember that."

"Let me refresh your memory. The next day Ben fired him, and he ended up on your doorstep crying and begging you to intercede."

Pauline giggled. "Well, I did, didn't I? After all, I'm just nasty, not heartless. And he was nice. If you know what I mean. Anyway, I felt bad for him. He had a pregnant wife."

"Like hell. He wasn't even married."

Pauline just laughed. She didn't really care. Not that it was impossible to hurt her, but the long lonely nights without the heat of another body hurt her even more. Of course, drugs helped and so did alcohol, but in the end it was only the contact of flesh that really allayed the horror, if only for a moment. For the horror was so great, nothing could fight it long.

"Still, he was nice," Pauline said wistfully. "And as big as a . . ."

"Enough!" Elizabeth barked angrily. She'd been trying not to listen, but it had become impossible. She supposed that Pauline had wanted her to. "Your brother's sixtieth birthday there is. And I won't have you spoiling it."

She glanced over at her daughter-in-law, Angela, to see if she'd been listening to all that had passed, but it was impossible to tell. Angela was just looking off into space, her little hard nutlike face impassive. Still, Elizabeth supposed she had heard and enjoyed it. Angela seemed to enjoy her mother-in-law's pain, and Elizabeth supposed, truth be told, the reverse was true.

"By the way," Dyer said amiably, "where *is* the birthday boy? I haven't seen him in a while."

This time Angela was listening. "He's probably in the basement printing up money to pay for all this."

"He'd better be," Dyer answered somberly. "I hate to think what this party's costing."

Pauline patted at her hair and smiled. "Oh, well, you're only sixty once. Except me. I'll never be sixty. Besides, he can afford it."

"Don't be so sure," Dyer said. "At least not if he keeps up like this. Midwestern is in trouble, big trouble. But of course you wouldn't know that. I doubt that you've ever even looked at the balance sheets we send you."

"Just the check stubs, nephew dear. As far as I'm concerned, as long as my money keeps rolling in, my brother can do what he likes."

Elizabeth said angrily, "Aye, and relieved he'll be to know that you approve."

Dyer chuckled and took another drink of his scotch. "Say what you like, Grandmother. Not even motherly love can deny the balance sheets. And Midwestern Steel is in trouble."

Just then Dyer looked up, and for a moment he thought he caught sight of Ben, walking up the elegant winding staircase to the bedrooms. Only a few seconds later a tall attractive blonde followed. Dyer glanced at his grandmother to see if she'd noticed, but if she had, she gave no sign. And anyway, Dyer didn't know if he had really seen Ben and the girl, or if it was merely what he had expected to see.

James waited outside the house a long while before he entered, but still the foyer was crowded with people. The two nuns were there now. James wondered what they must think of the clutter of fake French antiques, Greek statues, and Romanesque arches. He suspected that they thought it was beautiful.

James had always hated his father's taste. It was almost as if Ben prided himself on not knowing any better. He supposed to Ben it was masculine not to be able to distinguish between the beautiful and the ugly, and for all James knew, perhaps it was. He had problems enough in that area, so maybe it was macho to lack taste, except in women, and in that Ben had impeccable taste, running to an elegance and sleekness he'd once found in his wife and then lost forever, as if he were trying to obliterate her from his mind by duplication. It had been twenty years since James's mother had left Ben. And still the string of women, all pale and slim and rich looking. In many ways Ben was obsessed with women. He didn't love them; he didn't even seem to like them much, and he rarely saw them more than once. Perhaps what he enjoyed was rejecting them.

James looked around the foyer for his father, but he was nowhere in sight. Relieved, he pressed through the crowd and made his way to the bar, ordering a scotch and drinking it down thirstily. He could see his family across the room, but he stayed where he was. He would go to the family corner eventually. First he wanted to nurse his drink and his anger.

The two nuns had materialized next to him and were ordering ginger ale, looking around the room with shy pleasure. James felt sure this was the highlight of their year, possibly their lives, and oddly he found himself envying them that. But James supposed this was just part of his childish wish that at least someone in this world lacked the sophistication he increasingly hated but worshiped.

One of the nuns smiled uncomfortably at James. It was true what they said about nuns having peaceful eyes, or at least this one did, brown and soft behind her thick glasses. The other nun turned away, but for a moment James thought he saw a sadness behind the embarrassment.

"Isn't this a lovely party?" It was the nun with the soft brown eyes. Her voice was surprisingly feminine, almost sensual. "Mr. Savage is such a generous man. They say he invites everyone who works for him to his house at one time or another."

James nodded and took a drink of his scotch. She was just another of Ben's collectables. Ben was known as a man who took in all strays, beggars, thieves, nuns with charity on their minds, and they all adored him for it.

She stared at her drink. A maraschino cherry seemed to stare back like a bloodshot eye. "Do you work for Mr. Savage?"

"And how." There was a bitterness to James's tone that made the nun look up from her drink questioningly, and even the other nun lifted her eyes and fixed him with a probing stare.

James tried for a smile. He was losing it tonight. First Henry, now the nuns. Once again he glanced over at the family corner. His aunt Pauline was no longer there. He supposed she was headed for the room with the rock band. It seemed she liked youth more as she lost it herself.

The nuns were still watching James. Finally the one with the soft brown eyes said, "I can hardly believe it. I came to the door last week to get a donation for the Children's Home and Mr. Savage asked me to his sixtieth birthday party. I was so surprised by the whole thing that I accepted."

The other nun ventured. "For both of us."

The nun with the warm eyes shook her head and laughed. "Mr. Savage is a very kind man."

"There are those who'd disagree."

The nun's soft eyes were going over James's face. "Do you know Mr. Savage well?"

James was instantly sorry. "No. Not very. The truth is, I really don't know Mr. Savage at all."

James tried to take a drink of his scotch and discovered he'd finished it off. Life was full of disappointments. He ordered another, smiled at the nuns, then turned to leave. But before he could, he caught sight of his cousin, Dyer, steaming toward him, his sharp eyes fixing James like knives. It was too late for escape, and James waited for the inevitable like a lamb at the slaughterhouse gates.

"Seen your old man yet?" Dyer asked, holding out his glass for the bartender to fill.

"I only just arrived."

Dyer smirked. "He's been looking for you all evening."

"Henry told me. He said Dad seemed anxious that I wouldn't come."

"He was. You two have a fight or something?" Dyer's eyes too seemed to be probing.

"For a change? No, actually we didn't have a fight, at least nothing more than usual. We don't really fight much anymore. But then we don't have to. We know it all by heart. One of just has to say one word, then the other can write in the rest. It's a real time-saver." James laughed emptily. "Well, I guess I'd better pay my respects to the old cannibal. I don't suppose you know where he is now."

"I thought I saw him slinking off to one of the upstairs bedrooms with some chick."

Dyer shot James a look of jealousy, but James knew it was a pretense. In fact, he doubted that Dyer had any appetites except for work. It was only when he was hunched over the phone or sitting around the conference table that Dyer gave the impression of enjoying himself at all.

"Anyone else comment on my lateness?" James asked.

"Everyone noticed, if that's what you mean, but no one said very much. Except Pauline, who at this point isn't noticing much besides one of the welders from the mill. She's probably in the bedroom next door to Ben. Good old Pauline was higher than a kite and talking about, well, the only thing she ever talks about. And poor Grandma just pretended like she was going deaf. Jesus, I thought she was going to have a heart attack right there. But Pauline just kept repeating herself with this blissfully stupid expression on her face."

"Yes indeed," James said. "Another typical night at the Savages, full of spite, anger, and cruelty."

Dyer smiled tightly. "Drunk already?"

"Not yet. But I have plans."

Dyer held out his glass for the bartender to replenish. "Well, let me know when you are. I want to talk to you."

Fifteen minutes later James had paid his respects to the family corner and was feeling sufficiently drunk to talk to Dyer. But there wasn't enough liquor in his father's house to prepare him for their conversation.

The garden was empty of people now; the cars jamming the driveway were all stacked along the quiet neighborhood streets. The doors to the living room were thrown open, and Dyer and James could see the press of people illuminated, like an animated doll's house.

Dyer was staring hard into the darkness. "We would be in it for different reasons. But the outcome would be the same."

James looked at Dyer blankly. "I don't know what you mean. I don't even think I want to know what you mean."

"Sure you do. You want to get your father. I want to make him mine."

"Now I'm *sure* I don't want to know what you mean. You're talking about taking my father's business away from him."

Dyer laughed, but there was a tinge of anger in it and, under the surface, fear. "Don't overdramatize. I just want to spread some of the control of Midwestern around."

"I fail to see the difference."

"They didn't teach you much at Harvard."

"We were expected to be gentlemen. Gentlemen aren't supposed to know anything."

Dyer smiled, amused. As a boy he'd envied James's easy self-deprecating humor, his educated upper-class manner, and though he knew what a curse it must be to be James, still there was an attraction to it.

"I'm serious," he said finally.

"I know," James answered. "That's why I'm joking."

"Look, Midwestern is in trouble, right?"

James stared out at the garden. "We can ride it out."

"Like hell. The recession is killing us. Our orders are down twenty percent from last year, which was no record year either. To make matters worse, there are those lousy Japs who believe employment is more important than profits and are only too delighted to take a loss just to keep their coolies working. Between the big steel companies and the Japs, our nuts are being squeezed in a vice."

James didn't answer, and Dyer became angry. "Just look at the figures. Have you looked at the figures lately? We're thinking of shutting down one of our ovens. You do at least know what that means."

Dyer was hulking over James. So much like Ben, it was startling.

"Okay, okay, so we're in trouble. We've been in trouble before."

"This time is different. This time we could go under."

"You don't really believe that?" James asked. He was mildly surprised, but in truth he didn't care. He wondered if this was because he, like everyone else, had unlimited trust in his father, or if he really didn't care. James had no idea what it would be like to be poor, but he supposed it couldn't be much worse than things were. Of course all that was easy for him to think when to him being poor was having a woman in to clean only twice a week. Briefly he considered how Dyer would fare being poor. He decided he probably wouldn't even notice it.

"The answer is to diversify," Dyer continued, as if James had not said anything. "Buy chicken franchises or rental car agencies or whorehouses, whatever. We can use our losses as a fairly attractive tax advantage. It could be done so easily."

"Except for Ben. 'Midwestern is steel and only steel,' " he quoted.

"He's a god damn dinosaur. He'll ruin this company."

"Well, it's his company to ruin. He built it."

"From my mother's money and my father's soul." Dyer paused. He rarely mentioned his late father, Evan, and when he did, the emotion it called up was powerful, especially when it was in relation to his uncle, Ben. "Besides, it's not his company to ruin anymore. It's a public company."

"He owns fifteen percent."

"Sure, and Grandma has ten. You own five. I own five. And there's Aunt Pauline's five. Not to mention the fifteen percent my father left. For Christ sake, even your mother received one and a half percent in her divorce settlement."

"And Ben controls it all."

"We'll see if he controls as much as he thinks. Blood may be thicker than water, but it isn't thicker than money. And they all like their money. Aunt Pauline. My mother. Your mother. Even Grandma."

James shook his head. "Life isn't as simple as that."

But Dyer just smiled slyly. "That's where you've always made your mistake. Life is exactly that simple." Dyer turned away. "Think about it," he said. Then abruptly he left, striding across the lawn back toward the house.

James didn't move. Dyer had shown his hand without considering that James might betray him. He was surprised, faintly flattered, and very scared.

Suddenly all the lights in the house went out. There was blackness for a moment, then a flash and sixty tiny bright lights gleamed fairylike from a procession of birthday cakes. There was the sound of two hundred voices singing "Happy Birthday" to Ben. And James wondered if indeed this would be a happy birthday for Ben.

TWO

Midwestern Steel crouched at the edge of town like a huge prehistoric beast, gated against the world by barbed wire and fences, glittering cold gray and rust in the quickly gathering morning light. Great steel structures, open on all sides, sprawled endlessly down the network of company roads. They looked like skeletons of long extinct creatures, only bigger, much bigger; one of them stretched so far into the horizon that the curvature of the earth had had to be taken into consideration when it was being constructed.

Many of the skeletonlike buildings were fed by a procession of railroad cars, steam shovels, and giant cranes, dipping into mountains of coke and taconite, then disgorging their contents into them. Suddenly furnace doors were flung open and brilliant molten flames shot across the silent gray landscape.

It was like the beginning of the world. There was a boom as of

Family Passions 27

thunder, intense, deafening, and the blast furnace lay exposed to the world. All at once everything was alight with molten steel, licking red, yellow, orange, blue-white, green-white, throwing sparks into the air. It was all liquid and moving cataclysmic light, shrieking with power and heat and noise.

Then once again the doors closed and Midwestern became gray and muffled, a world of rusty steel buildings, piles of coke and iron, long empty company roads.

Though the morning shift was just beginning, there were no people around. Most of Midwestern was run by unseen hands, hidden well away from the terrible heat and noise, encased in the silence of glass booths. Still, signs of the men were everywhere: a discarded Coca-Cola can clattered over the silty ground; a torn jeans jacket hung over a rusty steel beam.

Far up on a catwalk that stretched the entire length of the mile-long hot, rolling mill, Ben Savage hung over the railing watching the enormous ingots of steel being tortured into thin sheets. Wearing a construction helmet, cobalt glasses, and company overalls, he didn't look different from any of the strong, tobacco-chewing men who fed the furnaces. As he leaned against the railing, his ears filled with sound, his eyes startled by the brilliant flaming steel, Ben felt as he had at fifteen when he was just one of the bakebrains, the band of crazies who used to feed the inferno of the blast furnace.

Ben turned and saw the men in the soundproof booth behind him trying to catch his eye. He knew all of the men by name, he even knew the names of their wives and their children; they were like family to him. He gave them the thumbs-up sign, then the finger before he turned back to the sight of steel.

Even at sixty, Ben Savage was a magnificent man, tall, gray haired, blue eyed, with a broad strong chest. His arms were thick and muscular, his hands wide and scarred with remnants of long-ago injuries impossible to recall, some not even noticed at the time in the brawling heat of the furnace. He was a steelman, a true steelman, not the Harvard-educated businessman of today whose sole knowledge of steel came from press releases or slightly phony P&L statements. Ben loved steel, the feel of it, the look of it, the fire that never burned out. He'd built an empire out of it, small perhaps by U.S. Steel standards, but thriving and solid. Midwestern was something quite remarkable in the multinational world of today, a family-run, if not owned, steel company, and its prosperity was due almost entirely to Ben, forged from a single-mindedness that had left friends, enemies, and even lovers either shattered or dead.

Ben watched as two red-hot ingots were released. They fell onto the rollers and with a crash were hurtled back and forth, roaring with noise as they collided like two giant suns, shooting glittering sparks hundreds of feet into the air. Ben felt a shiver pass through him; every muscle in his body was alive, and he leaned even farther over the railing, almost as if to touch the molten mass.

Tom Lindsay spotted Ben and agilely climbed the ladder to the catwalk. Though he was close to sixty-three years old, tall, with stooped shoulders and thick glasses, looking almost like a professor, he too was a steelman and physical activity came easily to him.

Tom stopped when he came to Ben, but his eyes were on the crashing ingots, staring at the brilliant cataclysmic light as if it were the first time he was seeing it. Even now that Tom was head of Research and Development with his own pine-paneled office, well-stacked secretary, and well-stocked bar, he still lived most keenly when he was out on the floor. He had been a laborer, and laboring was the great divider. Somehow if a man had sweated to earn money it made him a different kind of person, or at least he thought of himself as different, which came to the same thing.

"Look at that, will you?" Ben said after a while. "You know, I've seen it for forty-five years, and I still get just as big a kick out of it as the first time."

Tom smiled. "Like sex, huh?"

"Better. You don't have to talk to an ingot in the morning."

"Or discuss your relationship."

Ben laughed. "And they don't get pissed off when you've got to work late."

Tom sighed. "Yeah, lad. And even when you're eighty years old and your dick's as dried up as a prune, they'll still be around."

"Speak for yourself, you limp Scot. I plan on dying at a hundred and five in the arms of a woman, shot by a jealous lover."

Tom was watching Ben with a look of understanding and love that reached back forty-five years. "And I thought you didn't plan on dying at all," he said after a while.

"Hey, reality encroaches after a while. No, I'll settle for going out with a bang."

"I want to die peacefully in my sleep, my whole family around me."

"How morbid."

"Well, you're the one who brought it up."

"I was talking about something dramatic, being shot or maybe self-immolation." Ben paused and suddenly there was sadness in his voice. "Yeah, I don't know how I'll die, but it'll be a grand death, I promise you." He fell silent, then finally he said, "I read your report on Anti-Cor."

"I think we'd better drop it, Ben. It's just too expensive to produce. It's cost a bundle in research so far, and we're no farther along than the day we started."

"Maybe if we modify the hot rolling."

"Maybe pigs can fly. Do you have any idea what that'd cost?"

Ben smiled. "Hey, that's your department."

"Thanks a lot. Well, you can take it from me it'd be a lot. If this Anti-Cor is ever going to be cost effective, we're going to have to change it at the formula."

"So then alter the formula."

Tom sighed and put his weight against the railing. "As you well know, that's just what I've been trying to do. With nil success. Maybe the whole thing is a bum idea. Maybe we'd better just drop it and cut our losses."

"You don't believe that."

"No. Not really. But I'll tell you what I do believe. I believe we haven't got the facilities to develop it. We're a small company. U.S., Bethlehem, Armco, they can afford to blow a lot of money. We're chickenshit compared to them. We'll bleed ourselves dry."

"Sounds to me like you're angling to get more money allotted for development."

"I wish that were true. No, I'm not angling for anything. Much as I hate to say it, I think we should drop the whole idea."

Ben hesitated. "There's a chance to get a government contract with it."

"What exactly do you mean by government?" Tom asked warily.

Ben avoided his eyes. "Remember? They're the guys who take all that money at the end of the year."

"Cut the shit."

"Okay, okay. Army, Air Force, you know."

"That's what I figured. You're better off without those jokers."

"Don't tell me what I'm better off without. Have you seen this month's figures? Detroit is on its ass. Everyone's selling. No one's buying. For Christ sake, this country's getting worse than England, and the Japs are becoming the new Americans. Jesus, Tom. I don't know. Sometimes I begin to think I just don't understand this world anymore. I swear to Christ, Arabs climbing off the backs of camels and settling into the front seats of Rolls-Royces. What's happened to Yankee ingenuity? Hell, no one even hates us anymore. I went to Mexico last week, and you know what? I didn't see one 'Yanqui Go Home' sign. Shit, why bother? They're all over here, selling us oil."

Tom held to the subject like a bulldog. "I'll give you business isn't good, lad. But I still say it isn't worth it. One of the best things about Midwestern is we don't deal with the military, just home appliances and Detroit. Well, good for us."

"Jesus, Tom, don't tell me you're going hippie on us."

Tom laughed. "You're a little behind the times, Ben. That was the sixties. No, look, in the end, the American economy will come around. Sure, defense is big now. But the next administration can take it all away, just like that. With a government contract, you're exposing yourself to the winds of change even more than with business."

"Bullshit. I don't believe that's your objection."

"Okay, have it your way. I'm a hippie. But whatever, Anti-Cor isn't going to save Midwestern."

Ben tensed. "Save Midwestern? Things aren't that bad, you know."

"I know. But I don't like the past few months' financial reports."

"Like? What's there to like? But let's not commit suicide over them. Midwestern's had some scrapes before."

"Not like this."

Ben shook his head. "No, Tom. Exactly like this. Only they never used to spook you. You're starting to act like an old man."

"Haven't you noticed? I *am* an old man. And so are you."

Ben laughed. "Like hell I am."

"It'll catch up with you, lad. Christ, some mornings I feel like Methuselah. Of course there are other mornings when I only feel a hundred and five." Tom was silent, thoughtful, then finally he asked tentatively, "You don't ever think about the old days, do you, Ben?"

"Once a thing is past, it no longer exists for me."

"Well, I think about the past."

"You aren't going to give me that malarkey about being happier then and it's the struggle that counts, are you?" Ben asked.

"We had our good times."

"Aye, yeah, we had good times. But we've got them today. You've got a wife and children and even grandchildren, and a big fancy house on First Street and a sailboat on the Ohio River. You can't tell me the good old days aren't right now, today."

"It's different. Not that it isn't good, but it's different. Hey, Ben, you remember the day we walked out of old man Healey's office and we knew we had him, he was going to back us in our own company, and we weren't going to be dirty steelworkers anymore? Jesus, Ben, remember? We ran all the way to your mother's house, sliding on the ice, banging and hitting one another and shouting. You, me, and Evan. Screaming like a bunch of drunks, though that was one Saturday afternoon we were stone-cold sober. And remember we bought sweet potatoes off that old guy Pergament, on the streets, and how crusty and hot they were? And sweet. My God, why did food taste so sweet then?"

"It still does, Tom. No, I remember it like it was a dream, another life. The only thing that counts is today. And maybe tomorrow. The past is for old men."

Ben fell silent, then turned back to Tom. "Hire on as many people as you need. I want Anti-Cor and I want it quick."

Tom shook his head. "Even if we do that, and it works, we aren't going to be ready in time for any government contract that's coming up for bids now. Even if you ran overtime, which would be economic suicide, we'd never make it."

"Not if we expand facilities meanwhile."

"And push our costs up even higher? Whatever we gained by changing the formula would be put back into retooling. It's too expensive to produce, leave it at that."

"Let me worry about it."

"Until the balance sheets come rushing in like the Red Sea." Tom tried to catch Ben's eye, but he was staring into the molten light, his expression well hidden. "Maybe Dyer's right. Maybe it's time to start thinking about another way out, like diversifying."

"No!" Ben snapped.

Tom waited for Ben to continue, but he was silent, staring straight ahead into the heart of the fire. "Just no, huh? No explanation?"

"I don't need to give any."

Tom's voice was becoming tense and tight. "Hey, Ben, since when has Midwestern Steel been a dictatorship?"

Ben turned on him. "And since when have you started doubting my ability to run it?"

"I'm not doubting you, lad. I'd trust you with my life. More, I'd die for you. But you're fallible. And anyway, since when have you doubted my ability to know what's worth pursuing and what should be dumped?"

They had reached an impasse, and both of them knew it. Though neither of the men had raised his voice, the tension had grown. Usually when they disagreed, they screamed and shouted at one another, and then it was over. But this time was different, and they were both aware of it and feared it.

A voice came over the intercom. "Mr. Ben Savage. Call on line one."

It took Ben a moment to break from Tom's stare. He moved to the wall and hit the intercom button. "Tell Carrie I'll call whoever the hell it is back."

There was a hesitation, then the voice returned. "Ben, she says it's important. Senator Morrison from Washington."

Tom was shocked. His face grew tight with irritation. "You've been talking to Morrison about Anti-Cor?"

"In general. I told you before, there's nothing to worry about." Ben stopped. Anger was making red blotches on his face, but his voice was calm and even. "We need Anti-Cor, Tom. I'll give you anything you want, but make it work."

Tom was silent for a long while. "I'll do my best," he answered at last. "No guarantees, but I'll try."

Ben smiled, but still the angry blotches of red remained on his face. "That's all I'm asking."

The men watched as the two new ingots fell to the rollers and began crashing and pulling apart, and when Ben turned back, all the tension of before was gone.

"You know, Tom, I wonder what happened to that old guy Pergament. The one who sold sweet potatoes on the street."

Tom shook his head sadly. "Dead, Ben. They're probably all dead by now. Don't you realize that was over forty years ago?"

Senator Morrison's voice boomed through the phone, rich and well fed. "Ben, you old dog! How in the heck are you?"

Ben hit the buzzer for his nephew, Dyer, to come into his office, then, cradling the phone between his shoulder and neck, he leaned

Family Passions 33

back in his swivel chair and clasped his hands behind his head. "Never been better, you thief!"

Ben was smiling broadly, his big burly body relaxed and confident yet thrilling with anticipation. This was business, and there was little that made Ben feel as good as business. "I assume you called because news travels fast," he said heartily.

"Well, there is a rumor that Midwestern's interested in bidding on the new F four twenty-three."

"My, my, you just can't keep anything secret these days."

"I'll bet you didn't exactly try either. I hear you have some new kind of process."

"Alloy, John. Alloy."

"Well, whatever. Always glad for some fresh blood. In fact, I've wondered why you didn't join the fray before." He hesitated. "So when in the heck are you coming out here?"

"I hadn't really thought about it." Ben's voice was sly.

"Well, think about it. I've got a couple of places I could take you that would make Midland look like the hick town it is."

"Midland suits me fine. I always seem to find everything I need here."

"Yeah, I'll just bet you do. From what I hear, you're the eighth wonder of the world when it comes to finding what you need. But it still might be a good idea if you came down here. Pronto."

Dyer walked in, and Ben motioned for him to sit down. Dyer noted that Ben's eyes were sparkling with delight, and he raised his eyes in response. He was listening.

"Yeah, sure, John." Ben said heartily. "How's the beginning of next week?"

"ASAP, if you know what I mean," Morrison answered. "Look, Ben, I'll level with you. I carry a lot of weight over at the Pentagon."

"Don't I know it. I can't go anywhere without seeing your ugly puss splashed across the TV screen. By the way, you've put on weight."

"Haven't we all," Morrison said stiffly. "Look, I want you to understand what I mean. I can't promise you this contract, but believe me, I know exactly how important it is to you, and I could put together a little meeting. There's me and Senator Weinstein of Illinois and Representative Persky of New York. We're all interested in seeing Midwestern do well."

This stopped Ben. Suddenly his face became tight and the blood began spreading through it. Dyer watched Ben closely; he could tell something was wrong, though he couldn't be sure exactly what it was.

Ben sat up in his chair, clutching the receiver tightly; his body was rigid and angry. "You aren't saying what I think you're saying?"

Morrison retrenched. "Look, Ben, come down here and we'll talk."

"Now just hold on. I want to know what you mean."

Dyer was leaning forward, trying to read the expression on Ben's face.

Morrison's voice had become softer, less healthy and robust. "Ben, it's okay in Ohio to play by schoolboy rules. But Washington is the big guys. It's major league and it's tough."

"But rewarding?"

"That's not the point."

"Then what is the point? Or am I growing senile?"

"Look, Ben, I'm not going to argue with you. I know exactly what Midwestern needs, and I can tell you how to get it."

"And it isn't necessarily by coming in low man on the bidding."

"For Christ sake, Ben. You can't come in low man. Okay? You've got problems with Anti-Cor. It's too damn expensive to produce."

Ben was shocked. "How in the hell do you know that?"

"I know. That's enough. So you've got three choices. Either bid high and lose the contract. Bid low, get the contract, but lose your pants and probably the company in the process."

"Or?"

"Sweeten the pot."

"I'm hanging up the phone now, John."

"Think about it, Ben."

"Like hell, John!" Ben slammed down the phone, his eyes wild. "Fucking bastard wanted a bribe. Can you believe that?"

Dyer didn't flinch. "You should have given it to him."

"What are you, crazy? First off, Midwestern is clean, and it'll stay clean. Second off, even if I were so inclined, which I am not, it's too damn dangerous."

"Not if you're careful."

"Jesus Christ, you been on this planet the past few years? Haven't you ever heard of Abscam, for example?"

Dyer shrugged. "They were just stupid."

Ben stood and walked to the window. He stared out at the soot-gray mill that lay just beyond the glass. There was nothing like the sight of a steel mill in full blow. It was something he never tired of watching.

He said softly, "Am I going nuts or is everyone else?"

"Hey, come on. You can't play Mr. Clean with me. I've been here for years. I've seen you at work."

"I've never given a bribe in my life. Not even when those EPA jokers were creaming in their pants, and I knew I could save Midwestern millions of dollars."

"Everything is relative. You've done other things that weren't exactly kosher."

"There's a difference."

"Like hell there's a difference. You've made a big mistake turning Morrison off like that."

"I told you, Midwestern doesn't give bribes."

"It just goes bankrupt?"

"Yes, if necessary."

Dyer sneered. "Well, I'm glad at least you're not being rigid about it."

Ben glanced at his phone to let Dyer know he wanted him to leave. It was a hint Dyer was delighted to take. As he stood and headed for the door, he began to get the feeling he might win this one. Ben was watching him, his eyes hard and probing. For a moment Dyer worried that Ben knew what he was thinking, but then he relaxed. Ben was a man who was totally consumed by his own thoughts and dreams; he couldn't see beyond himself.

"Well, it's your company," Dyer said as he stopped at the door.

There was something in Dyer's tone that caught Ben. He turned and watched Dyer smiling pleasantly at him. Dyer's huge body was hulking at the doorway; he seemed almost too large for the room. In every movement, every muscle of Dyer's body, Ben could see himself and his mother, his whole family and all the generations he knew of only from half-heard stories, back to the trees when the Savages had lived up to their name. Yet behind the jarring familiarity of movement and gesture was someone Ben didn't recognize, a stranger, and a dangerous one at that. He wondered for a moment who that stranger was. He felt sure he was someone he knew but couldn't place. And then the look was gone, and Ben wondered if he had seen it at all.

"That's right." Ben's voice was full of a warning that surprised even him. "It's *my* company. And don't you forget it."

Dyer laughed. "How could I? You're always around to remind me."

There was something in Dyer's laugh, just as there had been in his movements, that gave Ben a feeling of intense foreboding. As Dyer left the room, Ben quickly turned back to the window, trying to shake off the presentiment, blocking out all the questions to which he had the answers. It was probably just that he'd been feeling edgy lately. He supposed with the figures being so bad it made sense to be edgy, especially after the phone call he'd received from Morrison.

Ben stared out at the gray and rust world outside the window, his mind revolving over the problem. If Tom worked hard and luck was with him, maybe they could get Anti-Cor off the ground before all of the bids were in. Licking Anti-Cor would solve all of Ben's problems, even his misgivings about Dyer. There wasn't a stockholders' meeting for another nine months, by which time they'd be going into production, and any concern he might have about Dyer's making a frontal attack would quickly evaporate.

Ben felt himself relaxing. Tom wouldn't let him down. He never had; he never would.

THREE

Elizabeth Savage prowled her Victorian monstrosity of a house like a rancher his land. Night was just beginning to close in, and the red light of evening threw highlights across the dark heavy living-room furniture and onto the patterned carpets. Elizabeth looked around the old-fashioned room with little attachment. Though she had lived in the same house for over thirty-five years, she still felt like a stranger in it.

In truth, Elizabeth always felt detached from her surroundings. The only place she'd ever felt completely comfortable was the house Ben had bought her in Wales. And now she couldn't even visit it anymore; traveling was too hard, the loneliness and silence of the Welsh countryside too frightening. The fact was, she was scared of dying there, alone, uncared for, and at this point dying played a great part in her thoughts and plans. Not that she really believed she was going to die. It seemed impossible that one day her world would cease and there would be dark shadowy sleep forever. But of course it wouldn't be dark restful sleep; it would be something far less poetic, a corruption, decay. She shuddered violently. Better to stick to the lie of the centuries and call it sleep.

She wondered if anyone really believed he was going to die. Certainly as people got older, they spoke about it all the time; certainly they must know it was true. But to believe that everything you worked for, dreamed of, and did would end suddenly, finally. No, it was impossible. She supposed half of life was pretending. You pretended to grow up, to be parents, to be grandparents, to run companies, and so old people were probably just pretending that they were going to die. But believing in it was something else entirely.

Elizabeth glanced at her watch. It was six o'clock, time for her to start cooking dinner. She didn't feel much like eating, but then she never did. It wasn't just the usual lessening of appetite that old people had, but the pain. She could feel her meals moving through her crippled old body, churning in her, sometimes even tearing at her insides. Still, she knew if she didn't eat, it would be the beginning of the end.

Elizabeth felt as if she were perched at the edge of a precipice, the fall to senility and death a constant danger, so she watched vigilantly for signs of weakening. She didn't allow herself a maid, only a cleaning woman. It seemed vital that she continue to care for herself, feeling if she started allowing people to do things for her, to take over her life, she would lose herself. She would already be dying. But as long as she cooked and cleaned and ate her meals, no matter how difficult it might be, she would still be Elizabeth. She was still winning.

Elizabeth walked to the kitchen shakily, leaning on the walls for support. Her arthritis was bad tonight, and her stomach felt very hard and round. She shut out the pain and thought about Ben. Sometimes in the evening he would stop by after work. He rarely stayed long, just enough to have a drink and review the day with her, but it had become a focal point to her. Though she never knew when he'd pay these visits, she preferred it that way. Otherwise she might be tempted to pull off her clothes and go to bed right after dinner, another sign of weakening. This way she stayed dressed and fighting long into the evening, only half watching television, but up and about nonetheless. This way she still existed as a person.

As Elizabeth looked into the refrigerator, her stomach contracted sharply in response. She closed the door, but quickly forced herself to reopen it. She took out two eggs, one slice of bread and some butter, walked over to the stove, lit the gas, and swirled the butter in a frying pan. The smell of melting butter was thick and heavy, and her stomach turned wretchedly, but she made herself continue, taking comfort in at least the soothing ritual of cooking.

Often she asked herself why she clutched so crazily to life. Why not, when everything was so difficult, just slip slowly into the quiet of old age? The answer never changed. It was the family, always the family. Oddly, it wasn't even individual members of the family that meant so much, rather the family as a whole, the name, the concept of family. What else could justify her fighting through everything, the terrible voyage to America with its sickness and filth, the long trip from New York to Ohio with its hunger, the terror of the great sprawling country called America that didn't care, and the grief of losing her husband, Wynn? Why had he died if not for the family? Without the family, her mourning and loss and loneliness and bitter disappointments—everything that went into making a life—meant nothing. But with it even the pain and suffering became something magnificent, and nothing could diminish the splendor.

It was this, much more than the so-called life-force, that made Elizabeth want to live. Deep inside she feared that once she was gone, there would be nothing to keep the family together. Everyone was pulling away from each other; with every passing year the fabric of their family was tearing, and she alone was the cement. Her death would mean more than the loss of her life, it would mean the loss of the justification for ever having lived at all. And so she pressed herself on, day after day, year after year, because she knew it was worth it.

Elizabeth cracked the eggs into a pan, placed the bread in the toaster, and made up her tray. The eggs began splattering and she was overwhelmed by the warm sickening smell of food. She forced herself to ignore it and think about Ben. If Ben came over tonight she would tell him about Dyer's visit, though what she would tell him about it, she didn't know. Why had he come? What was he after? Dyer was not a man to waste his time on old people; he was not a man to waste his time on people at all, unless he wanted something. The question was, had he gotten what he wanted from her? She wasn't sure. They had talked about the troubles at Midwestern, the recession, the figures. But he had asked nothing of her. Yet he had wanted something. Again she wondered if she had given it to him.

Dyer had laid out papers on the dining-room table, placing them in orderly rows, like lines of soldiers before the battle. Was that what it was, a battle? Elizabeth thought it was. Most of the papers and reports were ones Elizabeth had seen many times, yet in a line they told a story she had not allowed herself to see before.

Dyer went through them slowly, yellow light spilling onto his head from the overhead chandelier, making his blond, close-cropped hair almost disappear.

"Look here, Nairn." When they were alone, Dyer always used the Welsh word for grandmother. "In the fiscal year 1977–1978, Midwestern spent a total of—"

Elizabeth interrupted him. "Aye. You can stop it right there. Old news these figures are, and none the wiser I'll be when you're finished."

"Like it or not, these figures speak the truth."

"And what truth is that then?"

"Midwestern has to do something and do it quick."

Elizabeth stared at him. "Something, is it? And what is this something when it's at home?"

"Diversification is one answer. And I think the best. The point is, we shouldn't just be heading bull-like in the direction we're going. And Ben has to be made to see it."

Elizabeth laughed sharply. "To me you've come to persuade Ben Savage? I couldn't persuade that boy of the color of the sky from the moment he was born. Twenty-seven hours in labor I was. Twenty-seven hours, lying there all in a sweat and a heat, saying all kinds of crazy things, trying to persuade him to come out. But Ben Savage was sticking where he was, all warm and cozy, and he didn't come out till he had a mind to. Then out he came, all in a rush, announcing his coming to the world with the scream of a banshee. Make no mistake, from the day our Ben was born, no control did I have, unless it was something he wanted in the first place."

She fixed Dyer with a cold stare. "Besides, not sure am I that I want to persuade him. Diversification has a nice ring on the tongue, but that means nothing. Bad times there are now, bad times and recession. But it's ever like that, good times, bad times, then good again. Wait till you're as old as I, then you'll see. Everything passes, both good and ill. Today is hard times, but tomorrow the sun will be shining."

"Not for steel. Steel is dead."

"And what will they be making cars out of then, cow dung?"

"No. Steel. Japanese steel. And why not? They'll all be Japanese cars."

"I never thought to see it. Prepared you are to give in without a fight. But no. That isn't it. From the moment you came in I've been tickling my brain to figure out what you're up to." She turned on him. "What are you up to, then, Dyer?"

"I told you, diversification."

"Diversification of what? Power? Is it a fight you're looking for, whilst pretending to avoid it?"

Dyer's eyes grew cold. He began packing away the papers in his briefcase. He could feel his grandmother watching him, but he didn't turn back to her. Then suddenly he felt her hand on his shoulder, and he jumped instinctively.

Elizabeth sighed. "So nervous are you of your old nairn that you shrink at her touch?"

Dyer tried for a smile. "Of course not. I've just been working too hard."

"Aye," she repeated. "Too hard."

Dyer left shortly after that, and Elizabeth had felt unsettled ever since. If Ben stopped by she could discuss it with him. He would know. And yet she sensed that he would not know, and that she and only she could understand. Elizabeth had feelings about things, as if the older she became and the farther she grew from the world, the more she understood about it.

Elizabeth prepared her tray, took it into the living room, and set up a table next to the television. The local news was still on, and she watched the long procession of fires, robberies, murders, and rapes as she slowly ate her dinner. It seemed appalling to sit chewing, while the agonies of life were paraded before you. But she supposed it wasn't all that different from the legends she'd listened to as a girl. She could imagine the children sitting openmouthed in front of the television, listening to tales of Vietnam and the assassinations of presidents as she had listened to the legends of King Arthur.

* * *

The doorbell rang just as Elizabeth finished her dinner. Ben was leaning against the threshold, a smile on his face. His jacket was slung over his shoulder, his tie was off and his collar unbuttoned; still he looked as if the day were beginning, not ending.

Elizabeth turned from him without a word and began making her way back to the living room, showing little pleasure, though in fact she could feel her energy returning, her pain receding, and even her brittle bones felt less fragile. "I expected you," she said flatly.

"I wouldn't be surprised. You're getting spookier by the day." Ben was smiling. Despite the coldness of his mother's greeting, he knew how much his coming meant to her. He went directly to the liquor cabinet, poured himself a scotch, and flopped into a chair.

Elizabeth allowed herself a sherry and sat savoring it as she did the prospect of the visit. Finally she said, "Our Dyer was here earlier."

Ben drank some of his scotch. "Yeah? What did he want?"

"Your neck, I think."

Not a muscle in Ben's face moved, and yet Elizabeth thought she saw something close to pain flickering across his eyes. He took another sip of his scotch and stared at the window though the curtains were drawn against the night.

Finally he turned back to her. "Well, did you give it to him?"

Elizabeth smiled. It seemed impossible that Ben could think she'd do anything like that. She looked at Ben but he was staring at the window again, and suddenly she realized that he wasn't worried that she'd sell him out on purpose or even by mistake. There could be only one reason she would desert him—for the good of the family, for Midwestern.

"I asked, did you give it to him?" Ben was still turned away from his mother, but she could sense the strain in his face.

"Better than that you know me, Ben Savage." Elizabeth fell silent. Though she loved Ben fiercely, violently, she loved him without any insipid tenderness, and she had to continue. "Still, what about the figures? Terrible they are, make no mistake. I didn't need Dyer to tell me that."

"Did he talk to you about diversifying?"

"Roughly translated. Hard it is to tell with Dyer, though blunt and to the point he is at the same time."

"You know I'm against it."

"The question is why."

"I've been through the reasons a dozen times. We know nothing but steel. The only way we could successfully diversify is by bringing in new people, allowing control of Midwestern to slip from the family."

"That's the argument you give to me, because you know it's one that will appeal."

Ben smiled at Elizabeth. Though he never underestimated her, sometimes her caginess did catch him off guard, and at those moments the years fell away, and the ancient stringy woman was transformed to what she had been.

"Say what you like," Ben answered. "It's true nonetheless."

"Perhaps it would mean the end of Midwestern as it is today. But the worry there is if we don't do it, will it spell the end of Midwestern altogether?"

Ben laughed tightly. "I love my company. Do you think I'd let it go under?"

"For your own ego. Perhaps." Elizabeth fixed him with her ice-blue eyes.

Ben was becoming angry. "Look, I guarantee we won't go bust. Okay?"

"My son you are, and I love you as on the day you were born. But sometimes you do talk. Old enough you are to know in this life there are no guarantees."

Ben turned from Elizabeth's gaze. Though he knew she loved and respected him, any crack in her devotion bothered him, and for a moment he felt abandoned. Though usually he took his mother's love for granted, he knew it could be withdrawn.

"I won't diversify," he said at last.

"No other options can I see," she said softly. She smiled sadly at Ben. She was sorry she'd brought it up, yet at the same time she knew she had no choice; it was her obligation.

"Hell, there are millions of options," Ben answered. And with that he began to relax. "The Japanese are after me to form a little merger, for one."

"I don't like Japanese."

"You don't have to like them."

"It's all the raw fish they eat. Cold and clammy it makes them." She laughed heartily, then looked sharply at Ben. "You aren't really serious about the Japanese then?"

"It's a sweet deal they could make." His face broke into a grin. "Of course I'm not serious."

He sat forward eagerly, his eyes sparkling with excitement. "But I'll tell you what I am serious about. I've got Tom working like the devil on Anti-Cor. It would be perfect for a new government contract that's about to go up for bids."

"The reports I have read. And well do I know it's the cost that's the trouble. Anti-Cor is just too dear."

"Tom's working on that."

"But the problems are enormous—"

Ben cut in. "Tom'll solve them."

"A genius is our Tom. Always did I say that. But problems there are that even geniuses can't solve. Or at least not on time. And time is important, I'll wager."

"If you're talking about a stockholders' meeting, there won't be another one for a long time."

"Nine months is hardly an eternity."

Ben took another drink of his scotch and sat back, his smile cagey and hidden. "Of course, there *is* another way to make sure that we get that contract."

Elizabeth didn't answer. She stared at Ben, silent, waiting.

"Well, do I have to spell it out to you?" he asked finally.

"If you don't mind. I am an old woman."

"Only when it's convenient." Again there was that sly smile. "Look, the bids are closed. Who knows why these contracts are awarded to certain companies?" He paused, leaning closer to Elizabeth. "I've been approached by several people in government."

Elizabeth sat bolt upright. "Bribes, Ben? Shame on you!"

Ben laughed. "Don't worry. I turned them off. But Dyer favors it. The way he figures it, Abscam has scared business clean away from Washington. Now's the time to make our approaches while everyone's hurting for money."

Ben was laughing again, but Elizabeth didn't pick him up. "Dyer. Always Dyer." She touched Ben's arm with crippled fingers. "Worried I am at the sound of his name."

"I can handle him."

"Aye. But clever he is and ruthless to boot. I can feel things, Ben. I can feel there is something in the air. Something I don't like."

Ben shook his head. "Are you about to give me that old-woman superstitious crap?"

"No superstitious old-woman crap there is coming your way. Talking I am of plain common sense." Elizabeth stopped. She knew

Ben hated any hint of instincts. He wanted facts, only facts. But life wasn't just a list of interrelated facts, life was subtle, and Ben lacked subtlety. The lack was a New World trait. Americans didn't understand, couldn't make use of subtleties. And her son was an American.

She looked over at Ben, but he seemed far away, locked into his own world.

Finally he said, "Make no mistake about it. Midwestern is mine and will stay mine."

"Yes," she answered slowly. "But if I were you, no mistakes I'd be making either."

Ben smiled and finished off his drink. But inside everything was tight and edgy. For he too could feel things, and though he couldn't understand them, or even admit them to himself, still they sat there, heavy and dark, a shadow on the horizon.

FOUR

The emergency whistle was sharp, piercing. It set teeth on edge, it fried the brain, it reached all the way back to the startled alarm call sounded through the ages, and heads jerked, mouths opened, the moment the men heard it.

A frantic voice came over the loudspeaker. "Gas emergency. Number-two precipitator. Upper deck."

Everyone was frozen, aware of the lack of movement in others but unable to do anything himself. Time seemed to dribble slowly, fractions of seconds stretched. Time was passing, passing, and no one could do anything about it.

Ben was in the computerized booth of the hot rolling mill, watching the men as they worked, the smell of coke and silt still in his nostrils, the burning heat of steel sealed into his clothing, though he was now in the atmospheric calm of regulated air.

"Gas emergency. Number-two precipitator. Upper deck."

Ben could see it all; he was immobilized like the rest, but his

Family Passions 45

mind was clear and sharp. There was an accident. They never happened anymore, not like the old days when the company hospital used to be filled with the flotsam of making steel. Now their safety record was exemplary, spectacular. But there was an accident. The chilling sound of danger he remembered through the years had returned.

Suddenly everyone was in motion. Ben could see men's mouths working, barking orders, but he knew underneath their words what they were thinking: *Thank God it isn't me.* And he knew he was thinking that too.

"Gas emergency. Number-two precipitator. Upper deck."

It was just in the next building. Ben sprang out of the booth and across the ramp, down the stairs and into the courtyard. Outside it was all noise and swirling people, studied confusion, purposeful mayhem. The maintenance staff was running around, preparing to take down the furnace on the other side. There was the terrible cry of ambulances. And still the emergency whistle pounded at the skull, setting up vibrations in the mind.

Men were yelling, "Anyone in there? Anyone hurt?"

"Shit. I don't know" came the answer. "Christ, I hope not."

Ben heard and saw it all, but it was very far away, as if in a dream. He was running to the number-two precipitator, going in to help, without planning it, without even being totally aware of what he was doing.

As Ben passed the first precipitator, he saw the mistake. He was at the round hatch that led into the tank, and inside, in the corner, were two men, one lying over the other, protecting him from the gas. Neither of them were moving. Ben couldn't see if they were breathing.

Everyone was heading away to the number-two precipitator. Ben yelled, "Over here! The leak is over here!"

He couldn't tell if he'd been heard, nor did he wait to find out. There was a moment when he thought he shouldn't go in and tried to hold himself back, but something was driving him forward. And already his body was moving, quickly, efficiently.

He opened the round hatch, no longer trying to think at all, only acting automatically. The two men were almost hidden on the other side. They still weren't moving, but Ben could see the eyes of the man on top, and they looked startled, unseeing. Still, there was something about them that told Ben the man was very much alive.

Ben was just moving forward when he realized something was wrong. All at once the world slowed and he was drifting, as if underwater. There was a terrible weakening; his limbs felt very heavy and soft, melting. His body was out of control. He was aware of everything that was going on, but there was nothing he could do about it. The leak wasn't in the back of the tank at all. It was just above him.

He wanted to scream out, he wanted to run, but he was slipping down to the ground. In a hazy mist he saw everything shifting; the world turned and lurched as he fell.

"Gas emergency. Number-two precipitator. Upper deck."

Time passed. He could hear the loudspeakers giving out the warning, and his heart clenched, because he knew the orders were wrong. The gas was eating at him. The sounds around him became lower, slower, strangely far away and meaningless. He could hear that there were men's voices outside, but it all seemed too distant and unimportant. Vaguely he could feel that he was losing consciousness, but the sharpness of fear was fading.

Time passed. He couldn't move anymore. There were lapses. His eyes were open and he could see everything, but it lacked immediacy. It lacked reality. There was only one thought in his mind now: Things were happening too slowly, much too slowly, and he was going to die.

Suddenly, as if awakening, he realized there were men inside the precipitator; he could just barely make them out at the back of the tank. His heart lurched, racing with joy and relief. But it was only momentary. They were on the other side, removing the two men. They hadn't seen him lying near the hatch. They hadn't come to rescue him at all.

Ben tried to scream, but no sound came from his lips. He tried to move, but all control was gone. And still time passed. He could feel the gas eating into the heart of him, and he knew as a distant shadow that his brain was drinking it in, allowing it to cripple him and kill his cells.

Terror gripped him, and he wanted to cry out in pain and grief, "I'm over here, God help me, over here!" But he could do nothing, only stare crazy-eyed as his life was strangled from his body.

Oddly there was a cooling period, a moment of great clarity when everything seemed painfully sharp, outlined in black; and then the whole universe seemed to jerk forward again, moving quickly, crazily, and he was falling, falling off a high peak, until he hit a great hole of blackness.

It was then they finally found him.

BOOK TWO

THE EARLY YEARS
Ohio, 1937

FIVE

"Come you now, Ben," Elizabeth shouted up the stairs. "I won't have you late like this every morning. Your father and brother'll be docked, and then where will we be?"

"Starving in the streets," Ben called back. But he didn't get out of bed. He rolled over, feeling the soft warmth of his sheets wrapped around his legs. Evan was up already and he could spread out full. It was a wonderful feeling, and he groaned and closed his eyes, lying in the luxury of a warm bed, his morning erection stirring thoughts of the night before at the Four Leaf Clover Bar. He had been sitting so close to Lizzy, he'd almost been able to feel her warm breath disturbing his neck; the smell of her perfume had enveloped him, until there was nothing but the sound of her laughter. Lizzy wore high heels; her body was soft and rounded, sluggishly feminine. She worked in the offices down at the mill, which put her in a whole different class from the men.

As Ben had sat next to Lizzy, sending urgent hot messages to her, he'd felt the beer going to his head, and he'd known in a moment if he weren't careful, the whole room would go spinning out from underneath him. He'd wanted then, more than anything in the world, to be able to lean to her and whisper to come back to his apartment. He could imagine himself mixing gin cocktails and then drinking them naked in bed. But he didn't know how to mix a gin cocktail and even if he did, he had no apartment. He could hardly bring her back to his home with its dingy cracked paint peeling onto the floor like dandruff, and his mother and father huddled around the kitchen fire, drinking tea, staring into space. Still, in his mind he could imagine his finger sliding slowly over her swollen nipples.

"Damn you, Ben. Get up!" Elizabeth yelled.

"I am up," Ben called back. Still, he didn't move. His hands were slipping down over Lizzy's round curving belly to her dark triangle.

Elizabeth called, "Oh, aye? And where are those footsteps? The sound of feet on the floorboards I don't hear. Watch you, boy. I'm coming up there in one minute, and then you'll be sorry, I promise." Elizabeth's voice was high and shrill and full of anger, but in truth she knew she couldn't threaten Ben. He was eighteen. He was a grown man.

Ben inched his way up in bed, trying to shake off the thought of Lizzy and her soft yielding body. If he had an ounce of sense he'd move out of the house and take his own apartment. A few of the men had done that, and they told heady tales of gin cocktails in bed and women with mammoth breasts, but his parents needed the money, and he couldn't move out and leave them to struggle alone. Still, the vision of Lizzy and her hot thrusting body disturbed his mind, and he consoled himself with the thought that next year he would move out and damn his conscience.

Ben stuck one foot out of the covers. The whipping chill of morning slapped at him, and he withdrew it. But he could hear creaking on the stairs, and he knew Evan was on his way up, and he could tell he was angry.

Quickly Ben got out of bed. The floor was so cold his feet almost stuck to it, and there was a cracking sound from the frozen floorboards. He supposed Andrew Carnegie had had to suffer in just such a way too. Ben had read all about Andrew Carnegie for a book report in school; it was the only book he'd really read through, and the parallels seemed unmistakable. The strong, determined mother, the beaten father, the young boy coming to America so full of curiosity and a zest for life. Carnegie had started off as a messenger boy and ended up one of the richest men in the world; he'd sold U.S. Steel for the largest sum ever in history. Not bad for a messenger boy, Ben thought as he scrounged under the bed for his shoes.

Evan appeared in the doorway. Though Evan was only a year younger than Ben, he was a great deal smaller, slim like his father with the same large round eyes, very sad but lit with an optimism and innocence long ago beaten out of Wynn in the deep dark coalpits of Wales and the red-brown air of Ohio steel.

"Excuse me, your majesty," Evan said and bowed deeply, "but your presence is required downstairs."

Ben threw on his shirt. "Outta my way. I gotta take a leak."

"It's not fair you keeping us waiting like this," Evan said, but he stepped aside and let Ben make his morning run down the stairs, through the kitchen, and out into the yard.

The kitchen was still shadowy, steamy from cooking, with patches of yellow light thrown by the wood stove and fireplace and little rounds of light ringing the kerosene lamps. It was a large room; counting the scullery, the largest in the house. At one time the walls must have been white, but now they were dingy gray, cracked in so many places they looked like the back of an alligator.

Elizabeth was standing over baby Pauline, trying to get her to swallow a large spoonful of cereal. She didn't even bother to look up as Ben dashed past. "And use the outhouse," she yelled at him. "A fine lot we look, you peeing in the yard like a dog."

But Ben was already outside, unbuttoning his fly, making little yellow patterns in the snow. Elizabeth shook her head and pushed another spoonful toward Pauline's mouth. Pauline turned away, her eyes on the doorway, bright with anticipation. Ben was awake.

"I might as well be talking to the wind," Elizabeth muttered, as she jammed the mealy mush into Pauline's cheek. Pauline let out a shriek of irritation, but Elizabeth ignored her and shoveled the glob of food across her face and into her mouth. Then she went to the table and lined up the three lunch pails.

Elizabeth was waiting at the kitchen door when Ben came back, hands on hips, her large face twisted into a frown of consternation. In truth, she and Ben kept up their abrasive banter more as a sign of love than anger. Still, underneath there was an electricity that could one day explode into a brutal argument. Both of them knew it, and both of them avoided it, though they allowed themselves to come very close. It was a form of excitement, coming that close to an explosion, and the danger of it kept their relationship alive.

Sitting quietly in the corner of the kitchen, Wynn sipped his morning tea, staring into the fire. He sat totally still, silent. Only the sound of breath rattling through his chest came from him and, every once in a while, a terrible cough that he tried to swallow.

Even with his winter coat on, Wynn looked fragile and thin. His shoulders were stooped by the years of working a coal seam only four feet high. His skin was transparent, worn and bluish gray, and in the seams there was a permanent darkening, an etching of silt and black smoke that no soap could cleanse. Though he heard the bustle in the kitchen around him, it seemed very far away, like a faded old picture. He was dying and he knew it. He seemed only to want to do it quietly, with as little fuss and bother as possible.

As Ben bounded through the back door, he made a grab at the loaf of bread on the counter. Elizabeth chopped his hand away. "Too late, it is. The dining room's closed."

Ben laughed, then grabbed his mother's arm and pretended to gnaw on it.

"I'm not laughing," Elizabeth said peevishly. "Truly I am not. More special than God Almighty our Ben thinks he is, but down at the mill, it's just another bakebrain." Nevertheless, she tore off a chunk of bread and tossed it to Ben.

"And what's wrong with being a bakebrain, then?"

Baby Pauline had her arms up, hoping Ben would notice. He did and pulled her up to him. "Our mother treats me bad, she does." He danced her around the kitchen, while she squealed with delight.

Elizabeth grabbed Pauline back from Ben, hiking her up on her hip like a piece of baggage to be hauled around unnoticed. "Nothing upstairs does it take to be a bakebrain. A bunch of wild men you all are. Frying your brains out in the furnace, just like an animal. A brain is a wonder, a gift from God. Think you we came all this way across the world for you to go throwing snowballs filled with excrement and other disgraces, instead of reading books and trying to learn like our Evan?"

"Aw, Ma, we were just horsing around."

"Since when is that an excuse? To think a boy of mine . . . I didn't know what to say to Mrs. Morris when she told me. And blame it I do on that pack of animals you work with."

Ben was gnawing on his chunk of bread. "Yeah, well, being an animal earns me more than Pa or Evan for all their brains."

Elizabeth walked to the sink and began clattering dishes, still holding Pauline. "That kind of attitude ends up in jail. Make no mistake about it."

"Oh, aye? I'm in jail already," Ben muttered. He picked up his lunch pail from the table, strode to the door, and opened it angrily. Wynn stood wearily, and Evan came sprinting into the room; they followed him to the door.

"Well, that's where you'll be," Elizabeth yelled as they disappeared through the doorway. "And don't be expecting me to be helping you escape when you're there," she called furiously. But she was yelling to an empty room.

*   *   *

The area around the mill was called Bonetown because that was what its inhabitants ate, at least on Sunday, bones and potatoes and heavy, grainy breads to sop up the gravy. Bonetown was no more than a few blocks deep, but it was a crowded few blocks, with row upon row of houses, all three-story dingy red brick, hunched up together, one on top of the other, so that there was no room on either side for so much as a blade of grass to grow. Still, to the people who lived there it was a whole world, with its own shops and schools, doctors and lawyers, as separate and distant from the vast sprawling mansions around the edge of town as any man is from his rich relations.

The sun was beginning to rise, and it stood out cold white against a dead sky. The mill was close to a mile away, but it could be smelled everywhere, a burning acrid smell that stuck to a man and his clothes and took years to clear from the nose. The sky was stained with smoke, and pieces of soot fell from it like black snowflakes to the few trees that tenaciously tried to live there. There was a tree in front of the Savages' house, but it was so twisted and stunted that it was impossible to tell it was an elm. Almost miraculously in spring a few withered green buds would appear on its crippled branches, and in June there would even be a few leaves, brown and sickly, waving in the sooty breeze. In midwinter it looked like a gnarled dwarf.

Ben and Evan were moving quickly, coats open, lunch pails swinging. Already the streets were crowded with men, laughing and calling to one another, greeting their friends, complaining about the cold, their bosses, their girls, and mostly about old man Healey, the owner of the mill, who wouldn't allow them a union. They rushed forward, tearing at pieces of bread, their hands and noses bright red from the cold, a swirling mass of soot-gray overcoats flapping in the icy wind.

The whistle sounded, shrill, piercing through the cold gray morning, and the men picked up their pace, butting the wind, shoving bread into their mouths.

Without anyone's noticing it, Wynn dropped back. The cold air was stinging his throat, burning his lungs. He thought he was going to vomit. A shudder went through him, and the earth seemed to be slipping beneath him. He slowed even more, until he almost stopped, and in the rushing stream of men his stooped frame became like a rock in the middle of a river.

For a moment one of the men paused as he passed him, glancing back with concern. But almost immediately he picked up his pace again. Being late meant a loss of money, and there was no time for worrying about others when your own life was as cold and barren as the winter of Ohio.

Evan looked back expecting to see his father, but the crowd of men were pressed closely together, and the rush and urgency to be at the mill on time kept the crowd surging too quickly toward the entrance for any individual to stand out.

Tom Lindsay had caught up to Ben and Evan, and he helped speed the pace, his long legs striding forward easily. Tom was smiling, and Ben noted the smile with envy. Tom was the only one of them who had a wife, a short pudgy girl made even rounder by her pregnant belly. No wonder he was smiling, Ben thought bitterly. He would too if he were getting it every night.

Still, Ben found himself smiling. Steam was pouring from his mouth, and it felt damp and warm against his skin. The heat of his body and the pleasure of motion stirred him on. He loved this run to work, watching all the men rushing forward, a giant wave. Many of the other workers nodded to him, some he didn't even know but who knew him by sight. After all, he was a bakebrain, one of the crazies, and that went for something at the mill. A cocky grin covered Ben's frozen face. He liked being who he was. At moments like this he wanted nothing more, except maybe a woman. Yes, definitely a woman. But other than that he was happy.

The coldness had gone from Wynn now, and he was beginning to feel very warm. He pulled the scarf from around his neck and unbuttoned his coat. The men had all passed him, and he could see the back of the crowd receding into the distance. He was late; for the first time in all these years, he was late. He knew it would mean a docking of pay, maybe even the sack, but still he didn't move. Everything felt hazy and distant, very unimportant. The warmth was all around him now, and he was surprised to note that the heavy wheezing breath that usually tortured his chest didn't seem to bother him, the bruised feeling around his lungs was not nearly so painful. He wasn't even coughing.

Mostly he felt tired; it was like the soft warm feeling before sleep. Wynn tried to spur himself on, but he couldn't; all he wanted to do was go to sleep. His mind drifted to Elizabeth, standing in the center of the kitchen, the steam of cooking all around her. Elizabeth was a magnificent woman, strong and hearty, almost frightening in her hunger for life. She reminded him of Boadicea astride her scythe-wheeled chariot, leading her tribe of early Britons in revolt against the Romans. Watching her had always filled Wynn with wonder. Right from that first moment in the hills of Wales.

The street was quite empty now. He could see the women through the windows of their houses, cleaning up after breakfast. He heard the babies crying and the scolding of their mothers. He realized he'd never known what went on in the world after the men left for work; it had never occurred to him to think about it. There were so many things he had never thought about, strange and beautiful things. How much had he missed by shuffling mulelike up and back from work? For the first time in years Wynn felt the joy of life moving through him, and he walked over to the curb and sat down, gazing up and down the street with wonder.

At the gates of the mill, a long black Ford was pressing through the crowd, moving quickly, horn blaring, forcing the men to scatter to the sides of the road. As it passed the men stopped, watching the car make its way to the gates. Inside the shriveled silhouette of Nicholas Healey could be seen, almost enveloped by the plush leather seat covers.

Nicholas Healey was dressed in black, his small, nutlike face was sharp and quick, peeking out from under his tall hat like a ferret. He kept his little brown eyes straight ahead, staring at the back of the chauffeur's neck as if he found something terribly interesting there. Next to him sat his daughter, Angela, with an identical ferret face. Her thin dishwater hair was tied back, and she too was wearing dark colors, a younger if no less unattractive version of the original.

As the car passed, several of the men pulled off their caps and made mock angry bows to it. Nicholas didn't seem to notice; he turned his eyes neither right nor left, but kept them tightly forward. Only Angela seemed to see, jerking her head around, her eyes wide and disturbed, as if discovering for the first time that the press of men who fed her father's mill might have feelings about it, about them—in fact, about life in general.

Ben and Evan were stopped just short of the gates, and they watched sullenly as the black car closed in on them.

"Make way for the king," Ben said under his breath.

Evan nodded. "You ever wonder what goes through that bastard's mind as he pushes us peons off the street like he was the lord of the manor?"

Ben grunted, his eyes on the shiny car. "Well, it's his street, isn't it?" he answered.

Evan flared. "Like hell it is. The Healey Mills starts at the gates. Everything else belongs to the city or county or maybe it's the state of Ohio."

Tom laughed. "Make up your mind, Evan. Which is it? You're the one who's supposed to know all the facts."

"Laugh if you want, but it isn't fair."

Ben was watching the car dreamily. "Five'll get you ten, old man Healey doesn't eat stale bread for breakfast."

Tom sighed. "Too right, lad. I'd have steak every morning."

"Steak, hell!" Ben's eyes lit up. "Me, I'd have lobster, dripping in butter."

"Lobster?" Tom sneered. "No one eats lobster for breakfast, you idiot."

Ben poked Tom in the ribs. "Oh, yeah? Look who's calling who an idiot. When was the last time you had steak for breakfast?"

"Well, if I was old man Healey I would. Idiot!" Tom shoved Ben hard on the shoulder, but he didn't budge an inch, and once again Tom wondered at the size and strength of his friend. He was immovable, like a great wall. Tom supposed only time would erode Ben, and that would be slowly.

Evan's eyes were on the black car; they were serious eyes, full of repressed anger and disdain. "You're both idiots, if you ask me. Arguing about what you'd eat for stupid breakfast if you were old man Healey. Because you aren't old man Healey. You aren't even his dog. But there you are talking about stupidities that aren't ever going to happen when there's a way to change things right in front of your eyes, and you're just too blind to see it."

Ben groaned. "Oh, oh. Here comes the old union horseshit again."

"Shhh!" Evan stiffened. It was said old man Healey had infiltrated one hundred scabs into his mill. Evan was looking around cautiously, but no one seemed interested in what was being said; they were too busy trying to get to the mill before the final whistle.

"Will you look at the big hero?" Ben sneered. "Shaking in the old hobnails every time someone as much as says the word 'union.' "

"Oh, yeah? And what exactly is it you think I'm scared of then? Getting hit on the head?"

"Aye, yeah. That. And losing your job."

Evan turned on Ben, the muscles in his thin jaw were tight with anger. "Scared I am all right. But not for fear of my skin. It's fear of hurting the union that silences me. After the Homestead riots, who wouldn't be scared?"

Ben roared with laughter. "Homestead? Homestead was over thirty years ago, long before either of us was thought of. Besides, those steelmen gave the Pinkertons something to remember. Stole a cannon from the center of town and shot right back at them. Killed two at least. Why, those people ruled over that town for over five days."

"Until the state troopers moved in. Forty dead, one hundred sixty-three injured."

"But what a way to go!" Ben said, doing a little dance.

Tom warned, "Now, Ben. I'm not going to laugh with you over Homestead. It was a tragedy."

"Big deal," Ben said belligerently. "It took time, but now they've got a union at U.S. and Bethlehem, don't they? We'll get a union one day."

"Don't bet on it," Evan answered. "U.S. and Bethlehem are big steel. They've got stockholders to keep them in line. We're little steel. No one gives a damn about us. Little steel doesn't have to answer to anyone but itself. And old man Healey's the worst of the lot."

The black Ford was parallel, horn blaring. Ben pulled off his hat and made a mock bow. "Will you look at him? As dried up as a prune and none so pretty."

Tom pointed. "Look at this, lads. There's a young lady beside him. Well, who would have believed he'd be able to shift the old codpiece?"

"Forget it," Evan said. "She's got a puss like his worship. I heard he had a daughter. It's probably her."

Inside the car, Nicholas was staring straight ahead, avoiding the sight of the workers who surrounded the car, their seamed dirty faces an unnoticeable background to his life. And yet he was aware of them, more aware with every passing day. The change in this sea of faces was unmistakable. No matter how much he tried to avoid it, he couldn't help noticing the growing anger. The voices were lower, more sullen. Everything was running slower and more stupidly, a kind of retaliation for not allowing them a union.

And why should he? Nicholas thought to himself. The problem was they had it too soft. Give them too much and all you did was make things worse. At U.S. and Bethlehem they'd made that mistake, and now their workers were lounging around all day, picking their teeth and drinking their wages. They were all the same. Allow them an inch and they took a square city block. The trick was not to give in to them in the beginning; the minute you did, you were weak, and then there was nothing you could do. It was like trying to hold back the waves.

Nicholas sat up even straighter; his scrawny neck and back made a perfect line. Besides, there were no workers starving. They were lucky to be working at all. If they didn't like it at the Healey Mills, let them try their luck outside, see where that got them.

The car reached the gates and came to a halt. The crowd of men was so tight, it could barely move an inch.

"Lean on the horn," Nicholas barked at the chauffeur.

Angela was looking out the window, her eyes large and frightened. She seemed barely able to distinguish faces in the crowd, only the great sprawling mass. Then, oddly, she focused in, and she was looking at Evan.

It was only for a moment, but Ben saw it. He glanced at Evan to see if he'd noticed. Evan was standing still, his eyes on the car, and there was an expression on his face that told Ben he had indeed seen. Ben snickered to himself. It would be excellent material to tease him with later.

Finally the crowd parted and the car was able to inch forward into the silty courtyard, then over to the administration building. Again Ben saw Angela turn back and look out the rear window at Evan, and when he saw Evan's face, he knew he had seen it too.

Then suddenly the crowd started to move fast again, and Ben forgot everything but the fiery heat of the blast furnace and the hot liquid movements of the day.

Wynn had lost all track of time. He could hear running water and the clatter of dishes. Several women were leaving their houses, shopping bags under their arms, well-bundled children toddling beside them. "Come on, hurry up," said the rushing women to their children. The sound of their voices was reassuring and soft to Wynn. It reminded him of his own childhood, the warm coziness of kitchens, the rhythmic regularity.

The sun was higher than before, but it was cold and very watery. Snow began to fall, white, feathery, covering the gritty ground with a soft film that would be black within the hour. It didn't occur to Wynn to ask himself why he was sitting where he was. He had no idea how long he'd been there, perhaps an hour, perhaps only a few minutes. Everything seemed so unreal, and yet for the first time so intensely real. He just watched the snow falling all around him, thick and damp. There was beauty in it; there was great beauty in it.

It reminded him of Wales. Wales had been beautiful with the snow hard on her. Sometimes it had snowed so heavily the miners had had to bed down at the pits for days on end without going home. But what a world it had been outside the windows, and in spring all the snows had fed rivers until they were bursting from the mountains, and all the valleys were tender green.

Close to the mines had been an abandoned pit. It was said it had been sunk in Roman times, and worked from time to time through the years. The pit was close to seventy-five feet around, cut from the rocky ground, a deep shadowy hole, overgrown with clinging trees and grasses, oaks and ashes and silvery birches. He had often walked by on his way to the mines and stared down at the weathered rocks left from the ore, looking for something to tell him that indeed the pit was from Roman times, perhaps a shard of pottery or a piece of jewelry.

Often as he stood looking down into the blackness, he wondered about the men who had once worked the seams. Were they heathens or Druids, Roman slaves? He was an uneducated man with only a dim idea of where Rome lay. It was impossible for him to reason out these things. He supposed Elizabeth knew. But by that time he'd been too tired to ask.

He remembered trudging home from the mines, his thoughts on Elizabeth. God, what a woman she'd been. He could see her, waiting at the threshold, her belly as large and full as a great mountain. He'd know from that first time out on the hills that Elizabeth wasn't like other women. How lucky he'd been, how infinitely lucky. He'd never understood why she'd picked him out, but always he was grateful for it. Even through the bad times. That night on the hill he'd seen in her eyes what strong sons she'd make. And it was true. Two sons and a daughter and only one other dead.

The unborn child had been the first thing he'd lost to America, but it wasn't the last. There had been the months of cold and fear, the looking for a job without a penny in his pocket and no friends and relatives. And even Elizabeth had grown scared. He supposed she'd felt responsible, though he'd never blamed her, for he'd known she was right. But there had been the nights they'd slept in the cold, holding the boys to them for warmth. There had been the days without eating and everything black and harsh and unfriendly around them. They had been strangers in a strange land. He supposed

America had undone him, because he hadn't been right after that. But Elizabeth had survived it all.

He could picture Elizabeth carrying a bucket of water to the wood stove, magnificent, hearty. She wasn't a woman, she was a mountain, as strong and immovable as nature herself. She carried them all like she carried that bucket to the stove, her strong shoulders and arms holding them all up. America had broken him but not Elizabeth. Still, he supposed even that had been all right, because in the end it would be good for Ben and Evan and Pauline. It had been what Elizabeth had dreamed of and wanted, and he couldn't have refused her what she wanted, so grateful was he at having been chosen.

Still and all he missed Wales, especially on a day like this, with the snow falling and the sound of children and mothers behind their frosty windows and a kind of peaceful hush on the streets.

Tiredness enveloped Wynn, and he lowered his head to his knees. He watched the snowflakes falling all around him with a childish delight. His chest was beginning to feel even heavier than usual, but he didn't seem to mind it as he had. All he could do was watch the snowflakes and listen to the morning sounds.

And then slowly everything began to fade. At first all color was gone from the already bleak landscape, becoming black and white, then gray, then monotone and pale. Wynn slipped to the ground until he was lying on the pavement. The snow fell all around him, catching at his body, sticking in the folds of his overcoat and turning the little man a soft white.

SIX

Miss Ballen was rushing behind Nicholas Healey as he walked briskly and purposefully toward his office. She clutched the morning mail to her stringy chest and said shrilly, "Mr. Harris phoned and asked you to return his call."

"The hell with him," Nicholas barked.

Miss Ballen was becoming breathless from the run down the

corridor, and she could hear Angela Healey behind her, high heels clicking against the tile floor. "Mr. Basser at Beckland also called," she continued.

"The hell with him too."

"And a delegation of workers have asked for a meeting in half an hour."

"To hell with all of them. I don't give a hair of my nose for the bunch of them."

Nicholas Healey entered his office, opened his window several inches, slipped into his large leather chair, and pulled himself to his enormous leather and mahogany desk. Instinctively he brushed off his suit, though he knew the soot of steel could no more be brushed away than the uneasy feeling he'd been having every day as he went through the gates. He watched silently as Miss Ballen placed his mail in piles before him, then he reached into his pocket, carefully pulled on his glasses, and with pursed lips began going through his correspondence.

Angela had followed them into the office and stood in the center of the room, unsure what to do. She knew her father had forgotten that she was there, and she was terrified to remind him of her presence. Miss Ballen retreated to the door and waited to make sure there was nothing else her boss might demand, then quietly she slipped from the room.

Nicholas scribbled some notes at the bottom of a letter, then carefully placed it at the edge of the desk and went on to the next letter. His movements were precise and quick, neatly efficient, and Angela wondered if he was doing this for her benefit, or if even when he was alone, he went through life with such precision. She knew nothing about her father. Though her mother had died when she was a baby, they had lived a strange separate existence from one another, and his world was unknown to her.

She watched as her father scribbled another note on the bottom of a letter. Angry lines scored his forehead, and his jaw stiffened. Angela could tell he was becoming upset, and it made her feel even more anxious and unsettled, but there was nothing she could do; she couldn't even move. Angela was terrified of her father, and though she was aware this terror made him despise her even more, she couldn't control it.

Ever since she was a little girl, she'd known that her father disliked her. She had been a quiet, ugly child, dull and frightened. She remembered well her father's infrequent visits to her playroom, how she had awaited them in an agony of fear and also intense excitement. She could remember the scratchy wool underwear she'd been forced to wear, the coldness of the room, which had made her fingers bleed from rawness. Usually she'd be having dinner, sitting at her little table and chairs that had long ago become too small for her. She remembered how she'd tried to hide her reddened hands from her father's gaze. Sitting there, uncomfortable in her scratchy underwear, her legs sprawled awkwardly under the table, she'd watch him enter briskly. He'd stand over her, glasses on nose, lips pursed, and then would come the questions, formal, condescending, and totally without interest in the answers. A moment later he was gone, and Angela would feel desperate and despairing until the next time, building up his visit in her mind until she was torn with anxiety and excitement. Angela felt a chill go through her. Though there had been brief feelings of rebellion, vague hints that the existence she lived was perhaps not the world, these momentary sparks had been extinguished almost immediately in a house that was cold and dark with no one to point out the sun.

Nicholas had moved on to the next letter, but in fact he was well aware of Angela's presence, and he resented it. It was a ridiculous idea of hers to learn to become his secretary. By her age she should have had her own home, been raising her own family, though with her unattractive face and embarrassed manner, even the Healey money couldn't make a dent in her social schedule. Still, something might have been done if only she hadn't been so recalcitrantly dull and sullen. He supposed in anyone else, he might have found it admirable that a woman should want to earn her own living and be useful. But Nicholas had always disapproved of everything his daughter did. It had become a habit. Perhaps if there had been anything lovely or graceful about her, as there had been about her mother, he might not have begun his angry dislike.

Vanessa had been the only living thing in what his parents made sure was a solemn, austere life. She had been a blaze of light that seared the corners of his mind and obliterated the shadowy places. He had stood, stunned in her warmth and beauty, idolator to her sun. And suddenly, terribly, as she lay screaming in childbirth her light had flickered, and then it was gone, leaving a darkness even blacker than death and a bitterness in his heart against the one who, in her greediness for life, had taken Vanessa from him.

No, Angela was nothing like her. There wasn't anything about her to stir tender feelings, no feminine charm, no softness of voice or manner. She was a dull, hard-muscled woman, emotionless and ugly. Though she was only twenty-one, already she had the mannerisms of a spinster, revealing nothing to inspire a man with dreams or hopes or longings.

Again Miss Ballen entered, looking around the room furtively, her thin weedy body hunched and bowed, her hollow face wizened. She paused next to Angela, moving ever so slightly to alert Nicholas that she was there without disturbing him.

Nicholas didn't look up from his correspondence, but there was irritation in his voice. "What is it, Miss Ballen?"

"The delegation of workers is outside."

Nicholas scribbled a note and took up another letter. "How nice for them."

"There are ten men."

Nicholas interrupted. "How very nice for all ten of them. I hope you made sure they wiped their feet. I wouldn't want them tracking dirt all over the new carpet as they leave."

Miss Ballen hesitated, her bony face a sea of lines, and Angela was struck anew how terrible it must be to work for one's living, always treading lightly, unsure whether you were about to give offense and lose the little money you earned.

While always Angela had understood she was lucky to be rich, the thought had had little impact on her. Her own life had seemed so bleak, so unrelentingly hopeless, that other people's misfortunes played only lightly across her consciousness. But from her twenty-first birthday, the moment when in desperation she had begged her father to allow her to work for him, everything had begun to change.

Ever since Angela was a child, she had always had a premonition she would die before she was twenty-one. It was a secret thought, one she knew was unreasonable, yet one she deep-down believed. Her twenty-first birthday surprised her, filling her with despair. And as the day dragged on with its usual emptiness, Angela knew she had to do something, anything, rather than fulfill what was likely to be a life sentence of another forty years.

It had seemed at the time a limited decision, yet now standing in her father's office, watching the fear on Miss Ballen's face, she began to feel the repercussions of it.

Miss Ballen looked down at her feet, then offered tentatively, "They seem very impatient. I'm not sure what they'll do if I say you refuse to see them."

"Why are they here, Miss Ballen?"

"I believe—" she paused, licking dry lips with an equally dry tongue. "I believe they want to discuss a union."

"Not while the wind goes in and out of me. Is that clear enough, Miss Ballen?"

"Yes, sir. But it's just that I've told them that so many times. And now they refuse to leave without seeing you."

Nicholas continued working on his mail, slowly, precisely. Once again the silence grew until it had become momentous; only the ticking of a wall clock and the rustling of papers disturbed it. Angela looked from Miss Ballen to her father, as if caught between them, frozen in her own anxiety and by the dread on the secretary's face. Angela turned away, but still that look of Miss Ballen's remained in her mind. As terrible as her own fear was, Miss Ballen's seemed so much worse. At least she knew she would eat; no matter what, there would be food on her table. And with that thought came a crack in her terror. There was something worse than her father's disapproval.

"Father," she said softly. "I think you must see them."

"What's this?" Nicholas's small ferret face jerked from his correspondence, and he fixed Angela with an angry stare.

"They might become rowdy. I think you must see them."

"I *must see* them?" His face drained of blood.

Angela had rarely seen her father angry, and then never at her. It was as if Nicholas saved his emotions for important events, and certainly she was not one of those. But this time he was angry at her. Oddly, rather than feeding her panic, it gave her a strange sense of power, as if an emotion, any emotion, even anger, gave her a human dignity she hadn't had before. It meant she existed.

"You had better meet these men," she said. Her voice was gaining strength. "I saw the looks on the men's faces as we came into the mill this morning. I felt their anger."

Miss Ballen was watching Angela; the look of intimidation was still on her face, but now there was the beginning of a smile.

Nicholas noticed this, and it only increased his anger. From just outside he could hear the low murmur of voices, and he knew that the men had moved closer to the door, impatient, burning. Angela was right; he should see the men. Yet by being the one to say it, she had made it impossible.

Angela was watching her father. She could almost read his thoughts; she could feel his conflict. She'd never seen her father as a person before. It had never occurred to her to see him as having motives and needs. But he was a person, with motives and needs and wants and defects, neither totally good nor totally bad, simply a human being, and in that one moment of recognition, her fear faded. Her father was just a man.

Angela continued, "At least if you agreed to see the leaders and sent the others away, they might not get any more mud on the carpet."

Nicholas's expression didn't change, but clearly he understood all that had passed, Angela's sudden rebellion and her release. She was letting him off the hook, helping him to save face in front of his secretary. It was intolerable, yet he knew he had no choice but to go along.

"Indeed," Nicholas answered, placing a paperweight on his mail and leaning back in his chair. His face had reset into a superior blankness.

Miss Ballen looked from Nicholas to Angela, knowing something had passed, but not precisely what it was.

Nicholas tapped his finger on the desk impatiently. "This week, if you don't mind, Miss Ballen. Before it's time for me to retire."

He smiled to himself as he watched Miss Ballen's fearfulness return and she went scurrying out of the office. Well, he thought, he would see these men because it was necessary that he do so, but they would get nowhere with him. In fact, he rather looked forward to the opportunity to turn them down.

Angela moved to the window and looked out at the gray dusty grounds of the steel mill. In the distance she could see the mountains of coal and iron that fed the fires of the mill. Black clouds of smoke were rising from the fires, almost obliterating the sky. As she stood there, gazing out through the thick glass, she could feel in her body the crashing power of the red-hot ingots, the grinding of gears, the screeching of the railroad cars that ran between the ovens and the rolling mill. She looked down on the men as they stamped their feet against the cold or wiped the sweat from their faces with their arms. The extremes of temperature amazed her. But she would learn all that soon. She promised herself she would learn everything now. When she turned back from the window, she was smiling.

Three men had entered the office, feeling dwarfed by its size, though in fact they were far larger than the man who occupied it. It was only then that Angela remembered the intelligent-looking man she had seen at the gate. It was an important time to see him again.

Somehow he became enmeshed in her moment of triumph, as if the woman, newly born, was opening her eyes for the first time and seeing Evan.

Elizabeth stood at Wynn's grave, rigid and erect, her face set into dull blankness. But underneath, the sorrow had solidified into hatred, though what it was directed against was unclear. Perhaps it was the fates she was cursing, the indifferent presences that controlled human life. Certainly it wasn't the men who owned the steel mills and coalpits. Ironically they seemed even more distant and lofty than the gods.

Ben and Evan too stood erect, their faces somber but questioning, as if trying to understand the significance of a man who meant so little to their life that his death was merely the passing of a shadow. As they stood there in the snow watching the minister drone his few words, only Pauline seemed to be feeling any emotion, and that was merely impatience. Pauline was cold and hungry and bored. She had tried to play with Ben, grabbing at his hand, pulling at his nose, but Ben hadn't wanted to play. Everyone was less attentive than usual, though she didn't know why. She'd been told her father had gone away on a long trip, but this wasn't in answer to any question. She hadn't even noticed his absence.

Except for the family, Tom was the only one at the gravesite. Making friends was not a talent of Elizabeth's, nor did she consider it a virtue; she rarely talked to neighbors, kept mostly to herself, and since she had little to offer to the tradesmen of Bonetown, none of them had felt an appearance was necessary.

Ben was the first of the children to throw earth on the grave. The dirt was packed hard from the cold, and there were little glittering ice crystals sparkling coldly against the blackness of the earth. He watched the dirt fall on the grave with a strange detached feeling, as if he were encased in glass. Evan was next, then Ben helped baby Pauline, and it was all over.

After that they went back to the house, pulled off their heavy coats, and sat down to lunch. Ben and Evan were back at work by eleven o'clock. Tom had already gone back. With a wife and a child on the way, he couldn't afford the loss of another hour's pay.

Once back at work, Ben thought very little about his father, and his name was not mentioned that evening. It was only later, as he

Family Passions 69

lay in bed, Evan next to him in the dark, that he thought about Wynn. But it was not because of anything his father had done or said in his life, but because of what he had left behind. From the next room, they could hear the muffled sounds of crying, and for the first time Ben realized what Wynn's passing meant to his mother.

The two boys listened in silence for a long while, and Ben felt resentment rising inside of him, unexplained, undefined, but strong and powerful for all its mystery.

Finally Evan broke the silence. "It'll be hardest on Ma," he said softly. "Nineteen years is a long time. She'll miss him a great deal."

Ben answered angrily. "There was nothing in him to miss."

"In the early days there was," Evan answered. "Remember how he was when we were young? Always singing. A right cocky man he was. A smile on his face and a swagger when he walked, hoisting us up on his shoulders, playing 'sack of coal.' Do you remember, Ben?"

"No. I don't remember anything about Pa except the stoop and the shuffle and the coughing. Never talking, never doing anything but going off to work, then coming back again, sitting in front of the fire, all bent and broken, coughing his guts out."

"And you blame him for it?"

"Who should I blame?"

"You could start by blaming the mining companies. You think getting black lung was his idea?"

"Others survived it."

"An unforgiving man you are, Ben. Hard and unforgiving."

"Maybe. But he never did anything for his family except drain off all hope and strength."

"There was much magic in the man. And love, Ben, love."

Ben stared at the ceiling angrily. "He let them beat him."

"Them?"

"The world. He let the world beat him. Sure he had black lung. So do a lot of them, but still they go to the bars for a pint and a laugh, still they come home with a smile. My God, they don't sit there like a corpse by the fire. He was weak and . . ."

". . . And he frightened you."

Ben laughed too loudly. "Frightened me? How could I be frightened of that bag of bones?"

"Because like it or not, we are a part of him. We've got his blood in our veins. And if he can be beaten, then maybe we can too."

"Codswallop!"

"It's not codswallop I'm speaking, Ben. It's the truth. You hated him not for what he was, but for what you're scared you are."

Ben pulled the covers around his ears. "I'm not listening anymore. Honestly I'm not. If you and Ma want to make a saint of the man, go right ahead. But do it without me."

From that moment Ben put his father out of his mind, but never again did he sit in the corner where Wynn had passed his evenings, staring at the fire and coughing up his dreams.

SEVEN

Ben could hear Evan calling to him from downstairs. He opened an eye and peeked out at the dawn. His head felt like the inside of a Bessemer converter; hypothermal explosions lit his aching eyes. Cloudily he remembered that close to three quarters of a bottle of whiskey had passed into his molten bloodstream. But with that thought came the memory that it had been in celebration of today, Memorial Day, a day off.

Ben groaned with relief and rolled over on his stomach. His liquor-sodden brain began working on a new hot dream. This time he was Andrew Carnegie, showing a whole group of women around his steel mill. There was a little redhead with knockers that just didn't stop.

Slowly he became aware that his sheet was slipping from the bed. With half-closed eyes he reached for it, but felt nothing. He opened his eyes and discovered Evan standing over him.

"Time to get up," Evan crooned.

Ben grunted. "Give me back my sheet, you bastard."

"No."

"Give it me back or it's your life."

"I'm shaking in my boots. Don't you remember what day it is today?"

"Damn right I do. It's my day off."

"Wrong. It's the day you demonstrate for the union."

Ben shut his eyes and fell back, turning toward the wall.

Evan warned, "I'll throw cold water on you."

"You do and you're taking your life in your hands."

"I'm on my way to the kitchen for a bucket."

Ben rolled back, but he still didn't open his eyes. "You wouldn't dare."

"Wanna bet?"

Ben opened his eyes and whined. "I don't believe in the union, for Christ sake, and I certainly don't believe in it on my day off."

"Well, I do. And I'm one of the leaders, and I'll be damned if my own brother isn't going to be there."

"I don't understand. What the hell is all this going to do except lose us our jobs? Jesus, Evan, you know as well as me that old man Healey isn't going to stand for picketing around the mill." He sat up in bed. "You want to know what I think? I think he's going to call the police. I think there's going to be trouble. And then what? We'll all get gassed and beaten up, and we'll be right back where we started, which isn't that bad, eh? I mean, we earn okay money. We've got our buddies and our Saturday nights."

Evan sat down on the edge of the bed, his eyes very serious. "But don't you want more?" he asked softly.

"You bet I do. I want to be a millionaire like old man Healey."

"Oh, sure. Fat chance."

"You watch," Ben said brightly. "I'm going to get there one day."

"Okay, Mr. Andrew Carnegie. And how exactly do you expect to accomplish that earth-shattering feat?"

Ben smiled. "To tell you the truth, I haven't figured that part out yet. But I will. Hey, it's the land of the free, home of the brave."

Evan shook his head sadly. "You're crazy, Ben. You've got no education, no money. All you're trained for is the furnaces. How are you ever going to get anywhere? You're going to end up like everyone else. You're going to end up like Pa."

"And you think a bunch of idiots waving banners and singing 'We Shall Overcome' is going to change any of that?"

"Yeah, I do."

"Then you're even crazier than I am. All you're going to do is get your head flattened a couple of inches."

Evan was staring down at the floor, his jaw clenched with

determination, and Ben could see how important this was to him. Slowly he got out of bed. His head felt as if he'd been clubbed already.

"All right, all right," he muttered. "I guess I'd better go. I don't trust you to have enough sense to come in and out of the gas."

This made Evan smile. "Just wait. You'll see. Old man Healey isn't expecting anything like the demonstration we're going to put on today. We're going to close that mill tighter than his asshole."

"Yeah, sure." Ben reached around on the floor for his clothes from the night before. "You're really going to show him. He's going to say, 'Evan, my man, you've pointed out to me the error of my ways. Now I understand. And I'm going to give you one million dollars a day to act as my employee advisor.'"

Evan smirked. "I didn't say I was looking for a miracle."

Ben pulled his trousers up and buttoned his fly. He was subdued, thoughtful. "You know what? I am."

"Then you're in for a big disappointment."

Ben put his arm around his brother. "Well, then that makes two of us."

Angela Healey lay in bed, staring out at the rising sun. It was a huge red ball in the east and as it rose she could feel the heat begin. It had been in the nineties all week, and the temperature at the mill had been astounding. Damp, acrid-smelling coal dust and soot had stuck to everything. Her hair was thick with it; it was under her nails, on her clothes, in her mouth. She couldn't imagine what it must be like outside of the offices, in the furnaces, but she could see from the men's faces what it must have been like, and she was sure the heat was helping to fan the flame of rebellion. She had been watching the men from that first day at the mill, but always on the other side of windows, car windows, office windows. Yet, isolated as she was, she could feel their anger, sense their cornered lives and the need for destruction.

Several times men representing the union had tried to speak to her father, but he'd never let them into the office again. She'd watched as they left to return to their jobs, each time their bodies more taut, the anger and frustration burning deeper into their faces. There would be trouble today. She could feel it.

Standing at her window, she wondered at her turning into what

Family Passions 73

her father would call a bleeding heart. Until that first day at the mill, she had thought of little but the emptiness of her own life. Isolated as she had been, she'd counted the seconds as they slipped by with only the occasional visit or walk to break the gray useless monotony. How different her life had been from the aching round of activity of the men outside, and yet in a way, how strikingly similar. They too watched their lives pass them by in steady futility. They too were numbed against all thought or hope. They too lived in a prison, and though they were each separated from the other by windows, both in different ways held in by them, the more she watched, the more it seemed to her that in some way their destinies were intertwined.

There was, of course, another reason for her watching out the window. She was looking for the man with the intelligent eyes. Angela was well aware how ridiculous that made her, a dried-up, harsh little woman spying on a common laborer. The shame became astounding, but so did the obsession. She could not stop herself, nor could she forgive herself for it. She was brutally torn by the forces within her which were made all the stronger by their newness.

Angela glanced at the clock by her bed. It was only six thirty, and a day off. Still, she couldn't stay in bed, even though she was tired, nor could she pull the bell for the maid to bring her breakfast as she had before. Increasingly she was finding the luxury around her repellent. She couldn't shake from her mind that only a few blocks away, her father's workers were hunched in gloomy rooms, making a meal of a chunk of bread. Who was she to have warm rooms and maids and hot breakfasts brought up on trays? Was there something inherently more valuable about her? Had she lived another life and done something so splendid? And her father, what wonderful thought or gesture or moral fiber gave him the right to live as he did?

Angela ran cold water in the basin and splashed her face with it, then she looked at herself in the mirror. She had never spent much time looking at herself. Usually she would just wash her face, brush her hair, and get dressed. Rarely did she bother with lipstick, and even when she did, it was gone in the hour, easily forgotten in her uninterest in anything about her looks. But today she looked in the mirror. It was her father's face that stared back at her, small, brown like a hazelnut, with a thin pointed nose and small hooded eyes. Water ran down her face, collecting in beads under her eyes and across the bridge of her nose. She was an ugly woman, hard and angular. She couldn't imagine anyone looking at her and feeling anything but indifference. Angela shivered and turned away from the mirror, but the dull pain of this thought followed after her, sitting on her chest and eating her soul.

Quickly she moved across the room, pulling on her clothes. She wondered if her father was up yet. She supposed he was not. Though he was well aware the men were planning a demonstration, and had in fact arranged for police protection at the mill, he was determined to pretend that nothing was going on. Every time she brought up the Memorial Day demonstration she could see his face darken, but there was no anger there, not even fear. On the contrary, he looked quite calm. A strike was unspeakable; therefore, he didn't speak of it. Nor did he appear to think about it. He seemed to feel if he didn't acknowledge the problem, it didn't exist.

Angela glanced out of her bedroom window. The sun was no longer red but white-hot and glaring. The problem did exist though; it wouldn't disappear, and slowly a feeling of impending doom came over her. There would be trouble at her father's mill today. She could feel it, and there was nothing she could do.

Though it was only eight o'clock in the morning, the mill was already sealed off. Police had been brought in from all the cities around. They formed a line completely around the mill, shoulder to shoulder and, at the gates, two deep. They were still wearing their winter uniforms, and the heat was so intense that already beads of sweat stood out on their faces. They were nervous too, wearing guns and cannisters of tear gas that they kept touching to reassure themselves. There had been trouble at Homestead; there could be trouble here.

Ben helped Evan and Tom form the union men into a long line just outside the front of the Healey Mills. Placards were handed out, as were warnings. There was to be no trouble today. Trouble would only bring retaliation, and what they wanted was change.

By nine o'clock the line was already four deep. Ben was astounded by how many men turned up and how peaceful they were. But under the peacefulness there was a strength and resolve; these were men who knew what they wanted and were willing to go after it. Ben had never felt proud to be a part of anything even resembling a group, but he felt proud to be one of this wall of determined men.

Just outside the mill, where the streets of the town began, a large crowd was beginning to gather. With every passing minute, more arrived, until the streets were packed with men, women, even children. Many of the people were dressed up as if they were going to a party; some had brought picnic baskets.

As Ben stood among the line of picketers, a thrill passed through him. He felt as if he were an actor on a stage, and everyone had come out to watch him alone defy the power and wealth of old man Healey. Standing tight in the line, looking out at the growing crowd, for the first time he could almost believe that something might come of all of this, something miraculous.

Angela spent the morning in her sitting room trying to concentrate on a book of shorthand, but her mind wasn't on it. She kept finding herself leaving her desk, moving to the windows, and peering out at the empty treelined street below. Her father had arisen late. She heard his footsteps on the stairs at eleven thirty, and his tight high voice calling for his car to be brought around. He had not come to her room nor left a message, though she supposed he was going to the Park Lane for lunch. Her father spent all his holidays going over his correspondence during the morning, lunching at the Park Lane, then returning home to do his bookkeeping.

She picked up her shorthand book again, but a moment later she was back at the window. The sun was overhead and there was no wind, not even a breeze to relieve the relentless heat.

It was not a conscious decision, rather a cessation of all thought, or perhaps she had known what she was about to do all along and had chosen like her father not to think of it. But all at once she turned from the window and ran down the stairs. She paused only for a moment in the cool of the entryway, then opened the door and walked out onto the quiet treelined street.

Once outside, it seemed impossible that there would be trouble. The line of mansions with their well-manicured lawns and pruned trees seemed to promise only graciousness and order, the tranquility of the first summer holiday where the only battles lay on the tennis court or who would be the first to propose a toast at lunch.

Angela turned toward the mill. As the houses grew smaller, boxier, the streets less shaded, the heat grew in intensity. Her clothes began to feel heavy and awkward; her shoes pinched as her feet swelled. Still, she picked up her pace, pressing herself closer to Bonetown and the outskirts of the mill, with no thought to what she was doing or why but merely driven forward, instinctively, by a force she didn't understand.

At the outskirts of Bonetown she became aware of a strange noise, almost like the buzzing of insects, far off, but coming closer with each step she took. As she moved, the sound seemed to change, becoming louder, stronger, more like the noise of animals than insects, though what kind of animal she had no idea. The closer she came to the mill, the louder the sound became, until she was aware it was changing again. This time she stopped walking, and she was tempted to rush back to the safety of her home. It was the sound of voices, human voices, she'd been hearing. It was the sound of a crowd.

Angela paused on the hot pavement, her ears filled with the distorted hum. The sun beat down, stinging her eyes with its glare. Yet suddenly she found herself moving again, quickly, her heart beating with anticipation and fear.

The crowd started several blocks from the mill. The people were standing in doorways and on the sidewalks; some of them were sitting on the curbs. All up and down the streets, people hung out of the windows of their cramped houses, calling down to those below, waving shirts, trousers, even long johns, like giant handkerchiefs to soldiers going to the wars. The bars were open, and men were pouring out of them, carrying bottles of beer to the accompaniment of cheers from their friends. Children clutched their mother's skirts, then darted at one another, teasing and laughing. It was a circus atmosphere, a day's outing, yet despite the gaiety there was a feeling of tension, for in a life sentence of toil, this was only a reprieve.

At the edge of the crowd, Angela could feel the heat of human bodies adding to the fiery glare of the sun. She could smell the poverty, an acrid mixture of beer, garlic, and sweat.

Angela pressed forward, eyes down. The closer she got to the mill, the tighter the crowd. She could not see individuals, only the stunning mob; she could not even pick out separate languages, only the clatter of strangely shaped words, the noise of foreigners. Several times she heard people laugh, and she was sure it was at her, but she didn't look up and confront their eyes or stay long enough to try to pick out what they were saying. She was becoming frightened now, frightened of the indistinguishable wash of faces, the chaos of sound, the sharp human smell.

Brilliant sun glanced off the buildings. Angela felt her clothes dragging at her, pulling on her back, choking her neck. She still couldn't see the mill, though she sensed it was close, but it was impossible to see more than a few feet ahead of her, and then all she could make out was the mob.

She stopped. Now she was completely surrounded by people, and they were jostling and shoving her; their strange languages clattered in her ears; the heavy smells oppressed her. She had never been so close to people before; their breath rushed against her face; their flesh and muscle pressed against her. Being rich was an insulation against the world, but here in the crowded streets of the poor, there was nothing to protect her.

Suddenly she panicked. No longer could she feel the injustice of poverty; all she could feel was the threat, growing more terrifying. She was a stranger, a person with no value. Worse, she had become part of a giant wave, an existence where births and deaths and great thoughts and acts went unnoticed.

Angela turned and tried to wedge her way back through the streets, but even in those few minutes, the crowd had grown, and she was held in by people, unable to move at all. The voices had become louder, and there was a tense anger to their sound, as if they sensed something terrible was about to happen.

Over the noise came a loud crack. At first Angela couldn't be sure of what she'd heard or if she'd even heard anything at all. But suddenly the crowd shifted; their eyes seemed to flash with terror. Men were shouting to one another, gruff, anxious shouting, and though Angela couldn't understand what they were saying, she sensed their tone, and it was then she knew what she'd heard and what it meant.

Once again there was the crack of a rifle, and this time the crowd turned, crying out, their voices sounding danger like a herd of wild animals.

Angela was shoved back violently, the force of the turning crowd throwing her off balance. For a moment she was afraid she was going to fall, but there was no room for it. The crowd jerked around, and Angela was sent hurtling forward, pressed to the mob until she was joining them in their desperate surging to get away.

Ben was just outside the gates of the mill when the police began firing. It was sudden, unexpected, and he had not seen what caused it. But all at once several of the police were pointing to the marchers, and he hardly had time to register that fact when there was the first crack of a bullet.

The demonstrators stopped, startled into immobility. The police were fumbling for their guns and tear gas as they moved forward. It all happened so quickly, Ben saw them only as a wave of dark blue, animallike in their gas masks.

There was a yell. Ben couldn't be sure which side it came from, but suddenly there was another shot, and this time the bullet came closer to him. He thought he saw a man drop to the ground, though everything was moving so rapidly he still wasn't sure what that meant. He could see the police badges glittering savagely in the sparkling heat; he could see their blue uniforms moving forward, but none of it made any sense to him; all he knew was he was in danger.

Ben turned, looking for Evan and Tom. The men were scattering now, running toward the spectators, throwing their picket signs to the ground, trampling them under their feet, unaware that their running was only making things worse. For a moment Ben wondered if he should stay where he was and hope the police would pass him by, but the panic was growing inside of him and he couldn't stop. He knew nothing except he had to get away.

The police had moved up just behind the running men. There was a loud shout, and then they were reaching for their cannisters of tear gas.

A pop, and the tear gas rose in a thick blue haze. A scream went up from the men, a scream of anger but full of animal fear. It was chaos. Everyone was running crazily, pushing and shoving, fighting each other and even themselves in their hysteria to get away.

Again a pop. Tear gas was spreading across the crowd like a thick cloud. Everyone was choking now, convulsed, bent, and tormented by the crippling gas. Men were staggering, trying to force themselves forward by tearing at each other. Some women had been left behind to fend for themselves, and they clutched their children and wailed. No one stopped to help them. They were just obstacles.

There was another shot, and this time Ben saw blood splatter through the crowd. Still the people pressed forward, hardly noticing it in the howling moment of panic. Ben could see everything, the crowd in chaos, the women and children mixed in with the frightened men. There was blood everywhere, blood and vomit, and there were people being trampled. He could hear them crying out. And behind him, someone was whimpering, just whimpering.

Then the tear gas took hold, and Ben's throat caught fire, pain tore at his eyes until he couldn't see. His legs felt very far away, feeble and uncontrollable. He fought, but the pain was growing, burning out all thought or feeling or anything except its own intense white-hot agony. It was taking over his body, sapping all control. He was like an animal.

His legs gave out, and he felt himself slipping to the ground. Panic-stricken, he pulled himself up, but with the panic came some strength. He turned quickly and began staggering to the side of the street and out of the way of the crushing crowd. When he reached the sidewalk, he felt everything give way again, and he thrust himself toward a building, grabbing hold of a wall, clutching it, head down, eyes closed.

Angela looked up and saw the blue haze rising behind her, spreading quickly across the crowd. Behind her she could hear the sounds of choking and retching. Terror gripped her, and she wanted to scream out, but no sound came from her mouth, and even in her frenzy she knew that there was nothing her screaming could do; she was part of the faceless, meaningless crowd. The police had released the gas and it was spreading rapidly through the hot summer air, tearing at the throats and eyes of the people, burning them until they fell to the ground. Then suddenly Angela realized she too was screaming, sharply, animallike. She could hear her voice mixing with the terrible hysteria around her, and she was moving erratically, fighting against the crowd to keep her balance.

There was another series of popping sounds. The haze spread thickly across the sky. Angela could see it over them, hunching just above the ground. She shuddered convulsively, her throat caught fire, and suddenly everything seemed to be jerking crazily around her. The choking and screaming of the crowd began to slip away, the shoving seemed almost from another world. The only thing real to her was the gaseous fire tearing at her throat. She clutched herself, as if her hands could protect her from it.

Distantly Angela felt herself being shoved violently back and forth, but she could no longer fight it. There was only the pain, splitting through her, pulling her apart until she was no longer aware of what was happening to her or if she existed at all.

* * *

Slowly Ben's head began to clear; the tearing pain receded. And with its passing, he began to see what was happening around him. The crowd had passed by; only a few of the wounded lay on the ground where they had dropped, choking from the gas or trampled by the frenzied mob. There were several policemen left behind, but most of them had followed the crowd. There would be more bloodshed.

Slowly things began to make sense. In his mind he relived the sight of the police closing in, gas masks obliterating all signs of humanity, guns drawn without any provocation. But he had seen those same policemen earlier; he had seen the fear in their eyes; it was no less than that of the people they were chasing. Terrified crowd. Terrified police. All battling, while the man who had caused it, the only one who benefited, was tucked away in comfort and privacy, somewhere far from danger. It was this that had caused the events of today; it was this that Evan had been trying to explain to him for months. They were all caught up in the web, and there was nothing any of them could do about it.

It was a moment of terror and deep despair, leaving scars that would last forever. For that was the way the world worked. There were men like his father who struggled in the mill and fought the choking blue haze, then there were the others, like Healey, who watched the struggle from behind tinted glass. The reality of the world tore at Ben. For he too was part of the choking, swirling mass, and he hated himself and everyone who had put him there.

Through the lifting haze, Ben could see Evan and Tom, handkerchiefs tied around their mouths, trying to pick up the wounded, though they too were coughing and unsteady on their feet. Shakily, he stood free of the building and began moving forward to help.

As Ben came closer he saw Evan reach for the figure of a woman on the ground and take her in his arms. There was something familiar about the outline of the woman, the small hard face, the drab clothing. Ben startled as he watched Evan moving toward him with the body of Angela Healey. And in that moment he knew exactly who she was, and he saw the possibility of redemption.

EIGHT

"So who are you staring at then?" Ben called out. "Something funny about our faces?"

Angela was standing, partially hidden by the administration building. The minute she heard Ben yelling, she shrank even farther into the shadows.

Ben leaned to Evan and laughed. "I told you you'd made a big impression."

Ben and Evan were taking their break, sitting cross-legged on the sooty ground just outside the blast furnace, lunch pails open before them. It was a breach of the rules to be sitting out there, instead of in the doghouse, but it was a rule that was being overlooked for the moment in the aftermath of the Healey Mills riot. It was a small concession, of course; the union was still banned, but it was a concession nonetheless, another indication that a change had been begun that Memorial Day. The wave was on the move.

Ben looked back at the administration building. Angela hadn't come out of the shadows, but she hadn't gone away either. Ben called again. "Well, there must be something up, the way you keep watching us and all."

Evan shot Ben a dirty look, but this did nothing to discourage him. He merely snickered and whispered to Evan, "Oh, my darling, I owe my life to you."

Angela came out of the shadows. "I'm sorry, but I wanted to thank you again for saving my life and . . ." She stopped, feeling awkward and foolish.

"Wasn't nothing," Ben yelled back. "Was it, Evan? All in a day's work." He began nudging Evan to get up and go over to Angela. "Talk to the lady," he whispered. "Let her express her gratitude. Maybe with a check for a million dollars or something."

"You're disgusting," Evan whispered back.

"Oh, disgusting am I? Well, excuse me." He laughed heartily, then nudged him again. "You go over and talk to her or I'll say something disgusting again."

Angela could tell they were laughing at her, and she stood in an agony of embarrassment and shame. She couldn't blame them for laughing. She'd had no business being at that demonstration. She had risked their lives, all the men's lives in fact, for if something had happened to her, there was no telling what the consequences would have been for the men.

"I wanted to let you know if there's anything I can do to repay you . . ." Again she fell silent.

Ben chuckled to Evan. "Too right there's something. Tell her what she can do for us, Evan boy."

Evan threw a murderous glance at Ben, but he could see there was only one thing he could do to stop him from making a fool of both of them and that was to talk to the woman. Reluctantly he got up and, dusting the soot from his trousers, walked toward Angela. He dreaded talking to her. She seemed such a lady in her dark tailored suit, a creature from another world, so out of place in the filth of the steel mill. He felt dirty and sweaty, an awkward working man.

He stopped when he was several feet away, aware of the smell of work and steel on him. "How are you feeling, ma'am?" he asked. "You got quite a bumping around."

"I had no business being there. I must seem very stupid to you."

"Well, you ought to be more careful from now on," Evan answered. His voice sounded strange, and there was a tight feeling in the back of his throat. He didn't look at Angela, but he was aware of her expression, and he felt oppressed by it. He wished she would go back into the shadows and the cool cleanliness of the offices.

Angela blushed and looked around, confused. Of course she must seem stupid to him; she must seem foolish to them all. Who was she to pretend an interest in the workers when she had her big luxurious home to return to, with her clean sheets and fresh nightgowns and breakfast in bed?

Evan felt angry and embarrassed. "I saw you the other night at the union meeting," he said at last. "You shouldn't have been there. It was no place for a lady."

"I wanted to know . . . I wanted to feel what was going on." How ridiculous she sounded to herself, stammering and stuttering. "I didn't approve of what happened." The blood rushed to her face; she felt she had betrayed her father by this statement.

"What exactly is it you didn't approve of?"

Family Passions

"I believe in the union. I believe my father should allow it," Angela answered softly.

"And have you told him that then?"

Angela shook her head. How could she explain to him that she hardly spoke to her father, that she was as scared of him as were the men who risked their lives at the mill, that in many ways she was similar to Evan? He would have laughed. Mental fear wasn't anything like physical fear. What did she know, she who had never gone cold or hungry; what right did she have to believe in the union?

Finally Evan stiffened. "Well, it doesn't matter, ma'am. I don't suppose there's any reason for you to get mixed up in it."

"It wouldn't make any difference what I said," she answered desperately. "He wouldn't listen to me."

"It isn't your fight."

"But it *is* my fight. You don't understand. If people like me don't back the union, then nothing will happen."

Evan drew back. "The union's done all right without your help so far, ma'am. I know we aren't much to look at and we're not educated, but we can still make things happen if we stick together."

"I didn't mean it that way." Angela felt herself shaking. What a fool she was!

"No, no, it's okay, ma'am," he answered stiffly. "You're right about there being people like you and people like me. But that doesn't mean we can't change things. After all, people like you need people like us. You aren't all that enchanted about climbing into blast furnaces or cleaning your houses or tending your lawns or taking out your garbage." He fell silent. There was no use getting angry with types like Healey's daughter. They would only laugh at the way he spoke or cringe from the way he looked. Even the best of them moved away instinctively when one of the men came close. And do-gooding ladies? He supposed they didn't really see people like Evan as existing as men. They were just another species to them, a curiosity to view, perhaps even to aid. But to count as having value? Never.

Angela's voice was shaking. "I put that all wrong. I didn't mean to imply I was better than you; honestly I didn't, though I suppose you have every reason not to believe me. You must be thinking that I have no idea what you're going through. You must be thinking that I'm just playing at it."

Evan didn't answer. Although it was exactly what he was thinking, he knew better than to say it. After all, she was the boss's daughter, and there was no telling what kind of trouble she could make for a man stupid enough to be honest.

Angela moved up cautiously. "I know that's what you think. I can see it from your face. But you're wrong. I want to help. If there's anything I can do, please tell me."

The whistle blew and Evan looked back at Ben, who was quickly gathering up the lunch pails. He turned back to Angela. "Well, thank you very much, ma'am. I'll certainly keep that in mind."

"But I mean it." Angela felt desperate.

"Yes, ma'am. Sorry but that was the whistle. If I don't rush I'll get docked, if you see what I mean."

Angela saw exactly what he meant. She nodded at Evan, but he was already turning away, running back to the mill.

Slowly she walked back to the administration building, feeling the sting of Evan's last words. In the end that was the important thing, his running back scared to the choking dust, worried that he would lose money, and her heading back slowly to her father's office, where a hot meal would be waiting.

"We're never going to get anywhere with that Healey," Tom said, as he pulled up a chair and sat at the kitchen table across from Ben and Evan.

Elizabeth was standing over the sink, washing potatoes, but she was listening to the talk attentively, noting every gesture, every mannerism.

Tom continued, "I just don't know why we're wasting our time. It's like the big demonstration. What the hell did we get out of that but several bashed heads, some gassed lungs, and a whole lot of bad feelings? I gotta pinch myself to believe we've still got our jobs at all."

Evan was rigid. "So what do you think we ought to do, Tom?"

"Just take our paychecks and be grateful. I think we ought to forget the whole idea of coming up with some new alloy that's going to put us on easy street. 'Cause it ain't gonna happen. We aren't even going to get into old man Healey's anteroom."

Ben laughed angrily. "You know, Tom, I think it's your optimism that keeps me going."

"It's called realism, Ben. And if you ask me, you could use a bit more of it."

"Realism is for peasants."

Evan grimaced. "And since when have you become a member of the landed gentry, Ben?"

"Not yet. But I'm planning on it." Ben leaned back in his chair and sprawled. He was feeling good and smart and lucky. "Now let's take a little look at that invention of yours, and you just let your uncle Ben worry about the Healey part."

Evan shot Tom an exasperated look. "Ben, how many times do I have to explain, we don't have an invention? We have a *new blend* of steel."

"Excuse me, gentlemen. Then please let's have a look at that brilliant new improved blend of steel that we're going to march into Healey's office and knock him over with."

Evan was astounded. "Ben, first of all, I've explained before that this new alloy is not better or stronger or cheaper than anything on the market today. The only advantage is that its components are not under the control of the Axis, and should there be war, they can't cut off our supplies. Second of all, there are no samples."

"Hey, Evan. I gotta show the man we can make a damn good steel."

"Jesus, Ben," Tom said. "How the hell are we going to do that? We can't exactly go into the kitchen and whip up a batch."

"So then how do you know it's good?"

"I can tell by the formula."

"Let's say you're right and it's good. Let's say it's great."

Tom frowned. "Evan told you before it's not great."

"All right, Tom. Let's just say it's adequate. Now you know it. And Evan knows it. And I know it. Wonderful. But how do we prove it to old man Healey, who happens, just happens, to hold our destinies in his scrawny skinflinting fist?"

Again Evan shot an exasperated look at Tom. "Ben, anyone with a knowledge of metallurgy can look at this formula and get a pretty good idea."

"Really? You mean you can look at a bunch of stupid elements like val . . . whatever the hell it is, and know what it's going to come out like?"

Tom answered evenly. "Not entirely. Of course it's just an indication, but you can use your imagination and knowledge to predict."

Ben's face was a tight knot of concentration. "And what makes you so sure Healey'll understand? For Christ sake, when I look at all those garbagy symbols, it's Greek to me."

Evan shot out, "And since when have you become the intellectual standard?"

"I don't need to bother with that stuff. That's your part. I've got business instincts. That's enough."

Evan looked skeptical. "It wouldn't hurt if you spent a little time on it too, you know."

Elizabeth was leaning against the sink, watching. It was clear she wanted to enter the conversation and was fighting to hold her tongue.

"Hell, I fall asleep if I even pass the library," Ben said sourly. "You just worry about your valhoozium . . ."

Tom corrected, "Validium."

"Fine. You just worry about it, and I'll worry about the business aspect."

"The big businessman," Elizabeth interjected sharply. "Why don't you listen to your brother for a change? Something you might learn about what you hope you're selling."

"Hope?" Ben got up from the table and walked over to Elizabeth. Standing face to face with her, they looked like two carved mountains. "This isn't just a hope, Ma," he said intensely. "This is it. The end of washing potatoes and chasing after Pauline and scrubbing floors and counting pennies every time you go shopping. And we'll get a maid, and you'll say, 'Fifi, I want you to make dinner for a hundred or so people tonight.' "

Elizabeth's eyes were sparkling with humor, but she tried to keep a serious expression on her face. "Fifi?"

"Well, okay. So maybe we won't get a Fifi. How about Jemima? I saw this movie once where they had a maid called Jemima . . ."

"No one do I want to do things for me when I can very well do them for myself, Ben Savage. So forget you your Fifis and Jemimas."

"Fine," Ben said with great dignity. "Have it your way. But I won't have you scrubbing floors or peeling potatoes."

Elizabeth shook her head. "Getting a wee bit ahead of yourself, you are."

Evan laughed. "Ahead of himself? Why, he can't see his own backside for the distance."

Tom nodded. "We aren't even going to get over the threshold of Healey's office, let alone convince him to start us in a company."

"Now that's what you leave to me," Ben shot back.

Elizabeth folded her strong arms across her chest and fixed Ben with a sharp stare. "And since when has ignorance got anyone ahead in this world then?"

"I'm not ignorant."

"Pretty close to it you are. And no great beauty either."

"Just 'cause I don't know a bunch of dumb facts about steel doesn't make me ignorant."

"They are not dumb facts," Evan answered heatedly.

Elizabeth nodded. "Andrew Carnegie knew a bunch of dumb facts and look what happened to him."

"I'm just as smart as Andrew damn Carnegie," Ben said, but his voice was subdued. "Well, okay, so maybe I will read a book about steel. But just one book. And I can't promise I won't fall asleep."

Tom sighed. "You can read every damn book in the library, and it isn't going to get us into Healey's office."

Ben turned on Tom angrily. "Well, then, why don't you just shuffle on home to your wife and kid? You want to spend the rest of your life sweating like the rest of the insects of this world, go right ahead."

"He's right, Ben," Evan said. "It doesn't matter how good our formula is; we couldn't get in to see old man Healey even if we were the guys who'd invented the wheel."

"We'll get in," Ben said impatiently. "In fact, it's our Evan who's going to get us in."

"Me? Now how in the heck am I going to do that?"

"Old man Healey isn't going to turn away his future son-in-law, is he?"

"Son-in-law? Ben, have you gone nuts?"

"Hey, you can't tell me Miss Angela Healey isn't sweet on you."

"What's this?" Elizabeth asked, surprised.

Evan blushed. "Now I know you're nuts."

"Oh, am I? I saw how she looked at you that first time from the car. And for Christ sake, you saved her bloody life. She's always looking at you all soft-eyed." Ben minced across the room and chucked Evan under the chin.

Evan fought to control his anger. "She's grateful I saved her life. That's all."

"Well, you're going to give her a chance to show her gratitude."

"You're disgusting, Ben. You really are."

Elizabeth was looking from one of her sons to the other. "I want to know what's going on."

Ben smirked. "I'm just being disgusting, Ma. But I'm going to be rich and disgusting."

"I don't want any more of this talk about Miss Healey."

"You're blushing, Evan," Ben teased.

Evan stood up; his face was bright red and angry. "Stop it, Ben. Or I'll punch you out, brother or no. I swear I will."

Elizabeth's voice cut through. "What's this Miss Healey business, then?"

Ben walked back to Elizabeth and leaned against the sink next to her. "It seems our Evan over here has made a conquest in the person of Miss Angela Healey, daughter of, and I'll bet sole heir to, the fortunes of Mr. Nicholas Healey, owner of the Healey Mills no less."

Elizabeth was stunned. "Is this true?"

Evan shouted. "No, Ma. It isn't true. It's just Ben's overactive imagination."

"Is not! He saved her life at the demonstration. He carried her right out of the teargassing and took care of her until she was fine, then he made sure she got back home safely. And she was making eyes as soft as a plum in August at him. I could see it half a block away."

Elizabeth turned to Tom. "And what do you think about all this, then?"

"I think Ben has a point. But no daughter of a millionaire is going to do more than perhaps flirt with a steelworker. So it doesn't matter whether she's soft on him or not."

"Oh, yeah?" Ben said. "Well, I think she'd be damn lucky to get our Evan."

Elizabeth was thinking. "Yes, certainly. A king can look at a cat as easily as a cat a king. But still and all, in this country a millionaire is no closer than the Prince of Wales was back home."

"Look," Evan said. "If you're all through deciding my future, I'd like to talk about the formula. That's why we're here, remember?"

Ben waved Evan's words away. "The hell with the damn formula; we can discuss that later."

"Damn formula, is it? Well, all the conniving in the world doesn't mean a thing without my damn formula."

"And all the damn formulas in the world don't mean a thing without my conniving."

Elizabeth laughed. "Aren't either of you ever going to grow up?" She turned to Evan. "Why are you getting so hot under the collar about this Miss Healey business?"

Family Passions

"I'm not getting hot under the collar."

"Like hell you aren't." Ben sneered. Evan moved closer to his brother, and for a moment it looked as if he might start a fight.

Elizabeth boomed, "Now stop it! Both of you."

Ben and Evan turned from each other and watched their mother. Though they were both grown men, she still had power over them.

"The way I see it," Elizabeth continued, "if this Miss Healey wants to help, why should you object?"

"But she doesn't want to help, Ma. I haven't said more than a few words to her."

Ben simpered. "Like I love you."

Evan was red-faced and moving toward Ben again.

"Stop it, I said!" Elizabeth waited, watching them angrily. "Now, Evan, all peculiar you're acting about this Miss Healey business. And I've a feeling you just might care for the girl."

Evan shook his head. "You don't understand, Ma. You can't call a millionaire's daughter a girl."

"What else can you call her, may I ask? Take it from me; a girl she is, and there's no reason in the world why she shouldn't have a case for you."

"You don't understand."

"Oh, aye? Well, as far as I know, millionaires' daughters get babies just like the rest of us."

Ben was nodding his head. "All you gotta do is stop being so damn shy. Talk to her, you know. Sort of start slow, like about the weather and what not, and before you know it . . ." He snapped his fingers.

"That's right," Elizabeth said. "Where's the harm in it? It's clear you aren't set against the girl."

"How can you back him up like that, Ma?"

"No reason do I see not to try."

"No reason? She's a rich man's daughter with a rich mind and she wouldn't look at me. And even if she did, I wouldn't do it because it'd be using her."

"For Christ sake!" Ben exclaimed. "Everyone's using people. That's the way the world works. Take a look around. Healey's using his foreman and his foreman is using us and we use the new boys, and we're all scrounging and scratching around so we can get out from under and be used as little as possible and use as many as we can."

Evan was shocked. "What the hell's happening to you, Ben? What kind of talk is that?"

Tom smiled. "He's becoming a cynic. It comes with growing up."

"Well, I'm no cynic," Evan said self-righteously.

Ben's eyes narrowed with suspicion. "What's a cynic?"

Tom ignored him. "Maybe that's part of your problem, Evan."

"In other words, you think Ben's right?"

Ben whined. "Isn't anyone gonna tell me what he just called me?"

"Quiet you, boy!" Elizabeth warned.

Tom continued. "It isn't like you hate her or anything. Using her would be if you hated her and every time you went to screw her you wanted to vomit—"

"Stop you, right there!" Elizabeth demanded. "That might be the way you talk around your house. I can't help that. The boss you are at home, though Lord only knows you're still young enough to need a da yourself, rather than being one. But there it is. And in the Savage household we don't talk like that."

"Like what? I didn't say anything worse than Ben or Evan say."

"That'll be enough." Elizabeth pushed up her sleeves and walked to the center of the kitchen. Her large imposing face was lined, her eyes thoughtful. "No more do I believe that we should talk on this subject, for all we're doing is setting Evan against the idea just to spite us."

"Yeah. He's a real pain in the ass," Ben said.

Elizabeth glared at him. "More than enough we've heard from you, Mr. Big Mouth. I don't notice you coming home with any millionaires in your back pocket."

Evan was furious. "Am I going crazy? I don't have anyone in my back pocket. The woman smiled at me, and you have us waltzing down the aisle all of a sudden."

Elizabeth commanded. "Tom, don't you think it's time you went home to your wife and new son? Good there is not in leaving a new mother all alone, and on your day off." Then she looked at Ben. "And time it is to wake our Pauline. Take her out for a walk. Poor child hasn't been out in the air all day."

"I'm not leaving here till that stupid brother of mine changes his mind."

Elizabeth shot an angry look at Ben. It was a look he remembered all too well from his childhood, and for a moment he felt like a little boy, frightened of his mother's anger. Tom too withered under her glare. He got up from the table and made for the door.

Ben sighed. "Hold up, Tom. Pauline and I'll walk you home."

Evan was about to follow, but Elizabeth caught at his arm. "No, stay, Evan. Stay you here."

Evan looked up at his mother's face, and he too felt the power of her stare. He sat back down, watching the others leave with envy; he dreaded the confrontation he sensed they were about to have.

Elizabeth took a seat next to him; her arms, red from hard work and water, lay across her huge lap. "A story there is I want to tell you. Never have I told you this, nor talked to anyone, even your da, though he knew it anyway as he was there. And what need is there to talk of things that are known and never can be changed?" She sighed. "But your da and I didn't talk much ever, even at the best of times. Understood by a look, we did. And what do you need with words, when it's in the eyes?"

She fell silent, and Evan could see it was hard for her to continue. "Never have we talked about when we came over from Wales," she said at last. "There is very little I'm supposing you remember, so young you were. Not much above four years. Aye, and a lark it must have seemed to you then, not knowing enough to worry."

Evan had expected an argument, and his mother's sad tone surprised him. "There's very little I remember about that time, the feel of the ship, a new kind of cookie you bought me, small things. But I do remember the excitement and the newness."

"Aye. There was that in it." Elizabeth laughed, though her eyes seemed very far away. "But more too. Hard it was. Very hard. I had saved up money, not much above fifty-five pounds, but it had seemed a lot, so young and cocky was I and wanting to come to America. Though what I hoped to find, I did not know. But an obsession it was with me. Feeling if only we could get ourselves to America then everything would come out right. And hard on the subject was I to your da, nagging and pleading and whining till all hours." She smiled at Evan. "Not much have I changed from those days, have I?"

"You get your point across."

"Aye. A curse it is to be a strong woman. Always you must ask for what you want. Begging and wheedling for what is rightfully yours. But that's all you've got and use it you must, even knowing the clatter you make. Anyway, my mind I had set on coming, and there wasn't a peaceful moment with me from that time on. I cried. I screamed. I nagged. I whined. I was silent. And always just one word, America, America, America. But scared was your da. Scared of the passage and finding a home and a job. Good reason he had to be scared too, though I had not the sense to see it.

"Then one day his pit closed and the men were being transferred to another one ten miles away, and the time seemed right, and he had to give in. Ben was five, and a regular tyrant even then. And you were just a *crwt* of a boy, no heavier than a sack of flour. And there was another on the way."

"You were pregnant?"

"Aye. Six months gone and as big as a house. But the minute your da nodded his head in agreement, out was I booking passage. And fair play to me, packed up and ready to leave in a week was I. Of course the mess left behind was nothing you'd care tell about. But truth be known, we didn't have all that much. And proper up in the air with excitement was I, so I would have left everything behind at a moment's notice. I just knew this was going to be the beginning, a dream come true. We were going to have grand carriages and drive through the streets like royalty. Aye." She laughed. "For your da I bought a white shirt. Beautiful white it was, and as dear as all the rest of our clothes put together. But look you, it was white, clean white. For in the mines it didn't pay to wear anything but gray. And never again, thought I, would he lift the haft of a mattock."

She smiled at the memory, but there was great sadness beneath. "Not all that different from our Ben, you're thinking, and you're right. Just as silly." She sighed. "Of course cheated we were, just as everyone who came over was. But no use there is dwelling on that. Thinking about sad things does not change them one bit. A mistake there was with our passage and we knew we were being cheated, but by that time no choice did we have. All of us were being shoved on the boat like a herd of cattle, and sickness there was, days and days of sickness. Evan, never have I seen the like of it, and I hope to God I never do again. Like animals they lived, like animals they died. And though used was I to see people dying from living in the country and all, this kind of dying I never did see. Throwing up their insides until they were down to nothing. And still they sicked up, and then they stopped, and one day they just didn't move at all."

Elizabeth paused and turned her eyes from Evan to the floor. It took her a long time to continue. "Six days out it was when I began to sense that which was going on in my belly wasn't good. The

Family Passions

pains they came, as strong as birth itself. And then I knew. A girl she was, all curled in on herself, and tiny, sad tiny, but peaceful too, and sleeping in a sense, though that wasn't how I saw it then.''

She clenched her reddened hands. "Can one so young have a soul? That I wondered and many other crazy things as I lay ill." She was silent again, her eyes on the table where she traced circles with her rough finger. "And then New York there was, and without a soul as the devil himself. No one did we know, nor even were we sure we could get in. For your da was beginning to cough about that time, though not a word did he say. But his face told the tale when the spells hit him. And scared he was, like he wished he'd never been born. And scared was I too.

"Well, we stood on those docks, our things all around us, though little enough there was left. The white shirt was gone, used to stop the sick, and much else too, either stolen or borrowed. For a long time we stood, looking out at the rotting buildings. Oh, Evan, nothing do you see from the docks of New York but rotting piers and rotting buildings. Old, terrible old, far worse than anything in Wales, like they'd been standing since the beginning of time. Dockhands there were, all around, yelling at each other and at us to go away. But nowhere was there for us to go. No more money had we, no more food. Nothing had we, and that we had in plenty. Your poor da was coughing, and weak was I, fresh from losing the little one. You and your brother weren't crying anymore; you were sleeping on a sack of clothes, dark circles under your eyes and all thin and sad. And I thought to myself, standing there, what a fool I was, what a wicked, wicked fool, for pushing this move that left us homeless, friendless in this terrible land. And I cursed myself and my tongue and my will that had made me so stiff-necked."

She hesitated for a moment, and suddenly she smiled. "Then it was that farther down the dock a great white ship I spied. Oh, Evan, beautiful she was. More sleek and elegant than a lady from Cardiff, and the size of a mountain, a great glittering mountain of ice. Like nothing I ever saw in all my life. Getting ready to leave was she. With people crowding all around. And 'Hark!' I said to your da. 'Look you very carefully and you can see all the ladies in their fur coats and the gentlemen in gray jackets. Great steamer trunks there are and ribbons and balloons. Stewards in sparkling white uniforms.' And your da screwed up his eyes and looked. Well, just then, the ship sounded her foghorn. Oh, Evan, what a sound! It went right through me. Goose bumps I get just thinking about it."

Her voice grew hushed. "And then it was I knew; the realization shook right through me. For just about everyone boarding that ship had started out like us, coming to America, scared and homeless. And I said to your da, 'Good is the dream. Good and right, and never again will I curse it, but get down to work and everything will come out well.' And your da laughed, because funny it must have seemed with me such a fright and talking about dreams and hopes and things like that. But that didn't bother me. For I knew he laughed out of love and respect. So a bit of a laugh never hurts when it's mixed with love."

Again she stopped and fixed Evan with her hungry eyes. "A great deal did I lose along the way. That trip was the end of my little 'un, and it was the beginning of the end of my husband. But listen you, Evan, nothing there was that was wrong with the dream. The dream wasn't at fault."

"Then what was?" Evan asked, and there was anger in his voice, for while he knew much of the fault lay in the world, he also believed that some of it lay in the dream.

"Nothing there was at fault. It all went as planned. Ben and you are here to carry on. You've inherited that dream, the both of you. And a responsibility you have to it. Otherwise it makes no sense. For the soul of your da and your baby sister lie waiting. Give up the dream and what do their deaths mean? All the pain and suffering and sacrifice, it's got to mean something, doesn't it?" Elizabeth's eyes were pleading. It seemed more as if she were asking that question to the powers of light and darkness than to Evan.

Then she took Evan's hand and held it tightly. "Son, never have I asked you to do anything that is repellent to you. This life is yours and not for me or your da or your unborn sister or all the generations behind you to live. But if the offering is there and you fancy it, don't turn away. There's a knack to living, and being able to take is a large part. Taking is so much harder than not."

She opened Evan's hand and held it before her. "A good hand, yours is, when it's open like that. So much stronger than a fist. For an open hand will hold much and be of much use. While a closed hand will hold nothing but itself."

She sighed deeply. "Oh, aye. Life is a lot of sorrow and trouble, but there can be great pleasure in it. Great, great pleasure. It is up to you."

Elizabeth stood abruptly, but her eyes were still on Evan, and she leaned to kiss his forehead as she had when he was a child. "I love you, Evan, as ever I've loved anything. And happy I'll be whatever your choice."

NINE

Angela stopped and looked at the red brick house with excitement and also apprehension. "So this is where you live," she said to Evan.

"Aye. And not much to look at either."

Evan glanced away from her. Though he and Angela had been seeing one another for the past month, there had been little time to build trust, and he felt bringing her to his house would shock and sober her. And perhaps that was why he did it.

Angela smiled gaily. "I'm trying to imagine you coming out the door every morning, lunch pail in hand."

"Running's more like it. As late as an old maid's reward."

Evan was wearing his Sunday suit and feeling uncomfortable in it. Yet there was pleasure in his discomfort, as if everyone on the street could see what was happening and envied him. Angela was wearing a dark dress and hat, but she had pinned a cluster of silk roses at her neck, and her face had changed; it looked younger, fuller. But also, Evan could tell, she looked scared.

"Shall we go in then?" Evan asked, taking her hand in his.

Angela drew in breath. "Are you sure you want to?"

Evan held her hand tightly, trying to read her thoughts. "Oh, aye, if you do."

"Yes, I do want to," Angela said determinedly. "I want to very much."

Elizabeth was startled when the door opened. She was standing at the sink, her arms red and steaming from the hot water, and she drew back a moment in embarrassment, almost dropping a plate. Then quickly she motioned for Evan to come to her, and when he had neared, she pulled him to the sink, clutching his arm. "You could have told me she was coming," she whispered angrily. Then, forcing a smile, she turned back to Angela, who was still in the doorway. "Well, don't just stand there, gel. Come in."

"Mrs. Savage, I'm so sorry to barge in like this," Angela apologized. "But Evan invited me and I wanted so much to come."

Elizabeth turned on Evan, her eyes speaking her irritation. Then she remembered herself and tried to temper her voice. "Well, glad I am that he asked you. Though well would it have been had he told me. The house is a mess, what with three children and one of them still small. And nothing there is to eat, I warn you."

She wiped her hands on a towel. "A nice pie I would have made. Three of them, when it comes to that. Apple and a nice jam, maybe even a plum if the greengrocer had had any good ones."

Evan laughed but he was clearly uncomfortable. "That's why I didn't tell you, Ma. I didn't want to put you out."

"Put me out, is it? And what may I ask is it now, with the house all rumble tumble, and your visitor scared to come over the threshold lest she get a disease?"

Angela realized with mortification that she was still standing at the door. Yet she didn't move. She was terrified of the large woman. While Evan was delicate looking, darkly intelligent, this woman was broad and thick and threatening. For a moment she was reminded how she had felt on that day at the demonstration, and she was instantly sorry for that thought. Still, she couldn't move. She was caught where she was, feeling very frightened and alone.

"Well, bring her in then," Elizabeth said. "And sit her down if you can find the room. Tea I can make and something sweet, though I can't promise much."

She went to the cupboard and began clattering cups and saucers, trying to calm herself. After all, hadn't she been the one who'd encouraged Evan to pursue Angela? What possible difference could it make that she hadn't been warned of this visit? And yet it did make a difference. She felt jealousy rising in her, unreasonable but strong and hard like a knot in her throat. She felt betrayed.

Evan winked at Angela, then came to the door, took her arm, and led her into the room. He was smiling at her, and she tried to find some comfort in his eyes, but she could tell by the set of his shoulders that he also was unsure.

Elizabeth put water in the kettle, lit the stove, then opened a cookie jar. Belligerently she piled cookies on her best blue plate.

Every once in a while she glanced over and, from the corner of her eye, scrutinized Angela. Finally she turned around and watched her openly. "Is it too cold for you then? A fire I can lay if there's need."

"It's very comfortable, Mrs. Savage. Thank you."

Elizabeth's eyes didn't waver. "You won't be needing your coat then, will you?"

Angela flushed and pulled off her coat. She looked over at Evan. He was still smiling but the nervousness was clearly there. And suddenly she felt very angry with him. After all, she was his friend; he should have been worried for her, not his mother. Then quickly she caught herself. Why did she feel she had any special importance, so much so that he should no longer consider his own mother's feelings? Was it because she was the boss's daughter? Tears of shame came to her eyes. No wonder the tall broad woman with the angry blue eyes didn't want her there. Undoubtedly his mother could read just what kind of a person she was.

Elizabeth poured boiling water over the tea leaves and carried the pot to the table. She glanced at Angela and forced a smile. But she noted that Angela hadn't offered to help, noticed and disapproved, though in fact she suspected she would have been just as angry if she had.

"Our Evan's been telling us all about you," Elizabeth said, as she placed the cookies in front of Angela. She sat down at the head of the table with a weary sigh.

"All good things," Evan said with a laugh, but his laugh sounded false in his ears, and he was angry at his mother for making him feel so nervous. For a moment he almost forgot that Angela was there. The world had shrunk around him; he felt enclosed by it.

"Aye. Good things," Elizabeth echoed. She began pouring tea, trying to do it gracefully, as if she were used to having rich company. Every once in a while she glanced over at Angela but she said nothing. She could feel the air in the room growing thick with tension, but she didn't care. Who did she think she was to come barging in without so much as a word of warning? It was Evan's fault, of course, not the girl's, though a girl of that sort should have known better. But deep down she knew it was not this that was making her angry, it was something much more important.

As Elizabeth poured the milk, she stole a glance at Angela. She was much too thin, like a broomstick. In bed she'd be all nobbles and bones. It surprised her that her son could find beauty in anything as sorry as Angela. She glanced over at Evan and could see how uncomfortable he was becoming, perhaps even having second thoughts. Well, if he was, she couldn't blame him. For sitting next to her, the girl must have seemed a bloodless stick.

Once again Elizabeth pulled herself up short. Hadn't this been her own idea? Wasn't she the one who'd told Evan to reach out for life? Still, if this was life, she didn't know what death was. Again she stopped herself. But no, he said he was fond of the poor wretch, and useful she could be, very useful. She could be the beginning of the dream.

"Have some cookies then." Elizabeth held out the plate to Angela. "Just shortbread they are, but homemade, not store bought. And plenty of good butter and sugar there is in them for all that."

"Thank you, Mrs. Savage." Angela took a cookie, though the thought of eating made her ill, and she knew if she did, it would stick in her throat.

Elizabeth's eyes were on Angela as she took the cookie and put it on her plate, watching pointedly until she had forced Angela to take a bite. Again she pressed the plate on her. "Go on, take more than that."

She turned to Evan. "She doesn't eat, this one. Make her take some cookies home. No good it is for a woman to be so thin. Strong and healthy she should be for when her time comes."

Angela flushed and looked at Evan, but he was staring at the floor, his jaw set tightly as if barely holding back angry words. Elizabeth glanced from one to the other, and there was a gleam of triumph in her eyes.

"Where're Ben and Pauline?" Evan asked after a while.

"Ben took Pauline out for a walk," Elizabeth answered. "Poor little gel hasn't been out all day. Soon it is they'll be back, I expect. Though they'd be here now if you'd told us you were bringing your lady friend."

"Don't worry, Ma. It's better this way. It gives us a chance to talk quietly."

Elizabeth smiled. "Aye. Quiet it isn't when Ben's around. Do you know our Ben?" Elizabeth had turned to Angela and was grilling her with her stare.

"Yes, Mrs. Savage. I've met him a few times. He's very nice."

Elizabeth laughed. "Nice is it? What a word for him! Not a nice bone in his body has our Ben. But good he is, good for all his ranting and raving. And so is our Evan, though a bit stronger in the

Family Passions

nice area. It's a good family you're visiting, Miss Healey. Not rich, but good."

Angela nodded and felt the tears coming to her eyes. She wished she were anywhere but sitting at that table, with Mrs. Savage trying to be dainty, her large bulky body betraying her at every turn. Angela's very presence was making this woman feel uncomfortable, and in her own kitchen. It didn't seem fair.

"Relax, Ma," Evan said. "Angela knows what kind of family I come from."

"It's a wonder she does, dragging her in like the cat with no preparations made."

"What is this preparations stuff, huh? Just stop it."

"And since when is it we have that kind of backtalk in my house? Just because you're bringing a lady around now, you still are living under my roof. And I won't have it, Evan. Really I won't."

"What are you getting so upset for, Ma?"

Elizabeth hesitated. She didn't know why she was so upset. It made no sense to be angry at Evan for doing precisely as she advised. But still the feeling of desperation held her and drove her tongue on. "Aye. Upset I am. And with good cause. For I don't like you bringing your friends around to look down their noses."

Evan yelled, "Stop it, Ma!"

Angela stood up. "It's my fault, Evan. I should never have come." She grabbed her coat. "I'm sorry for barging in like this, Mrs. Savage. I hope you'll forgive me."

Evan got up angrily. "Now see what you've done, Ma? You've hurt Angela's feelings." He stopped Angela with his hand. "I'm sorry, Angela. Really I am."

Elizabeth sat like a boulder at the table. "What's all this fuss about then? Sit down the both of you and stop all the dramatics."

Evan held Angela's arm. "Dramatics, is it? You were being rude, Ma, and you know it."

Angela touched his arm. "It's not your mother's fault. It's mine. I'm the one who's disrupting the household."

Elizabeth didn't turn around, but the rigidity was gone from her back and her tone had softened. "Always disrupted this house is. So no offense should you take. It's nothing to do with you. Sit you down and we'll start again."

Angela looked questioningly at Evan, but he was staring at his mother's back, his face flushed with anger.

"Come on," Elizabeth said. "Sit you back down here. The tea's going cold."

Elizabeth turned her head and looked back at Angela. For the first time Angela realized how upset she was. Elizabeth's stark broad face was creased with lines, and her eyes seemed heavy like stones. She was terrified of losing her son. Though she knew she was losing him whatever she did, she was scared of losing him this way, in anger and pettiness. Yet she couldn't say so. She was caught in her pride. Just turning her head around had pushed her as far as she could go. Women like Mrs. Savage could never manage more.

Angela touched Evan on the arm. "Let's sit down, Evan."

"Not till she apologizes to you."

Angela shook her head. "There's no need for apologies."

"Well, I think there is."

Elizabeth was turned to the wall, but Angela could see from the set of her back that she deeply regretted all that had passed and was unable to do anything about it. Angela broke from Evan's hand and walked to the table, then she sat down in her place and began to eat one of the cookies.

Elizabeth was drinking her tea slowly, deliberately, staring straight ahead of her, but Angela knew she had seen what had happened and was relieved.

Finally Elizabeth turned to her. "A bit of roughness you could do with, gel. A bit of roughness and rudeness and flesh. Never did it hurt anyone to put a little meat on their bones and blood in their veins. Aye, yeah. Savage is our name. And savages we sometimes be. But it's from savages that this world evolved. All the churches and art galleries and libraries and bridges and all the dainty ladylike world started with the monkeys, as that man Darwin says. So it can't be as bad as all that to be a savage sometimes. There isn't a baby in this world that came from polite conversation, eh?" She put her rough meaty hand on Angela's shoulder and smiled, heartily.

And Angela found herself smiling back.

Nicholas Healey loved Bach. It was a passion with him, in fact, the only passion he could bring himself to enjoy since his wife had died. As a young child he had played the cello, wrapping his small body around that large instrument like a cat around a tree trunk. He had been neither good at it nor had he ever tried to play an instrument again, but for that one year, at the age of twelve, he had sawed away with a concentration and energy that today he reserved solely for his business. There had been a woman behind it, of course, a teacher named Miss Morgan, a tall, dark-haired woman with a wonderful laugh. She'd brought to her class an enthusiasm that quieted even the class jerks, and she'd brought to Nicholas in particular a glimpse of the world, not gray and circumscribed, but full of color and depth and romance. She'd only been at the school for a year and had disappeared without an explanation. For a long while Nicholas had waited patiently, expecting her to come back, but she had never returned and eventually he'd quit the waiting and the cello, and then the memory of her too had faded, and once again the brightly colored world had shrunk and grayed.

But she'd left behind her love of Bach. Interestingly, she could not have left behind her a love of the more romantic composers like Liszt or Brahms, but Bach she could leave. The structured order, the completeness of Bach fitted into the gray world that was around Nicholas; even the grandeur could appeal because it evoked the austere presence of his father. But the passion in the music could be ignored, and Nicholas had never again wanted to feel passion. For the brief two years with Vanessa, he had been stunned by the discovery of emotion. But he had been like a flower that while opening had been cut down by frost. And with her death all softness and beauty had died in him too. The rest of his life he'd followed an orderly pattern; he'd ruled over the Healey Mills, raised his daughter according to form. But Bach remained, an indulgence allowed between dinner and bedtime. In moments of great disturbance it was to Bach that he turned, on the Gramophone or radio, never in concert, as if to a friend for advice. Sometimes he even used his friend Bach as an informal business partner, to distract, to emphasize, and to dismiss.

Nicholas turned down the volume on the Gramophone, but kept the music clearly in the background. Tonight Bach was to act as a partner. The majestic strains went well with the austere gloom of his paneled study where no book postdating the last century or, worse yet, a novel dared to intrude. His desk was of mahogany, undisturbed by clutter and as large as a life raft. It glistened darkly in the dim study, and above it there was only one overhead light, forming a cone of yellow that captured Nicholas Healey in its center.

As the three men were shown into his study, Nicholas motioned to the high-backed chairs lined like supplicants in front of his desk. Then he sat back and pretended to be deep in contemplation of his partner Bach who was busy recapitulating his first theme. Upstairs he could hear the floorboards creaking. Undoubtedly Angela was pacing her sitting room in a frenzy about what was going on below. It was an intriguing situation, him downstairs scrutinizing the three rough steelworkers through half-closed eyes, her upstairs, caring desperately, without any idea of the outcome.

It was the man called Evan who cleared his throat and shifted in his seat as if he were about to start. Nicholas knew from an earlier meeting that he was part of the union conspiracy. He certainly looked the type. Why were union men always so damn thin and miserable looking? From the choice of hundreds, only a silly woman like Angela would have picked this one.

Evan was sitting, eyes downcast, picking at a loose thread on the pocket of what was obviously his only suit jacket. Finally he spoke, and though there were traces of nervousness in his voice, there was a clear strength in it too that Nicholas hadn't expected.

"I don't know if Miss Healey explained why we're here."

Nicholas didn't answer. He merely closed his eyes as if in ecstasy over Bach.

Evan continued. "We feel there will be war in Europe any day now."

Nicholas opened his eyes. "War is unthinkable, even for those monkeys across the sea. They learned their lesson in the Great War. And a tough lesson it was."

"If you'll excuse me, sir, I'm not sure they have learned their lesson; at least that's how it seems to us. Germany is on the march, and I believe she will not stop. Nor will England and France stand idly by. As to Russia, well, your guess is as good as mine. But all I can see is that it will be like 1914 again. Except that this time we won't hesitate so long."

"Bullswoggle!" Nicholas waved war aside with his hand. He leaned over, turned up the volume on the Gramophone, and once again attended to his partner, Bach.

Evan had not expected to encounter an objection before he even proposed the plan, and this time his voice was less sure and steady. "But as you well know there are many who would disagree. Why, just yesterday there was an editorial in the *Tribune* that stated—"

Nicholas snapped, "I don't need a lecture on world affairs. I read the papers too. And let me tell you something: If there's a war, and I say *if*, it will be because of those scoundrel journalists who are frightening the pants off of everyone just to sell that load of chicken scratchings they call a newspaper."

"Perhaps," Tom ventured slowly. "But whatever the cause, there is a growing hysteria for war, and once that starts to spread, very little is needed to set things in motion."

Nicholas cleared his throat, then turned over the record. "Well, all right, have it your way. I'll give you your war in Europe if you must have it, but America has more sense than to get involved again. And on that point I won't argue."

Evan started picking at the thread on his jacket. He forced himself to stop. "The problem is, will we have to be involved in certain ways? After all, our economies are interlocked."

Nicholas brightened. "Indeed! And let me tell you, my friend, a war could be most interesting from that aspect."

Nicholas sat forward, his eyes on the three men. He was, in fact, quite sure that there would be war in Europe, and the ramifications had not missed his scrutiny. "If there is a war, mind I say *if*, the demands for steel would be enormous. Nearly every major and minor part of military equipment requires it. And that is very good news indeed."

Evan too sat forward. For a moment he managed to lift his eyes to the little man's face, but quickly they retreated to the carpet. "That's the point; the demands would be enormous, especially for alloys. And that's where the problems begin. Looking at a map, you can see it all. If Germany is half as strong as I think she is, she could overrun Russia, or worse they could become allies. And Russia is where we get our manganese. Or take Japan, for example. She could cut off eighty-eight percent of our tungsten."

Nicholas smiled thinly. "I don't think I need a lecture on geography either. In fact, I suggest you look at your map again. I see no reason for Japan to cut off our tungsten. Germany wouldn't dare attack Russia. Who would? It's far too cold and too crowded with those dreadful Russians, and the food is diabolically bad. Even Germans have better taste than that. But here is the point. Since we wouldn't be fighting, what the hell would any of that have to do with us? If you ask me, leave them to it. Sell what can be sold and sit back and watch the fireworks."

"Take the money and run," said Evan. "Yes, if possible that is the best course. But who would have thought we'd be involved in the last war? And yet we were."

Nicholas opened his eyes; his face tightened, and he glared across the desk at the three men. He could almost see them shrinking under his gaze, and he enjoyed that immensely. He could still hear Angela pacing the floor upstairs, and that too added to his enjoyment.

But then his eyes traveled across Evan and Tom and stopped at Ben. For the first time he noticed that he was not like the other two men. He had lumped all three of them together, seeing their reactions as the same, just as he saw all the workers at the mill as being one person with the same needs, desires, the same bad habits. But this one was different. He wasn't shrinking under Nicholas's gaze, and his eyes were not downcast. Nicholas couldn't remember his having said anything; he just sat there, large and thick, his eyes alert, and with an air of cockiness that was almost a challenge.

Nicholas could feel himself growing angry. He stared at the man across from him, waiting for him to avert his eyes. But Ben didn't change his expression or show in any way he was disturbed. He seemed immovable.

Evan broke the silence. "I think at least that America must be open to the possibility that anything could happen. After all, we could go to war or our sources could be cut off or destroyed; certainly trade could be disrupted. The world is explosive. With any luck we can avoid getting caught up in it. Yet can we be sure?"

Evan reached into his pocket and pulled out the piece of paper outlining their plans for the new alloy. It had become bent at the corners, covered with lint, and there was a rumpled patch where it had been folded. It looked like the paper of a workman. Evan hesitated. How could he have dared to go along with Ben and arrange this meeting? How foolish he had been. He too could hear Angela's footsteps as she paced above, and he was painfully aware he was letting her down. He supposed he'd known all along he would.

It was a long while before Evan became aware that Tom was watching him, motioning for him to hand Nicholas the sheet of paper as planned, but Evan couldn't move; his sense of inadequacy held him breathless. His being there was worse than foolishness; it was a betrayal of Angela. Yet he knew that by not going, he would have betrayed her too.

Tom could wait no longer. He reached over, took the paper from Evan's hand, and put it on the desk in front of the shriveled little man.

Nicholas turned up the volume on the Gramophone and let Bach swell through the room. He was well aware of the crumpled slip of paper on his desk, but he pretended that he was too carried away by the music to notice it. He closed his eyes and his forefinger traced patterns of sound in the air.

Tom looked over at Ben. He hadn't changed expression since he'd entered the room. He looked almost amused. Sometimes Tom hated Ben's arrogance; it was as unrealistic as Evan's fear, and he felt alone, unaided, cast adrift in the dim vast room and the swelling of Bach.

Nicholas's finger stopped in midphrase and jabbed at the air accusatorily. "And have you tested it out?"

Tom said blandly, "On paper it looks as if it might work very well."

"But you do not know for certain."

"We don't have the equipment to make steel, of course," Tom answered softly. "But I know enough about it to have a fairly good idea."

"But you do not know."

"There's every reason to think this alloy is strong and flexible, maybe even better than the one we make today."

"I repeat! You do not know."

"No."

"Eureka! A one-word answer. No. You do not know." He reached over and grabbed up the piece of paper, then slowly he pulled on his glasses. "There are no percentages here," he said, allowing the paper to fall to the desk.

Ben answered. "That's right."

Nicholas looked up quickly. Those were the first words Ben had spoken since he'd entered the room, and of course it would be he who spoke them.

Nicholas cleared his throat. "You realize, of course, that you are not the first to come up with the idea. I believe they are calling them National Emergency Steels, and several companies are toying with them."

"But the Healey Mills is not testing out any National Emergency Steels," Ben returned.

"Perhaps for good reason."

"Perhaps," Ben answered.

Nicholas fingered the sheet of paper, but his eyes were on Ben, and this time he looked him over very carefully, as if he were not a common laborer but a man to be dealt with. The other two men sitting beside him were acceptable looking for steelworkers, perhaps even intelligent looking. He supposed that if dressed properly they could blend into the men's bar at the Park Lane Hotel, at least if one didn't look too closely. But dress the tall broad one up in the most expensive tailoring that London or Paris had to offer, and he would still look exactly like what he was, a bakebrain. Put him in society, and he would undoubtedly offend the ladies and disturb the gentlemen. On purpose. With delight. It was this that held Nicholas.

Ben's eyes also were on Nicholas, and there was a trace of a smile as he watched the old man's anger rising. "The point is you could get caught with your pants down. If your supplies are cut off and the other companies are all set to go with National Emergency Steels, it will be too late for you to start testing."

"And if the supplies are not cut off, then I won't have spent a great deal of money for piss all."

"Aye. It's a gamble. And if you aren't a gambling man there's no reason for us to be sitting here. I guess we'd better leave."

Ben could see both Evan and Tom desperately trying to catch his eye, but he ignored them. He was playing this one on instinct, believing that Nicholas Healey had become interested enough in him that he could risk showing a little strength.

Nicholas caught all that was passing between the three men. With a smile, he turned the volume on the Gramophone even higher until the whole room was shuddering with Bach. He'd had enough of steelworkers.

Ben watched Nicholas, trying to discover if he was indeed as little interested in gambling as he seemed or if it was all an act, but he could not tell. Ben was caught at the edge of his seat. Big mouth that he was he'd said they'd leave, and now Healey was calling him on it. Ben didn't move. One thing was sure; he wasn't about to slink out of the most important meeting of his life, his false pride slightly tattered but intact. If he did, he'd come out with nothing.

Ben smiled tightly and tried to control his voice. "What we're proposing is you try our new alloy, hold off producing it until world events take a turn for the bad, but be ready to produce it at a moment's notice."

Nicholas began humming along with the recording. He broke off suddenly. "And what's in it for you?"

"A percent of the gross profits and a certain amount of control over production."

Nicholas roared with laughter. "In other words, you propose to spend my money to make a jackass out of me."

Family Passions 107

It was out before Ben had a chance to stop himself. "You won't be needing our help with that."

Nicholas jolted forward. His face had become ashen, and the end of his nose was scarlet. Evan's and Tom's eyes were riveted to the floor, desperation drawing lines all across their young faces until they looked twice their age. Only Ben appeared to be calm. He was watching Nicholas with a smile, as if he were enjoying a secret joke.

Nicholas remained silent for a long while. It was the arrogance of Ben, the will as strong as, perhaps even stronger than, his that held him. Here was a man who would have what he wanted one way or another, and that fascinated Nicholas. There were so few of them these days. Rarely did a man cross the path of a winner, and when he did it was usually as an adversary. Here was one who proposed to be an ally. Nicholas worked it over in his mind. Of course, men like Ben were not to be trusted, that was quite clear; they were to be controlled and used, but never trusted. The only problem was it might require so much energy just watching your flanks that you spent more time outfoxing the fox than doing business. No, he decided, it wasn't worth it. He would dismiss these men, then get down to work and try to come up with a National Emergency Steel of his own.

Nicholas continued to watch the three men in silence. He could just barely make out the creaking of wood upstairs and he sensed that he would almost enjoy depriving Angela of the one thing in the world she'd ever asked for, the one thing she'd wanted with anything resembling passion. Recently her eyes had seemed on fire; her whole body had changed. And he resented her even more than ever for that; it made his own loss sharper. Of course, she could run off with her steelworker friend and live penniless, hanging out her wash on the line in a sooty breeze. He doubted that she had the backbone. Still, it was an interesting thought, and Nicholas considered it with a clinical detachment not unmixed with relish.

Again Nicholas looked down at the sheet of paper on his desk. Even supposing this new alloy was better than the steel he produced today, he was sure there were other alloys that could be made. If other companies had come up with their own, this was clearly not the only solution to the problem.

Still, Nicholas remained silent. Though he'd come to the decision to dismiss these men, he couldn't quite bring himself to it. His partner, Bach, had also fallen silent, and the record revolved on the turntable, the needle scratching along the last groove. Never before had anyone spoken to him as Ben had, and for it to have come from one of his own workers was unthinkable. Nevertheless, the seconds were passing, and Nicholas found to his amazement he hadn't thrown them out onto the street.

Again he found his eyes drifting over to Ben, taking in his cocky, calm expression, summing him up. And slowly he began to realize, that he couldn't do it. If he rejected this new alloy, he'd be losing something far more valuable than a simple metal or a daughter; he'd be losing the big burly man sitting so boldly across from him, who, he decided, was a man and a challenge he couldn't resist taking on.

BOOK THREE

OHIO
Fall, 1980

TEN

The Learjet sat at the edge of the runway, power rushing, waiting for the precise moment when the pilot would unleash it. Suddenly the plane shuddered and began its surge forward, gathering power, eating up the ground, until all at once it lifted into the air.

Inside the plush cabin, fine crystal and bone china vibrated; platters that usually held ham and pâté and French cheeses inched forward in the galley. Most of the plane had been emptied out for the medical equipment; the humped shapes of the gurney and respirator, the wiry frame of the drip, looked almost prehistoric in the darkened cabin. There was only one row of seats left standing, and in them two people sat motionless.

As the plane climbed steadily into the clouds, the nurse reached over and opened the window shade. Outside the city tilted crazily then receded, and the great rolling earth appeared and disappeared between the quickly shifting clouds. The nurse leaned to her patient and loosened his seat belt. Ben Savage didn't move, a stony, hulking figure, completely paralyzed, towering in the seat. His almost transparent blue eyes stared straight ahead, as if he couldn't feel the urgent thrusting of the plane or hear its roaring power. It was as if he were living another existence.

As the plane leveled out, Mrs. Mided scanned her patient. Though the sight of paralysis was something she'd grown used to over the years, there was something about this patient that was more grotesque and disturbing than usual. Perhaps it was the insistent reminders of sheer normalcy. For covering the inhumanly still body, drawing attention from the senseless empty face, were all the trappings of a man. He was dressed impeccably but lovelessly, his tie slightly askew, the collar of his silk shirt bent under the left corner. His massive hands were laying on the chair arms and a five-carat diamond sparkled on his broad third finger. There was no expression on his strong face, and yet in every line there were traces that great animation had once been there. Now it was as if he'd been changed to stone; suddenly he was merely an enormous bulk that needed feeding and changing, not much more than an overgrown baby. He looked neither intelligent nor moronic; rather he was a shell of a man, a body still strong but becoming flaccid from inaction, a brain damaged by carbon monoxide. He seemed already to be dead, a great stone monument to himself. But perhaps that was where the grotesqueness lay, not in what he was, but what he had been.

She watched Ben a moment longer, wondering if it wasn't a blessing he didn't know who he was. Then she put it out of her mind. Life went on.

As Mrs. Mided turned her attention from her patient and took up a magazine, Ben tilted his head toward the window. Sitting there in the prismatic sunlight, he seemed almost like the man he had been. Suddenly there was a look of stark terror on his face; his mouth opened and his eyes seemed lit from within. Then a moment later it was gone, and once again his eyes were transparent and dead. Only the shadows of passing clouds and the dappling of sunlight played across his expressionless features. He seemed a man with no thoughts or feelings, hardly even a man.

But inside the enormous hulk that appeared so inhuman was still a man, and Ben could see clearly every detail of the plush private plane that his mother had arranged for him, and all the preparations that had been made to transport him to her home in Wales. He could see them, but he didn't care. Images flashed cruelly across his brain in great angry strokes. Only a few weeks before he'd been a man of great power and influence, and now he was paralyzed, close to death. From his prison of stone, he'd heard the doctors tell his family that he'd been damaged beyond repair, that he was about to die. But even if they'd said nothing, he would have known. He'd been exposed to carbon monoxide for over three minutes, and that was considered a lethal dose.

The plane was cruising at maximum altitude and the clouds were stacked below. The sun glinted off the windows, forming little shafts of light in the plane. Ben felt the sun tearing at his eyes, and they burned in response, but it all seemed very far away and unimportant. All that mattered lay below under the bank of clouds.

He had lost Midwestern; he had lost everything, and there was nothing he could do about it. It was beyond impotence. It was beyond even death.

Family Passions

Mrs. Mided glanced up and adjusted the window shade so that no light pierced the cabin. Still Ben didn't move; he seemed to be staring at the window senselessly, but his mind was alight with visions of the past and the beginning of the end for him.

He had no idea how much time had passed since his accident. All he remembered was one day he'd become aware that he had passed through death. At first he had lain in blackness, floating in the darkened void, as a piece of driftwood gently rocks in the ocean. Gradually a shore had appeared, not softly, but in flashes of illumination, startling in their glaring light. Consciousness had crashed suddenly, then disappeared into the rocky annihilation, and with these eruptions of life there'd been a vague awareness of what was going on around him, sudden frenzies of lungs collapsing, the glimpse of a bottle dripping somewhere, again a flash and the image of an arm, though whose arm he'd had no idea; of who or what he was he'd had no understanding. He'd been a piece of driftwood; his only desire had been for the shadow. Gradually these moments of illumination had grown longer, whiter, and with them had come some understanding. His heart had been very weak, his lungs had collapsed twice. But there'd been no pain, and so if he'd tried very hard he could still float as driftwood; if he'd tried he could still remain in the void. Until one day when the flash was upon him he'd remembered Ben Savage.

It had come sharply, powerfully. It had come with a pain and a light far more agonizing than anything he'd ever experienced. He'd felt a terrible cry inside of him, a cry of horror and anguish, a cry of the damned.

Slowly he'd become used even to the anguish. He'd watched the succession of trays lined with needles and probes, glass bottles filled with colored liquids, machines mathematically reducing his inner functions into numbers and blips of light. When his lungs had collapsed again, he'd been totally aware. He'd watched the racing, controlled hysteria around him as a piece of theater. Machines had clattered down the hallway; nurses and doctors had appeared, shouting instructions to one another.

But this had been the last emergency. After that everything had stabilized. The machines had disappeared, rooms had been changed, groups of physicians had trooped by, probing, testing reflexes, visitors had stared down lugubriously.

And slowly the horror had set in. Understanding had come in fits and starts, panicky stabs of reality that had been uncontrollable and intense. Visions of himself as strong and vital, so alive, had appeared in the white hospital room. He hadn't been able to move. He hadn't been able to scream. The grief had been locked within, unexpressed in the prison of his body. After a while the void of before had seemed his only escape; the black limitless ocean, the floating driftwood had been a memory that had comforted him, and he'd tried to struggle back to it, discovering how to loosen his ties to a world that had brought only intense anguish. The damage to him had been more than physical, it had been spiritual, and already he'd no longer been a man.

Vaguely he'd become aware of voices and the fact that everyone around him had not known he could understand them. He'd been able to hear the nurses chattering cheerfully as they'd moved his large immobile body from side to side, sliding clean sheets under him, bending and stretching legs that would never move again. Ben had half listened, as to a radio program coming from the next room.

"All his vital functions are now stable. He will continue to live in this condition for an unpredictable length of time, but he will not recover. His heart is very weak. Immobility makes him subject to serious respiratory ailments, viruses. Eventually he will succumb to one or more."

Ben had allowed the words to drift by him like newspapers on a windy day; they had made no sense, they'd had no relevance. After a while Ben had realized the only control he'd had over his own life was the denial of it. To the world he'd been dead, to himself he'd been dead, and though the shell of what had once been Ben Savage had remained alive, he could kill the inside.

He'd resolved to die. Though his thoughts had been bouncing crazily back and forth, he'd silenced them. Though he'd been able to hear voices, he'd refused them. Though he'd been able to see, he'd taken note of nothing. He'd allowed himself to be shoved back and forth like a heavy sack of flour with neither embarrassment nor anger. He'd watched his mother standing over him, her face masking her anguish, but even she had no longer had the power to reach him. He had resolved that he was dead.

And slowly the world had receded. But try as he might, it had always come back. Ben closed his eyes against the thought, for willing himself into death seemed a kind of life, and he did not wish to go even that far.

ELEVEN

Ben lay motionless in a lumpy old-fashioned bed, looking around the bedroom. He had bought this house in Wales for his mother many years ago, but he'd never seen it, never even been tempted to in the frantic rush of living. The room was like his mother, large, primitive, devoid of frills and fancies, serviceable. Yet all around were surprising touches of femininity and warmth—embroidered antimacassars, handmade hooked rugs. Lined up on the bureau were pictures of everyone, old sepia photographs of his father, pictures of all of the family as children, adolescents, and grownups. There was even a portrait of his wife, Dylan, holding James as a child. When Dylan had left Ben, he had burned every picture of her, and it was unsettling to see her image on his mother's bureau, but less painful than he would have thought. It was another life.

Ben's eyes stayed with the photographs, scanning them slowly. They seemed to be arranged haphazardly, a mixture of sizes and shapes. Behind them all, taller and older than the rest, as if overlooking the family, was a picture of his mother and father on what must have been their wedding day. He had never seen it before, never even known such a photograph existed. It was startling, not so much because of its unreal color or his parents' awkward pose but because underneath it all there were traces of the people he knew. There was his mother's proud carved face, dark against the white of her dress, looking as if she'd just gobbled up the world, and his father's thin sensitive body almost overshadowed by his mother's massive form. Yet in the end it wasn't this that held him. It was something in his father's stance that came as a surprise. There was a pride in it, an animal leanness and sinewy strength that Ben had never seen in the vague shadowy man who had hardly dented his childhood and slipped into death unnoticed and unmourned by him. His father had been a handsome man, but more important he had been a man. Never before had Ben understood what his mother had seen in the withered husband who'd coughed by the fire and shuffled back and forth from work, but looking at the photograph Ben could see what it was that Elizabeth had loved. Again his eyes traveled to his mother's face. How happy she seemed under her studied scowl. With a shock he realized she was probably thinking about the night to come. Though Ben's mother had often told him about that evening on the hill and how she had chosen Wynn from all the other men, it had never occurred to him to link passion with them. But yes, she must have felt great passion for Wynn. It was an unsettling thought, wide and vast and scary.

He wondered if there were other things about his mother he didn't know. Was it possible there were secrets, lovers long dead, skeletons in the closet? Was his mother a woman he'd never bothered to discover? The thought surprised him as much as the room. It hadn't occurred to him that people were more than the faces they presented to the world. He had never had the time nor the caring.

Ben looked around the room again. There was only a small gas fire, and the air was very cold and damp. From the distant past came a memory of cold damp mornings in the dark hills of Wales. It wasn't really a memory even, just a feeling of being young and running in the misty morning. Though Ben had left Wales at the age of five, he had never remembered anything about it. In fact, Ben remembered almost nothing about his childhood at all; it was almost as if he'd begun life at eighteen. They said that when a person lay dying he remembered his whole life, but as Ben had lain in the hospital on the brink of death, he'd remembered nothing. All that had gone through his mind was the accident, flashing horribly across his consciousness like a vivid dream. But now memories were stirring in him, memories he'd never had before.

Ben closed his eyes and again drifted back into his death; he didn't want to remember. Slowly he became aware of a noise; there was the sound of a doorknob turning and the rustling of a skirt as a woman opened his door and crossed the room.

"It's time to wake up, Mr. Savage." It was a Welsh voice, musical and lilting, but with none of the guttural sounds of his mother's accent.

There was the creaking of shutters being opened, and light flooded the room. Ben reluctantly opened his eyes.

A woman was standing in the morning light, a tall, slim redhead, perhaps thirty-five, perhaps older. She had large green eyes and a very pale skin; she was pretty, and yet that wasn't the first thing that struck Ben. Despite her height and the healthy flush of her face, there was a frailty about her. It was more than just her slimness or any delicacy of feature; it was an impression from within, as if she'd been wounded once, and though now it was invisible, it had never completely healed.

She leaned against the shutters, haloed in light, and there was a smiling, knowing look in her eyes that was very disturbing. "My name's Tally, and I'm your nurse," she said brightly. "I'll be alternating with Mrs. Mided, the nurse you brought with you from America, who is, by the way, quite hopeless." Again the disturbing look.

Ben stared blankly, but he was watching her. A feeling of wariness pressed in on him and a muscle began twitching in his jaw.

Tally was looking at the muscle. It took her a long while to speak, then softly she asked, "You understood every word I just said, didn't you?"

She was watching Ben's face probing his eyes, and there was an arrogant knowing look to her that Ben didn't like. He stared straight ahead and emptied his mind. Darkness drew in around him, and once again he was dead.

"Mrs. Mided told me that you were a bit less aware than a turnip, but she didn't have a clue what was going on, did she, Mr. Savage? I saw you when you came in last night and you were too tired to hide it. And I saw you just now. You *are* aware, aren't you?"

Ben refused the sound of Tally's voice; he blotted out the words. Around him was the comforting darkness and silence.

Tally crossed the room and moved toward the bed. She stopped when she came to the dresser. It was an idle gesture, looking at the photographs, but once she started she was arrested, held by the little shrine to the past. She guessed the big peasantlike woman to be her patient's mother. Swiftly her eyes took in the fierce sardonic face and the starched white dress, a girlish touch that seemed ridiculously out of place on the strong woman. She decided she liked the woman, but she felt sorry for her too. She could sense her pride as she stood in her ill-fitting dress waiting for life to begin. It was a look of completeness, a victory over life, as if for the first time she felt she truly existed, that having a man made her real. Tally laughed to herself. She supposed as the years went by that too had faded, like the photograph, an awkward sepia memory.

Tally's eyes shifted to the pictures of her patient and traced him through his childhood to a quite recent press photo of him accepting some kind of award. He was his mother's son, all right, that same big frame, that same fierce rich bloodedness. Tally responded to people like that, but also she was frightened of them. It was like eating red meat all the time, too rich, too bloody; there were times when all one wanted was white meat.

She turned back to the bed and looked at the stone man, lying there so rigidly. He'd made his fortune young and used it well from what she could see, and there must have been a gaiety under the fierceness that he'd inherited from his mother.

Still her eyes went back to the snapshots. He had been a handsome man, he had been a fierce man, a man who'd attacked life hungrily. There was a look of discovery about him, as if every day he lived was his first. Yes, life must have been an adventure to him. And now it was over.

Tally went back to the bed, her eyes on Ben's face. "You did understand me before. I feel sure of it."

The muscle was still twitching and Tally watched it. She moved closer to the bed until she was standing over Ben. It was as if she were waiting for an answer. "And I suspect you have some feeling in your body too."

Ben was stone, his transparent eyes cold and dead. Yet she stood over him, watching, waiting.

"Of course I could test my theory by pinching your arm or tickling your stomach." She laughed, and still there was the feeling that she expected an answer. She seemed so sure, so disturbingly smug.

"Quite right," Tally said after a while. "I wouldn't dare. I need the money too much to risk my job. Nevertheless, I suspect I'm right about your having feeling in your body, and I know I'm right about your understanding me. You do understand me."

Tally reached over and softly touched his cheek. She smelled of lavender soap and fresh air. It was a childish smell, simple and of the country, and her hand was very warm. "The question is, why are you hiding it?" Again she seemed to be waiting for a response. "You know exactly what you're doing too. And you're doing it on purpose. But you'll just sink deeper and deeper into yourself until there's no coming back. Is that what you want to happen?"

Tally was silent, watchful, but Ben just stared blankly, an empty shell devoid of feeling or emotion. Tally shook her head and walked to the door, then she stopped and turned back to him.

"Of course an even better question is, why should I care? It's really much easier dealing with a vegetable. Just bathe and change it, wrap it up warm, shove custard and baby food down its throat, and keep it alive as long as possible. It's a cushy job with very little work and no backtalk. But you see, Mr. Savage, I can't do that. My job is to save lives, and as strange as it might seem, I take my job rather seriously."

She held the doorframe, her eyes on her patient. There was something about him that was making her angry. Perhaps it was his stony belligerence. Perhaps it was because her last patient had been young and handsome and he'd wanted to live more than anything, but despite everything Tally had been able to do, he'd slipped slowly into oblivion and then death.

As Tally stood in the doorway, she realized how foolish she was being. He probably was dying, and she was just trying to see things in him that weren't there at all. But strongly she felt that he had understood her; strongly she felt his will fighting against her from behind those transparent eyes.

She stood watching him for a long while, her interest in him surprising her. What was the fascination in this unmoving, almost inhuman man? She had been a nurse for many years; she had seen many men die, and watched them not with coldness, not even with equanimity or resignation, but the original horror had faded; the feeling of injustice that she had felt in the beginning had become assimilated. She had never found a philosophy to explain death to her; she had never found peace in resignation; rather she had tired of her anger at death and had stopped thinking about it all. In truth, she'd stopped thinking about a lot of things. But perhaps that was age; it took the edge off of things. You didn't like them any better than when you were young, but you became fatigued from worrying about them. Yes, probably that was it. She was forcing herself into middle age, not because she looked old, not even because she felt old, but because there was an attraction to the peacefulness of it; the order and predictability were soothing. She supposed it was a kind of death, but how soft and gentle it seemed to her now.

Yet though she'd made that choice for herself, she still found it intolerable in others. Perhaps even more so. When you were living hungrily for yourself you didn't have time to seek it in those around you.

Tally glanced back at the bureau with its clutter of photographs. "What kind of man were you, Mr. Savage?" She said this out loud, and she was watching him shrewdly. "You look like a fighter to me. What happened to kill that? Why have you given up?"

She laughed, embarrassed at herself. "You're telling me with your eyes that you didn't give up, that you don't understand what I'm saying. But I don't believe it. All I'm asking is for you to send me a sign that you do understand, that you do have thoughts and feelings."

Ben didn't move; he kept his eyes blank and staring.

"Fine. Have it your way. But don't think I'm going to give up on you so easily, because I won't."

Quickly Tally walked into the hallway. Ben heard her calling, "Mrs. Mided. Please have the patient washed, dressed, and in a wheelchair in an hour." Her voice echoed above the clicking of her heels against the wood floors. She sounded very brisk and very angry.

Tally moved around the living room, pulling open the curtains, letting in the gray rainy light. Ben was turned to the window, staring blankly, only partially aware of what he was seeing. Outside was just a mist of gray, gray trees clinging desperately to gray grass, bare twisted branches raised to a leaden sky. He was aware of Tally bustling around the room and his American nurse, Mrs. Mided, standing at the door, but they too were no more than passing shadows on a characterless canvas.

"Until I say otherwise, Mr. Savage is to remain here." Tally's voice was cool and efficient; it was once again the voice of a nurse.

Mrs. Mided remained at the threshold. She neither liked Tally nor approved of her, though she couldn't put her finger on why. She supposed there was an arrogance to her; Tally pressed things. She was the type who didn't understand the smoothness of life but tugged at it, making things uncomfortable. Mrs. Mided had set her mind on a nice easy assignment, but Tally threatened to disturb the ease. She wouldn't leave things alone. It was more than a difference in age; it was a difference in point of view.

Mrs. Mided looked disapprovingly around the room. "I'll go tell the maid to serve breakfast in here."

"Don't bother. Mr. Savage won't be taking breakfast." Tally opened the last curtain, then settled herself in a chair by the window.

Mrs. Mided smiled tightly. "But he hasn't had anything to eat since the flight."

"I know. Mr. Savage isn't hungry right now. And when he is, I'll take care of it."

Tally watched Ben in silence for a moment, then continued. "If you want to take the day off, you can." Tally kept her eyes on Ben. "There's a village less than half a mile away, not much by American standards, but it's the best we can offer. Otherwise the town of Maesteg is a few miles down the road. There's a proper cinema there and several restaurants."

Mrs. Mided stiffened. Clearly Tally was trying to get rid of her. But why? Her imagination sped crazily through a long list of terrible possibilities. She stopped herself. No, it couldn't be. Tally might be a troublemaker but she wasn't that kind. Then what was she up to? Mrs. Mided tried to put it out of her mind, and after all, she really wouldn't mind getting some fresh air.

"If you're sure he won't be hungry," Mrs. Mided said, throwing one last suspicious look around the room.

Tally was amused. "I'm sure."

Mrs. Mided shrugged then left the room, closing the door softly behind her. When Tally had heard her footsteps recede down the hall, she turned back to Ben.

"No," she said. "I'm sure Mr. Savage is not hungry. In fact, I suspect he won't be hungry for a very long time."

She got up and began walking around the room. There was a smug, knowing smile on her face; even the way she walked showed an ease and assurance. "You see, Mr. Savage is not going to have anything to eat or drink until he communicates with his nurse, Tally. And I have a feeling that our Mr. S. is going to be very stubborn."

Ben continued to stare out the window. Beyond the gray trees there was a gray stone farmhouse with a slate roof. The barn and the stable were attached to the main building, squared around a muddy courtyard, curled in upon itself, perhaps in protection against the desolation of the hills. Next to the farmhouse was a church. It looked very old, possibly even Roman, and there was a hilly cemetery surrounding it. But other than those two buildings, there were only the hills and the rainy sky, a barren landscape filled with neither life nor death, but a suspension of the two.

Tally had returned to her chair. "It would be so much easier for both of us if you would just give in now."

Ben wasn't listening. All he knew was that he had lost everything and was dying. His whole life had been torn apart in three minutes; such a short time, and yet how long it had seemed then.

There was a clock ticking far off, and he listened to the mechanical sound of it. Wind was whipping at the rain, sending it against the window, rattling at the frame. Once more his mind shifted to the cold outside, and he saw himself as a young boy, running through the damp grass. It all seemed so real that for a moment he was stunned by it. He could feel the urgency of running, the clear clean movements of a boy in motion. He could smell the frosty air with its traces of coal dust from the mine. He could see the sky above, dramatic dark clouds against the blue; he could feel the sting of winter through his gloves and trousers. He had been happy running through those fields. He had been truly happy.

Then once again his mind was tossed back into the room, and he was in a wheelchair, an old man dying.

Ben awoke from the shadowy corridors of his mind with a start. He had no idea how much time had gone by, but he supposed he'd been drifting between sleep and wakefulness for quite a while.

The rain had stopped, but still huge black clouds hung low in the sky, moving quickly to expose small patches of blue. Light spilled through the cracks in the clouds, illuminating the rolling hills and valleys outside. The church was sparkling in the liquid light, its ancient windows glittering with vibrant color. Even the little cemetery surrounding it seemed brighter, the stones a mottle of hundreds of shades of gray. The farm complex too was patched with color, and it seemed cozily folded in on itself, surrounded by its blanket of hedges. There was smoke from its chimney, spilling up to the sky in billows that thinned softly until they were only wisps disappearing into the clouds. It was a different world outside the window, beautiful and wild, old and solid, with a simplicity that surprised Ben. He wondered what it was like to live in that farmhouse, with its quiet daily rounds, a place where you could see the clouds and feel the shifting of the seasons. Never had he thought about what it would be like to live another life. He had only thought of his own as inevitable and certainly the best possible, but now he wondered.

Across from him, Tally sat knitting. Rays of sunlight fell all around her, making the room pink and soft; her hair gleamed warmly.

Ben became aware of a pinching in his stomach and remembered he hadn't had anything to eat since the night before. He wondered briefly what the nurse sitting across from him was up to. Then that thought too faded.

There was a small child in front of the farmhouse now, but it was impossible to tell at that distance if it was a boy or a girl. There were birds on the gnarled tree, and he could hear them complaining to one another, arguing over a perch or perhaps a tender bit of worm.

And then even that faded, and once again Ben was dozing, images whirling in his mind. The door opened and Ben awakened as Mrs. Mided came bustling in. For the first time Ben looked at her. She was less old than she seemed, perhaps not more than fifty, yet everything about her seemed dried up. Her skin was pale, almost powdery, and her crisp gray hair looked parched.

Mrs. Mided moved around the room fussily, then she looked down her nose at Tally. It was a long thin nose, well suited for aiming. "Well, I can't say all that much for your village," she said primly.

"No. There's not much to see. You should have gone into Maesteg. It's a proper town. There's quite a lot to do there."

"I did go into Maesteg."

Tally laughed. "Maesteg isn't exactly a village. There are five thousand people there. But I suppose after America we must seem rather small to you. Still, it's an interesting area. That church you passed is Roman, and there's even a legend attached to it. It's all about unrequited love, a Romeo and Juliet theme with a little Camille thrown in. The Welsh seem to be obsessed with unrequited love. I've never understood why. Perhaps it's just that we're a passionate people, and the sun and fields and trees and sad young girls stir us most."

"Well, I wouldn't know," Mrs. Mided answered. "It didn't look any too romantic to me, just a bunch of coal mines."

"Ah, now, that's where you're wrong. There's romance in coal mines. But perhaps only to the Welsh."

"Yes, I'm sure." Mrs. Mided hovered around the door, looking down her nose, and Tally went back to her knitting. There was a tension between them that grew in the silence, and Mrs. Mided felt strongly that Tally didn't want her there, which made her stick almost boulderlike. She didn't like being dismissed by anyone and certainly not by someone younger and no better than she. Finally she said, "The maid asked me to tell you dinner'll be ready in ten minutes."

Tally smiled. "I'll be having my dinner in here." She was still working on her knitting, but her eyes had shifted to Ben.

He could feel her staring at him, as if she could read his thoughts. Ben tried to block out the sight of her, but his mind was in the room, and he could not stop himself from feeling the power of her probing eyes.

Mrs. Mided asked coldly, "And what about Mr. Savage's dinner?" She scanned the room, passing over Ben as over any other object.

"Mr. Savage won't be having dinner."

Mrs. Mided walked to Tally, standing directly over her, demanding her attention. "Just what are you up to?"

Tally sighed. "I suppose a resurrection of sorts. I'm attempting to bring our employer back from the dead, you might say." Tally lay her knitting on her lap and turned her eyes back on Ben. He appeared not to notice. He was looking out the window blankly, but Tally sensed he was aware of every movement in the room, aware and listening.

Mrs. Mided pulled herself up with dignity. "Well, I hope you know what you're doing. I'll tell you one thing; if his family hears about this, they'll be good and angry."

Damn right they will be, Ben thought to himself. Then he wanted to laugh. Because he knew in fact that most of them wouldn't care at all if something happened to him.

Tally had turned to Mrs. Mided. "Are you just lodging a formal complaint or does that mean you're going to contact his family?"

"To tell you the truth, I don't know," Mrs. Mided answered.

"Would it help if I asked you please not to?"

Mrs. Mided shook her head, but her face had become softer, more caring.

Tally turned back to her knitting and tried to sound nonchalant. "Have you met his family, Mrs. Mided?"

"I was interviewed by the mother."

"What was she like?"

"A very old woman. Actually more of a war-horse than a woman. But admirable in a way. You know, salt-of-the-earth type. Of course she's rolling in money; all of them are. It's just money seems an uncomfortable fit on the old, so you notice it more."

Family Passions

She stopped and watched Tally with a concerned, almost motherly expression. "For goodness' sake, why don't you just take your salary and be grateful? We can't afford to become so wrapped up in our patients. It just doesn't make sense. All it'll do is drain you dry and leave you with nothing in the end. Take my word for it. What do you care whether he can think or not?"

"But I do care. I can tell he's aware. Perhaps a lot more than aware."

"Even if you are right, which I doubt, it's a personal choice. And if you are not right, you could do a heck of a lot of harm."

"But how can I leave him to waste away? I have an obligation."

"To whom?"

"Why, to him, of course."

"Of course," Mrs. Mided echoed, and it was clear she didn't agree with Tally. "But maybe you ought to consider another explanation. Just ask yourself, who is he to you?" She stared hard at Tally for a moment longer, then turned and left, closing the door quickly behind her.

Tally did not pick up her knitting for a long while. She was looking out the window at the red sun sinking behind the brown hills. Then she looked over at Ben, tracing the contours of the large stonelike man whose eyes she was sure held intelligence and life. She wondered indeed why she should care about the angry presence before her. Who was Ben Savage to her?

The door opened, and Ben was aware of the maid bringing in one dinner tray. The food smelled rich and meaty and homemade, as it had when he was young. Again he felt his stomach pinch with hunger. He half expected Tally to make teasing, smacking noises while she ate, like when he'd been a child trying to tantalize a friend out of a secret. But Tally no longer seemed to notice him. She ate slowly, staring into space; her delicate features seemed very sad once again.

Ben turned back to the window. In the end there was nothing that had the power to hold him for long, and as the light slipped from the little square of the world encased in his window, Ben's mind drifted back to the darkness.

A cock crowed, breaking through the silence. There was a terrible moment of disorientation. Ben was caught in time, unsure where he was, unsure even who he was.

The room was dark, with only a hint of light coming through the window. He could just barely make out the shape of the hills and the crippled outline of a tree, but he could no longer see the farmhouse or the church. Disoriented as he was, he wondered whether it was evening or morning.

Across from him, Tally was asleep, sitting in her high-backed chair, her head on her shoulder. Her knitting had fallen from her lap and lay in a heap on the ground.

Ben's body felt cramped and aching. It was the first sensation he'd had in his body since the accident, and it startled and angered him. In the beginning the knowledge that he was paralyzed and dying had shattered everything he'd believed in, then slowly he'd been able to reconstruct things. Since he was dying and there was nothing he could do about it, he had hoped at least that there would be no pain, that one day he would merely drift from the half-life he was in into the stillness of death. But if some feeling came back, then there was the possibility of pain, and with the pain came a kind of life. And that was something he couldn't bear.

Ben became aware of his hunger again, and that too angered him. He hadn't felt hunger since he was young, perhaps even since the beginning in America. It was an intense feeling, and he tried to reject it.

He looked at the tall frail woman who slept across from him, and she too angered him. The shifting of emotions came with a start. They were the first feelings he'd had for anything outside his anguished memories since the accident, and they tore through him brutally, forcing him to the moment with a vivid power. Everything converged—the hunger, the discomfort, and the irritation at Tally— until he felt anger rising, strong and hard, in his belly.

His muscles tightened in response. For a moment there was the sensation of movement, abrupt, purposeful; his weak muscles seemed strong. Everything stopped inside Ben. It was impossible, and yet his body seemed to be thrilling with motion, reborn instantly, wholly. His feeling of excitement was close to madness.

Again there was the sensation of motion. Quickly he looked down at his body, but there had been no movement, no movement at all. He sat exactly as he had, every part of his body still and dead.

The blow came savagely. For a moment he felt as he had when he'd come to consciousness and realized he was paralyzed. It was happening all over again, the terror, the fury at the vast dim prison he lived in. Ben tried to force himself back to resignation, to rush back to the darkness, but the possibility of before was burning in him and could not be extinguished. He had felt motion; he felt sure of it. The man he had been returned, and the longing for the darkness weakened.

Ben gathered all his energy. This time he pressed at his muscles violently, trying to push himself into motion. There was a momentary shuddering in his arms. But it was merely a trembling, brief, ineffective, and then there was nothing.

The anger in him grew, feeding on his inability to move, making it stronger because he was unable to express it. Again he tried. There was a shudder in his arms, longer this time, swelling, then fading. His arms felt very painful now, heavy and aching; his heart was beating rapidly, and it hurt him too. He thought about his arms, once so powerful, now turned to useless stone, and the realization of what had happened came back to him. He tried to blot it out, but it stayed there, solid and hard in his center.

With all his will he ordered his right hand to move. He could feel sluggish muscles begin to respond. It was a terrible, painful feeling, and yet in the pain there was life. Haltingly his left hand began to close over the arm of the chair, clawlike, stiff, almost as if it were carved from wax.

It was stunning. The wrong hand had moved, but still it was movement, and the sheer magnificence of that held him. Again he concentrated on his right hand, feeding thoughts to it in a constant stream. His left hand began to shiver, then slowly close. Everything was all haywire inside of him, yet it was clear there was something inside him that was working. Then again came the truth; though he might quiver and twitch, it was a far cry from moving.

Tally shifted in her chair. "I thought so," she said. She was smiling.

It was the knowing smile and the fact that she'd only been pretending to sleep that turned the anger into rage. Ben watched her, smiling so cockily, and he wanted to get up and rush across the room. He wanted to tear her from her chair. He wanted to hurt her as he'd been hurt. It was the injustice that burned most strongly inside of him. Why should he be suffering, while the world continued, smiling, unknowing, with neither pain nor discomfort, so very alive?

Ben focused everything in him on his muscles, tearing through damaged pathways until his flaccid muscles trembled. He could feel everything taking hold. Energy pulsed through his body, and when he looked down, both of his hands were closing over the arms of the wheelchair, and even his legs had begun to quiver. His hands tightened. He could see his fingers closing, and they no longer looked so waxlike and unreal. His legs were trembling, and then they too took hold and he was beginning to move upward, pushing down on his arms, forcing himself out of his chair. It was stunning. It was beautiful. It was life.

Tally remained where she was. She saw the look of concentration on Ben's face and, just beneath the surface, the anger. She knew she was provoking him with her smile, feeding the fury until it gave him life.

Ben commanded his legs to stop trembling. He could feel them jar violently, then catch hold. It was exquisitely painful. He pushed himself farther, thrusting down on his arms, using them as leverage, trying to lift himself to a standing position. His legs were tightening now, grasping at the floor, muscles clenching, and he was rising upward, slowly, very slowly. His heart was pounding heavily but strongly, and it was not giving out like they'd said; it was pumping life through his veins.

Then all at once his muscles gave way, his legs weakened, and Ben was tumbling forward, collapsing onto the floor.

Tally didn't move. Though she wanted to rush forward to help, she sensed that would be the worst thing she could do. "If you want my help, just ask for it," she said softly. "Show me with your eyes."

Tally was watching Ben with detachment, and he closed his eyes against the sight of her. He lay on the floor, his whole body stunned with pain, but even more agonizing was the impotence, growing like a terrible cry inside him. He felt his face shudder; then all at once tears stung his eyes. He thought to himself, *You pathetic old fool. Now you're even crying.*

Tally repeated, "Show me you need my help."

Ben lay motionless. He didn't even attempt to get up. The excitement of before was turned inside out. His was a crippled body, and any movement he might regain would only serve to cause him suffering before his death. The tears were like waves inside him, and he wondered why he hadn't been killed in the accident. It would have been so much easier if only he'd died, quickly, finally.

Tally saw the look of grief in Ben's eyes and knew she'd gone too far. She moved to him rapidly, hooking her hands under his arms, trying to lift him back to his chair. She strained against his weight, pressing her arms tightly up on his body, but Ben was too heavy, and he slid up less than an inch. Tally could feel her whole body being pushed to its utmost. Trembling, she tried harder, but the weight of Ben fought against her, until her muscles too were giving, and Ben slipped back to the floor. She waited for the aching in her arms to subside, then once again tried to lift Ben to his chair.

Suddenly Ben saw how funny it was, him lying on the floor, a huge boulder of useless weight, and Tally pulling and pushing at him, her face growing red from the effort.

Ben's lips began to tremble. The humor gathered, and with it the quivering, and then he realized he was laughing. What had seemed so painfully tragic only moments before now seemed only ridiculous. He felt stupid and impotent, yet oddly no longer ashamed.

Tally was stunned. She remained where she was, watching the huge stonelike man. A raspy sound broke from his lips, and his face moved stiffly. He was laughing. She watched the ugly awkward movement, and it was breathtaking to her. The vulnerability was astounding, like watching a creature being born. But there was something terrifying about it too, for she no longer knew what she was facing. While Ben's body did move, and there was even sound coming from him, she had no idea what kind of damage there had been to the brain. She couldn't tell if he was thinking at all, or only reacting as a senseless being.

Ben was staring at her now, laughter breaking from his stiff lips. Then through the laughter came sound, a voice. It was hoarse from weeks of silence, distorted by the paralysis. "Get a crane," he stammered weakly.

Tally recoiled. She tried to hold down the panic. That he could speak amazed her, but the words seemed to make no sense; they were just random sounds put together, perhaps memories set free in the jumble of his mind.

Ben was still staring at her, his eyes filled with humor and what seemed to be an intelligence and understanding. She repeated to herself the words he'd just said, but she could gather no meaning from them; they were merely senseless syllables strung together.

Then suddenly as she leaned toward Ben's heavy body and began straining against his weight, his words made sense. He was making a joke about his weight.

It was a powerful feeling. It seemed impossible that she had even questioned whether he could think. He could do better than just think; he could see humor in his tragedy. It was a sign of great humanity, stunning and quite beautiful.

A smile broke across her face, and she felt laughter rising inside of her. She allowed the laughter to take over, calming the panic of before. "Never mind a crane," she answered finally. "This time you're going to help me."

Ben's lips quivered. His eyes were sparkling with humor and embarrassment. "Like it or not?"

The laughter slipped from Tally's face and was replaced by determination. She looked very strong and efficient, not at all the woman of before.

"Oh, no, Mr. Savage," Tally answered firmly. "I guarantee you're not going to like it. It's going to be a great deal of hard work and pain, and you're not going to like it at all."

TWELVE

Midland, Ohio

"Hey, son, what's going on over there?" Mason Josephs's voice on the telephone sounded cheerful to the point of idiocy, but anyone with a passing knowledge of Wall Street knew that it masked a finely tuned brain that had made him one of the world's most successful investment brokers. For over thirty years that brain had been ruling the Over the Counter market, where they didn't have an array of sophisticated computers to make decisions for them, just men with good instincts.

Dyer kept his tone as playfully amiable as Mason's. "Dunno. But I suspect you're about to tell me."

Mason laughed. If possible his laugh was more fatuous than his voice, but Dyer could imagine his small hazel eyes moving behind their shield of horn-rims. There was nothing idiotic about those eyes; they were carnivorous.

"Well, son, there's a hell of a lot of activity going on in Midwestern shares back at the schoolyard, and I wondered if you were aware of it."

To Mason the "schoolyard" was the Over the Counter market.

Dyer felt himself tightening with anxiety. Mason could pick up the slightest whiff of trouble while other brokers were still looking over the morning papers. And he'd be right too. Mason wanted to know what was going on and that was a question Dyer couldn't answer; his silence hardly gave the impression of a strong hand on the reins of Midwestern. He waited for Mason to deliver the bombshell.

"So you weren't aware, huh? Well, there's buying. A heck of a lot of it too."

"And you just thought I should know?" Irritation had crept into Dyer's voice. He fought to control it. Whatever was going on, it wouldn't do any good for Mason to get the impression he was worried. But he was worried. Why should someone be buying Midwestern stock in volume, especially now with Ben ill? It made no sense, or rather the sense it made, Dyer didn't like at all.

"Sorry I called?" Mason asked.

"No. Just thinking. Who's doing the buying?"

"Your guess is as good as mine. I can tell you who they sez is doing it. But that ain't gonna help you."

"I see." Dyer heard himself sigh. "What is it, a dummy company?"

"Companies. Mit an 'es.' And third parties too."

Dyer could feel the sweat starting to pour off of him; he was glad Mason couldn't see through the telephone. "Exactly how much activity are you talking about?"

"Hard to tell. You've got to separate the real stuff from the phony baloney."

Dyer pressed. "How much?"

"Roughly four point nine percent."

"Roughly, huh?" Dyer laughed sharply.

"Well, as you know, according to the Securities Exchange Act of 1934, over five percent and they have to register with the SEC."

"Indeed I do know," Dyer said pensively. There was no use now in trying to hide the fact that he was worried; anyone in his right mind would be.

"So obviously whoever it is would like to remain quietlike."

"And within the law," Dyer added.

"Exactly. Of course, the question we're presented with isn't just who, it's why."

Dyer was silent. Of course that was the question. Was it the beginning of a take-over bid? Dyer thought that was possible, though he didn't see how they could bring it off. The real problem was, now that Mason knew about it, what would he do? It seemed likely he'd do a lot of damage; Mason had a mouth on him almost as big as his brain.

"Maybe," Dyer answered evasively. "But it seems to me that whatever the reason, it won't make much difference to us over here. Four point nine percent is not exactly a controlling interest."

"Though sometimes it can be an indication."

Dyer laughed, but even he could hear the falseness in it. "Oh, yeah? Of what?"

"Of many things, son. You know that as well as I."

"Yeah, well, this time it's just an indication that Midwestern's a good investment." Dyer was losing his cool; he could hear it in his voice, and he suspected Mason could too.

"Hey, relax, Max. I called because I thought you'd be interested. I didn't call to pry."

"But any information you might gather."

Mason pressed jovially. "I won't deny that with Ben ill there's been some talk. If there weren't such an animal as gossip, guys like us would be out of business. I'll tell you the truth, son. There are those who say it's strange you haven't had the court appoint a conservatorship. Ben has fifteen percent of the stock; no company can exist for long with that kind of volume outstanding."

Dyer felt trapped. He had hoped not to have to go to court and divide the family; he had hoped to keep the stockholders from becoming too concerned while he solidified his position.

"That's right," Dyer answered. "We haven't gone to court."

Mason pushed. "Which means provisions for voting his stock were made before? A presigned proxy or power of attorney?"

Dyer hesitated. "As you said, no company can exist with that kind of stock outstanding. You answered your own question."

"Yeah, ain't I smart." Mason laughed affably. "Still, I'm surprised you're not interested in who's behind this buying business."

"I didn't say that."

"In so many words."

The conversation had clearly shifted now, and Mason had declared outright that he was on a fact-finding mission. It meant that any more information Dyer was going to get would be in exchange for what he gave. And that he wasn't prepared to do.

"You've got me all wrong, Mason," Dyer returned. "All I said was that I wasn't worried. And I'm not."

Mason was quiet for a moment, and this time when he continued, the cheerful foolishness was gone from his voice. "Look, son, what goes on at Midwestern isn't of all that great concern to me, if you know what I mean. It ain't exactly a giant conglomerate that's going to make or break my reputation. But I've known your uncle a good long time. We go back to when he first went into the OTC market with a little half-ass firm that was hardly big enough to register with the SEC. I like him. I like Midwestern, and I called to tell you something's going on. Take it for what it is, a discreet warning."

"Which won't go any farther than the two of us?"

"My loyalty is to my clients. If something looks fishy, I'm obliged to tell them."

"I can promise you there's nothing fishy going on here."

"Maybe, son. Maybe. Still, there's the decided tang of salt in the air. And for one reason or another, my shoes are getting damp." He laughed, and once again his tone became cretinous. "Anyway my phone's got more flashing lights than the Christmas tree at Rockefeller Center, so I better get off and earn my keep. Give my best to your family," he said bluffly. "Especially your grandmother."

Dyer hung up the phone, but he stared at it for a long time. There were plenty of good explanations for this unknown buyer, plenty of explanations that shouldn't concern him in the least. Yet he could feel the tension gripping his chest. With Ben ill, this was a perfect time to stage a take-over, and though the attempt might seem doomed to failure, Dyer knew it could be enough to bring him down.

Dying sunlight reflected off of the windows of the administration building of Midwestern, making it look as if it were an inferno inside. The night shift was coming on, and the secretaries and executives were all going home to frozen macaroni-and-cheese dinners in front of the TV. As the spectral shadows of evening crept all around the quiet mill, sealing it in, only one light in the building remained.

Dyer sat in Ben's office, hunched over a legal pad. Packing crates were all around him, the debris of a move from his own office made only a few hours before. Dyer stopped writing and looked at the list of stockholders' names he was compiling. There were ten men on the list, all with varying degrees of financial capability, all with varying degrees of foxiness. But though each of them might have been able to purchase the extra stock, none of them stood to gain enough.

Dyer wadded up the paper and left-hooked it at a wastebasket across the room. It ringed the edge, then fell to the floor. It had been an easy shot, and Dyer took the miss as an omen. He pulled himself from behind the desk, retrieved the ball of paper, then made a feint, this time executing a perfect shot.

He was feeling better as he went back to his desk and glanced over Tom Lindsay's monthly report from Research and Development, but that didn't last for long. Soon his mind drifted back to his conversation with Mason Josephs, and his eyes wandered over to the wastebasket. It occurred to him how unwise it was to leave evidence of these thoughts for anyone who might care to snoop, and he got up quickly, stooping to the wastebasket.

Just then James burst through the door. "Well, what do you know? Body's not even cold yet." James pushed past Dyer and fell into a chair across from his desk.

Dyer couldn't move. A picture of himself squatting over the wastebasket, clutching a wad of crumpled yellow paper, flashed through his mind, and he felt foolish. Holding the paper in his fist, he rose and slowly walked back to his desk. He wondered if James had seen what he'd done; he rather suspected he had. James wasn't an idiot, he was simply a fool, and there was a very great difference between the two.

"I am acting president of Midwestern," Dyer answered once he was safely behind his desk.

"You're telling me? You're acting president all over the place. This is Ben's office."

"Was."

"He's not dead yet."

"Look," Dyer said evenly. "I'm not going to sit here and argue your father's condition. Believe me, I'd rather stay where I was. But I needed to use your father's secretary and his files, so I had myself moved in. There's nothing symbolic or ulterior about it. In fact, I hate the feeling."

James laughed angrily. "Too many ghosts?"

"Not ghosts. Implications. It looks bad for me to be here. But it looks bad for the office to remain empty. I was caught in between."

"Tsk, tsk, poor cousin Dyer."

"Is that all you came here for?" Dyer asked impatiently.

James sat forward in his seat, and there was an angry rigidity to his body. "Not exactly. I thought we two cousins should have a chat."

"As I remember we had a meeting at eleven fifteen, lunch in the cafeteria at noon, and bumped into each other innumerable times in the corridor."

"I'm well aware of my schedule. In fact, I'm hurt you haven't noticed just how devoted I've become to work these past two months."

"I've noticed."

Dyer's tone stopped James. It was clear that if Dyer hadn't noticed before, he was beginning to be aware of it now, and though James didn't know what Dyer was thinking, he could see that he was, and he liked the interest it implied.

"I'm not talking about that kind of chat," James continued. "I'm talking about a more intimate one. Like at my father's sixtieth birthday party where we really got to know one another."

Every word James said sounded pointed, though at what, Dyer wasn't sure. If he hadn't been so busy recently, he might have noticed that James had been acting differently since his father's accident, and if he'd noticed, he might have been prepared. As it was, he was caught off guard.

"Have you been drinking?" he asked with superiority.

"Not a drop."

"Well, start then. You're better when you drink."

"For whom?"

Dyer watched James in silence. For the first time it occurred to him that it might be James behind the stock buying. Dyer laughed at the thought. James wasn't capable of pulling off a panty raid, let alone a stock manipulation.

"All right, I give up," Dyer said amiably. "What's with all the sarcasm and jaunty quips? It isn't that I'm not amused by them. I'm always amused by you, James. But tell me what's bothering you, because you caught me at a very busy time, and I'd like to get home at a reasonable hour."

James's eyes shifted to the piece of paper Dyer held. "So I noticed."

"For crying out loud! Speak! Or is this going to become an all-night bull session?"

"What a great idea. Just like when we were kids and slept over at each other's houses."

"Yeah, terrific. You used to keep me up all night with your tossing and turning."

"And you used to keep me up all night with your jerking off."

James his face bright red with anger, was staring at Dyer. It occurred to Dyer that perhaps James was crazy. Then suddenly James smiled, and he no longer looked crazy at all; he looked very sane and in control.

James reached to Dyer's desk, picked up the pad of paper Dyer had been using, and began writing numbers on it.

"You want to know why I came here?" he asked when he was finished. "I'll show you. It's a simple matter of arithmetic." He flipped the pad on the desk so that it was facing Dyer. "What you're looking at is a complete list of the family stock."

"I never could have guessed."

"Oh, I have no doubt that all those nice little figures are engraved indelibly on your brain. But bear with me. It gets much more interesting." He resumed deliberately, pointing like a schoolteacher at the figures he'd written at the top of the paper. "Basically what we have here is a reasonably typical OTC picture. Fifty-five percent of the stock is retained by the family, forty-five is in the hands of the public. But what we're concerned with here is the fifty-five percent."

"Forty percent. You're forgetting that Ben isn't exactly voting his shares at the moment. No one is."

"Unless I have a proxy."

"Unless pigs can fly. Ben didn't believe in all those morbid necessities like presigned proxies or powers of attorney or trusts. He thought he would live forever. So now his stock is useless."

"Unless, of course, you go to court and get yourself appointed conservator. But you aren't likely to do that, are you?"

"I don't see how I can avoid it. So far we've been keeping things stable without going that far. But Ben has fifteen percent. He's a major stockholder. In fact, he could be considered a statutory underwriter. A court would have to appoint a conservator."

"But not necessarily you." James smiled. "She'd fight you, you know. Grandma'd fight you."

Dyer didn't bother to deny this. For years he'd known that his grandmother didn't trust him, and while it had always hurt him deeply, he'd also seen a certain justice in it. "She might," he answered slowly. "But she'd lose."

"Perhaps. Of course I could fight you too. And there's an excellent chance that I *wouldn't* lose."

Dyer sneered. "The question is, would the fight be worth it? There'd be enough carnage left behind to make World War Two look like a border incident."

James turned pale. Though he had feared Dyer would stop at nothing if he opposed him, and knew he was vulnerable on many fronts, he had hoped that Dyer's devotion to his grandmother would keep him in check. But now, looking at the expression on Dyer's face, James doubted whether his grandmother could reach him. No one could. "Is that a warning?" he asked.

"Is one needed?"

"Not for now. I have other things on my mind."

James withdrew into silence, waiting until he had recovered. But when he began again, his voice was softer, less sure, and he could feel a tic in his right eye. "Okay, for argument's sake we'll call it forty percent. Whatever, the picture is the same.

"In 1951, Midwestern stocks were divided into what must have seemed at the time equitable blocks. Both of our fathers received fifteen percent. Grandmother got ten. Pauline, you, and I got five each. Later my mother received one and a half percent, but that didn't come out of the family stock. Still, it counts, since Ben has her proxy, so in effect it's another one and a half for him. And Tom has a little too, also not in the family group and not enough to worry about."

"All this is fascinating, James. But what's the point?"

Dyer was looking around the room, making a display of his impatience, but James could see it was an act. Dyer hated the unexpected, and he had been thrown off balance. James could tell he was getting to him, and that made him feel much more in control.

"When your father died," James resumed, "his stock went to your mother, which meant it really went to you." James pointed at the next block of figures on the pad. "So there you are, voting twenty percent to Ben's sixteen and a half. Of course all that means nothing, because Ben really voted for Grandma and me and Pauline. So we're back to you at twenty percent and Ben at thirty-six and a half. Until the accident."

"Now let me see if I can figure out what it is now. Very difficult, James. Thirty-six and a half minus fifteen. Is it twenty-one and a half?"

James grinned. "It's something much more fascinating than that, Dyer. It's, shall we say, fluid. A question mark. For the moment we're all sticking by you. We have to. After all, it wouldn't look good. But, and here's the really riveting bit, you'd better mind your *p*'s and *q*'s. Stay a puppet and you control all forty percent."

"Forty-one and a half if your mother stays true to form and keeps out of family business except at dividend time."

James ignored his remark. "But if you should get it into your head to take independent action, like moving toward diversification, the entire picture changes." He smirked at Dyer. "Getting any more interesting now?"

"I'm spellbound."

"Well, you should be, Dyer, because from now on, it's all unknowns, and I always find the unknown so much more fascinating than the known. Don't you?"

"Oh, indeed."

"Good! So here you are. You've got your twenty percent, plus Grandma's ten, plus Pauline who'll stick by her mother."

"You're forgetting your five percent."

"Wanna bet?" James laughed. "But we'll put that aside for a while. Now as I said, there's Grandma. And what an adversary she'd make! My guess is you'd like to take her on even less than all the stockholders and the SEC combined. At least they're bound by rules; they'd fight clean. But Grandma, God bless her, would use anything and everything in her power. And she'd believe in her perfect right to do so too. Plus, and here's an interesting plus, what happens to my father's stock when he dies? Who gets his fifteen percent?"

"I'd put my money on Grandma."

"So would I. But Grandma's eighty-six years old. What happens to her stock?" Again James took up the pad of paper and began scribbling some numbers. "You see how interesting this is getting? Will she divide it up between the two of us? In that case it gives me only seventeen and a half percent to your thirty-two and a half. With Pauline's floating. Or will she leave Dad's to me and divide hers between the two of us? That puts us both at twenty-five. With Pauline's stock becoming quite important."

Dyer watched James in silence for a while. The suspicion was back full force. He said slowly, "Unless of course you decide to buy stocks on the sly."

James looked surprised. "I could do that, I suppose. But I don't see the point. You'd only buy up more trying to match me. It would be a losing proposition in the long run. Still, as I said before, it's all a big question mark. Who the hell knows about any of it?"

Dyer relaxed. Indeed, what James had just said made sense. On the other hand, even if James were planning something, Dyer had let him know that he was being watched.

Dyer lit a cigar and looked out of the window impatiently. "So after fifteen minutes of discussion, we're back where we started. As you said, it's all a big question mark. I don't see exactly what we accomplished."

"I wasn't sure that you knew that I knew."

"That's it? That's all you wanted to prove?"

"And did I?"

Dyer smiled. "Yes, you did, as a matter of fact."

"And it comes as a big surprise, I'll bet."

"Okay, I'll give you that too."

James was watching Dyer cagily. "So now what?"

"Indeed. So now what?" Dyer was growing unsettled again.

James sat back in his seat and allowed the silence to play around Dyer. Finally he leaned forward. "I want in," he said earnestly. "I want into the family business."

Dyer laughed. "You are in. Unless you call five percent of the stock, a title, and a healthy salary out."

"I've been on the outskirts of the family business all my life. A dumb empty title, in charge of dumb empty bullshit."

"Public relations."

"Like I said, bullshit. Just holding up the clients' balls after you and Ben chop them off."

Dyer let out a long stream of smoke. "So what do you want? An ax?"

"That's right. I want an ax."

"I see." Dyer paused, pressing on the wad of paper in his hand. "And in exchange you offer your five percent?"

"You're forgetting Ben's shares."

"But for the moment, five," Dyer answered. "And in exchange for some, I don't know what."

"Power, Dyer. Remember it? It's the stuff you're so hungry for. And I don't offer you my five percent. I offer you a working relationship, where maybe if you're good you can use my five percent. In other words it's equal time, just like we were partners, or at least almost like we were partners, because you're as slippery as hell and it'll be all I can do just to keep up with your scheming."

Dyer was watching James cautiously again. There was no question that James had changed, or at least was making an attempt to change, and Dyer needed time to absorb it. He assumed it was related to Ben's accident; he'd seen that kind of thing happen before. Dyer contemplated the turn of events with a certain amount of relish. He enjoyed a fight, especially one he had absolute confidence in winning.

"All right," he agreed finally. "But you'll have to buckle down. No more fooling around."

"I thought you got the picture before. That's all over since Dad's accident."

Dyer nodded. "Okay, fine. You'll have to give me time to figure out how to do this. It'll take a lot of moving people around. Meanwhile, we'll get you an assistant, someone really good, and if you want to move into my office, you're welcome to it."

James frowned. It was a bribe, of course. But no one had ever thought him even worthy of bribing.

"Okay," he replied. "That'll do for a start. But just to sort of cement this new relationship, I want you to show me the piece of paper in your hand."

James was prepared for an argument and was surprised when without a word of protest, Dyer tossed the wadded-up paper over to him.

THIRTEEN

Though Angela was an old woman herself, as the younger of the two, it was her obligation to visit Elizabeth. It was never the other way around. Elizabeth never phoned and never visited. She just waited for her daughter-in-law to make the first move. Elizabeth knew this irritated Angela, and suspected that it was for this reason she always telephoned before she came, setting up a formal appointment rather than just stopping in as the rest of the family did. While to outsiders it might seem a sign of respect, it was quite the opposite. There were rules in every family, unspoken but strict rules peculiar to them, and one learned early on how far one could go and what a breach of them meant.

How much of life is unspoken and only implied, Elizabeth thought to herself as her eyes moved over the coffee table. The little table was filled with plates of smoked salmon sandwiches, little bowls of olives; there was a cut-glass decanter of sherry on the sideboard and cups and saucers for tea. To the world it might seem a happy scene, a rich old lady entertaining her daughter-in-law, nicely, respectfully. But Elizabeth knew it was thrust and parry, silent strokes of anger.

Angela resented offering guests anything when they came to her house, and therefore Elizabeth made it a point to be lavish, not to teach her a lesson—the two of them had gone much too far for that—but to reprimand her. She knew Angela understood every olive, every tea sandwich, and resented them intensely. Elizabeth also knew that Angela considered her a fool. For at twelve dollars a pound, smoked salmon was a very expensive admonishment. So Elizabeth's delight at her abundant table was always diminished. Yet she did it. It was strange the silent battles people waged with one another.

The doorbell rang, and Elizabeth gave a last anxious look around the room, making sure that everything was as it should be, then slowly she went to the door.

Angela stood ramrod straight; her small frame had shrunk through the years, and she looked brittle, as if the merest hint of a breeze would toss her from the doorway. But the tight stiff way she planted her feet, the firmness of her thin pale lips, showed a determination to remain fixed to the ground; only a hurricane would dislodge her.

"Good afternoon, Mother." Angela quickly moved into the house, imposing herself on the hall. "And how are you feeling?" She walked into the living room and moved briskly to the couch, sitting down without the usual groans and fusses of older women. Though she had seen the sandwiches the moment she'd come into the room, indeed had expected them, she kept her eyes well away.

Elizabeth poured two sherries and handed one to Angela. It was part of the ritual, though neither of the women drank them, and it was only when Elizabeth had settled herself in her chair that she answered.

"Well enough. Though this year there'll be no running of the marathon for me." She laughed. "Still and all, at eighty-six, drawing in air is something of a miracle, so thankful I am for that."

Angela pressed her lips even more tightly together. Never in all the years had Elizabeth asked after her health, though in fact she'd had terrible bouts of illness and had even been close to death once from tumors in her uterus. She remembered bitterly that when Dyer had been born, Elizabeth had appeared without so much as a flower, and she'd never asked about her labor, though everyone knew it had been a hard one.

Angela asked sharply, "Any news from Wales?"

"Under a week it's been, and any news I would get would only serve no purpose."

"Now, now, Elizabeth. We mustn't give up hope."

Elizabeth ignored her. "I expect I'll hear soon enough. That Mrs. Hoozits promised she would write weekly and call if something important happened."

"Mrs. Mided," Angela corrected. "But, dear, I still don't understand why you sent him away. It's at a time like this when a person should be near his family, not stuck off in some godforsaken country halfway around the world."

Elizabeth interrupted, "Have some smoked salmon sandwiches. Made they were especially for you."

Angela looked down at the sandwiches with studied disdain, but in truth she was a woman torn. She adored smoked salmon, and it was a treat she never allowed herself because of the price. She looked up and saw Elizabeth watching her as though she were a laboratory animal, and she knew her mother-in-law could see everything, her temptation, her desire to resist, even her eventual defeat. For Angela was well aware that she would give in, not because she was so weak willed—she'd rejected far more enticing temptations in her sixty-five years—but because refusing might cause a breach, and she didn't want to go that far.

Angela placed two finger sandwiches on a plate and set it on her lap. She could smell the tangy meaty fish and allowed the odor to tease her before she ate. Since she only had smoked salmon sandwiches when she visited Elizabeth, it was important that she enjoy them to the fullest, and she knew only pleasure delayed could bring the sharpest delight.

Angela carefully chewed and swallowed one of the sandwiches before she continued. "I always thought you should have sold that house long ago. It's just a drain on your resources. And it's not as if you can visit it anymore."

"Ben's there now."

"Yes, but—" Angela paused, trying to find a delicate way to say what she felt she must. She decided there was no kind way. "It isn't as if he's getting any pleasure out of it," she said at last. "And certainly he'd get much better care in America."

"No way there is to guess the pleasure of others. Perhaps he knows where he is, perhaps not. But clear it is if he did know, it's where he'd want to be."

"Stuck away from everybody?"

"Aye, yeah. Away." Elizabeth could hear the sorrow in her voice and stiffened. She always kept a close watch over herself when Angela was around, guarding every feeling from her penetrating gaze. To Angela emotions were a weakness to be exploited, and especially now, Elizabeth had to protect herself against any chance of being used. Though Angela seemed to the world a shadowy and frail creature, it was she who, through her seeming weakness and self-denial, had molded her family's life. It hadn't taken long for her to gain power over Evan, and as time went by and he became weaker, she seemed to grow in strength, as if she were sapping it from him. After Evan had died, she'd switched her influence to Dyer.

Elizabeth knew that in many ways both of them used their sons as shields in the invisible war between them. The irony was that neither of them really needed shields; both were quite capable of waging battle themselves.

Elizabeth watched as Angela nibbled her smoked salmon sandwich. How smug and satisfied she seemed since Elizabeth no longer had Ben. For years Dyer had been the weaker of the two, but now he was the only one left standing.

"I'm sorry I brought this all up," Angela resumed, startling Elizabeth back to reality. "But you must understand I'm only saying it for your own good. You have enough to worry about at this time without your son five thousand miles away."

Angela glanced down, embarrassed, and truly she did seem sorry she'd brought the subject up. Instantly Elizabeth felt guilty about her cruel thoughts; sometimes she could be a very disagreeable old woman.

"And how is Dyer then?" she inquired, trying to be amiable. "Long it is since I've seen or heard from him."

Angela sat forward, her face screwed up with interest. "Dyer's been working very hard, Mother. He's taken over Ben's work as well as his own, and that's taking a great deal of time, as you can imagine. Of course he was always kept up to date on everything Ben was doing, but just the sheer volume—"

Angela stopped herself abruptly. She knew her talking was only reminding Elizabeth that Ben was no longer the head of Midwestern and that it must be hurting her deeply. It was something Angela could understand. Life without Dyer was unimaginable.

Angela looked out the window nervously. "It's gotten quite cold recently. I'm beginning to believe we're in for one of those white Christmases they go on about."

"No need there is to change the subject. A perfect right you have to talk of your son to me. My loss should not subtract from you. For Ben is as dear to me as anything, but all my anger, jealousy, and tears aren't going to change facts. Nor, for that matter, all happy and gay will I be if you do not mention his name. My suffering remains, no matter what you say or do."

Elizabeth stared at her hands, embarrassed that she'd slipped and displayed her grief. Never before had she allowed the layers of propriety to peel away in front of Angela, and it alarmed her as a sign of age.

Quickly she rose and went to pour tea at the sideboard, her mind tightening. She was resolved to bring up her guard again.

Angela took two more sandwiches and placed them in readiness on her plate. "I do know that Dyer is worried about the annual stockholders' meeting."

"And what has he to worry about then?" Elizabeth snapped irritably. "Certain it is that he'll be voted in as president."

"That of course is my hope."

"Only a hope then?"

Angela laughed snidely. "Well, the competition is hardly fierce. But one never knows."

While Elizabeth knew this last remark was directed at James, and indeed she agreed with Angela's assessment of his competency, she took it as a personal rebuke. Elizabeth hated when Angela made comments about the inadequacies of anyone in the family. She was an outsider; she had no rights.

Elizabeth's voice was very cold. "So what does Dyer have to be concerned about, may I ask?"

Angela fixed Elizabeth with her eyes. "You."

Elizabeth laughed sharply. "Too old I am to run for president of Midwestern."

Angela took a sip of tea and stared into her cup for a long while. Then finally she put it down decisively. "Look, Mother. Perhaps it's time you and I spoke frankly to one another. After all, it's been so many years, so much pain and tragedy, and we're the only ones left from before. In a sense it's this, even more than the family, that links us. There is no one left but you and I who've been here from the beginning."

"And Tom! You're forgetting Tom."

"He isn't family." Angela answered quickly, but she paused and smiled sadly. "Yes, of course, you don't think of me as family either, do you? But I am a Savage, Elizabeth. I'm a Savage as much as you are."

Elizabeth felt a dangerous anger rising inside of her. She tried to control it, but it seeped from her, tightening her mouth, narrowing her eyes.

Angela was sitting forward in her seat as if she were asking for something. Elizabeth wondered what there could be that she needed. Dyer was on the ascendancy; there was nothing she need ask for. But Elizabeth knew that wasn't completely true. She controlled her own stock and that went for a lot. Dyer might be acting president of Midwestern, but it was clearly on her sufferance. And Angela understood that very well.

"Whether you're a Savage or not is not in question," Elizabeth answered. "A proper wife you were to Evan. Never have I given you reason to believe I thought otherwise."

"Yes. But I'm more than Evan's wife. I'm Dyer's mother."

"Aye. And that you have done well too."

"But there is still more. I have served the family. I have always given as much, if not more, than any of them."

Elizabeth stiffened. She knew Angela was implying that it had been her marriage to Evan that had started them all. "In equal amounts have we given. And in equal amounts have we taken. Your father's business never suffered from the Savages. For hard work and brains were our share."

Angela retrenched. "That wasn't what I meant, Mother. You're twisting my words." She stopped, playing with one of the smoked salmon sandwiches. But she had lost her appetite. "I think the time has come that we discuss openly what you certainly must have suspected for years," she said at last.

"No use have I for suspicions. That is not my way."

Angela continued as if Elizabeth had not spoken. "I know you must have suspected, though you've never betrayed your thoughts." She paused and her face softened; she looked almost four decades younger, almost as she had when she'd sat across the table from

Elizabeth that first time. "I loved Evan, you know, perhaps more than any woman should love a man. He was everything to me, truly everything. It was as if I didn't exist before him." She sighed sadly. "It's as if I no longer exist now that he's gone. But I doubt you can understand that."

"I understand."

"No, it was different for you. I've always envied your ability to live on your own. But for me there was only Evan."

There were tears in Angela's eyes, and this startled Elizabeth. She wished more than ever that Angela would leave and take her grief and her accusations far away. Elizabeth was frightened of this plea for understanding, frightened and slightly sickened. Still, she could not send Angela away; it was part of the rules, and also she suspected that Angela was about to tell her the truth, and Elizabeth had an obligation to listen to the truth whether she liked it or not.

Angela looked down at her clasped hands and she was crying, tears slipping down her cheeks without her even bothering to wipe them away. "I would have done anything for him. Really I would have."

Elizabeth watched her coldly, hoping that at least the tears would shame her into stopping. But Angela just allowed them to slide down her cheeks, then eventually subside.

"We'd been married five years," she resumed calmly. "And I remember thinking it was impossible anyone had ever been so happy. It seemed an enormous secret that only the two of us shared."

Elizabeth shifted in her seat and her face became creased with pain. A spasm had passed through her body, leaving her even more anxious and angry. But Angela didn't seem to notice Elizabeth's grimace of pain. Or perhaps it was that for once it was she who didn't care.

Angela pressed on softly. "Except that we didn't have any children. We never spoke of it. But it was there, between us, always. Or maybe I shouldn't say between us, because it was never like that. There wasn't any blame. I assumed, of course, it was my fault. I was too thin, too brittle. I was too small. I suppose I felt I wasn't equal to it. I knew that Evan wanted a son desperately. And the more time went on, the less he talked about it. But you could see it written all over his face; you could see it was eating into him. And I thought he was sorry he'd ever married me. I grew frantic about that. I'd watch his face, trying to guess his thoughts, reading every expression that passed over it for signs of his regret. But remember!

Family Passions

All this was unspoken, and probably because of that, even more terrible. Finally I couldn't bear it anymore, and I spoke to Ben. It was he who suggested that perhaps Evan was the one who couldn't conceive a child. It was he who arranged that I go to a doctor secretly and find out."

She stopped and once again began to cry. Elizabeth could see her shoulders shaking, and she despised her even more.

Then Angela's tears subsided, and she continued. "When I knew the truth, the rest seemed so clear, so right. You can understand that, can't you?" She didn't wait for an answer. It was as if she were speaking to herself. "Ben was against the idea at first naturally. He said it was a betrayal, that if Evan found out the truth it would be the end of the two of them, the end of all of us. But it seemed so unlikely that he'd ever have to know. I persuaded Ben eventually. And though he had doubts, I never doubted. Not for a minute. Not for a second."

Angela looked up at Elizabeth and her eyes were clear and strong. "To you it must seem strange, perhaps terrible. But even today, after everything, I still believe I made the right choice. Because in the end there is Dyer."

Elizabeth didn't answer. Although she'd suspected what Angela had just told her, she'd kept her suspicions far away, blocking them firmly from her mind. But now Angela was forcing her to face the truth, and she hated her for it.

Elizabeth's voice was very weak and at the same time very angry. "I don't understand why I had to know this."

"Don't you see? So that you'll love Dyer as I do. Dyer is more a Savage than any of us. Ben was the beginning, and it was Evan who raised him."

Elizabeth's eyes narrowed. "And what about you then? It seems you also had your finger in the pie. In both pies, to be precise."

Tears came to Angela's eyes. "There was never anything between Ben and me."

Elizabeth watched her coldly. "Nothing between you is it? To me it sounds like something of a very particular sort arose twixt the two of you."

Angela was sitting rigidly, glaring at Elizabeth. "It was done as a duty. On both sides."

Angela paused, allowing the anger to subside, but still her soft reasonable tone barely concealed her annoyance. "We met secretly until I was sure I had conceived. But there was no pleasure in it for either of us."

"Not quite accurate can that be, my dear. For without a certain degree of pleasure the mechanism doesn't work." Elizabeth laughed wickedly. "Old I may be. But not so old I can't remember that much."

Angela stood up and began gathering her things. "I just felt you should know."

"Oh, aye?" Elizabeth sighed wearily. "And what have you accomplished by it?" She too stood, slowly, weakly. She was feeling very old and tired.

"Dyer is more of a Savage than any of us. I wanted you to see him as such. I wanted you to trust him."

"Hard it is to see how this should make me trust him the more. Only you the less."

Angela turned from Elizabeth and began walking to the door, her small head held rigid. But there was something about the set of her back that told Elizabeth she felt she had won, though what her victory was, Elizabeth still didn't know.

Elizabeth followed her to the door, and it was only when they had reached it that either of them spoke. It was Angela who broke the silence.

"Think about what I just said. I know when you do, you'll understand why I told you." Then she opened the door and quickly left.

Elizabeth didn't move. She could feel the breath stinging her fragile lungs, and it made her feel very weak and alone. But as she stood at the door, gasping for air like a dying fish, she did begin to understand why Angela had come and why she had told her what she had. For if Dyer was Ben's son, not his nephew, and Elizabeth believed this to be true, then his claims on Midwestern seemed stronger than before. It was an important point, more important than anyone knew. Years ago Ben had signed a secret trust, putting Elizabeth in control of his stocks should it become necessary, and though time had passed, he'd never changed it; Elizabeth still held title.

Elizabeth stood at the door, listening to the sound of her own breathing. She was an old dying woman; she was foolish in many ways, but no matter which way she looked at it, Angela was right. What she now knew did alter her feelings toward Dyer, toward everything, and she could never again view her family in quite the same way.

FOURTEEN

Every day Dyer Savage worked until nine P.M. exactly, then drove across the bridge into Midland to his small efficiency apartment. There he'd have a sandwich or a casserole the maid had left in the oven, several beers, watch television until after the news, then go to bed. Weekends were the same, except during the football season when he'd stay home for the Sunday games.

It was a life-style that was austere, not because Dyer was frightened to spend money—he'd always been rich and couldn't conceive of being otherwise—but because on the whole, he needed very little to please him. Once a year he took a vacation, but every day of the two weeks he was away, he would call into the office first thing in the morning and always he was available by phone. Even on those occasions when he did spend time with a woman, he would have to fight to concentrate on what he was doing. It wasn't that he had problems in that direction; he supposed you had to care enough to have those kinds of problems, and Dyer hardly cared at all.

There were times when he thought about marriage and children. He knew that because James was as he was, he ought to make a try. Occasionally he would even resolve to do it, but always the call of his neat efficient life was too strong, and he returned to it gratefully, feeling a magnificent peace as he closed the door to his apartment and padded around the kitchen making his sandwich, opening his beer and preparing himself for another fourteen-hour day of work.

But tonight Dyer was breaking his rigid schedule by leaving early, and as he walked out of his office and down the long corridor to the parking lot, he wondered why.

He paused at the gates. The sun was just beginning to set, and the mill was haloed with rosy light. The fire of the blast furnace sent up brilliant orange waves that melted into the red air, making Midwestern look like a fiery planet. Dyer breathed in the air that smelled of steel. There was no one around; only the noise of machinery disturbed the quiet, and at that moment, Dyer thought Midwestern must be the most beautiful place in the world. Yet Dyer knew in the end he could give it all up for the chance of winning over Ben. Even though Ben lay dying, he needed to win against him. He supposed in a way to justify his own existence.

Fifteen minutes later Dyer was looking for a parking place along the side streets of the Park Lane Hotel, where his aunt, Pauline, kept an apartment she used only three months a year. Long ago Dyer had heard that Pauline's three-month stay in Midland was part of a bargain struck between her and Ben. The story had been told both ways, that she was paid to spend three months near her family, that she was paid to spend no more than three months. From what he could tell, it was the latter. Or perhaps what they said about Ben and Pauline was true. Dyer shut this out of his mind. Ben had been many things, some of them not very nice, but Dyer doubted Ben could ever bring himself to do something like that.

The door to Pauline's apartment was ajar, and he walked in, standing in the gilt and pink living room, looking around awkwardly, like a poor relation. Scarves had been thrown over the lamps and the lighting was soft, probably from pink light bulbs. It was said Pauline was rarely seen before seven o'clock in the evening, preferring the light of dusk because she looked younger in it. Pauline called herself a vampire and left it at that. Dyer thought both probably were true.

He put down his briefcase, poured himself a scotch at the bar, and sat on the couch. He could smell the expensive French perfume Pauline always wore, and was sickened by the warm heavy sensuality of it. But mostly it scared him. He wondered briefly why Pauline frightened him so much, then blocked it out of his mind.

"Pour yourself a drink, Dyer," Pauline called through the closed bedroom door.

"I'm way ahead of you, Aunt Pauline."

She laughed. "Don't bet on it." It was a throaty laugh, full of the sound of too many cigarettes and too much booze.

"I was surprised you called me," she said through the door. "This is a first."

Dyer could imagine her sitting at her dressing table, painting on makeup, sipping at a large scotch, her hair tied back with an elastic band. Pauline always smelled of perfume and scotch. It was a sickening, sweet smell, full of ease and decay.

The door opened and Pauline walked into the living room. She was wearing a long silk robe that flowed as she moved, and she was vamping it up like an old movie star. Oddly enough Dyer sensed she knew how much he hated her performance and was doing it to make him angry. She stopped in the middle of the living room, her tall, overdieted body poised nervously, like an eagle perched on a high branch overlooking the field below. There was much of the predatory bird about Pauline. Though she still looked amazingly young, probably as a result of face-lifts, close up there was a shiny deadness to her skin, a brittleness to her expression that came perhaps less from the surgery itself than too many nights spent anxiously searching for another pretty face.

Pauline poured herself a drink, then settled into an overstuffed chair opposite Dyer. "To what do I owe the honor of this visit? I assume it must be business. Certainly it isn't social, since you don't have the vaguest idea what that means."

"That's right," Dyer answered coldly.

Pauline smiled. "Ah, chatty as ever. Dyer, you really are my favorite nephew. I like you so much better than James whom I understand all too well. You're an exotic. I haven't the foggiest idea what makes you tick." She laughed. "Tick. That's exactly what you do. Just like a clock, a large, efficient wall clock. Or one of those new kind that is always accurate to the second."

"Are you finished?" Dyer took a sip of his scotch and tried to appear as casual as possible.

"No. I'm not finished. In fact, I believe I haven't really begun."

Dyer picked up his briefcase and placed it on his lap, clicking it open. Again Pauline smiled, and for a moment Dyer was surprised by the anger in that smile. He was not a man who was used to investigating the motives of others unless they had to do with business, but sitting there in the overheated, perfumed room, Dyer saw Pauline as a person, cruel, angry, and terribly unhappy.

Pauline caught his expression. "Why are you staring at me like that?"

"You look like you're mad at someone. I was wondering who and why."

Pauline laughed. "For heaven's sake, don't start trying to understand me, Dyer. It's so out of character." Pauline paused, taking another drink of her scotch. She was looking at Dyer sharply, as if trying to decide about him. Then all at once her whole face changed, and she appeared almost as a child, terrified of disapproval yet expecting it always.

"I *am* angry," she said after a while. "In case you haven't noticed, I'm a very angry woman, though I believe the word today is hostile, or have they gone back to using angry? Anyway, I suppose from where you sit it must look like I've been given everything, with nothing demanded in return. You've seen me be rude to my mother; you've heard rumors about my bad behavior. Well, there's more than one side to that little story. You never saw how little your grandma cared about me. How little *any*one cared about me."

Dyer shrugged. "Grandma isn't my greatest supporter either, you know."

"Don't I ever. And you're angry as hell about it. Have you ever noticed how people react differently to anger?" She smiled to herself. "No, I don't suppose you have. But I like to watch people; they disgust me really, but I like to watch them. Maybe because they do disgust me."

Pauline got up and poured herself another drink, and for the first time, Dyer realized she was drunk.

"Anger is really interesting," Pauline said, as she sat back down in her chair. "There are only two basic reactions to it. Some people hold the anger inside and spend the rest of their lives trying to prove others wrong about them. In case you don't recognize yourself, that's you. Then there are the rest of us who spend our whole lives trying to prove others were right. That's me. The family thinks I'm a wasted person. Well, all right, fine, I've gone out of my way to prove them right."

"You're forgetting about the people who ignore the problem altogether and just go on living."

"Name one."

"Ben."

Pauline laughed loudly. "You're joking." She watched Dyer for a while, as one watches a child, surprised and slightly touched. "You really mean that, don't you? Well, talk about your hero worship. You actually think that Ben is sane. I'll be damned. No wonder you're angry. Well, I'll tell you something. I hope you're wrong. But you could be right. It's not fair though, is it, if he isn't suffering? It just wouldn't be fair."

Pauline downed her drink quickly, then got up, took Dyer's glass, and poured them both another drink. When she returned to her chair, she said, "We never really talked, do you realize that? It's strange. I guess you could say as far as families go, we're a close one. I mean, we all grew up together, and even today we live near one another, and we're all in the same business. Yet I don't think any of us have really talked to one another. Not ever. Maybe everyone's like that, living their own lives, only guessing what the other person is thinking."

"Maybe."

"You don't think about things much, do you?"

"Not if I can help it. Thinking about things is an excuse for not doing them, and I believe in doing things."

"Like Ben."

Dyer didn't pick this up. He hated being compared to his uncle, yet at the same time craved it. It was strange and awful this love/hate relationship he had with Ben. He supposed Ben ruled his life. In many ways he ruled all their lives.

Pauline tucked her legs under her and sipped at her drink, watching him dramatically, and Dyer found himself despising her for her studied gestures, her mannered pauses. The heat and the smell of perfume were pressing in on him; they made him feel sick.

"Remember when you were a young boy and I was sent away?" Pauline asked.

"I was only four or five."

"But you do remember it."

Dyer shook his head. "Not really." Once again he felt a wave of nausea press at his throat. He tried to turn his eyes from Pauline, but she was holding him with her predatory stare. Her mouth was twisted in a cruel smile, and it made Dyer feel even more sick and scared.

"I suppose you heard the rumors about me and Ben."

"I've heard them," Dyer answered softly.

"And do you believe them?"

"Of course not. You hear a lot of things about Ben, you know that. But I never listen to them."

"They're true."

Dyer felt everything spinning beneath him; the fear was a tight knot in his stomach. Pauline was looking at him with that same cruel, teasing smile. He knew she was lying to him.

"You don't believe it. But you're curious. You're thinking to yourself, is this really true? And if so, why is she telling me? Or if, in fact, it's a lie, why is she telling me?"

"Pauline, I said to you before, I don't think about people. I came here on business." The room seemed even hotter than before; the smell of scotch and the faintly decaying scent of Pauline were crushing in on him. He wanted to leave, but he knew he had no other choice except to stay; he needed Pauline's support. So he clutched his briefcase tightly, staring stupidly at his aunt.

Pauline sipped at her drink reflectively. "You see, Dyer, I think it's time we talked to one another, told one another the score. Then we can do business together. I always think it's better to do business after you've reached an understanding."

Dyer interrupted. "Why are you doing this to me?"

Pauline grinned. "For fun. I have a reputation as a troublemaker to keep up." Then she thought for a moment. "I really don't know why I do things like this." She brightened. "But there it is. Now, where was I? Oh, yes. Ben and I and that dreaded word. Incest."

She shifted in her chair seductively, and this distrubed Dyer even more. He wanted to scream out, but he couldn't move; all he could manage was to hold even tighter to his briefcase, struggling for control.

"We were discussing whether it's true." Pauline was slurring her words. "Now personally I think it's true." She laughed, almost hysterically. "There I was just sixteen, a poor innocent girl who looked up to her older brother like a father. After all, I hardly knew my own father. He died when I was very young. And Mother never paid any attention to me. Not when she had sons to worry about. So, there was Ben, successful, newly married. Dylan was pregnant. There's something so sexy about a man whose wife is pregnant."

"When you were sixteen, James was already born."

Pauline laughed. "Was he? Oh, yes, that's right, he was. Well, never mind. There's something so sexy about young men with children."

"Look, why don't you stop right there, Pauline?"

"It all began at my sweet sixteen party, though of course not much could happen there. But that was where it started. And the next week I went out to the mill for dinner."

"Look, I don't know or care why you're doing this. I just want it to stop. Now!" Dyer's voice was shaking with anger and, just beneath the surface, fear.

Pauline shrugged. "Then leave." She smiled. "But you aren't going to leave, are you? After all, you have business you want to discuss with me. And I have this I want to discuss with you. Don't you see? I have to tell you these things. That way we can reach an understanding, and you'll know you can trust me." Pauline reached out her hand and touched Dyer on the knee. "Because you really can trust me."

Family Passions 155

Dyer shrank from her touch; nausea gripped him. There was something more than business that was holding him, something about the terrible perfume and overly dramatic sexiness that was riveting him, making his mind close down. Pauline didn't move her hand for a long while, and Dyer was painfully aware of it and the heat that spread through his knee.

"You don't remember Ben then. But I remember him very well. He was just thirty-two, and he was so strong and handsome. I had gone out with many boys by that time, but Ben was a man; he was the only man I knew. Maybe he still is."

"Really, Pauline. I don't want to know all this. I came here to talk about Midwestern."

"You're looking to take over Midwestern, aren't you?"

"No, not really. But I am looking for your support."

"Really, Dyer?" Again her hand touched his knee, resting there lightly. She was smiling, and Dyer could see all her little teeth behind her parted lips. Suddenly the room seemed to fade. All there was was that terrible parted mouth and the feeling of her hand resting on his knee.

"Ben gave me a drink," she said softly. "A bourbon and ginger ale, and we sat in his office discussing steel. I felt so grown up with my drink, sitting there in his office, discussing important manly matters. I wasn't really interested in steel, of course. I was only interested in my brother's description of it. Did you ever notice that when Ben talked about steel, his whole face lit up? Well, it did, and his eyes used to sparkle."

Pauline's hand was still on Dyer's knee, but she wasn't looking at him; she was staring into space, her face alive with memories of the past. "It wasn't ugly at all. It was very beautiful." She turned back to Dyer. "Can you understand that?"

Dyer didn't answer. He was shocked and frightened, yet held tightly to the moment.

"Now do you believe me?"

"I don't know." Dyer broke his eyes from Pauline and glanced down at her hand. It was still on his knee, and he felt her tighten her fingers around him. Electric hot waves moved through his leg.

Then suddenly Pauline laughed sharply. "Well, you shouldn't, because it's a lie. I made it all up." Her fingers tightened even more and again her voice was very soft. "Anyway, it doesn't matter whether it's true or not. The point is it could have happened."

Slowly Pauline moved her hand up Dyer's leg. He wanted to cry out for her to stop, but he couldn't move; he was held tightly, the heavy scent of her perfume closing in on him.

Her hand lightly traced the contours of his leg, and she was looking up at him, her lips parted, the pink light glancing off her face, illuminating her cheekbones and small straight nose.

"It wasn't ugly at all," she said softly, almost hypnotically. "It was beautiful, very, very beautiful."

FIFTEEN

Mr. Hamayoshi looked down from his hotel room window at the gathering rush-hour traffic below. It had been a long trip with several delays, and he felt tense and tired, too tired to even attempt going to sleep. In Tokyo he would have gone out for a shiatsu, then a light Japanese meal, and after that, home for precisely seven hours sleep, never longer; more than that would make him even less alert than he was now. But Hamayoshi wasn't in Tokyo, and he'd spent enough time in America to know that towns like Midland had neither Japanese massage parlors nor sushi bars, and he'd have to content himself with a hot bath and a soggy club sandwich.

Years ago Hamayoshi had made the mistake of remarking about his devotion to shiatsu to a pork-faced P.R. man from International Tin Plate Inc. With nationalistic fervor, the man had explained the wonders of American massage parlors and insisted that he accompany him to his favorite place. Hamayoshi had been appalled. The masseuse had been, if possible, even more porcine than the man who'd brought him. There was even the odor of uncooked bacon about her, and she had prodded and poked at him with the delicacy of a hog rooting in the mud. Finally she'd brought him off with an inimitable style, staring blankly at the dirty peeling walls, looking into the TV set of her mind, and then he'd been sent packing, feeling even more on edge than when he'd arrived.

But a shiatsu was something quite different. It was an intricate ballet performed on the muscles of the body. First there were the hot-water baths, then a small, clean room with indirect lighting. He'd lie on a mat, waiting in quiet. There would be the soft rustle of a woman entering the room, holding towels and oils. Then she'd kneel by him silently. What came next was a subtle manipulation of muscles that took an intimate knowledge of anatomy and pressure points. Afterward she might bring him off or not, depending on the place, the girl, and how he felt. But that too was delicate, expert, and infinitely subtle.

A variety of conclusions could be drawn from the difference between the two massages, conclusions Hamayoshi had drawn long before his encounter with the porcine masseuse. Hamayoshi had been educated at Harvard and NYU. For several years he'd served his apprenticeship in the business world at Bethlehem Steel in the accounting department, and the difference between the two cultures had not escaped him. He'd watched life in America with the fascination of a child at the zoo. Today he still watched, though his original excited curiosity had dulled into a scientific contemplation. In a sense no longer like a child visiting the zoo, but an old man returning to it, still keenly interested, but with a detached amusement at what lay on either side of the iron bars.

If Hamayoshi had to name what part of the zoo he felt like he was at as he stood looking down at the pattern of traffic and the hurrying pedestrians, he supposed he would have to pick the monkey house, the big apes in particular. For Americans were a brawny, passionate people, totally lacking in any of the subtle, deeper layers so prevalent in the Eastern cultures or even the European.

They had an expression for it: What you see is what you get. And indeed this was true for Americans. Nowhere was this clearer than in business. While the Japanese played the game strictly by the rules, and what a complicated set of rules they were, each player adhering to his rigidly prescribed part, Americans didn't seem to follow any rules, didn't seem to even know that such things existed. This curious difference had made for many surprises for his Japanese colleagues, and it was from this that they wrongly concluded Americans were wily. In fact, they were dense.

On the other hand, Hamayoshi had developed a great respect for denseness. While it might be perspicacity that had started many wars, it was invariably the strength which came from denseness that won them.

So as Hamayoshi moved from the window to the telephone it was with all his wits about him. He glanced in the gold-flecked mirror and tidied his already impeccably combed hair, as if he could be seen as well as heard over the telephone wires. Then he dialed, slowly, precisely, and without checking his address book.

"I'd like to speak to Mr. Savage, please," he said when Dyer's secretary, Carrie, answered. "Tell him my name is Mr. Hamayoshi. I'm one of his stockholders, one of his major stockholders. Four point nine percent to be exact."

SIXTEEN

Wales

Ben hadn't moved in days. At first there had been the pain from forcing himself out of his wheelchair. It had been brilliant and electric, and it had seemed to tear every muscle of his body. Even after it receded, there was another kind of pain; this one was dull, imprisoning, and it never seemed to leave him. Ben wasn't sure whether it was real or imagined, but it didn't matter. He felt emptied out and bitter. It was as if the effort it had cost to pull himself from that chair had weakened him to the point of annihilation, as if he'd had only that one burst of energy and resolve, saved from weeks of inactivity, and now he had finally run down forever.

He spoke rarely; his odd, mechanical-sounding voice scared him too much; just hearing himself try to speak made the reality of what he'd become fresh and startling. He had not tried to move, for his movements were those of a cripple. Immediately he'd retreated to his own half-life, willing himself from the pain and the anger, though always he was aware it was there.

At first Tally had tried to rouse him from his depression by pressuring him. But she hadn't tried to provoke him again; what she'd done before had shaken her too much. She had seen Ben as a human being rather than a patient, and once she'd seen that, it'd become impossible to treat him with the same cold objectivity.

Ben had resisted her urging, remaining slumped in his silent

Family Passions

fury, and after several days she had stopped altogether, ignoring Ben, allowing Mrs. Mided to bathe and change him and push his wheelchair along the gray path to the little churchyard for their afternoon walk.

The morning before Ben had heard Tally's car pulling away from the house. She had been gone for hours, and when she'd come back there'd been the roar of a truck following, and the banging and clattering of something being moved into the house. Ben had wondered briefly what was going on, but his wondering had been only superficial, and it hadn't lasted for long. Mostly he'd sat in his bedroom, staring straight ahead, trying desperately to return to the warm rocking ocean and the little bobbing piece of driftwood that was his soul.

At nine o'clock the next morning, Mrs. Mided was sitting next to his wheelchair, feeding him like an infant. Ben's mind wandered vaguely as he allowed Mrs. Mided to put the humiliating spoonfuls of porridge in his mouth. He was aware that he had not seen Tally that morning, though he'd heard her footsteps hours before. It occurred to him that she was trying to punish him by her absence, and he found that somewhat amusing.

It wasn't until eleven o'clock that Tally did appear, and when she did, her manner was brisk and efficient, almost angry. Without saying a word to Ben, she kicked off the brake on his wheelchair and began pushing him out of the room.

Ben wanted to ask where he was being taken but he refused to be drawn in. It wasn't so much that he resented being treated like an inanimate object to be shifted wherever was convenient; he'd grown used to that at the hospital and in fact preferred it to the alternative. At least if he was not spoken to, he could ignore what was going on around him. He even saw some justice in it, for he knew he was little more than a useless lump of flesh and bones, just waiting to die. What he resented about Tally's treating him this way was that he suspected there was more to it, that she was making some kind of point by it, so instead of being able to ignore the world around him, he became even more keenly aware of it.

Tally wheeled Ben into the corridor, still saying nothing, and pushed him toward a room he had not seen before. He presumed it had been a dining room, but all the furniture had been removed and now it was filled with what seemed to be rehabilitation equipment. She stopped his chair at the edge of the room, and though he didn't turn his head, he knew she was smiling.

He forced the words out. "What is this?"

"I ordered the equipment yesterday." Tally walked to the side of his wheelchair, but her eyes were on the room, and she looked very proud of herself, very sure.

"I don't want." There was humiliation in this, humiliation and also fear. It was too difficult to speak; the intense anger he was feeling was missing from the words; he sounded only like a ridiculous computer. And at that moment he hated himself and Tally, and everything that had made him what he was.

Tally answered evenly, "Now, Mr. Savage, you know perfectly well we need to build up your muscles."

"No!" Ben's voice was stronger, but still there was the dead, mechanical sound to it. "I won't."

"I'm afraid you must. How else do you expect to recover?"

Tally's voice was professional and calm, but there was a snap to it, and Ben could sense the anger in her body. She began walking around the room, touching the parallel bars and massage table, testing the pulley weights hooked to the ceiling.

"I've been thinking it over all morning, and I've decided that we should work together at least two hours a day. If you'd like I can tell Mrs. Mided about what happened the other day and we can both work with you." She glanced nervously back at Ben, but he was looking away, his face set in stony belligerence.

She continued quickly. "Actually I have to admit Mrs. Mided isn't all that bad. We didn't get on at first, but that was my fault as much as hers. I suppose we both felt we were in competition. I really don't know why. But that kind of thing happens everywhere I expect. At any rate, with a little bit of goodwill, we should be able to work together, if you'd prefer it that way."

Tally stopped. She'd been chattering to defuse the situation, but when she looked back at Ben, she could tell he wasn't listening. "It's for your own good," she said softly.

Ben fought to speak, but he couldn't. Just getting the words out of his mouth took too long; his brain was racing far ahead of his body and he felt trapped inside himself. Finally he blurted, "I want nothing."

Tally walked to his chair and stood in front of him. "I'm not interested in what you think you want. I'm only interested in what's good for you."

Ben's voice screeched. "Leave me alone!"

Tally didn't flinch. She stood, watching Ben coldly. "I told you before, I can't do that. If I leave you alone you'll just wither. If I leave you alone, there's a very good chance that you'll die."

Ben laughed bitterly. But it was a mechanical laugh, frightening even to him. "Die anyway."

Tally's face softened. "We don't know that, Mr. Savage."

"Doctors know."

There was a terrible deadness to his response and Tally shivered at the sound of it. Still, she answered calmly, as if she were having a perfectly normal conversation.

"If you'd been a nurse as long as I, you'd know that doctors are not omniscient. In fact, I've seen almost more miracles than not. That's what they call them when they've made a wrong diagnosis. They say it, looking heavenward, when it's only that they've made a mistake. It's really too bad we all can't use that excuse when we're wrong."

"No!" Ben screamed. The urgency pierced through the dull tone of his voice. "Let me die!"

Tally turned away. She couldn't bear to look at Ben's eyes; they were the eyes of an animal, stunning with unexpressed fear. "In the end you'll be happy that I didn't listen to you. Honestly you will be." She sounded lame and silly even to herself. How could she be so sure she really knew what was right? In all probability the doctors' prognosis was correct; there was a very good chance her pushing would only hasten his death. Still, there was the responsibility to try. She had to believe in that.

Tally forced herself to look at Ben. "The truth is, I don't know your chances of recovery. Perhaps they're only a thousand to one. Perhaps even less. All I do know is you have to try. You just have to try."

Ben's eyes burned. "Why?" His voice was almost a whisper.

"I don't have the answer to that. All I know is you must."

"Why?" Ben repeated. "For you?"

"See here, Mr. Savage. Whether you live or die means very little to me, beyond of course, the obvious moral questions. As I told you before, your recovery would only give me more work to do."

Ben watched her cagily. "And purpose."

Tally stiffened. She tried to calm her irritation, but she could hear traces of it in her voice. "You know nothing about me. My life has quite enough purpose without you. And certainly if I were casting around for causes, a sixty-year-old, probably corrupt, most certainly spoiled American businessman would not be high on my list."

"Let me die."

Tally was silent for a long while, and when she spoke there was almost a desperation in it. "I won't feel sorry for you." She paused as if trying to regain something. "I'll try to help you recover to the best of my ability. And if, by some slim chance, you do get better and go back to your family and your business in Ohio, you can send me a thank-you card. And I'll be pleased to accept your gratitude, and that pleasure will last me precisely one hour, because I will be busy with my next patient."

Ben licked his lips, trying to force out the words. His eyes were wild and haunted. "Want to die!"

Tally felt chilled. "Perhaps now. But you'll feel differently later."

Ben didn't answer, refused to answer, though the look in his eyes seemed sufficient as one. He was silent and motionless, like stone, and Tally could see that all his strength and will was turning against life. A dreadful emotion was gripping him, and it scared Tally to be standing in the same room with it.

Ben lay in his bed, looking at the streaks of moonlight reflected on the ceiling. His body ached with the dull drumming pain that had appeared when he'd tried to move, and now since his argument with Tally, it had grown until it was so hard and constant he wanted to scream. It wasn't the pain itself that was so unbearable; he had suffered worse in his sixty years. It was the constancy of it. It was always there, sometimes worse, sometimes better, but everpresent, a great wall that blocked him in. Tonight in the darkness, he felt cornered by it.

Ben tried to turn his mind to the past, to the beauty and excitement he had only begun to remember, the little boy running through the fields of Wales, but his mind was driven to the pain, and he could remember nothing. He tried to think of the sea and the floating driftwood that had comforted him for so long, but the sea too would not appear, nor the rocking driftwood.

He scanned the room with his eyes, but that did nothing to relieve the pain. The night-veiled furniture and the photographs on the bureau seemed as far away as the driftwood. There was nothing he could do. He was alive, and he was in pain. That was all he knew. That was all he could think about.

Ben had always been a man who loved life, rushing forward to greet every moment with the unselfconscious greed of a child who does not yet know his own mortality. He had valued life for its seeming permanence. It wasn't that Ben had thought he would never die; there had just been a large part of him that believed it wouldn't happen for so long it hardly counted. But now he knew, and with this knowledge all joy was gone.

He thought of Tally and her insistence that he might not be dying, but that seemed somehow even worse. The thought of existing in a world where people walked and talked and laughed all around him, of being one who only caused discomfort and pity was breathtaking. To live was to live wholly. Ben had never been a man to compromise; he had expected it all both from others and from himself. But now there could be no living wholly and fully, only a partial awakening that would torture him constantly. He would be a freak.

Time passed, and the pain remained. Ben felt tears coming to his eyes, but not even the tears could bring any relief; nothing could stop it. He believed he'd rather suffer frequent intense agony, anything rather than this smooth, constant ache. It was like his life, heavy, stupefying, and inescapable.

As he lay there, cornered by the pain, once again he tried to deaden his mind. But the power to do it was gone from him. He was trapped, aware and alive, waiting for a death that might take years to come.

Ben had never considered the possibility of suicide, had never mulled it over objectively as most people do, taking it as an option to be rolled around in the mind, speculatively considering its contour and shape, then rejecting it. Ben had never given suicide a passing thought. But now it crashed in on him explosively, and perhaps the strength of it lay in the fact that the idea was so new to him.

To be dead seemed a great gift, a release. Death was the darkness and the ocean and the driftwood, only better, far better, for there would be no returning. All there would be was the void, endless and soothing, irrevocable.

But while death seemed preferable to life, in many ways it was farther away than at any other time in the past. The doctors had said death was near, but if so, it certainly was taking its own sweet time, neither creeping up on him nor crashing in, merely staying somewhere in the distance, mocking him. And there was nothing that Ben could do about it but wait. He couldn't lift a knife, much less stab himself; he couldn't get to stairs, much less throw himself down them. It was the final indignity. There was nothing in his life over which he had control, not even the end of it.

Ben felt tears of rage and frustration coming to his eyes, and he cursed life. Lying surrounded by his pain and his powerlessness, he no longer even tried to stop himself from crying. It didn't seem to matter.

His mind shifted to Midwestern. He supposed that by now Dyer was firmly in place, but even this thought had no power over him anymore. Let Dyer take over the business; he had ceased to care. He assumed that his mother would go along, deserting all Ben's beliefs and plans, regretfully but inevitably, and that too didn't disturb him. It made no difference what happened anymore, for he had no ties to the present or the future; he had even lost his brief connection to the past.

And in that moment Ben knew he was truly ready to die, swiftly and painlessly if possible, but to die. Yet always the reality teased. The question was how.

Still, Ben knew eventually the opportunity would arise. There would be a staircase left unguarded. There were mountains all around them; there were streams. The moment when he would be left alone would come. Even limited as he was, there would be a time.

Ben looked out the window. The moon had risen and it was haloed with light. He watched it with no regret, only the soft release of resignation. He would die. And with this thought, Ben closed his eyes and felt the warm ocean all around him, rocking him soothingly to sleep.

SEVENTEEN

Mrs. Mided had trouble sleeping. In the beginning she'd tried the usual remedies; eventually she'd started on sleeping pills. At first she'd considered taking the pills a weakness and tried to avoid them as much as possible. Now she took them every night. She knew she was hooked, but she rarely thought about it. They had become part of her life.

Ben had seen and noted the pills in her purse several days before, though he hadn't thought much about them until now. He could see Mrs. Mided's purse on the floor beside the chair she was sitting in. She rarely left her purse alone; she seemed the type to even take it to bed with her. His mother had once confessed to this, cornering herself with it as at least sharing the bed with something.

The pills had come back to Ben's mind the night before, when he'd first begun contemplating suicide. But the thought of killing himself with sleeping pills repulsed him; there was something so hysterical woman about it, and though he realized the alternatives were closed to him, he couldn't bring himself to that point.

He looked out the window at the gray countryside. The farmhouse had almost disappeared in the mist, and the church was only a vague smudge, a ghostly outline against the sky. He felt a shudder go through him, but it was an internal tremor, as unexpressed as everything in his life.

Ben tried to understand the difference between throwing himself off a cliff and taking the sleeping pills. The result would be the same; what possible difference could the method make? Still, he knew it did make a difference, perhaps not to him—he wouldn't be around for the repercussions—but to others.

Not that his mother would judge him by his death. To her it would be the dying that was important. He didn't know how James would feel about his death, let alone the method, but he supposed that James too wouldn't judge him. It was Dyer. In the end he wanted to die well for Dyer.

What a strange inside-out relationship the two of them had. How he had watched Dyer with anger, pride, guilt, so many conflicting emotions, so much force behind them. Had he been wrong all those years ago to have gone along with Angela? He still didn't know the answer, but there wasn't a hell of a lot he could do to change things now.

Ben's eyes shifted back to the window. The mist had grown heavier, obscuring the vague shadows of the buildings he had seen before. Even the tree had become invisible, though he could hear its bare branches scratching against the windowpane. It was a terrible, lonely world on the other side of the glass, full of gray shadows, and it made the vast emptiness he felt inside him even more unbearable. He knew at that moment he had no choice.

Mrs. Mided put out her cigarette but remained where she was, staring into space. Ben wondered how he could get her to leave the room without taking her purse. It seemed impossible. She looked like she and her pack of cigarettes were settled in for life.

Time passed, and Ben sat watching and waiting. The choice had been made.

Suddenly Mrs. Mided stood and with a little brittle stretching movement muttered something to herself. Then, casting a quick look at Ben to make sure he was comfortable, she left the room. It all happened so rapidly it took Ben a moment to realize that he was alone. And then the impossibility of the task hit him. The purse was halfway across the room; he could never reach it.

He listened to her footsteps recede down the hall. It seemed likely that she had gone to make herself a cup of tea; perhaps she'd just forgotten something in her room. Whatever had forced her to leave, it seemed clear there wouldn't be enough time. He could imagine her coming back into the living room and discovering him, her little beady eyes all aghast and accusatory; she'd take it as a personal affront. The worst part was that after that it would be impossible for him to ever try again. They would be careful of him; they would take precautions.

All of this passed through his mind and then disappeared. It might be days before he had the chance again, and he could barely tolerate the hours.

Ben forced himself to move. He concentrated on lifting his arms. There was a trembling, then suddenly his hands caught motion and stirred, moving upward from his lap. Everything was jerking uncontrollably, but still it was movement, and Ben fought back the pain, willing his arms to rise. His body shook crazily, but his arms lifted slowly, rigidly, until they were parallel with the rests on his wheelchair.

He stopped for a moment, then, pressing himself even harder, forced his hands to shift to the side of the chair. Pain spread outward, radiating through him; his chest felt heavy and hot. Still he brought his hands sideways to the wheels until he found them, and tightened his fingers around the tires.

Pain had become a searing hole in the center of him, and he wanted to cry out from it, but instead he pressed at the wheels, trying to push the chair forward.

The wheelchair rocked. There was a sensation of movement, then his hands gave way, and the chair slipped back into place. Ben tried again, using his body weight to help him. Once more the chair shifted, beginning to turn, then rolling back, pushing him even farther away than before.

Ben clamped his hands against the wheels. It was as if all thought had stopped; it was as if there were nothing for him but the pushing and the heaviness of his body.

The chair shuddered, then the wheels began to turn. Slowly, sluggishly the chair inched forward, completing one revolution. Ben paused. He was aware of the pain sharpening and quickening through his body, but it was as if it were happening to someone else; his entire being was concentrated inward, his mind forcing his arms to turn the wheels.

He thrust at the tires, throwing his body forward. This time the chair lurched ahead, rocking from side to side while it rolled. Ben felt everything give way; the pressure forward was intense, and the weight of his body collapsed him, folding him over onto himself. His hands weakened on the wheels as they turned; he had lost all control. All he could do was lie across himself helplessly, like an overgrown infant, while his brain screamed at his hands to grasp hold. He could feel the jumble of responses passing through his body, and the crazy half answers coming back.

The chair stopped rolling. But Ben's hands had lost their grip, and he was folded over himself, gasping for air, weak and helpless. He couldn't fight anymore, all he could do was lie collapsed, a feeling of hopelessness pounding through him.

Then slowly calm returned. As the pain receded, his mind cleared and movement came, shakily at first, but gaining in power, until his hands shifted back to the wheels. He mastered his fingers and closed them over the tires. Trembling from the effort, Ben pressed down against his arms, lifting his torso up slowly to an upright position.

Over a minute had passed since Mrs. Mided had left the room. Ben listened for her footsteps, expecting and fearing them. But there was no sound of her; only the brittle tree scratching against the window disturbed the quiet.

Ben looked down. The purse was only a few inches from the wheel of his chair. Had he been whole he would have been able to reach into it and grasp the pills easily. But sitting there, a rigid hulk of useless flesh, he knew he wouldn't be able to lower his arms to it. As impossible as it had seemed to cross the room, this was far worse.

Then once again Ben forced all thought from him, turning inward, concentrating his energy into his arm and willing it to drop to his side. As his arm responded and fell free, a sharp pain ripped through him. There was a feeling of flesh tearing, of muscle shredding. Ben gasped loudly; it seemed almost to echo through the room. He looked down at his arm through half-closed eyes. It hung free, as if it didn't belong to him, but he could see no injury; it was only the force of its own weight that tortured it.

Ben could hear his rasping breath; it seemed to fill the room. He waited, expecting Mrs. Mided to come rushing in; it seemed impossible that she hadn't heard him. But everything was quiet. There was only the sound of his breath in his ears, slowing, regulating, until it had become normal.

Ben's hand was just above the purse now. He looked down, trying to gauge how far he must reach before his fingers brushed the leather and found the little bottle inside. It wasn't far, only a matter of inches. But Ben was stretched to the limit; in order to move anymore, he would have to shift his entire torso, and that he knew was something he couldn't manage. Never before had he realized how much of his body he used for every movement. It had been a wonder just to reach out, a miracle to hold something in his hand.

Ben commanded his body to move. He felt himself shaking; the pain fired through him, but slowly he began to lean, feeling as if the whole world were tipping around him though he'd hardly moved at all. His fingers struggled, stretching, until the pull of them exploded into electric pain. He pressed farther and the chair creaked from the weight of him. Still he leaned, pushing himself downward, recklessly throwing all his weight toward the floor. And then his fingers struck something solid.

Ben took in breath. The purse was in his grasp, he could feel the bottle of pills resting on top of the clutter inside. But his stiff awkward fingers fumbled, brushing against the bottle of pills, pushing them deeper into Mrs. Mided's purse.

Ben froze, watching impotently, tears of rage and humiliation coming to his eyes. But desperation was driving him on, and again he jerked his hand down into the purse.

His fingers quivered crazily; all sensitivity was gone. His whole body was tipped to the side, pushing so heavily against the chair that he could hear it creaking. For a moment he thought he'd found the bottle, but whatever it was slipped immediately from his grasp.

Ben was crying now. Stupidly, shamelessly, tears were moving down his cheeks, and he was shaking from the sobs inside of him.

Nevertheless he reached even farther into the purse, blocking out the tears and the pain and the humiliation, pushing himself blindly on.

He touched something smooth. This time he took hold of it very slowly, carefully closing his fingers around the bottle, making sure he had a grip before he attempted to take it out of the purse.

The front door slammed. The sound of it echoed through the quiet house, and Ben froze where he was, his body hung over the wheelchair, his hand thrust deep into the purse. Everything stopped inside him. Tally was home now. It was the blocking of all exits, the certainty of discovery. She would find him, and she would understand.

Ben tried to force the fear from his mind and concentrate on bringing his arm back up, but he could hear Tally's footsteps in the hall moving toward the living room, and with the sound his hand began to tremble, a shaking took hold of his body. His grip was loosening, and there was nothing he could do about it; he was totally out of control.

Tally called to Mrs. Mided. Her footsteps stopped as she waited for a reply. Ben tried to concentrate on his arm, but the sound of her voice had unnerved him; it was as if she were making him give up.

At this thought, the anger returned and with it control. Ben shakily lifted his arm over the chair. Just as it was parallel with his body, he felt his fingers cramp.

Tally's footsteps began again until she was just outside the room. The doorknob started turning. Ben was motionless; he could barely breath. There was no longer any terror or despair or anything but a dizzying emptiness. He had failed.

His fingers gave way. The bottle tumbled from his grasp, striking against his thigh, holding there for a moment, then rolling sideways and falling into his lap.

Mrs. Mided called out to Tally. There was a brief stillness; the doorknob stopped turning, and he could imagine Tally poised, head turned back down the hall. Then once again the knob began to move, but this time it was shifting back into place. Tally's footsteps started up again, moving away. She was going down the hall to meet Mrs. Mided.

Ben didn't wait any longer. Holding the bottle of pills in his lap, he forced his arms to the wheels of the chair. The pain was searing, his whole body was reverberating with it as if he were palsied. Still he continued to push himself forward. He could keep the pills hidden in the folds of his trousers; he could wait. The hardest part had been done, and it would be over; soon all the pain and humiliation would be gone.

"Well, he's not dead yet." Dr. Waring stood away from Ben. He looked back at Tally and Mrs. Mided who were just behind him. "But I have every reason to fear that he will be before the night is out."

He moved briskly to his black bag, which gaped open on the bureau. "I've done the best I could. At least I've removed the drug from his stomach. But my guess is enough time has gone by to make that irrelevant. Too much has probably entered his bloodstream."

Dr. Waring shook his head angrily. He was a small hard man with sparse gray hair only slightly darker than his grayish skin. His lips were thinly pursed and bloodless, as if struggling against words. Finally he added stiffly, "I really think you should have expected something of this nature to happen."

Mrs. Mided shifted her eyes from the doctor. "I didn't think he was able to move, let alone this. As far as we knew he was almost completely paralyzed." She looked very scared and small, and she glanced back at Tally imploringly, as if begging for help.

Dr. Waring turned back to Ben and drew the covers around his shoulders. Whenever things were very bad, he always found himself trying to make the patient comfortable. He supposed far more for himself than for them.

The doctor's tone was pointed. "I noticed the rehabilitation equipment in the other room. It seems rather a waste on a patient who's completely paralyzed."

It was Tally who answered. She sounded shattered. "I knew he could move."

Mrs. Mided was astonished. "But that's impossible! We've been with him for days, and all we saw were a few responses, the turning of the head, swallowing."

"I saw him move that day you went to town."

"And you didn't tell me?" The terror was gone for Mrs. Mided, the fact that they were her pills totally forgotten. Suddenly she was the injured party. "Well, now I understand why you ordered all the equipment. I thought you were just trying to lift his spirits or something. I didn't figure anything like this!"

It took a long time for Tally to answer. "I was wrong."

Dr. Waring put his equipment back into his case. "Yes, I'm afraid you were very wrong." He snapped his bag shut. "You know, it might help if we put ourselves in our patient's place. How would you feel if it were you who awakened to discover that you were paralyzed? I like to think of myself as a man who loves life. But I have a strong suspicion I shouldn't like it quite so much if I couldn't do my work or go fishing or be with my wife." He turned back to Tally; his eyes were very angry. "To be quite honest, I think I'd do precisely what he did."

The doctor and Mrs. Mided were watching Tally, and she felt as if their eyes were imprisoning her. Everything seemed to be closing in. Waves of panic gripped her, and she wanted to rush at Ben and force him back to life; she wanted to make everything go back to how it had been. Ben lay before her, unmoving, not with the rigid immobility of before, but with the quiet of death, and Tally knew there was nothing she could do to change things; it was too late for that.

The doctor picked up his bag and headed toward the door. "I'll be back in the morning. Unless of course you need me before then."

Mrs. Mided was right behind him. "You haven't told us what to do, Doctor." She brushed past Tally and followed the little man into the corridor.

Tally didn't move. She stood over Ben, listening to their voices recede down the hall.

"Do?" she heard the doctor answer. "Well, I really can't imagine what you should do. I suppose you might pray, if you go in for that. After all, they were your pills he took."

The desperation had crept back into Mrs. Mided's voice. "But I didn't know."

"Yes," he answered. "Well, I'm not a great believer in sleeping pills myself. Nevertheless, if one must use them, then for God's sake, he should have the good sense to keep them under lock and key."

Tally heard the front door open. Mrs. Mided kept repeating, "I just didn't know." But the voices seemed distant; even Tally's guilt seemed unimportant. All that mattered was Ben, lying in front of her, his chest barely moving as he took in breath, and the terrible feeling of death all around him.

As she watched him she was struck by what a physical effort it must have taken to cross the living room and find the pills. What a terrible torment living must have been for him to try. Had he been suffering physical pain? She guessed that he had, but she felt sure it was another kind of pain that had driven him on, and it made her wonder if he hadn't made the right choice, if it wouldn't be better that he die rather than live as he was.

Tally stopped herself. She'd seen many people adjust to paralysis. In fact, most people did. She supposed something changed inside that allowed a person to accept it. Perhaps if Ben had waited, the same thing would have happened to him too; the acceptance would have come, the lessening of expectation, the dampening of desire. Perhaps Ben would have even become happy.

The question was, of course, what if the thing that changed was very important? What if something meaningful had to be lost? Perhaps to accept his being only part of a man, Ben would have to become part of a man, and that was a death in itself.

The thought went against everything she believed in. Tally had a reverence for life, no matter how flawed and halting it might seem. But what if she was wrong? What if the quality of life did matter? Certainly Ben had felt so. He had forced himself to death because the reality of what he was was so terrible he couldn't bear it. And in the end had the world lost much by it? The thought was brutal, cold, but it was a question he must have asked.

Tally took a chair and placed it beside Ben's bed. She heard Mrs. Mided creep back into the room, pause for a moment, then move just behind her. She stood there silently, unsure what to say, undoubtedly feeling guilty about how easily she had shifted the blame to Tally.

But Tally didn't care what Mrs. Mided had said or done. Her mind was on Ben and the question that had plagued him. The question to which he had found his own answer.

Mrs. Mided spoke softly. "I just can't imagine what we're going to tell the family."

Tally didn't even look up. "We'll tell them the truth, that he wanted to die. They'll understand or not."

Mrs. Mided moved closer. "I swear, it never occurred to me. Those pills were halfway across the room. They were low to the ground. I really don't see how he did it. Unless——"

"Unless what?" Tally asked with little interest.

"Unless he wasn't as damaged as he made out."

"He wasn't. I told you I saw him move."

"Moving is one thing, but this! No, he must have kept it a secret even from you."

"Or he wanted to die that badly."

"Then it's a darn shame he didn't want to live that badly."

Tally didn't answer, but she turned to Mrs. Mided, surprised. For that was the point. He'd been able to break through the paralysis and complete some fairly sophisticated motor actions. With the same energy directed toward living, he might have made a reasonable recovery.

She turned back to Ben, watching him, and he seemed almost to be answering her as he lay dying. He was not the kind of man to whom words like reasonable recovery applied. It was this quality that had made him who he was; once gone he would have lost himself.

Mrs. Mided touched Tally's shoulder softly, as if asking her forgiveness or absolution. "If you want, I'll stay with him for a while."

"I don't think I could sleep anyway."

"Are you sure?" Mrs. Mided was looking away, but Tally could tell she was very upset.

"It's nobody's fault," Tally said softly. "He wanted this. And who knows? Perhaps he was right."

Both of the women looked down at Ben, their eyes riveted to him, as if there were a kind of magnetism to death.

"It's never right to want to die," Mrs. Mided said finally.

It was the sureness of Mrs. Mided's voice that most struck Tally. "How can you be so positive of that?"

Mrs. Mided laughed uneasily. "I can't." She paused, her eyes still fixed on Ben. Then abruptly she turned away. "I guess being sure of things is just a heck of a lot easier than not. Besides, with or without our approval, he did it. I guess that's all that counts."

Tally looked back at Mrs. Mided, but already the little woman was leaving the room, and by the time Tally turned back, Ben had gone into convulsions.

EIGHTEEN

Midland, Ohio

Mr. Hamayoshi closed the door behind Dyer and moved to a tray of liquor, which had been set on the chest of drawers. "I'm delighted you could come on such short notice," he said ingratiatingly.

"Always glad to meet one of my stockholders," Dyer answered, as he strode to the center of the room. He looked around the Spartan suite, noting with approval the motel green curtains, cheap wood furniture, and slightly worn carpet. He too did not feel the need for luxury.

Dyer remained in the middle of the room for a long while, and Hamayoshi smiled to himself. He also made it a point to stride into a room. Psychologically it was a sign of control of the situation, and Hamayoshi knew very well that the unspoken moves in business were at least as important as the spoken exchanges.

What did surprise him, however, was Dyer's ready acceptance of their having this meeting in Hamayoshi's hotel room rather than the conference rooms at Midwestern. He took it as an indication of real confidence, and as he glanced back at the thickset young man he gained a great deal of respect for him. Nevertheless, Hamayoshi was well acquainted with the doublethink tactics of business, and he knew that it could just be a move to elicit exactly this response from him. Hamayoshi thought for a while but could come to no conclusion. He would have to wait before reaching an understanding of Dyer.

"What will you have to drink? A scotch?" Hamayoshi asked politely.

Dyer could tell from his manner he knew exactly what Dyer drank.

"Yes, thank you. No ice." Hamayoshi had not made a gesture toward the ice, and Dyer noted this too.

As Dyer took a seat and waited for the little man to bring him his drink, there was a pleasant smile on his face, but his mind was busily going over the little he knew about Hamayoshi and the consortium he represented. From what Dyer could gather, Hamayoshi was privately considered to be the head of this consortium. He was clever and he was prosperous. What he hoped to gain from Midwestern, Dyer didn't know, though it was clear he wanted something; men like Hamayoshi did not travel halfway across the globe just to pass the time of day. But Dyer knew he'd have to wait to find out. First there would be the obligatory chitchat. Hamayoshi seemed Western enough to cut short the formalities, though still Eastern enough to make a bow to them.

"When did you arrive?" Dyer asked, as soon as Hamayoshi had taken a seat.

"Yesterday afternoon." Hamayoshi paused, then continued pointedly. "You were the first person I called."

Dyer understood the pause, but he kept his face neutral. "Then you must be very tired. It's a grueling flight from Tokyo. I've made it several times myself."

"Yes." Again it was clear Hamayoshi wanted Dyer to know he'd done his homework.

Dyer took a sip of his drink and smiled. It was his turn to indicate he'd done his research. "But then you're used to traveling, aren't you?"

Hamayoshi's eyes twinkled with amusement. "Yes, after a while traveling becomes second nature. It's the returning that becomes hard." He sighed. "You don't have a family, but it is they who suffer most. A man who travels gets used to pleasing himself. Dinner on trays. Retiring at will. Never a need to ask or even demand. It makes a person very selfish and uncompromising. And it makes settling into a routine, even one geared toward you, quite impossible."

Dyer was surprised by this intimacy. Though he'd met many Orientals, they had always remained very private and distant.

He replied cautiously. "But I'm sure the rewards of family make up for the drawbacks?"

Hamayoshi raised his fine eyebrows. "That's what they tell us, but I'm not altogether sure. Let's face it, conventional wisdom rarely has the welfare of the individual in mind, only the survival of the species. I've often wondered if I wouldn't have been happier had I remained single. I'm a very solitary type, you see."

Hamayoshi stopped and smiled mischieviously. "I can tell I

surprised you with my candor. You expect only the Eastern formalities from a Japanese and not to glimpse the man. But I'm one of those anomalies. I was educated here, as you probably know." Again the smile, polite but with a prankish undertone. "I spent my early business years on the East Coast, and that famous American candor has rubbed off on me. I believe it comes from the fact that most Americans have no roots that define them. One cannot tell from a man's name or place of birth or type of business who he really is. There are no castes, no royalty, not even a real class system to give a man the feeling that he is understood. Everything is just too fluid. So one must go around defining oneself to the world." He grinned. "And since my own background is somewhat murky, as again you probably know, I find this need extremely attractive."

Dyer shifted in his seat; his eyes were very cold. "And no doubt useful."

Hamayoshi raised his eyebrows inquiringly, and Dyer laughed. "The unexpected puts a man off balance. And I'm sure we both prefer dealing with a man who isn't quite sure where he is."

Hamayoshi nodded soberly. He found Dyer increasingly intriguing. His instincts were excellent. But far from disturbing Hamayoshi, it delighted him. Hamayoshi enjoyed doing business, especially difficult business, with the relish of a man who knows that there is no more importance to it than anything else in life, and that it is only the energy applied that counts. Had Hamayoshi chosen, he could have attached himself to religion or love affairs or even fishing with the same zeal, for the pleasure was in the game.

"I like you," Hamayoshi said. "I had not expected to, but I do. Not that it makes a difference." Hamayoshi allowed his last words to sink in before he indicated a table and chairs that had been set up by the window. It was time for business.

Dyer felt a chill pass through him as he got up and followed Hamayoshi to the table. So it was to be like this.

There was a long silence as the two men reseated themselves. Neither of them took their eyes off the other's face, and they were both aware how their bodies were placed, anxious to give the impression of being relaxed and calm.

Finally Hamayoshi said, "I wish to buy Midwestern."

Dyer laughed, but it was clear from his eyes that he did not find it funny.

"For a very good price, I assure you."

"I'm afraid you've been given the wrong information. Midwestern isn't for sale."

"As yet."

"As ever. We have no intention of selling at any time."

"Mr. Savage, time is relative. I find even one day very long. Forever is incalculable."

Dyer took another sip of his drink, then smiled slyly. "Then that goes for you too."

Hamayoshi's eyes twinkled. "Yes, indeed. You are right there. But that's why we should talk this out fully. Perhaps there is a common ground that may be reached." Hamayoshi lifted his glass, but he didn't drink. "Now as I said before, I should like to buy Midwestern. For, of course, a very good price. More than would be paid by, say, Bethlehem or U.S. Steel, which, let's face it, are not much in the mood for making purchases at this time."

"If Midwestern were in the mood to be bought."

"Mr. Savage. Business is not spectacular. The future of Midwestern is less than cheerful."

"As you pointed out, even a day is a long time. Steel will be profitable again."

"Certainly. But what kind? Japanese steel is cheaper. When the demand becomes greater, it will be for our steel."

"Not necessarily. There's always defense. And the way the world's going, that might become increasingly important. After all, if the Middle East doesn't get us then Eastern Europe might."

"Let us hope not. War is bad, no matter what its effect on business." Hamayoshi allowed a silence to build, then he continued evenly. "I want Midwestern, with or without your consent."

"Do you now? Well, you ain't gonna get it."

"That remains to be seen."

Dyer took another sip of his drink, then stopped himself. Hamayoshi had not even tasted his. "How? A proxy fight? You own less than five percent of the stock. Hardly a staggering amount."

Again Hamayoshi's eyes sparkled with amusement. "That, Mr. Savage, was to serve only as a calling card."

"That, Mr. Hamayoshi, is your limit. To own more, you'd have to register with the SEC."

Hamayoshi shrugged. "It should present no hardship."

"Don't be so sure. The SEC might be very interested to find that a Japanese consortium is trying to take over an American company."

"Why? Because we're Japanese? It's been a long time since Pearl

Harbor, even for a country with such a short history as the United States."

"As you said, time is relative."

Hamayoshi's tone was still even, but there was a bite to it. "Japanese companies are buying in the United States all the time now. And don't American companies have their interests abroad?"

"What's sauce for the goose is not necessarily tasty on the gander."

Hamayoshi thought about this for a moment, then he shook his head. "I can see no problems. Midwestern Steel is not large enough to present a monopoly situation, and that is the only time the SEC can intervene."

It was Dyer's turn to pause pointedly. "And the Justice Department?"

"They too would have no reason to act. They'd only become involved in matters affecting the defense of the United States. Can openers, refrigerators, and cars are hardly vital to defense."

"But they both could tie you up with investigations."

"Yes. I suppose they could, but we could wait them out. No, Mr. Savage, let's face it, I'm quite set on having Midwestern."

Dyer smiled casually, but he was working on his drink again, and there was an angry tic beginning at the side of his mouth. "Fifty-five percent of the stock belongs to my family. And none of us will go along with you."

Hamayoshi returned his smile. "It's not quite that simple."

"It's exactly that simple. Even if I wanted to sell, which I most certainly do not, my uncle would never go along."

"Yes. I spoke to him about this matter once."

"And?"

"I believe his exact words were 'over my dead body.'" Hamayoshi beamed disturbingly at Dyer. "But let's face it, things have changed. Mr. Ben Savage is a very ill man."

"And when he recovers?"

"I have come for a real talk. Let's not waste each other's time establishing facts we both know to be true. Mr. Ben Savage is gravely ill. His mother is a very old lady. End of story."

The smile had hardened on Dyer's lips. "Well, since you seem to know so much about the family, you must also be aware that whatever happens, the stock will remain in the family and will probably be inherited by both me and my cousin."

"Which in effect is you. I'm sure by now you have your cousin well under control. I believe he has certain areas of weakness that make him easier to manage."

Dyer didn't answer.

"In fact, I would bet you've taken steps in that direction already."

Though Hamayoshi didn't continue, it was clear he knew a great deal more about Midwestern than just the business news.

"Have it your own way. I'll control a big chunk of stock. But you can't buy Midwestern without my selling. And I can't think of one reason why I should do that."

"Yes. That is the point, isn't it? Why should you sell to me? Not for money. You aren't a man who values money. Nor power. Not that you don't respect power, but you have it now, so that wouldn't be an enticement for you to sell. The reason, I believe, lies much deeper than that. Midwestern belongs to Ben Savage. It's as if his face were stamped on every ingot. Midwestern is not yours, will never be yours, no matter what you do. And, I think, more than anything else you want something that is yours, something you could afford to build on your own."

Dyer was silent. Often he'd thought that when his uncle was a boy, there had been new worlds to conquer, if not on the land then at least in business. Ben had forged an empire out of nothing. And while Dyer might run that empire ably, it would always be Ben's. Dyer would never know how he would have done if it had been he who stepped off that ship from Wales without a penny or a friend. Sometimes he tortured himself with the thought that he might have failed.

"Ah, you are becoming more interested. Good. I was growing bored with the preliminaries. So let's assume a sale is not totally impossible. Now, what do I propose?"

Dyer flared. "What the hell makes you so sure I'm interested in what you propose?"

"You're still here, aren't you? I didn't lock the door. I didn't hold you back by force." Hamayoshi's eyes were twinkling again. "Now, I suggest we do absolutely nothing, at least for a while. Our business here is to reach tentative agreement until your stock situation sorts itself out."

Dyer's eyes narrowed. "What you're asking is that in exchange for what I assume will be a substantial holding fee, I guarantee to sell to you when the time comes. Meanwhile I remain president of Midwestern, and you quietly run it from behind the scenes."

"I doubt that it will become necessary for me to be involved."

"But you'd like to be kept up to date just in case."

"As I said, I doubt the need will arise."

"For Christ sake, you're asking me to front like for a Vegas casino!"

"It isn't entirely illegal, you know."

"It ain't entirely legal either." Dyer stood, his cheeks burning and his head pounding.

Hamayoshi stood too, slowly, reluctantly. "What a shame. I should have liked doing business with you. We would have been most cutthroat together."

Dyer began to walk to the door. The anger was like a fist inside him. But he was aware that Hamayoshi did not follow him and was surprised to discover this disappointed him.

Just as Dyer reached the door, Hamayoshi called out, "Of course you know I'll merely go out into the open. I'll buy more stock."

"There's only so much you can buy."

"Enough perhaps to bring you down."

Dyer was caught at the door, unable to move. "Why?" he asked finally. "I don't understand why you want to buy us that much."

"We have need of a steel corporation." It was said like a man interested in acquiring a new sport jacket or a two-car garage.

This time Dyer did open the door, but still he hesitated, looking back at Hamayoshi.

Hamayoshi smiled. "Think it over. All I'm asking is that you think it over very carefully."

NINETEEN

Dyer's foot pressed tightly against the gas pedal. The lights of Midland sparkled in the darkening sky. It was a sight he saw every evening on his way home, but tonight the lights seemed to gleam sinisterly, drawing him in, taking over his mind and body until they were no longer under his control.

Dyer had fought many battles, and, more often than not, he had won them. But this battle was different. Always he had struggled against others, but now he was struggling with himself, and he was left weak and powerless, divided by what he needed and what he knew was right.

The Park Lane Hotel was the tallest in town. An annex had been built several years back, and the old elegance of the hotel was dwarfed by its shadows. At the top of the annex, hidden behind drawn curtains, muffled in pink light, was Pauline. The thought of her made Dyer's jaw clench with anger and also with fear. What had happened before was unthinkable, an aberration that could only be forgiven if it was never repeated. Dyer had vowed that night that it would never happen again. But he feared it was a promise that he could not keep. The draw was so strong he could feel it rising in his body until his hands were shaking and his mind was alight with the memory of Pauline's taut curves and the film of glistening dampness that had covered her body. He could see her hungry mouth parted, those predatory teeth, so dangerously erotic, and even as Dyer was heading back to his own apartment, he could feel himself giving way. The need was pulling at him, driving all thought and reason from his mind and replacing it only with instinct.

He stopped in front of his apartment building, staring into the darkening night. How long he was parked there he didn't know, but suddenly he was starting the car again, his heart pounding, his blood thick in his veins. Though he knew even satisfying the craving would do nothing to quiet the obsession and would only make it more intense, he headed back toward the hotel.

Dyer stopped just outside of the Park Lane. He could see that the penthouse lights were on, but Pauline was a woman who was careless and extravagant in all things. There was no guarantee that she was home, and certainly there was no guarantee that she was home alone.

As Dyer parked the car and entered the hotel, the thought that Pauline was with someone tortured him. It wasn't that he was jealous, for the obsession did not include loving or even liking; it was something else entirely, something much more akin to hate. Still, the idea that she was not alone ravaged Dyer. If she was with someone, she would send him off, and he would be left with this terrible hunger in the pit of his stomach, squirming and eating at him until he went mad.

Dyer knocked at the door. There was a long delay, and he debated whether he should force himself to go away. But he didn't move; he couldn't move, and a moment later Pauline's thick sensuous voice came through the intercom.

"It's Dyer," he said, trying to keep his tone from betraying his nervousness.

Pauline laughed softly when she heard his name, then opened the door to him. She was dressed in a silk pantsuit, designer scarf at her neck, and she looked as if she were about to go out for the evening. She said nothing as Dyer walked into the living room and headed for the bar, but merely watched him, eyebrows raised, her mouth parted just enough to reveal those powerful little teeth. And Dyer hated her more than ever; her dieted body teased him into a fury, so that he could not even look at her. He poured himself a triple scotch, then took it over to the couch and sat down.

She stood where she was, watching him for a long while, and she seemed very relaxed, very triumphant. Finally she too went over to the bar, though Dyer could tell from the way she walked, it was not the first trip she had made there that evening. She poured herself a large drink, took a gulp, then turned to Dyer.

"Just like that, huh?" She laughed. "You're awfully sure of yourself, aren't you?"

Dyer wanted to tell her he'd just stopped by for a drink or, even better, business. But he hadn't brought up his briefcase; he hadn't even thought of needing an excuse, so far had he been from rational thought. Time passed, but he still couldn't speak and the silence grew, until he was encased in it.

Pauline said petulantly, "I was planning on going out this evening. In case you care."

"Don't let me stop you." Dyer could feel the anger building in him and also the panic. He didn't want Pauline to leave; he couldn't allow her to leave. Suddenly he understood what was meant by a crime of passion. Always the term had seemed contradictory, but now he understood. The passion wasn't love at all; it was hate. Only the poets linked sex with love. The other was a far more compelling emotion, hate of the terrible control exercised by sex and the person who seemed to own it.

"Aren't you even interested where I was going?" Pauline asked. Dyer shrugged and concentrated on his drink.

She laughed. "I was going to your mother's for dinner. Ironic, no? But I'm sure she'd be delighted if I phone and cancel out. Or would you rather make the call yourself?"

Pauline smiled cruelly, then reached for the phone. Dyer wanted to run from the pink lights and the smell of expensive perfume, but still he didn't move.

Pauline dialed Angela's number and sat smiling, her eyebrows raised. When Angela answered, she gave Dyer a wink. "Angela," she said breathlessly. "I'm so sorry to call you like this, but I'm afraid I'm going to have to cancel our little dinner tonight."

She grimaced playfully at Dyer, then moved forward in her chair until she was perched at the end of it. She reached over and ran her forefinger along his knee. "Yes, dear. It's probably that ghastly flu that's making the rounds."

Pauline's finger kept moving along Dyer's knee, making little circles. "I can feel the beginnings of a fever." She said it with a sly smile.

Everything inside Dyer tightened, and he wanted to knock Pauline's hand away from him.

Pauline stifled a laugh. "Yes. I promise I'll go to bed the minute I get off the phone." She giggled. "Good-bye, dear." She replaced the receiver and sat back in her chair, contemplating Dyer through laughing eyes.

"Well, now, this *is* a treat," she said with a mocking sigh. "No one comes to visit poor Auntie Pauline very much anymore. And you know how much family means to the sad old dear."

"You're disgusting." Dyer was shaking.

"Oh, come off it. I'm disgusting? Is that why you come scratching at my door in the middle of the night like a god damn tomcat?" Pauline took another sip of her drink, and she looked very angry. "Why don't you climb down here with the rest of the pigs? It's where you want to be."

Then suddenly Pauline's face softened, and she reached over to Dyer. Slowly she teased her fingers along the side of his leg toward the inside of his thigh.

"You find me unbelievably attractive, Dyer, and you might as well admit it to yourself right now. The first time, well, maybe you could have found a way to stop. But now it's too late."

Her hand moved softly up his thigh, and she shifted off her chair and to the floor next to him. She was looking at him steadily; the smile was gone from her lips, and she was slightly flushed. Dyer could sense the fear in her eyes, and under the fear a revulsion. It was a terrifyingly needy face he saw, and he found his anger melting and a sadness and need of his own replacing it.

Pauline's hand moved to his groin, touching him so lightly, he could barely feel it, just enough to stir the waves of need. She closed her eyes and tilted her head back. Pink light caught at the contours of her face, and at that moment she looked very young, very lovely.

Dyer was motionless. The electric heat from her hand was inflaming his body, and as he watched her tilted face, his blood pulsed. Everything around him drifted away, until only her hand and the longing that was building inside him had any importance. He knew there was no use trying to fight Pauline; she owned him. Already the fire was growing, spreading through his belly, and he could hear the sound of his own breath being released from his lungs. It was a sigh, and he had no more control over it than he had over anything else.

He moved off his chair, lowering himself to the floor next to Pauline, and as he felt her hand tighten around him, an acute moan of ecstasy broke from his lips.

TWENTY

James cried out in his sleep, and the small part of him that was still separate from the darkness tossed him back into the world. Quickly he sat up and switched on the light. His sheets were wet with perspiration; his heart was pounding.

He glanced over at the clock by his bedside, hoping that he had only a few more hours of darkness and there wasn't enough time to slip back into his nightmare. But it was only one o'clock, and there were hours of shadow before the dawn.

He could no longer remember what he'd been dreaming, but he knew it had been terrible. The feeling was still on him; it was as if the dream were lurking in the corners of the room, hunching in the shadows, waiting, and all he had to do was reach out to remember it. Years ago, when he'd been in analysis, he'd been forced to remember his dreams. Wriggling on the couch like an overturned beetle, he'd relived all the agonizing chases, the misdialed phone calls, the drownings and empty rooms. But the analysis hadn't helped, nor the remembering, and gratefully he'd given up both.

Family Passions 185

James reached over to the bedside table, shook out a cigarette, and lit it with a gold lighter. He looked around the room, concentrating on every detail, clinging to the normality of furniture and carpet to hold him to the everyday world and keep the night horrors away.

James had been tortured by nightmares ever since he was young. They were probably his earliest memories; they were certainly his strongest. The dark shadowy presences that had crept into his child brain seemed more potent than any of the more usual first recollections. It was the giant grotesque bears chasing after him, cars bearing down on him while he was held paralyzed with fear in the middle of the road unable to cry out, that were the memories of his childhood, and though as he grew up his dreams became more sophisticated, the terror of them remained, haunting even his waking hours, until he was frightened to fall asleep. As a child he'd sat up in bed, rigidly awake, staring into the darkness, his whole body steeled against sleep. But always in the end he'd had to relinquish hold and slowly drift over the edge of awareness. Finally he'd given up even on wakefulness, succumbing to the night horrors as an inevitable punishment. Still, he always kept himself awake as late as possible.

As James sat smoking and looking around, the grip of his dream loosened, though the power of it remained with him, and he knew the moment he relaxed, it would be back.

James glanced at the clock. It was only five past one. If he hurried there would be enough time to get a drink at the Empire Club; a quick drink and a laugh would make him feel better. After that it would be easy to come back to the dark shadows; his tiredness would take him over; perhaps he'd be able to sleep undisturbed for a few hours before he had to get up and go to work.

James forced the thought away. It had been over two months since he'd been to the Empire Club. Ever since his father's accident he'd stayed away, knowing exactly what the bright lights, the crowds, and the pounding music pushed him to, knowing that it was even more disturbing than the terrible nights. Logically, of course, just because he went to the club didn't mean he had to come home with someone, but in reality, he knew it didn't work that way. Everything about the club was geared to helping its members push away the outside world. Once inside, nothing seemed important except what was going on right there and then. The Empire Club was a whole world, complete with rules and laws, strangely twisted, but more compelling than any outside its doors. That was why its members went there every night; that was why James was struggling to stay away. It was inevitable. With the strange inside-out world of the Empire Club came the other, and he'd vowed never to return to that.

James stubbed out his cigarette but immediately lit another. He remembered the night he'd made that vow, the night of his father's accident. He'd sat in the hospital waiting room and with a clinical detachment examined his life and what it had become. Up until then he'd been able to tell himself that his life-style was just a phase, temporary, enjoyable, and should he wish to, he could change it at a moment's notice. Always he'd been able to escape the truth by running around town, spending hours in busy idleness. But that night under the glaring hospital lights, he'd begun to see what his life was.

The memory startled James, appearing before him as strong and terrible as it had been then. Several times he'd been allowed into the intensive care ward to see his father, and he would never forget the sight of him, lying totally surrounded by machines, a shell of flesh bearing almost no relation to a man. He hadn't been frightened; his reaction had been something far worse. It'd been like looking at a portrait of one's ancestors, knowing that there was a man who was once very much alive, but now all humanity was gone, all faults and flaws had faded, and what was left was only the perfections and the responsibility they demanded. As James had stared down at his father, he'd been struck by how little he had given him, how much he had always let him down. This man who had angered and frightened him, this man who had in so many ways ruled his life, had also given him much. He had given him name, purpose; he had given him life, and James had a responsibility to him for that, one that had never been fulfilled.

Up until that moment having children had meant little to him. Certainly it was something expected in his family, and he had detected in his grandmother's eyes a sadness that he felt could be traced to the fact she must suspect he would never have children. While all through his childhood the importance of family had been drummed into him, he'd always been able to ignore it. But seeing his father dying had made it more real to him and he'd begun to feel the weight of his obligation, and how if he continued as he was, he would let it down.

It was such an old-fashioned concept, one hardly ever spoken of anymore, yet under the bravado how powerfully it had held him. As the hours had piled on top of one another, there'd been a dead-sounding echo to them, the sound of his own voice in his ears. He lived solely for pleasure and would die without a trace. He would make no life.

But it had been the next night, by chance, as he was sitting in front of the television, flipping through the channels and eating soggy fried chicken, that the obligation had changed in him and become need.

Why he had watched the program on childbirth he didn't remember; he had probably just been waiting for the next one to begin. But mixed in with the usual photographs of the development inside the womb had been one of a four-month-old fetus taken with ultrasound.

It had been nothing like the others. While in the rest of the pictures the fetus had appeared as a lusty colorful little creature, this had been a crude gray ghost, an almost transparent little form, floating, floating in what looked like a vast lonely emptiness. He'd been able to see the tiny heart fluttering, a ghostly limb stirring, but those movements had only seemed to emphasize the incompleteness of the fetus in its terrible lonely gray world where it neither understood nor received any understanding.

It had been impossible to put adjectives like sad or brave to what he'd seen on the screen. To even say vulnerable gave the indistinct phantom more substance and importance than it had. Even the word lonely gave it credit for being more than it was, because it would not know what loneliness was. The essence was it wasn't important; it was just a pathetic bit of cells.

He'd turned off the television, but he just hadn't been able to get the tiny phantom creature out of his mind. It had seemed less a baby than a naked soul, his soul, perhaps everyone's, alone, so alone, drifting in a vast emptiness. That night he'd cried, mostly for himself. But as the night had drawn on there'd grown in him a need to protect this little unimportant bit of protoplasm, to float with it so that it was no longer alone, perhaps not so much for the poor creature's sake, for he had seen clearly there was little he could do for it, but for his own, for the sake of the gray flickering transparency that was a part of him too.

From that moment on James had known exactly what he must do. It had all seemed so clear, as if he were standing away from the world and looking down on it. Suddenly he'd seen the purpose of everything and his place in it. He had decided he was going to lead a normal life, be just like everyone else. The word normal seemed to have such a magic and mystery to it. He would get married, have children; it all seemed so simple, so clean.

James lit another cigarette. His body was becoming heavy and drowsy from lack of sleep, but he forced himself to remain sitting up. He could feel the dream at the edge of his consciousness, waiting for him.

He turned his thoughts to the office, hoping to find some detail to interest him and keep the ghosts away for a little while longer. But the office had never been able to vanquish his nights; only the Empire Club had been able to do that.

For a moment he weakened. After all, he thought, it was just a bar and discotheque, the crowd was mixed, the young elegant of Midland. There was nothing in the club itself that would do him any harm; it all rested in his attitude. James stopped himself. Perhaps one day he'd be able to return to the Empire Club, but he knew that one day would not be now.

He finished his cigarette and his eyes began to close. Slowly the room dimmed for him, and his body slipped back under the covers. Almost imperceptibly the shadows in the corners of the room began to move, drifting across the carpet and lifting over the bed, until once again they held him, and he was screaming.

James got out of bed and quickly walked to the bathroom. As he showered and dressed he reassured himself that he would only go to the Empire Club for a drink or two, then when he was too tired and drunk to be scared, he would come home. But deep inside himself he didn't believe it, and he was frightened.

As James stood in the entrance to the club, he felt agitated and expectant. It was the feeling he always had just before he entered, as if something wonderful, almost mystical, might happen that night. Though in fact it never did, the feeling was always there, and perhaps this was the reason he used to come, night after night, standing for hours at the bar, chatting inanely with the attractive people who drifted in and out. It was the excitement of possibilities that drew him; the fulfilling of the promise was only secondary.

The bouncer at the door nodded to James but said nothing about his not having been there for a long time. People often appeared and disappeared at the Empire. They were all part of the vague young crowd whose lives and livelihoods were fluid, forever moving quickly, though where they were heading was rarely clear.

James used to wonder what happened to them after they were no longer young. Where did they all go to from there? Did they quickly change their lives, settle down, marry and have children? Did they go into hiding, ashamed of the affliction of age, for that was what it was considered at the Empire Club, a disease, disgusting, embarrassing, something only to be joked about but with a tinge of hysteria? James supposed he had been wondering more what would happen to him once his youth was gone. Whatever it was, he suspected it would be unpleasant. And he was one of the lucky ones; at least he had money.

Even at that hour the bar was packed with beautifully dressed people, both men and women, but leaning toward the chic gay crowd and those who clung closely to them, as something to be envied. As James looked around, he could feel the anticipation strengthening. He tried to stop it from taking him over. It was a dangerous feeling, more compelling than anything that could possibly happen, and for that reason it became almost addictive. Still, he moved through the crowd to the bar. There was the scent of perfumes and aftershaves mixing in the air, the warmth of many bodies around him; individual voices were deadened and muted by the sound of a hundred conversations. Close to the bar, the smells of the different alcohols blended with the perfumes, creating their own odor, at once sharp and smooth.

Suddenly James felt as if all his senses had come alive. It was a wonderful feeling, mindless, exhilarating, forcing out all resolutions and recriminations, leaving only intense happiness.

James ordered a drink and was staring out at the crowd when a voice startled him.

"I've been looking for you." It was Boris Tanderoff, James's new assistant, standing behind him. He was leaning against a post, a drink in one hand, a cigarette in the other, smiling as if this were the most ordinary of meetings, as if the Empire did not have a certain reputation.

"Well, you found me," James answered, less surprised than he might have been at seeing Boris. He supposed that his days at Midwestern were so separate from the rest of his life that he didn't really think of the men who worked there as existing outside the gates. To see Boris, comfortably standing with a drink in his hand, seemed a quirk of nature, a miscalculation in the scheme of things, but definitely not real.

"I asked at the front desk but they said you hadn't been here for a long time," Boris told James, as he moved to the bar next to him. "I suppose that must sound kind of strange to you."

"Considering that you have an office right next to mine? Yes, it does." James laughed, but he was watching Boris now. He was becoming aware of the implications of bumping into his assistant like this, aware of the implications and suspicious of the motives.

Boris leaned against the bar, his lean athletic body trying to look relaxed and confident, his handsome boyish face straining for a smile. But James could see the tension creeping in everywhere, tightening his shoulders, pulling at the corners of his mouth. Boris blew out a thick cloud of smoke and took a pull at his drink. There was something desperately stilted about his actions, a young man working so hard for sophistication that James found himself strangely touched.

"I didn't want to talk to you about business," Boris admitted nervously. "I wanted to talk to you about—well, I guess I just wanted to talk to you. But now that I've started I simply feel foolish." He stared down at his drink.

James was baffled by Boris's nervous confession and underneath it slightly flattered. Still, there was the suspicion that this chance meeting was more than it seemed, and he couldn't shake it. He watched Boris in silence, trying to discover what he might be up to, but nothing in the young man's smooth boyish face gave any clues.

Boris smiled shyly. "You can't imagine what nerve it took coming up to you like this."

"I'm that frightening, huh?"

Boris began to relax, and for the first time James was struck by how handsome he was. There was an animal keenness; his high cheekbones and large dark eyes had a deerlike beauty.

"You all frighten us, didn't you know that?"

James laughed. "We all? You mean the family?"

"Yes. The family." Boris was cautious. "I suppose it's something you aren't aware of. But Midwestern is divided into three groups—echelons really, or maybe even castes. There're the workers, and that's everyone who comes in contact with steel. Then there's the office staff, and that's me. Then there are the Savages. There's a big gap between all three, but the biggest is between you and us. More even than the workers. Maybe that's because they don't seem to recognize it. But we in the offices who see and speak to you every day do."

"The haves and have-nots, eh?" James grinned.

"No, not exactly. I don't think it has to do with the size of the paycheck. It's more to do with a difference in . . ." Boris paused, unable to find the word. "Maybe it's a difference in vision."

James groaned. "A difference in what?"

Boris watched him soberly. "I guess you wouldn't understand."

"I'm sorry," James apologized. "Try me again."

Boris's face flushed with embarrassment. "Well, you see, the rest of us are working for specific things, ourselves or our families or our mortgages."

"And we aren't?"

"Not totally. It's as if you are working toward something more than just today. Maybe it's for your family name or the good of the company. Or perhaps it's something else. Like I said, it's a difference in vision, so I'm not really sure."

"And you detect this difference of vision in me?" James was enjoying this immensely. It appealed to his sense of the ridiculous and also, if he were to be honest, to his ego.

"Of course," Boris said earnestly. "You're a Savage. Though I guess you could say that you're much more of an enigma to us than your cousin, and that makes the gap even greater."

"I've been thought of as many things, but an enigma was never one of them. I can assure you I am most ridiculously transparent."

Boris laughed nervously. "It's just that you seem different from Dyer Savage. Maybe even a little above him."

"Now that sounds very much like looking-for-a-raise noises."

Boris tensed. "I didn't mean it that way." He seemed to sink into himself. He finished the remainder of his drink and looked around the bar, as if for a place to retreat.

James sensed this and smiled warmly. "Don't worry. I'm not going to fire you for trying a little flattery on the boss."

Boris seemed upset. "The truth is I'm more worried about your disliking me than firing me."

James turned to the bar and ordered them both drinks, then he handed one to Boris. "Well, I'm not going to fire you or dislike you, so you can relax, okay?"

Boris was struggling to smile, but James could see he was off balance and scared.

"I don't understand why you should care what I think of you," he said to Boris.

Boris was staring at his drink; he could barely look up. "I suppose along with the feeling that your family is separate from us is a kind of admiration. You see, we care what you think of us. Not just on a business level, but in every way. I'm sure you'd be shocked to know how much of our time is occupied with talking about the Savage family."

"You mean gossiping."

"Sometimes, yes. But mostly just talking. At first I thought it was strange how much energy everyone put into worrying and discussing your family. But now I'm beginning to understand. Midwestern Steel is obsessed by the Savages, because the Savages are obsessed by Midwestern."

James chuckled. "And you think that I am obsessed by Midwestern?" It seemed impossible that even an outsider like Boris could so misjudge him.

"In your own way, yes." Boris was leaning closer to him, watching him so intently that James found himself shying away. Yet at the same time, he couldn't take his eyes completely off Boris. Once again he was reminded of an animal, though of which kind he was no longer sure. Not a deer, he was certain of that; it was a much less timid animal. A cat of some kind. And indeed, Boris's agile body seemed poised, motionless but full of energy, as if waiting to pounce.

"There are different kinds of obsessions," Boris persisted. His tone told James he understood him a great deal better than he'd suspected.

James turned back to the bar meditatively. He felt unsettled by Boris. There was something frightening about his understanding, but there was something comforting in it too. James had found little understanding during his daytime life at Midwestern, and even less in the evening.

"Well, this should make some hot gossip tomorrow in the cafeteria," James mocked anxiously.

"I don't use people like that," Boris answered. He said it with great dignity, but he was watching James with a worried expression, obviously feeling he had gone too far and regretting he had spoken so personally. His face was tight and unsure, his body electric. Now he seemed poised not to pounce but for flight.

It gave James a feeling of power to see Boris so frightened, almost awed by him. James had never before understood the pleasure of having power over another person. It was probably one of the reasons he was so ill-suited for being a Savage. But standing in the bar, comfortably smoking and drinking next to Boris, he felt the warm stirrings of control.

James said mildly, "I'm not worried about you. Besides, there's nothing to gossip about. Two executives from Midwestern having a drink together is hardly news."

Once again Boris relaxed; his slim body regained its feline ease and confidence. "That's right. Nothing would be more natural."

James was astounded by Boris. His moods changed so rapidly, flickering across his face, molding his body, and what was even more astonishing was they seemed to be dependent on him. Boris's whole being was, at least for the moment, controlled by James's reactions.

The silence between the two men grew, until both of them were very aware of it. Still, neither of them spoke. Oddly, rather than making James feel awkward, there seemed to be an intimacy in it that comforted and disturbed him at the same time. A shiver passed over James. For the first time he realized he was attracted to Boris. It was strong; it was compelling; and James stood rigidly, trying to fight it.

It was Boris who broke the silence. He repeated, "Nothing could be more normal. Two men from the same company having a drink together."

He smiled, and there was an ease and confidence in that smile that disturbed James. Then he put his hand on James's arm. It was an easy, natural gesture, just as the smile had been. "Even if they *are* having a drink at the Empire Club."

A shock went through James. He looked at Boris, warily going over his face, but there was nothing in it that showed he'd meant anything by the remark. He still looked happy, perhaps even excited to be standing next to James, as if this were an important event in his life.

The pressure of Boris's hand seemed to grow. Suddenly James could feel a thrill moving through his body. It was a dangerous feeling, and he recognized it as such. Nevertheless, he didn't move from Boris nor the feeling, and though he told himself he was only having a drink with an employee and it was perfectly normal, something that happened every day, he no longer believed it.

* * *

Shimmering morning light spread across the twisted sheets. Boris slept little-boy style, his body wrapped tightly in upon itself; his hair fell in damp curls onto his forehead. James lay awake, watching him with the same strange detachment he'd felt that night with his father in the hospital.

He didn't really feel anything. He wasn't even thinking. All he could do was watch the sleeping young man next to him as he pressed himself closer to his pillow and shivered in response to a dream.

How many dawns had he lain in bed watching other men? he wondered. But always it was with fascination or disgust or even indifference. This time was different though; this time there was a closed-in feeling, a finality to their lying together on the bed in their twisted sheets, and he knew that whatever had happened between the two of them the night before would be repeated. As he lay in the quickly gathering dawn, he felt strongly that he'd been drawn in, yet that knowledge did nothing to lessen the pull. It was still there, just under the surface, waiting until Boris awakened and smiled.

Suddenly James became scared. Always his men had been a diversion, and though he hadn't been able to fight the urge for them, the magnetism had been only to the act, not the person. But Boris was different. Boris had touched more than just the desire, he had touched the man.

Visions of the night before lit James's mind, and he felt everything inside of him stirring. He fought against it, turning from the sight of Boris, concentrating on the shadowy furniture as it glowed golden in the early morning light. But already he could feel the warmth spreading through his thighs. They ached hotly.

Slowly he turned back to Boris and traced the outline of his sleeping body with his eyes. Boris shifted under the covers; his lean body moved sensuously under the sheets. It was as if there were an invisible cord between them. As Boris moved, James could feel it tightening around him, swelling him; there was a heaviness in the pit of his stomach that responded to Boris's every movement.

Once again James looked away, trying to stop the need, but even as he did, he knew it was an aimless movement. Already he had resigned himself to losing the fight, and it wasn't long before he was turning back.

Boris's eyes were open, and he was staring at James expectantly but also with a tinge of fear. James pulled back the covers brusquely. Boris didn't move; he just watched James as he took in his body with his eyes, allowing them to move across his slim but muscular chest, down his tense stomach to his groin.

The two men watched themselves stir together. The sight of Boris's awakening tore through James. It seemed impossible that anyone could desire a woman, when her own desire was so well hidden, so secretive. How unsettling it was for a man to lie exposed in his feelings, without knowing the woman's reaction, how frightening. With a man, desire was a mutual exposure, an opening out.

James delayed touching Boris; he just watched him, postponing the excitement, holding it as a promise. He knew from the night before that when they came together it would be violent, animalistic, but for now the soft teasing intimacy was pleasing.

James waited until the heat had risen inside of him and his face was burning with it. Then he reached over and grabbed Boris by the hips. With a jerking movement, he pulled him upward, turning him over onto his stomach in one powerful movement.

James gripped tightly to Boris's slim hips, pressing himself against them. He dug his fingers into his flesh. He could feel the tension sear Boris's body as the pain gathered and he tried to fight against it, but also he could feel the pleasure just under the surface.

James tightened his grasp. Boris was shivering now, and a gasp escaped from him, but James could feel that the pain made everything sharper and more real to him, and that he wanted to be hurt.

James clamped to Boris's hips even harder. All at once he shoved them away from him, holding them at arms' length while he dug his fingers into Boris's flesh. Then rapidly he jerked Boris back toward him, until the two of them were jammed together. Boris took in breath and pressed himself against James, but already James was pushing him away and jerking him back, and there wasn't anything he could do but give in to the strong hands that controlled him.

James found the lubricant on his night table. With a quick movement he squeezed some onto his finger, then shoved Boris away and stared at the gentle line of his buttocks. There was a muscle twitching just under one of the little clefts. He clawed his fingers into Boris's hips and watched the muscle contract sharply as Boris exhaled with a gasp.

There was a moment of stillness. Neither man moved, waiting expectantly, then suddenly James tore at Boris's opening with his finger, lubricating him and opening him. Without giving him a moment to relax, James jammed himself in brutally, in one tearing movement.

Boris screamed. The pressure of James ripped through him, but he could not move from his grasp; he was held totally controlled, unable to do anything except submit. Still James pressed deeper and deeper, forcing the screams from Boris.

There was a glowing ache in James now, and it grew and grew until he too was groaning and screaming with Boris, in a blind animal frenzy.

It was only later as the two of them lay separate, their bodies glistening with sweat, the light of morning washing over them, that James felt the power shifting away. While in that brief moment of coming together James had controlled Boris's body, Boris now had regained ownership of himself, and James felt frightened. Though he knew he had power over Boris, he could sense that Boris had a power over him. For the first time in his life, he cared. It would matter to him if he lost Boris; it would matter a great deal. His control had only been temporary; Boris could take it away at any moment. And in that there was real power.

TWENTY-ONE

"It isn't that I'm not pleased to see you, James. It's just I'm curious why you're here."

Dylan Savage was sprawled in an easy chair, her eyes on the skyline of New York just outside the windows. In her Levi jeans and plaid flannel shirt she looked much younger than James had imagined. Though she was close to fifty, she still had the small-breasted slimness of a young girl; her thick wavy blond hair was tied back in a ponytail, and it did not show any gray. Only two thin lines at the side of her mouth told that Dylan had seen something of life and didn't like it very much. They were unhappy lines, burned into her face from years of holding herself together.

James turned from the sight of his mother, not because of the memories she brought up in him but because she seemed so much a stranger.

His eyes went over the living room. It was a nice room, beautifully decorated with parquet floors that were highly polished, good modern furniture, excellent paintings. A spectacular view of Manhattan hung like a backdrop at the windows. It was the apartment of an affluent New York woman of taste, but it had nothing to do with the mother he hardly remembered.

Coldly he began searching the room for signs of his mother's friend, Beth. Always it was implied, by silences or thinly veiled glances, that their relationship was more than just friendship. James had always written it off to his father's inability to believe Dylan hadn't left him for a man, not even a woman, just to get away from him.

Now as he sat looking around, he realized that he'd always wondered if his father weren't right, possibly as an explanation of himself. But there was nothing in the apartment to answer the question. Certainly signs of Beth must have been there, perhaps the paintings so tastefully placed, perhaps the brutally primitive wood sculpture. He'd heard that Beth had something to do with the art world, though he'd never asked what.

He had a feeling he'd spotted her leaving the building as he'd drawn up in a taxi. She'd looked quite ordinary, just another middle-aged, middle-class woman, a bit arty, a bit overweight. Yes, he supposed that was Beth, clearing out for the evening in deference to him, skulking around some movie theater or restaurant, in a frenzy about her friend. Yet still the question remained.

James turned back to Dylan. No, he knew nothing about her at all. She wasn't even related to him.

Finally he answered, "Yes. I can imagine you are curious why I'm here. I don't see you for twenty years. Don't even answer your letters."

"Desperate letters."

"I wouldn't know. I never read them."

Dylan cringed. She turned back to the window. The lights of the city were glittering cruelly against the black sky. The sound of an ambulance pierced the night.

James continued angrily. "Father never forgave you for leaving him, you know?"

"You mean your father never forgave me for divorcing him. The leaving part, well, he couldn't have cared less about that. We were hardly your basic happy couple."

"I can imagine."

Dylan flared. "You cannot imagine!" She stopped, trying to calm herself. "Oh, well, I guess it doesn't make a difference anymore."

"No. It doesn't make a difference."

There was a long silence. The two of them watched one another, each trying to guess the motives of a stranger. Yet underneath there was the disturbing feeling they could understand one another, that the distance of twenty years could be bridged, and if it were, it would be very powerful.

"I suppose I should feel guilty about leaving you," Dylan said at last, fighting to stay aloof.

"Do you?" It was a question James had asked himself for years, until the asking had become so painful he'd frozen out all thought of his mother. It was as if she'd died twenty years ago, and he hadn't seen her running from the house and into a taxi, never to return.

"Yes," Dylan said softly. "Even today I have dreams about it. Terrible dreams. Always I'm trying to get to you in a subway. Or I'm in a phone booth and I keep trying to talk to you, but you can't hear my voice."

She paused and again her eyes retreated to the windows. "It's not that I regret what I did. It was the only thing I could do at the time. But you were so young and unprotected. I knew you wouldn't understand. I don't suppose you do now either."

"You never gave me a chance."

"You sound very bitter."

"Surprised?"

"No. And I don't blame you." Dylan stopped. She could feel the tears just behind the words, and she fought against them, holding them back by her will. She didn't want to cry; she wanted this one chance to explain. "I had no other choice."

"You could have taken me with you."

"I didn't feel worthy of raising you. I felt . . ."

"So you left me. Running off without an explanation. Didn't it occur to you that Dad would try to ruin me like he did you?"

"It wasn't Ben who destroyed me. Don't get me wrong; he was no angel. But the destroying part came long before that. I married your father when I was just sixteen, a little girl, a very unhappy little girl. How unhappy I'm only now beginning to discover."

Her eyes were appealing to James, but he turned away from them. "Like you said, it doesn't make a difference."

"Yes." Dylan lit a cigarette nervously. "I'm sorry, James. If it's any help."

"None at all."

Dylan sighed. "Not much in the end, is it, after twenty years? But that's all there is. I *am* sorry. That you must believe."

Dylan sat up in her chair; she seemed to be gathering energy. "Well, there's your apology. I suppose that's what you came for."

"I didn't come for that."

"Then why?"

James didn't answer, and after a while Dylan began looking around the room. Her eyes finally came to rest on one of the brutal wood statues and stayed there, as if gaining strength from it. Then everything in her hardened, and she said, "Oh, of course, now I understand. Since Ben's accident you and Dyer have been running the company. I don't own much stock, just a measly one and a half percent. But it's nice to know it's in the bag. Well, you can relax. Dyer called me weeks ago, and I assured him that the less I heard about Midwestern Steel the better. So you can get on a plane and go back to Ohio. You've got nothing to worry about."

"That isn't the reason I came."

"Then what *is* the reason?" Dylan stubbed out her cigarette and stood, looking around the room frantically. But there was nowhere for her to go. James was everywhere.

"I don't know."

"But you do want something from me?"

James shook his head. "I don't know what I want." His whole body seemed to shrink into itself.

Dylan watched him sadly. It took a while for her to speak. "Life is very difficult for you, isn't it?"

James smiled ruefully. "The thing is it seems so damn easy for other people."

Dylan nodded. She'd thought that many times. "Like Ben?"

"Yeah, him and Dyer and even Grandma."

Dylan sank into her chair, her body relaxing. "I think in many ways life was easier for Elizabeth. Which is strange because she's the only one who had to suffer real hardships. But maybe that's the point. I've often wondered if life wasn't too easy for me. Maybe that's why I found it so difficult. Still, your grandmother is an amazing woman."

James agreed. "Yeah, she's worth more than any of us."

"You can say that again," Dylan answered, instinctively beginning an old childhood game the two of them had played.

James smiled. "Worth more than any of us," he repeated.

The two of them were quiet for a while, caught in the memory, and though neither of them looked at the other, the first tentative link had been established.

Finally Dylan asked. "How are they all?"

"The family? Oh, they're the same, only more so. Pauline's a moral cripple. Too much liquor, too many drugs. And, of course, men, mostly of the muscular variety. She's just about run through the entire steelworkers union. I think she's going for the world record. She spends only three months a year in Midland. The rest of the time she travels. But I have no idea where. Just anywhere, I guess."

"So sad. And what about little cousin Dyer?"

"Big cousin now. Like a bull, but with none of the charm. Actually he's more like a machine, a clever able machine, but a machine nonetheless."

Dylan laughed. "How very unpleasant! Well, it's no real surprise. He was a godawful child. Remember how he used to throw tantrums when he didn't get what he wanted?"

"He still does in his own way."

Dylan giggled. "Oh, James, you are cruel! And your Aunt Angela? How is she?"

"Ah, dear Aunt Angela. Well, she wears only dark colors, mostly black. In fact, she looks just like a crow. A gaunt hungry one. Very dangerous too. Did you know that crows sometimes pluck out the eyes of little children? It's the glittering they're attracted to."

"Oh, come on. Stop." Dylan was sitting cross-legged, her head thrown back with laughter.

"Yes, good old Aunt Angela. She disapproves of everything and everyone. Except, of course, Dyer, who's a chip off the old block, and she approves of him greatly."

"Nothing changes, does it? I don't know why I thought it would." She grew thoughtful. "And Tom. How's he?"

"Very sad. He misses Ben dreadfully."

"Yes. He must. I'll never forget Tom. He was a good man."

"He still is."

The conversation had wound down, the smiles were slowly fading from their faces, and they both sat locked in their own memories.

"I'm avoiding asking about your father," Dylan resumed softly.

"There's not much to tell. He's in Wales now. Grandmother sent him there."

"I know. Tom wrote to me. He's been writing to me all these years, though I don't suppose he told anyone that. Funny, it's probably the only secret he ever kept from Ben."

Again the silence built, long, awkward, heavy with questions.

It was James who broke it. "What's Beth like?"

Dylan looked away; her voice was very defensive. "What you mean is, is there anything between us? Ben would have told you there was. It was what he wanted to believe."

"I asked what she's like."

Dylan searched his face to see if this was true, but she could not tell. Finally she said softly, "I suppose you could say she's intelligent, witty, charming, you know. . . . But that doesn't answer your question, does it? You see, it just isn't that simple. She's a friend; she's been very nice to me. In many ways she saved my life, and yes, I love her for it. But that still isn't quite what you're asking."

She sighed and for a moment looked frantic. Then softly she continued. "Oh, it's all so complicated! No, James, it's not like that between us. It's as if that part of me doesn't exist anymore."

"Did it ever?"

Dylan lit up another cigarette with shaking fingers and silently watched the smoke and the question drift into the air.

Finally James said, "I think I saw Beth as I was coming into the building."

"Possibly. She wanted us to have time alone. I guess she didn't want to embarrass me."

"But you would have preferred that she stay?"

"When you called from the airport I was shocked, then scared. I guess I still am."

"What are you scared of?"

"I don't know what you want. I doubt that I can give it to you."

James thought about this. "I guess I wanted to understand you. No, I suppose it was more that I wanted you to understand me."

James turned away from Dylan, and in those few seconds he seemed to become frail. "I'm afraid I haven't turned out very well," he said.

"No thanks to me, I expect."

James didn't answer. He sat silently staring at the floor. He looked almost sick with self-hate and also with fear. Dylan watched him and understood. She was well acquainted with fear, it never being all that far away, just around the corner, just over the road, living next door, rattling loudly in the night and on long Sunday mornings.

"You've got nothing to be afraid of," she told him. "You have everything in the world. You're young. You're about to inherit a multimillion-dollar business that you don't even have to be very good at running because you have a cousin who is."

James hesitated. "There are things you don't know about me."

Dylan nodded almost before she understood. But she supposed she'd suspected it all along. Not that there was anything effeminate about James; it was more a difference in point of view. The guilt at that moment seemed unbearable, and she was glad that Tom had not written her about it. She doubted she could have lived with the responsibility for that. But perhaps she could have. People were a lot stronger sometimes than they wished to be.

She tried for a smile. "It's a different world today. It's not all that unusual anymore. You needn't be frightened of that."

"But I am frightened. I'm scared of everything and everyone. I'm scared of Dad."

"Of all the times not to be scared of Ben, now is the time. He's dying, James. In a month or two you'll receive a telegram and your father will just be a memory, a bronzed bust in the foyer of his blessed Midwestern Steel. Perhaps they'll name a school after him or a wing in a hospital. And then he will be totally forgotten forever."

James was turned away from Dylan, and though she couldn't see his face, she could tell that he was crying. It startled Dylan. She was unused to emotions in men, except for the more violent ones, but seeing James crumpled in his chair stirred in her memories of years ago, the little boy who had trusted and loved her so much, the boy she'd left, not without tears, not without eternal damnation, but left nonetheless, to fend for himself in a family of cannibals.

Dylan got up and stood in the middle of the room, wanting to walk to James and hold him, but unsure whether she had the right to touch her son, unsure whether she even had the right to be present for his tears.

Finally she walked to James and touched him on the shoulder tentatively. James looked up; his tear-stained face was scarred with lines of pain, his eyes grief-stricken.

There was no more thinking for Dylan, only instincts. She was his mother. She reached down and embraced him, taking him in her arms as she had when he was a little boy.

James could feel himself falling into his mother's arms, sinking into her body, and the tears came stronger, gripping him with their power until he was no longer James but only the fear and the grief and Dylan rocking him softly in her arms. His eyes closed and he saw only darkness and felt his mother's arms.

"Mommy," he said softly. "Mommy. Oh, God, Mommy."

Dylan couldn't sleep. She was aware of the warm body of Beth next to her and her hushed breathing, but she didn't feel the usual reassurance, the soft animal comfort of the night. Her mind was on James.

James had gotten up abruptly and left. Dylan had run after him to the door, but he'd pretended not to hear her and had taken the elevator down. Her voice had echoed in her own ears.

After that Dylan had been terribly shaken. She'd waited anxiously for Beth to return, desperately frightened to be alone, wanting to talk to her and tell her everything. But when Beth had returned, Dylan had said nothing, and Beth hadn't asked. They had sat at the kitchen table, drinking decaffeinated coffee, talking about the movie Beth had seen, anything to avoid the only subject they were thinking of. And Dylan had realized she wanted to be alone.

But once Beth had gone to bed, Dylan had felt the loneliness crowding in again, and she'd prowled the apartment nervously, unable to concentrate on anything, unable to sit still even for a minute. She'd smoked cigarette after cigarette, and in her head she'd tried to understand why James had come. But always the answer was unclear. She hardly knew James, only the boy he had been. Any clues were locked into a past she'd spent twenty years trying to forget.

Eventually Dylan had gone to bed, but she hadn't been able to sleep. In the darkness and the warmth, her mind had rebelled, and the past so long repressed had begun to reappear before her with startling clarity. She turned in bed, shifting her pillow, staring open-eyed at the shadows on the ceiling. But she could not dislodge the past. James had brought it with him when he came, and now even though he'd left, it sat heavy and demanding in the center of her mind.

She remembered the first time she'd met Ben. She'd been just fourteen, and he had been asked to dinner at her parents' house. Ben had been twenty-five then and virtually running the Healey Mills. Yet her father had treated him as an inferior, more, a strange new species of animal. Leon Wittiker had called Ben "the savage" and had treated him like a savage, but also with the curious kind of respect you would show a cannibal who was eyeing you for the pot. Which had been exactly what Ben had been doing.

BOOK FOUR

THE MIDDLE YEARS
Ohio, 1946

TWENTY-TWO

"So tell me, Mr. Savage." Leon Wittiker paused to eat a forkful of his dinner. He chewed slowly, delicately, and he didn't continue speaking until he was finished. "They say there will be a strike at the Healey Mills soon."

"We hope not," Ben answered. He was hunched over his food, cutting into the chicken Kiev. He drew back in surprise as juice spilled out.

Leon smirked and locked eyes with his wife, Martha. Though there was only the hint of a muscle moving in his face, she knew he was winking at her.

Martha smiled graciously and turned to Ben. "It's quite all right, Mr. Savage. That's chicken Kiev. It's supposed to be like that."

Then she turned away quickly, trying to coax her daughter, Dylan, to eat, deliberately avoiding her husband's gaze to keep from laughing. Still, her shoulders were shaking under her ice-blue crepe dress and there was a flush on her cheeks.

Leon turned back to Ben and resumed the conversation. "We all hope there won't be a strike at the Healey Mills. Especially after our talk today. The Wittiker Mines and the Healey Mills might have a very pleasant future together. After all, you need coal, and we need to sell it. We wouldn't want anything like a strike to interfere, would we?" He beamed.

Ben stabbed another piece of chicken. He could feel Leon's condescending gaze on him, and he hated him for it. It made him eat even more greedily, chewing loudly and rapidly in response. "There hasn't been a strike at the mill in nine years." He grunted. "We don't expect one now."

"Still, there *is* an atmosphere," Leon observed. "If you ask me, the mistake was allowing the union in the first place." His eyes sought out his wife's.

Martha agreed. "A very grave mistake indeed."

"I'm an old union man," Ben answered gruffly. "I can see their point."

"Yes, of course. But you're a practical man too. You're on the other side now. Rumor has it you're just about running the Healey Mills single-handed, and very successfully, I might add. I doubt that you'd be getting such good results if you were mollycoddling your workers."

"Unhappy men don't produce."

"Neither do completely happy ones. Keep a man a bit hungry, I always say."

Ben frowned. "My father died of black lung. He was not a happy worker, and we were more than a bit hungry."

Martha laced her fingers and smiled graciously. "But you prove the point, Mr. Savage. Look at you now."

Ben drank off his wine, but he hated the taste of it; he hated everything at the table. "There's no right to punish the body of a man to make a toaster or a car. Not one man'll be harmed because of the Healey Mills if I can help it."

Leon smiled. "Well, well, Martha. It looks like we have one of those dreaded socialists at our table."

Ben saw Martha shoot a warning look at her husband, and he flushed with anger. He resented Martha's attempt to save him even more than Leon's condescending smile. Only the little girl, Dylan, was watching him with anything resembling humanity. She sat, silent, eyes downcast, as if she were encased in glass. Her parents neither looked at her nor said more than a few words, and she seemed as much an intruder in her own house as Ben did.

Dylan looked up and discovered Ben's eyes on her. Quickly she turned away, blushing.

"I don't know about this socialist bit," Ben replied. His eyes remained on Dylan a moment longer. "I'm not an educated man and I don't understand politics. That's Evan's department, and he's welcome to it. Still, if you're saying that it makes you a socialist to value a man who puts bread on your table, then I guess that's what I am."

Martha raised her eyebrows. "Does that mean you're planning on giving in to the union?"

"I plan on negotiating with them. I'm sure in the end we'll reach what Evan calls a mutually unsatisfactory agreement."

Ben glanced up, and this time he caught Dylan's eyes on him, but the minute she saw him looking at her, she turned away. Blood rushed to her face; her cheeks looked as if they'd been smacked, and Ben thought he'd never seen anything so beautiful. He supposed it was her shy youth that fascinated him. It was like watching an animal newly born. He looked over at Leon and Martha, but neither of them had noticed what had passed. Their eyes were locked together, each finding in the other a reflection of himself.

Leon resumed. "Surely old man Healey doesn't feel that way. I'll never forget his handling of the Memorial Day strike. What was it he used to say?"

Martha reminded him. "He'd rather sell apples on the street than allow the union."

"Oh, yes, that's right. He didn't even turn up at the mill that day."

"I remember. I was there." Ben allowed a silence to explain which side of the police lines he'd been on. "Still," he continued, "everything changes."

"Indeed," Leon answered blandly. "But tell me, the word around is that old man Healey has just about given over all control to you, and he only comes in to pick up his paycheck."

"The word around is wrong. We all have our areas of responsibility. My brother, Evan, is in charge of production. Tom is Captain . . ."

"And you, Mr. Savage?" Martha asked pointedly.

"As you know, I run the business end. With Nicholas Healey's help, of course." He smirked slyly at Leon.

"Oh, yes, certainly," Leon agreed. He returned Ben's smile, but it felt tight on his lips, and there was a muscle jumping at the corner of his mouth. There was something about Ben Savage he didn't trust. For a moment he was tempted to break off negotiations, but always present was the knowledge of how much he needed the money; he needed Ben's money very badly.

Leon made room for the chocolate mousse the maid was placing before him. "Well, whatever the setup at the Healey Mills, a strike now would be very inconvenient."

"For us all."

"Let's not rush ahead of ourselves. I haven't accepted your offer as yet. There are details we still have to discuss."

Ben's eyes were very cold. "You'll accept. I'm offering to buy your coal for a very good price."

Leon's eyes rushed to Martha's, but this time under the condescension there was the beginning of fear, and he worried Martha had noticed it.

Leon answered slowly. "That remains to be seen. The Wittiker Mines are not greedy."

Ben turned to his chocolate mousse and began to eat. It was foamy and insubstantial, and just when you thought you could taste it, it was gone. Martha was delicately spooning small portions into her mouth. Under the hazy candlelight, she looked very beautiful, very genteel, and just about as satisfying as the mousse.

Once again Ben looked at Dylan. She was sitting quietly, as if under a drape, and though she didn't say a word, he could feel there was nothing insubstantial about her. He forced himself to turn away. Dylan was only a little girl. Her wrists were still rounded, her movements awkward, as if her hands were too large, like a young puppy. Her school uniform hung unbecomingly from her shoulders. Probably it was bought large for her to grow into. Yet his eyes returned; he didn't seem to be able to keep them away for long.

Dylan glanced up, and their eyes met. She startled, as if she were terrified, but underneath there was a hint of the woman not yet born who seemed to understand his gaze and return it. She looked away quickly and began playing with her mousse.

"You know, Mr. Savage," Leon intoned, "greed will be the downfall of America. We are a very greedy country."

"Some call it vitality."

"There's a fine line. But I'm afraid we're well on our way to stepping over it."

Ben looked around the dining room, taking in the crystal chandeliers, the highly polished woods and shiny silks. It was clear from his expression what he meant.

Leon laughed, but it was a tight laugh, full of anger. "Yes, well, we might just as well enjoy it before everything goes under. No use holding back from the table just because we know the dinner will soon be taken away."

"I'm a simple man, and I don't think much about the world," Ben rumbled. "But if I did, it wouldn't be like that."

"Though perhaps not as simple as you make out," Leon observed.

Ben's eyes glittered playfully. "Perhaps."

Leon leaned to Ben. "You know, Mr. Savage, you interest me greatly." He poured himself a glass of port though it was becoming clear from his voice he'd had enough to drink some time ago. "I sit here and wonder exactly what your game is."

"I don't play games. They're a waste of time."

"But if you did, I suspect you'd be very good at them."

Ben grinned. "Now who's playing games? You asked me to dinner. I accepted. I'm here because I want to buy coal from you. Pure and simple."

"I'm not so sure of that. You're offering a very good price. Perhaps too good a price."

"Well, can you beat that? This is the first time I've ever been told I'm offering too much. So you want to sell me your coal for less?"

"That, my friend, I most certainly did not say." Leon laughed but his eyes were hard and wary. "I'm just speculating as to why."

"Business is good. I need a great deal of coal."

It was Martha who answered. "There is no shortage of coal in America."

"I happen to like your husband's coal."

Leon was staring at Ben. "Mmm, I'm sure you do."

Martha made a move to get up from the table, but neither of the men seemed to notice, and quickly she sat back down and waited, her eyes far away, her thoughts well hidden.

Ben was watching Leon. "So am I supposed to take it that you won't sell coal to me?"

Leon spoke hesitatingly. "No. Not at all. I'd be delighted to take any extra cash off your hands."

"Good. That's real good," Ben boomed heartily. "You won't regret it."

Ben stood. He was hulking over the table, the remains of dinner scattered below him, and his eyes glittered hungrily.

Leon rose and moved to the door. "Yes, I'm sure I won't," he answered.

But as he opened the door, he suspected that he might come to regret it indeed; he might regret it very much.

Less than an hour later, Ben was walking rapidly through the night-dimmed streets, passing the large suburban houses with their green lawns and circular driveways. All up and down the street, windows were open to the hot night, and snatches of conversations and radio broadcasts could be heard. Dishes clattered as they were carried from the dining room to the kitchen. There was the rush of water being turned on, and the soft sounds of a maid singing. In one of the larger houses an argument was just beginning, voices only slightly raised but full of a tension that would soon explode. Farther along there was the sound of a young girl crying.

Ben picked up his pace. His body was tight and aching, and he was very angry. Sometimes when he felt like this he wondered if he wouldn't have been happier had he remained a bakebrain with its rough sweaty honesty, rather than try to fight it out with hothouse plants like Leon Wittiker. Though he knew he was good at business, he wasn't sure it was so good for him. It went against the grain, too many things unsaid, too much to be swallowed, and the revenge, though it always came, was often too late for release. The worst part was he suspected it was changing him, making him hard and brittle, making him no better than the people he hated. And yet he knew he could not give it up and return to his former life. Ben had never been able to give anything up; he only knew how to add.

He brushed away the thought and reviewed the evening in his mind. Everything had gone as planned. Leon Wittiker had taken the bait. Ben wondered what Leon was telling himself as he moved about his bedroom getting ready for bed. He suspected he was making up lies, probably only half-believed, but held to nonetheless in an attempt to postpone the inevitable awakening. When the blow came it might be swift and sharp, but it could not be wholly unexpected. Leon's business had been running at a loss for years, victim of its owner's arrogant extravagance and almost uncanny lack of business sense. Probably with each bad report he felt the urge to soothe himself by bleeding the company of even more of its capital, just as he bled the hills of its treasure of anthracite.

Still, when the blow came, Leon would undoubtedly play the injured party, symbol of a world gone mad, where laborers tore down the foundations of civilization and climbed to its pinnacle by their cracked and dirty fingernails.

Not that it was too late for Leon to recoup his losses. Basically there was nothing wrong with his coalfields. If he cut expenses and used the freed capital to modernize, he could emerge from his bad fortune lean and sleek and ready to undercut his competitors. A smart man would do this. Ben would have.

Presumably this was exactly why Leon was accepting Ben's inflated offer. But Ben knew that quickly Leon's resolve to economize would weaken. Without his even noticing it, his old life would return. There would be the grand parties, the new cars, the long sunny vacations. Everything would be just as it had been. Only Leon

Family Passions

would be growing more dependent on Ben's money to keep him afloat.

Then one day Ben would stop buying. It wouldn't take long for Leon to realize that everything was about to come crashing down around him, and it would be then that Ben would offer to buy him out. Leon would have no choice but to accept.

Ben stopped walking. The streets had suddenly become narrower, the houses smaller, older. Just ahead was the rambling Victorian relic that Ben had bought for himself and Elizabeth. It straddled the two neighborhoods, as they themselves did.

Ben paused, looking at the crooked outline of his roof against the night sky, then he turned around and walked in the opposite direction. He didn't want to go home just yet. Angry thoughts were still revolving in his mind, and also there was something else to think about, something far more complicated and far less clear.

Ever since dinner Dylan's face had been coming back to him in flashes, her childish mouth, her large blue frightened eyes. He tried to shake the image loose, but it kept returning to him, and with it, a crazy thought. He threw the idea off, striding it out on the darkened pavement, but it didn't take long to return. He could wait for her, he thought. He was still very young. In a few years the difference in age wouldn't matter so much. He could wait.

Ben was well aware that this sudden turn to romanticism was more a result of his feelings about Evan and Angela than the little shy girl who had not said a word the whole evening.

Angela was eight months' pregnant, and he'd never seen such a change in a person. All the sharp edges were gone; she was round and full; everything about her had softened; every movement was kind. She would sit for hours, contentedly watching her growing belly. For the first time she seemed happy, and there was a peacefulness in their house that disturbed and angered Ben. For he felt he'd been robbed.

After visiting them he would return to his room in his mother's house, and everything would seem empty and barren. He had never felt loneliness before, and it came as a sharp agony that he did not know how to ease. It wasn't that he wanted Angela, though there were moments when he almost convinced himself that he did. He wanted what she was giving Evan. It was his seed that had made the two of them happy, his child whom he never could claim, and he cursed himself for ever having gone along with Angela. He hated her sweet contentment. He hated how proud Evan was of himself.

He knew how wrong he was, and still the feeling of envy remained. And he felt robbed.

Once again Dylan's face flashed through his mind, and this time it stayed there, softly, sweetly, as if she were waiting.

As Ben strode his feelings out on the pavement, Dylan was getting undressed for bed. Ever since dinner she'd been feeling edgy and unsettled. Quickly she threw her flannel nightgown over her head, closed the window against the night sounds, and got into bed. She pulled the blanket up to her ears. But even under the covers she could hear her parents next door, the closing of doors, the footsteps, the murmurs of conversation, and it multiplied her loneliness, making her feel separate from life.

Dylan had always felt isolated from the world. While other children were reacting to life, seeing it only from their point of view, Dylan was well aware that a world existed outside of her sphere. She could see it from the windows of cars; she could hear it at night as she lay in bed waiting to fall asleep. Her parents inhabited that real world; so did her friends at school. It was only she who was excluded from it.

Dylan heard her parents' bedroom door close, and then there was silence. She rolled over and looked out the window at the moon. It seemed very far away, a cool face staring down on the darkened houses, and she wondered if it could see into her room as it passed by nightly.

She rolled back, burying her head in the pillow, trying to sleep, but she still felt on edge, and she knew it was connected to the man who had stared at her during dinner. It was as if he understood something about her that she hadn't yet discovered but could only imagine in the darkness of night. She lay awake for a long while, disturbed by half-formed thoughts and long ago memories. She tried to block them out, but she couldn't. And somewhere around midnight, the memory she was frightened of returned, the one connected with the man at dinner. And though she tried to hide under the covers, it stayed with her.

She remembered it had been late summer, when the days were hot and sultry but the nights closed in quickly with a dark chill. Dylan had only been seven years old. School had been out; camp had been over, and as usual her mother, who was always offending the household staff and having to do without, had found herself suddenly saddled with Dylan during the day. It'd been a familiar pattern. The maid would quit, then Martha, gulping her sobs, would rush upstairs and call all the employment agencies. Dylan would hear her voice, high-pitched and furious, then soothing and conciliatory, but each time she'd been told it would take several days to get a replacement. Eventually her mother would descend the staircase and tell Dylan to put on her best clothes, then the two of them would drive off in Martha's Cadillac to various houses for the visits that occupied her days. During these visits, Dylan's presence would be tolerated, as long as she sat quietly. Sometimes she'd been given lemonade and cookies, always she'd been completely ignored, and she'd stare out of the living-room windows, half-listening to the boring litany of names and places the women discussed.

But that day things had been different. That day she hadn't been made to dress up, and late that afternoon when her mother had driven her to a part of town she hadn't known, she'd been very kind to her. They had stopped at a bakery, and Martha had bought four buttercream cakes, Dylan's favorites. And when they'd pulled up in front of a dismal building, she'd even joked with Dylan about how out of place their big car must seem in the neighborhood. And she had laughed. Dylan remembered distinctly that her mother had laughed. Then still smiling, she had led Dylan up a dark winding staircase that smelled of babies and stewed cabbage and taken her to an unoccupied apartment.

It had only been one room, sparsely furnished, a small dirty kitchen merely indicated along one wall. Even today Dylan could see it in her mind, and she could smell the damp musty odor of disuse mixing with the odors of life just outside the door. But at the time, the small dingy apartment had seemed an adventure, and she had been surprised, pleased, and even excited by it.

Martha had left immediately, setting down the box of cakes without even warning her not to spoil her dinner, merely asking her to sit quietly while she had a chat with a friend down the hall.

It had been wonderful. Dylan had eaten the cakes one after the other, until she was in a stupor of sweetness and her belly pressed against the waistband of her skirt. Then she'd sat, licking her fingers and inspecting the box for any remnants of icing. Growing bored, she had gone to the window and pulled back the frayed curtains.

The streets below had been fascinating to her. Besides cars there'd been carts and horses, with a man selling fruits and vegetables. There'd even been a hurdy-gurdy. Young children had been running through the streets, laughing and playing, and women had been returning from shopping, carrying large bags crammed with food. Dylan had never seen anything like it in her life. The streets outside her home were quiet and empty, but these were full of life and color.

Then slowly she'd become aware that several of the women were calling their children in. The streets were becoming empty; the sunlight was fading and darkness beginning to creep in.

Dylan had walked to the door hesitantly. She'd been able to hear voices coming from other apartments, the clatter of pots and pans in preparation for dinner. As dark shadows had fallen all around her, it had become chilly. She'd been able to see lights going on in the building across the way and, in the little steamy windows, women setting their tables.

Dylan had kept close to the door, unsure what to do. She'd begun getting cold and frightened. The apartment, which earlier had seemed so exciting, had become full of shadows. But she hadn't dared open the door either, as the fear of displeasing her mother had been even greater than the fear of the quickly darkening room.

Time had passed; how much she hadn't known. Everything had seemed to be losing its shape and form; everything had seemed so alien. The room had grown darker and colder; the sounds from the other apartments had quieted, and she'd felt as if the world had died while she'd sat eating her cakes and looking out the window. She'd felt all alone.

Suddenly it had occurred to her that something might have happened to her mother; perhaps she was hurt or had gone away forever. Dylan's heart had clenched. The cold and the darkness had become unbearable, and she'd begun to cry. Finally she'd been able to stand it no longer, and she'd turned the doorknob and opened the door, slowly creeping into the hall.

It'd been less dark in the hallway, but it had been very long, and there'd seemed to be so many doors. She'd had no idea which one her mother was behind or if she was there at all. Shivering, she'd stood in the hallway, listening to the unfamiliar sounds, smelling the dark pungent odors, and she'd wanted to cry out, but she hadn't been able to make a sound.

Then all at once she'd heard her mother's voice coming from

farther down the hall. With relief she'd rushed to the door, wrenched the handle, and pulled it open.

At first Dylan hadn't realized what she was seeing, and when her mother had screamed, she'd thought her worst fears had been confirmed. She'd rushed forward blindly. But then her mother's screams had become words. "Get out, damn you!" she'd yelled. "Get out!"

It'd been at that moment Dylan had seen the man, thickset, covered with black hair. It'd been perhaps the only impression she'd had of him, but it was one she'd never forgotten.

Then suddenly she'd been turning, running from the room and back down the hall. Her heart had been beating crazily, her head had been pounding. When she'd reached the end of the hallway, she'd stopped, breathless, looking from the dark winding staircase to the long line of doors. She'd stood there, breath torturing her chest, cold penetrating her clothes, chilling her body, and she'd realized with dread that she had nowhere to go. Finally she'd walked back to the empty apartment and sat in the darkness on the rickety bed.

A few minutes later her mother had appeared in the doorway, her tall elegant frame fully clothed, her hair combed, cool and reserved, as if nothing had happened.

The incident had never been spoken of again, never even alluded to, and Dylan had been treated exactly as before. But she'd been able to feel that everything had changed.

Even then, though she had not understood what she'd seen, it had seemed to her a stain on the family, a hidden horror that the world could guess at a glance. And she too shared in that shame, for she had her own part in it. And the world could see that too.

She felt sure the man at dinner had discovered it as he stared at her from across the table. And as she lay in bed, watching the white distant moon cross the sky, she began to realize that she would see this man again, that he was lying in wait for her.

TWENTY-THREE

Nicholas Healey switched on his office lights, his small nutlike face pinched with anger. He placed a stack of files on his desk, then carefully hung his coat on a hanger and sharpened several pencils. Only after he had washed his hands did he sit down at his desk.

It was close to midnight, but Nicholas didn't feel tired. He was growing used to working late. He'd been coming in at the same hour for close to six months now, stealing in like a thief, bribing one of the guards to keep his secret. It seemed impossible that things had come to this. It was his mill, his name was over the gates, his name on the stationery, and yet there he was, sneaking in like an intruder.

He opened the top file and began reading through the correspondence. His fingers fidgeted with the cardboard folder, his tongue worked nervously at his teeth. A moment later he thought he'd found something. A little cry escaped his thin lips, and he sat up, muttering excitedly to himself. He reread the letter carefully. The figures seemed cockeyed to him, and he added them rapidly in his head. It was then he remembered Ben's telling him that because of a stockholder problem two separate letters, each with different figures, had been sent. He found the real letter just below. Nicholas's small anxious eyes ran down the set of figures. But there was nothing wrong with them.

He found this disappointing. Increasingly suspicion was taking over his life. Every night he came into his office, poring over the books, searching them for signs of collusion, any indiscretion that might tell him of a plot against him. He had found none so far, but rather than reassuring him, it had only fed his suspicion, doubling it until it had become an obsession. For he was quite sure that something was going on, and the fact that he could not find it only meant it was even more clever than he'd thought.

Nicholas lifted his spectacles and rubbed his eyes. They felt hot and burning and very tired. He knew it was age; the doctor had told him as much the last time he went there complaining of headaches. "Slow up," the doctor had said. "Go to Florida. Take a vacation. Better yet, retire."

"They can send my casket to Florida," Nicholas muttered to himself.

But he knew in fact his failing eyesight was a sign of age. He was getting old; he could feel it, not just in his body, but somewhere else. It wasn't exactly his mind, that was still sound. He rapped the desk superstitiously. It was those flashes of memory, those sharp disturbing jarrings that, without the least provocation, sent him hurtling back to some inconsequential moment in his youth. He could be walking along the street or straining in the bathroom, and suddenly he'd be ten years old, playing his cello. Whole pieces he'd known during that year would come back to him. He could virtually hear every note of the music; he could almost read them off the sheet.

Increasingly there were vivid flashes of his parents. He hadn't thought much about them since they'd died. In fact, even when they were alive, he hadn't thought much about them, nor they about him. But now he found himself remembering a look or a gesture, the sound of their voices, and the memories were so powerful and real that he'd start shaking. Looking at them again, the creases of anxiety pulling at his father's face, his mother's tired empty eyes, he could imagine them as people, contemporaries; he could see them as himself. All those years, he'd never understood his parents, but now he began to. They'd spent their lives building the Healey Mills. They'd never had a youth; everything had been for the future, and slowly from disuse they had dried up inside. But they'd thought they were doing the right thing, and from the vantage point of age, Nicholas believed they had.

But the most insistent flashes were of his late wife, Vanessa. It was only parts of her he remembered, a brief impression of voice, the illumination of a smile, echoes of her body. Yet these fragments stunned him more than memories, pounding relentlessly on his mind, casting shadows that were chill with remembered warmth.

He felt tears come to his eyes, and he shook his head to rid his mind of the image. It did no good thinking about people from the past or even the present. In his office were no pictures of Vanessa or his daughter, no bronzed baby booties or grinning likenesses of his grandson, Dyer. Nicholas laughed out loud. What the hell kind of name was Dyer? Welsh probably. Stupid name. And Dyer was an ugly slug of a kid. No, he didn't care about them. How could he?

He supposed it could be said that it was some deficiency in him, but there was nothing he could do about that.

Nicholas picked up the next letter in the file. It was full of malarkey about a pleasant lunch and hope we can do more business in the future, et cetera. Ben's usual horse manure. There was nothing in it to arouse his suspicion. Still he continued reading. One never knew what was buried within.

An hour later his door opened. Nicholas Healey's head jerked up, his eyes stunned and guilty.

Ben filled the doorway. "Kind of late to be working, isn't it?" Ben stood where he was, just watching Nicholas.

Nicholas didn't answer. He tried to stop the feeling that he'd been caught. He kept telling himself that it was his company; the files were his files.

Finally he spoke. "I didn't realize you were still in the building."

"Otherwise you would have dropped in for a chat?" Ben laughed and walked into the office. He stopped at Nicholas's desk. "Find anything?" he asked.

Nicholas's thin little face drew into a frown of confusion. "I don't know what you're talking about."

"I'm sure. Well, you won't find jack shit either. The Healey Mills isn't doing anything underhanded. At least nothing you don't know about."

"I'm merely going over the files. It's a perfectly natural thing to do."

"At one in the morning?"

"I was very busy during the day, so I thought I'd drop in—"

"The past six months?" Ben grinned. "Oh, forget it. It doesn't matter. Go over the files. Take them home if you like." He paused, then said, "Listen. Do you mind if I take a seat?"

"I was just about to leave." Nicholas closed the file.

Ben drew a chair up to the desk and sat opposite. "It'll only take a minute."

"Oh, all right. But make it snappy. I'm tired."

"You won't be tired for long." Ben sat forward in the chair; his big sturdy hands gripped Nicholas's desk. "Look, I thought I'd better come here and talk to you when no one else was around." Ben smiled.

Nicholas didn't move. He distrusted Ben's smile almost as much as he distrusted the man.

Ben watched Nicholas in silence for some time. "Evan came to my office today," he said finally.

"So what?" Nicholas hated when Ben played coy. "Evan is your brother and also your partner. It's hardly surprising that he came to your office."

Nicholas pressed his lips even more tightly together. He knew all too well that Ben was keeping him dangling, getting the point across that there was much more to say and that he wasn't going to like hearing it one bit.

Ben leaned farther forward; he looked as if he were about to pounce. "They want to force you out," he said slowly. "They want me to combine with them and press you into an inferior position when we issue stock."

Nicholas's little pinched face was full of derision. "They? Who are they?"

"Evan and Tom."

"I don't believe you."

"Fine." Ben shrugged and rose from his chair.

But Nicholas waved his hand. "Sit back down and tell me what they said. Not that I'll trust what you say for a moment."

Ben remained standing. "Look, it's late, and I've to get up very early tomorrow. Besides, you're not going to believe me anyway. So why don't we cut the discussion right here? I'll tell you one thing though. Don't come running to me when the shit hits the fan." He started toward the door. "Maybe they're right. Maybe you are getting too old."

"Is that what they said? Yes, that would be the approach. 'He's an old man. He doesn't do any of the work anymore, if he ever did.' " Nicholas slammed his bony fist on the desk. "Yes, yes, of course. I'd use it myself. But if they think they can get away with it . . ."

Ben had stopped at the door, watching him. "Think and *can*. That is, if I go along with them. Remember, the distribution of stock will be left up to the board of directors. But the vote doesn't have to be unanimous."

Nicholas's eyes became lost in the gray folds of skin around them. He was thinking. Then he looked up and fixed Ben with a suspicious glare. "So they asked you to go along with them, eh?"

"They need my vote."

Nicholas croaked. "The question is, why didn't you?"

"If I said out of loyalty to you, would you believe it?"

"Not on your life."

Ben walked back to the desk and slid into a chair. He was grinning. "Okay. I can use it to my advantage. Here's something that I'm sure you don't know. Evan and I have not been seeing eye to eye recently."

"Why?"

"The reasons aren't important. Just take it from me there are problems between us, okay? The truth is it's Tom who's been doing most of the work around here anyway. And you know that Tom doesn't want much of the action; he just wants to take it in salary. But even he's noticed a difference in Evan, though of course he's careful not to say anything. But that's neither here nor there. The point is I need a certain amount of power. And if it's up to Evan, I won't get it."

This seemed to please Nicholas. He sat back satisfied, like a wizened cat after a meal of kitchen scraps. "So you're looking to force Evan out, eh?"

"Eventually perhaps. For now I just want to gain a superior position. Evan's getting too frisky. He may be going after you now, but I'll be next. The truth is I need you as a buffer."

Nicholas shook his head in wonder. "Evan's after me? I didn't think he'd have the guts."

"Well, you haven't exactly been the kind father-in-law to him."

"What the hell does he want from me? One doesn't pick one's relations. Shame. But there it is."

"Personally I think it's Angela who's behind it."

"You do, eh? Angela? How interesting. How surprising. What difference should it make to her how much stock I receive?"

"I think she's bitter."

"Is she? About what?"

"Well, you know that better than I. I'm not one of those psychoanalysts."

"No. Indeed you are not." Nicholas paused. His face tightened; his eyes grew very hard and angry. "And let me tell you, if you were, you'd know that I'm not so stupid as to fall for a cock-and-bull story like you just cooked up for me. Evan's getting frisky? That wimp has the backbone of a two-day-old piece of parsley. He wouldn't have the balls to pull a stunt like that. And Angela? The idea is stunning in its stupidity."

Nicholas rose out of his chair very slowly; his face was white and his lips were trembling with fury. "Oh, no, my fine young friend.

Family Passions

It's you who's getting frisky. You who's trying to pull a fast one. Well, let me tell you, whatever it is that you're up to, you've outfiddled yourself. Oh, yes, you have. We'll see who combines against whom."

"You're making a mistake," Ben warned. "Why should I come to you if I were trying to force you out?"

Nicholas moved from behind his desk. "Get out!" he demanded. "Get the hell out of my office! I don't know what you're up to. But one thing I do know. You've picked the wrong person to have a fight with."

Ben left Nicholas's office without another word, slamming the door behind him. But the moment he was well clear, he broke into a grin. He could imagine Nicholas hunched over his files, muttering to himself, his mind revolving over the past few minutes like a top. Ben doubted it would take long for Nicholas to come up with the idea of going to Evan, telling him everything and asking for his help in forcing Ben out. It would, of course, be exactly the wrong thing to do. Ben was Evan's brother. He would never believe Nicholas over him, and finally the false loyalty Evan felt for his father-in-law would begin to dissolve; he would be willing to cut him loose. It was all going as planned.

"Your damn lying brother was in to see me last night," Nicholas said the moment Evan opened the door to him.

It was only six thirty in the morning, and Evan was still in his robe, the newspaper in his hand. From the kitchen Nicholas could hear the clinking of dishes as the maid set the table. He could smell the toast and coffee, and he could hear Angela trying to calm Dyer's crying.

Evan was surprised to see his father-in-law so early in the morning. In fact, he was surprised to see him at all; he doubted that he'd been to the house more than three times since they'd been married.

Nicholas walked past Evan to the living room. "I don't suppose there's any place in this damn house where we can have some privacy," he grumbled.

Angela appeared at the top of the stairs. Dyer was slung over one hip, snuffling the end of his tears; traces of his breakfast were all down his shirt.

Angela called down, "Who is it, Evan?" She looked concerned.

"Your father." Evan shot a look up to Angela.

"Is he okay?" She didn't wait for an answer. "I'll be right down."

Nicholas's voice came from the living room. "Stay where you are! I want to talk to your husband privately."

At the sound of Nicholas's voice, Dyer squirmed; his face grew bright red, and he began crying again. Angela hiked him up to her chest and made soothing sounds to him.

"Shut up, damn it!" Nicholas's voice overcame even Dyer's crying. "Damn kid is mentally retarded. I saw that from the moment he was born. I warned you to have him institutionalized right there and then. Do it. Before we all go crazy from the noise."

Evan shrugged to Angela, then walked slowly to the living room, like a man to the gas chamber. Though he'd become used to his father-in-law's tongue, it still had the power to hurt and anger him.

"Will you be staying to breakfast?" Evan asked as he sat on the couch next to Nicholas's hard-backed chair.

"This is not a social call," Nicholas announced ominously.

"No. I didn't think it was." There was a good-humored smile on Evan's face, the smile he used to keep their uneasy peace. "So what seems to be the problem?" he asked pleasantly.

"Your lousy conniving snake of a brother is the problem."

Evan laughed. "What's he up to, then?"

Nicholas's eyes were glittering. "He's trying to force me out of the business."

"That's ridiculous."

Nicholas smiled nastily. "He's trying to force you out too."

"Stop it, Dad. Ben has no intention of pushing anyone out. Everything is going well. We're running at a very high profit margin. Our expenses are low; our productivity is high. We probably have the most contented labor force in the whole steel industry. And we're thinking of expanding all over the place. So much so that we're about to go on the OTC market. As far as I can see, Ben is delighted. I'm delighted. And so should you be."

"Cut the crap," Nicholas snarled. "I'm trying to talk to you like a man. Your brother came to me late last night."

"Ben came to your house?"

"No. At the mill."

"You were at the mill late last night?"

"Damn right I was. I've been going in at night for over six

months now, looking over the books and the files. I knew something was up."

"Are you trying to tell me that Ben has been playing with the books?"

"No, damn you! Stop interrupting me. I knew something was up, but I wasn't sure what. The problem was I was looking in the wrong place. Playing with the books would require patience and cleverness. Neither of which your brother has. No, no, nothing as subtle as that. Not when he can get it in one stroke."

Nicholas leaned forward and grabbed Evan's wrist with his gnarled hand. His face looked as if it might crack into a thousand pieces. "The board of directors will meet next month to discuss the distribution of stock when we go onto the market. That's when he'll make his move."

Nicholas sat back with finality. There was a look of satisfaction under the anger, as if being proved right was more important than anything else.

Evan got up and began to pace the living room. He didn't want Nicholas to see the fury on his face. He had kept himself under control all these years for Angela's sake, but this time was different, and he feared he wouldn't be able to hold himself back. This time the man was attacking his brother.

"See here, Dad," he said firmly. "I don't know what gave you the impression that Ben is trying to push you out, but you have my personal reassurance—"

"Are you deaf?" Nicholas yelled. "Let me run through this slowly for you, because you seem to lack subtlety like your brother. Ben came to me last night and told me he was going to push me out."

Evan stopped pacing. "Ben told you that?"

"Not in so many words. What he did was far more devious. He accused you of cooking up a plot against me. He said that you had asked him to combine against me and squeeze me out."

Evan laughed. "Me?"

"Oh, yes, my dear son-in-law. You. Then he went on to tell me how you'd changed recently, and that you weren't doing any of the work, but that you were out to gain power. And how he was becoming sick of that, et cetera, et cetera. And the upshot was, in exchange for saving my ass, he wanted me to back him to get a superior position."

"Ben said all this?"

"Last night. In my office!"

"I don't believe it." Evan resumed his pacing.

"Well, you'd better believe it or you'll find yourself out on the street with the rest of the rubbish. And personally if my neck weren't in the noose, I wouldn't think twice about it. But I'm in this too. And I'm not about to let your thieving brother get away with it." He paused and glared at Evan irritably. "Will you stop your damn pacing?"

Evan did stop, but the anger was building inside of him, and he dared not look at Nicholas. He knew if he looked at him, he would explode.

"Now, the only way out I can see," Nicholas continued, his voice calmer, "is if I combine with you against him. Keeping it a secret, of course. Now it's up to you to go to Tom, have a talk with him. He'll listen to you. Meanwhile we both keep quiet, let Ben think he's okay. Then at the meeting, we spring it on him. Vote that bastard into oblivion!"

Evan was on the move again. This time he was moving toward Nicholas. He was shaking with fury, and his face was very pale. He looked almost sick with anger. "How dare you?" He was barely able to get the words out. "How dare you come here and accuse my brother of things that I know aren't true? And then to suggest that I combine with you? A man who has given nothing, no loyalty, no love, no comfort or understanding, only a wicked sharp tongue unlike any I've ever known. You expect me to combine against my own brother?" He laughed angrily. "And you call me a fool!"

Nicholas rasped, "You *are* a fool if you don't recognize the truth when you hear it."

Evan leaned toward Nicholas, and for a moment he looked as if he might hit him. He was struggling to regain control, nails biting into his fists, his teeth working at his lip. "I don't know why you're trying to pull this on me. Maybe you've gone crazy, maybe senile. Maybe you're just so evil you can't resist the opportunity to make trouble. But I don't want to hear it ever again, do you understand?"

Suddenly Nicholas's mind flashed on Vanessa's face, and in his ears he heard a passage of Bach. He could not get them out of his mind. Low voicelike sounds of his cello filled his head until he couldn't hear what Evan was saying. Vanessa was standing up, one hand extended to him, so he couldn't see Evan's mouth moving.

"Now, for Angela's sake I'm not ordering you out of this house. But if I were you I'd get up out of my chair and leave immediately!"

Nicholas was aware of Evan talking to him, but he couldn't understand what he was saying. All he could hear was the music, the clear rich sounds building in his ears, and the image of Vanessa reaching out to him.

Nicholas stood up, stunned and preoccupied. And without another word, he left the house.

"I knew it," Evan said to Ben as they drove together toward the mill. "When he told me that crazy story about you trying to force me out, I practically threw him out of the house. Well, in fact, I did throw him out. Christ, I enjoyed that. I really did. For years I've been taking that man's crap, just to keep the peace for Angela. Though God knows why she should care. He sure as hell doesn't give a damn about her. But when he started attacking *you* . . . How stupid does he think I am?"

Ben rolled down the window and put out his arm. He loved the feeling of the cool autumn breeze ruffling his shirt.

"It's not that," Ben answered after a while. "I didn't want to bring this up before because I thought we could keep it under control, but it's about time you and I did discuss him."

Evan sighed. "Yeah, I guess we'd better."

"He's getting old, Evan, too old. When was the last time he came up with a reasonable idea, even a suggestion? But fine, it's one thing that he's too old to work much. It's another that he's actually trying to ruin the company."

"I wouldn't go so far as to say he's ruining the company."

"What would you call it then? Causing dissension between us."

"Trying," Evan said. "He didn't succeed.'

"Okay. Fine. But what if one day he does succeed?"

"Don't be ridiculous. That could never happen."

"Maybe. But there's Tom too. Your father-in-law could slink up to him and start whispering in his ear."

"Tom wouldn't listen."

Ahead they could see the Healey Mills standing out against the hills, smoke rising from the stacks and lifting into the air in black clouds. Suddenly a thick red flame shot to the sky, then disappeared into black smoke again.

Ben slowed the car and pulled to the side of the road.

Evan glanced at his watch. "Hey, we're late enough as it is."

Ben stopped the car and turned off the engine. "I know. But now that it's out in the open, I think we'd better talk it through."

Evan nodded reluctantly. "All right. If we have to."

"Evan, he's going senile."

"I don't think so."

"Come on. It's me you're talking to. You know I'm right. All the signs are there: disorientation, paranoia."

"Since when have you become a god damn doctor?"

"Don't get angry with me."

"Well, Jesus, Ben, I'll give you Nicholas is an old flinthearted liar, but there's nothing wrong with his brain."

"Isn't there? Do you sneak in after everyone's gone home and go over the books?"

Evan was surprised. "How did you know that? I didn't tell you."

Ben hesitated, momentarily off guard. "I caught him at it last night. Didn't he tell you that?"

"He told me you came to the mill. But he said it was to talk to him about combining against me."

Ben laughed. "We had an argument, all right. But that was because I found him out. Maybe that's one of the reasons he's trying so hard to make trouble between us."

Evan was watching Ben cautiously. Though he knew that Nicholas had been lying to him about Ben's intent, he felt slightly uneasy about what exactly had happened. "Are you sure there isn't more to the story?" he asked.

Ben flared. "There you are. You see what I mean? Already the seeds of doubt are in your mind. Already Nicholas has made trouble between us."

Evan retrenched. "Oh, come on now, Ben. There's no trouble between us. I just asked a question."

"You doubted me. Admit it. For the first time you weren't sure about me." He put his hand on Evan's shoulder. "Look, I'm a bastard. I'll never deny that. But I swear to you on our father's grave, I wouldn't do anything to hurt you. Ever. I only have your good at heart. That you must believe."

Ben's eyes were going over Evan's face; there was almost a desperation in him, a child searching for any signs of loss of love.

Evan was touched. "Oh, Christ, Ben. I know that." He nodded to himself. "Yeah, okay. You're right. But I don't see what we can do about it. It's his mill, after all."

"There are ways of getting around that. I've become friends with Nicholas's trustees at the bank."

Evan recoiled. "Good God, Ben. You aren't considering having him declared incompetent, are you? I couldn't go along with that. I really couldn't."

"Hey, relax. Don't worry. It'll never have to go that far. Believe me. Now don't worry about it. Okay? Just let me take care of it."

Evan sighed deeply. "Yeah. Okay."

"You know that I'm right, don't you?" Ben started up the car and pulled back onto the road.

"Yes. I know that you're right," Evan answered.

But in fact, somewhere inside him, he wasn't sure. It wasn't that he thought Ben would try to harm him; he had total trust in his brother's loyalty, but he knew Ben's loyalty did not extend to his father-in-law and that he would indeed try to harm him if the opportunity arose.

Yet, though the doubt was there, Evan ignored it, partially out of devotion to Ben, partially for another reason, a reason he didn't even recognize, let alone admit to himself. He hated Nicholas Healey. He hated him for what he had done to Angela; he hated him for the way he treated them all. And it was this that pushed him on.

Not that he knew it as he watched Ben maneuvering through the gates of the mill, waving at several of the men. It was only later that he sensed what had happened and his place in it. And by that time it was too late. It had become another of the lies he'd told himself, another of the signs he'd ignored, until one day they all came back to ravage him, and he was too weak to fight them off.

The next week a whole battalion of lawyers and accountants rolled into the Healey Mills, representatives of the underwriters, representatives of the mills, all with enormous salaries and padded luncheon vouchers, all treading on each other's toes as they exercised "due diligence" in making up the certified financial statement necessary for the SEC.

Five months later, the Healey Mills, its name changed to Midwestern Steel to reflect a change in the corporate structure, went onto the

Over the Counter market with 200,000 shares being offered to the public at twelve and a half dollars per share. And by the next day the shares had risen to twelve and seven eighths. The following week Nicholas Healey, having resigned from the corporation, moved to the Sunaire Hotel in Miami Beach.

TWENTY-FOUR

Leon Wittiker was already seated at a table by the window of the Park Lane Hotel dining room when Ben arrived. It was the lunch hour, the busiest time at the Park Lane, and the pine-paneled room with its plush crimson curtains and faded tapestries was crowded with diners. Waiters dressed in red uniforms and turbans circulated around the room carrying flaming dishes to the tables of the elegant women taking a break from their shopping and the businessmen in pinstripe suits.

Ben was over ten minutes late, but Leon said nothing about it, and indeed stood to greet him, smiling, hand outstretched. They had been doing business for two years now, and Leon was no longer so careless about his disapproving looks, nor was Martha so coldly superior. In fact, it was with increasing respect that they opened their house every Wednesday evening to the savage. Still, Ben could see that Leon was angry at having been kept waiting, and he was agitated by it too.

Ben was delighted. He'd arranged to be delayed for exactly this reason. He always liked arriving at a difficult meeting just a bit late, not enough to give offense, just enough to put the other person out. A man who was angry but could say nothing was on edge. And Ben liked bargaining with a man who was on edge.

For the same reason Ben postponed discussing business for a long while. This too would put Leon off balance. He would be half-expecting that Ben was about to place a large order; he would be half-fearing that he was cutting back. So Ben spent a great deal of time over the menu, discussing the virtues of the trout versus the mutton chop, whether red wine at lunch gave one a headache, delaying, holding back, causing a tension to build. But there was another reason for Ben's lengthy pondering of the menu. He wanted to let Leon see how much he had changed from the burly man who had hunched over his chicken Kiev only two years before. Though Ben still viewed the social graces as a lion might regard a cage at the local zoo, he now knew how to use them when necessary. And he wanted to make sure Leon recognized it too.

Finally Leon began, trying to keep his tone casual. "Well, I doubt that you asked me to lunch just to discuss wine.".

Ben smiled pleasantly. "My goodness, Leon. I'm beginning to believe you've known me too long. You even can guess what I'm thinking."

"I wouldn't bet on that."

Ben ignored the irritation in Leon's voice. "How long is it that we go back now?"

Leon was watching Ben closely, aware that he was being drawn in, but unsure why. "Over two years."

"And we've done some good business together?"

"Splendid business." Leon relaxed. It did indeed sound like Ben was about to place a big order. He waited until the wine steward had filled their glasses, then raised his. "And here's to an even bigger and better future."

But Ben did not raise his glass. He stared soberly at Leon for a long while. "I'm afraid that's why I asked you to lunch. You see, I just got a call from the Caroline Mines. It seems they're willing to undercut you."

Leon flinched. "They always could have given you a better deal."

"I liked doing business with you, so I stuck, hoping that in time you'd be able to lower your prices."

Leon's wineglass was still raised. He lowered it and took a large gulp. "Like hell," he muttered.

"Well, what other reason could there have been?"

"I don't know. But I've got the feeling I'm about to find out. So you're going to start buying some coal from the Caroline?"

"Not some. All."

Leon startled. "All? You mean you're withdrawing your business from me completely?" He was no longer fighting to remain calm; he was clearly frightened.

"I have no other choice, Leon. You know what business has been like recently."

"What are you talking about? Business has been fabulous. Midwestern Steel just went onto the OTC market."

"We needed operating capital."

Leon's eyes became very hard. "For expansion, no doubt."

"We've been discussing something like that."

"What is it, Ben? Vertical expansion or horizontal?" It was clear he suspected the answer.

"Now, Leon, as you can imagine we have to be extremely careful about talk. But whatever, now that we've gone public, we need to keep as much cash in the business as possible at this time until we make a move."

"I asked whether your expansion will be vertical or horizontal."

"A little of both, I suppose."

"I suppose," Leon repeated. "But mostly vertical, eh? What you need at this point is to cover the whole process of steel. For example, a lime quarry might be helpful." He paused and then hissed, "Or perhaps a nice little anthracite mine?"

Leon finished off his glass of wine and motioned to the waiter to pour another. He leaned toward Ben angrily. "I won't let you have it, you know. I'd rather die than let you buy me out."

Ben's voice was ice. "I didn't offer to buy you out."

The appetizers came, glassy pink shrimp in dill sauce. Leon's stomach turned; he couldn't even look at them. The full impact of what was happening had begun to hit him, and he felt very sick. Still, he downed his wine and poured another glass. He was no longer waiting for the wine steward. He looked around at the other diners, the gray-haired men in their three-piece business suits, drinking their limit of two lunchtime bourbons, doing deals, cooking up plots, the women in their designer dresses from New York and Paris, trying to hold back their waistlines and the years, having their genteel little chats, probably with the wife of a man they were having it off with on the sly. Cut-glass crystal clinked musically; well-served meals steamed on their Spode dishes. There was the pleasant hum of voices over the orderly sounds of a string quartet. And his world was crumbling.

At the next table a waiter was officiating over the flaming of crêpes Suzette. The spicy-sweet smell made Leon feel even sicker. Everyone seemed so happy and comfortable in that room. He was dying inside; it was as if his whole body were collapsing inward, and all around him the world kept spinning merrily on.

"I don't suppose there's anything I can say to change your mind?"

Ben was eating his shrimp, dipping pieces of French bread into the mayonnaise. "You could reduce your prices."

"You know damn well I won't be able to undercut the Caroline's price, you bastard."

"Look," Ben said softly. "This is as unpleasant for me as it is for you."

"Oh, certainly. Your business is expanding and mine is collapsing. Just exactly the same."

"Now wait a minute. Your business won't collapse because you lose one customer."

"My biggest customer."

"I'm sure you'll find buyers to replace me. The thing to do, and you know this as well as I, is to cut back expenses and lower your prices, then go looking for new business."

"It's too late for that. I'm operating at a loss as it is."

"I didn't realize that, Leon. Jesus, I'm sorry."

"Like hell you didn't realize."

Ben hardened. "If you're operating at a loss, it's not my fault, is it?"

"In other words, I've run my business into the ground?" Leon was pale and he was shaking.

"You do spend a great deal of money."

"It's basically a sound business, Ben."

"I know that. You'll come through this just fine, I'm sure."

Leon was silent for a long time. "I won't sell to you."

Ben laughed in mock frustration. "What makes you think I want to buy?"

"It's the only answer. I should have seen it from the beginning. That's why you kept purchasing more from me. You were making me dependent on you."

"I was making you nothing!" Ben's own bitterness was just under the surface, and he could feel it threatening to break free. "You were doing it all to yourself. They were *your* yachts, *your* cars, *your* wife's fur coats. It wasn't me taking little trips to Europe. I was at the office, working my ass off."

"Bastard," Leon rasped. "You lousy bastard. Don't you feel any responsibility to anyone?" His voice had raised, and he could see several heads jerk around toward him, but he didn't care anymore. So what if he was disturbing the luncheon of the sunny women and smug clean-shaven men? He hated them all.

The waiter came and tried to place Leon's veal chop in front of him. "Take it away!" Leon snapped angrily. "I'm not hungry."

The waiter glanced at Ben for confirmation.

"What the hell are you looking at him for?" Leon's voice was very loud. "I'm the one who told you to take it away."

Ben nodded to the waiter who withdrew quickly. Then he leaned toward Leon and put his hand on his arm.

Leon threw Ben's hand off. His eyes were glittering blackly from out of his pale face.

Ben was really becoming concerned. "You'd better take it easy. Everyone's watching you."

"I don't give a shit!" Leon answered, but he did lower his voice. "You god damn cannibal. You savage. I won't let you get away with it."

This time it was Ben who flared. "That's all it comes down to, isn't it? If I'd been fat and rich, you would have taken it like a gentleman. You wouldn't have liked it, still, you would have taken it. But I'm not one of the boys, am I? It's not fair for me to win." He smiled resentfully. "But I *am* winning."

"I won't let you eat me up. I'd rather watch my business go under than allow you to buy me out."

Ben answered coolly. "If it goes under, so will you."

"I'll sell it to someone else first."

"You'd never get the price I could give you."

"I don't care."

Ben laughed. "And Martha? How will she feel? I can't see her cutting back, keeping the household money in a cookie jar, living in a bungalow somewhere not quite so nice. Does she even know there are cars other than Cadillacs?"

A shiver went through Leon. He felt as if there were no blood in his body. Abruptly he stood, trying to keep his dignity. But he'd drunk a whole bottle of wine himself; his legs were unsteady and weak, and there was a terrible crushed feeling in his chest. He was frightened that he was going to cry.

He steadied himself against the chair. There was nothing else he could do. He would have to go home and tell Martha everything. They'd sell the house, the cars, they'd cut back; they'd change.

He'd always said that it was greed that was killing America, but it wouldn't kill him.

In an age when monkeys climbed out of trees and put on business suits to take over the boardrooms of companies, he would be the one who was strong enough to fight them.

"Go get your sweater," Martha said to Dylan as soon as they were finished with dinner. "Mr. Savage is going to take you for a walk."

"Aren't you and Daddy coming?" Dylan glanced at herself in the mirror as she put on her cardigan. It had become too tight to button, and even open; it pulled across her shoulders. Once again she wished she would stop growing. She was only sixteen, but already she was five foot six, and if she stood really straight, she was much closer to five seven. Nothing fit her anymore. It seemed as if her legs were everywhere.

Martha moved behind Dylan and glanced at herself in the mirror. "No. I have a headache, dear." She patted her hair into place and tried to relax her mouth. But the lines remained there; she looked strained and tired; she was beginning to look old. Especially when she stood next to Dylan; that was when she really could see she was closing in rapidly on forty.

"And Daddy?"

"He doesn't feel much like a walk tonight," Martha answered tensely. "Now, hurry up. Don't keep Mr. Savage waiting."

She turned and left the room quickly. But Dylan didn't move. Again she looked at herself in the mirror, pulling down at the hem of her dress, trying to hide that it was well above the knees. All of her clothes were becoming too small for her, and for some reason her parents had not replaced them. Increasingly, Dylan felt as if everything were closing in, not just her clothes, but her whole world seemed to be shriveling. The chauffeur had been let go and not replaced, so had one of the maids. She was allowed to leave school, much to her surprise and delight, though nothing had been offered in its place, and for weeks she had been permitted to wander the house aimlessly or take walks in a nearby park.

Dylan turned out the light and walked to the door, but she didn't open it; she just stood there in the darkness, thinking. She didn't want to go for a walk with Mr. Savage. From that first time he'd come to dinner, he had made her uncomfortable, and even though he had been coming to their home for years, she still felt on edge in front of him. She couldn't remember him saying more than a few words to her, and they were always polite and kind, but he continued to stare at her, that knowing gaze that made her feel exposed. And when he did that, she was more aware than ever that she was wearing the body of a stranger.

Dylan had only a vague idea why her body was changing, gleaned mostly from the whispers of girls at school. Several of them had described the talks they'd had with their mothers, little lectures on things like babies. But they'd left so many questions she dared not ask. And somewhere hidden in the darkness of her mind was the memory of the man covered with black hair she'd seen when she was seven.

Three years before she'd been caught unaware by menstruation, and if one of the maids hadn't heard her crying, she'd probably still be convinced God was punishing her by making her bleed to death. The maid had shook her head disapprovingly and said it was time she asked her mother about "things."

But she couldn't ask then, and she couldn't even more now. Recently her parents had retreated almost entirely into themselves. Their tense conversations had stopped altogether, but this had only served to make the conspiracy between them stronger. The silence was complete.

Martha knocked at the door. "Dylan! You can't keep Mr. Savage waiting like this." Dylan could hear something in her mother's voice that told her it mattered a great deal that she go for this walk.

As she opened the door and walked past her mother, she wondered why she was being allowed to go out alone with the tall strong man they themselves called "the savage." Was she to be some kind of payment, a bribe of some sort? If so, she doubted that it was a one Mr. Savage would accept, and it also seemed unlikely that her parents considered her as being anything so valuable as an enticement. And yet she felt sure they did expect something from her.

Ben was waiting at the front door. Wearing a dark business suit, carrying his hat in his hand, he looked a very tame sort of savage. But as Dylan walked to him and felt her parents' eyes watching her from the top of the stairs, she became aware of the sheer bulk of the man, his massive chest and arms, his thick large hands, and once again she felt embarrassed and awkward.

Neither Ben nor Dylan said a word as they passed through the front door and out into the darkening suburban street. It was the time just before the streetlamps came on, when it was neither day nor night. There was no breeze; everything seemed to be caught in time, waiting expectantly, watching like her parents at the top of the stairs.

Ben walked purposefully, looking neither right nor left, as if he were going to some specific place, as if he were on a mission. Dylan had to hurry to keep up with him. She glanced back at her house with its little lighted windows. It stood out against the blue-black sky like a cardboard cutout, a backdrop with no substance, and she felt very much alone on the quiet deserted street.

Ben paused, waiting for her to catch up. Then finally he said, "I've been watching you."

Dylan didn't answer. Words kept flashing through her mind, but she refused them as either stupid or unimportant. She didn't dare look at Ben, but she was aware of him only inches from her; she could smell his aftershave; she could almost feel the heat of his body beside her. It stopped all speech, all thoughts, until the silence had grown too overwhelming, and it was impossible to find any words to break it.

Ben didn't seem to notice. He walked strongly, purposefully. He even seemed to have forgotten that she was there. Once again he began to move rapidly, leaving her behind, then, as before, he paused, waiting for Dylan to catch up. But this time he walked more slowly.

Ben continued as if there'd been no break. "And I think you've been watching me too."

"No, I haven't! I just always look like I'm staring. My friends tell me that all the time." Dylan was blushing, and she turned away so that Ben could not see it.

Ben stopped walking and looked down at her. He shook his head and laughed at himself. "You really are a little girl, aren't you?" Slowly he turned and began to walk back to Dylan's house.

Dylan didn't move. For the first time she realized she didn't want him to leave. "I did notice you staring," she blurted. "And I have been staring back at you too. It's been sort of a game with me, not letting you catch me looking at you. I've been doing it for a long time now." She stopped, shocked at herself.

Ben too was surprised. He moved back to Dylan, and his face was very serious. "That's the only reason I've been coming to dinner.

Certainly not to pass the time of day with your parents. Do you know what they call me?"

Dylan didn't look at him. "The savage."

Ben laughed, and indeed he did look like a savage, hearty and strong and very alive. His eyes were on Dylan, full of amusement and something else that Dylan couldn't name but could feel deep within her body. She was blushing again, and the heat of her blood was spreading through her until her legs felt weak and hot, and her heart was beating quickly.

Ben was staring down at her, his blue eyes full of humor; he seemed to be laughing at her, and once again Dylan had the feeling that he must know everything. She couldn't speak; she could barely breathe. All that kept going through her head was that she should run from those probing eyes. But she didn't run; she just stood there trapped, everything all jumbled up inside. She was frightened and yet, at the same time, intensely riveted.

Ben reached down and took her hand in his. "Is that what you think of me?"

Warmth rushed through Dylan's hand, spreading outward. Tears came to her eyes, and the urge to run became so strong she could hardly see.

Ben seemed to sense what she was feeling and in some strange way enjoy it. "Well, you're right," he said. "I am a savage." He laughed but there was a hint of bitterness in his laugh. "I suppose that's why you've been staring at me. You were probably real curious to see how savages eat."

"No. I didn't think that. They did, but not me."

Ben didn't answer. He too was having trouble speaking. He had come on this walk because he was amused at the idea of being alone with the little girl he'd been watching for over two years. But standing next to her, with the darkness surrounding them, isolating them from the lighted windows where people ate their dinners or watched television, he realized it was something much more than amusement. It was then that he knew what he must do. He must tell her how he felt. Once he told her, once he was honest, the two of them would be straight. Yet grown-up as he was, he felt a child in front of her.

Finally he said softly, "From the first time I saw you, I couldn't stop looking at you. I still can't."

He paused. It all seemed impossible. Dylan was looking up at him, her child eyes opened very wide and frightened. It was unfair of him to do this to her; she could hardly be expected to understand what he meant.

Still he continued. "I'm not a romantic man." He laughed. "Not by a long shot. But I noticed you that first day. I couldn't get you out of my mind. So I knew then that I'd wait for you. And that's what I plan on doing."

He touched her under the chin, a gesture to a child. "Now you're under no obligation, of course. It's just for me that it's like that. But you can do your growing and learning and know that I'll be waiting if you should ever decide you care for me."

He laughed, embarrassed. "For a man who isn't sentimental, I sure am making a horse's ass of myself. But anyway, I just wanted it out in the open between us. When you grow up, I'll be there if you want me."

Dylan was shaking. Ben was towering over her, a giant shadow obliterating the darkened suburban street, making her feel as if the whole world had faded and they were totally alone. She was hardly aware of herself, and when she spoke, it was as if it were someone else's voice. "My parents sent you out here, didn't they?"

"Your parents? Those two wouldn't . . ." But Ben didn't continue. "I don't know what your parents think about anything, let alone this."

Dylan was close to tears. "You've made some kind of deal, the three of you."

"I make no bargains. I didn't tell your parents how I feel. I wouldn't tell them a thing like that. What I just said is between us."

"But that's why they let me come, isn't it? My father is scared of you. I can tell. He owes you something."

"Your father owes me nothing. I bought his company last week. For a very good price. He's on salary to me now. But he doesn't owe me anything. Nor I him."

"You don't understand my parents like I do. They know everything. They arrange everything. They arranged this."

"Now why would they do that?"

Dylan sighed. "To get rid of me probably."

Ben laughed. "There are other ways, you know."

"No. It would be this way. You see, I know too much." As she said this, she became sure that it was true. She alone had proof that the loving glances between her mother and father were a sham. Once she was gone, there would be no reason for them not to convince themselves of the lie. While they wouldn't know it, they'd be letting her go with relief.

Ben didn't understand what Dylan had said, but instinctively he knew she was right. "Look, let's go back. I'm sorry." He began to move, but Dylan took his hand to stop him.

"I'm not sorry," she said softly.

Ben was caught off balance. "I think we should go back now."

But he didn't move, and Dylan could see that he didn't want to. She looked up at him. The feeling of fearful expectancy was growing inside her, widening through her body until she was gripped by it. His hand still held hers, and she could feel the warmth of it burning through her. Even if they had not been touching, she knew she would feel the pull of his body. It was that powerful. But she was no longer frightened. She could see that he too was feeling the force of the moment, unable to move, unable even to think, and it made her feel suddenly strong.

"Why wait?" she asked.

Ben didn't pull his hand away. He just stood, looking down at her, and Dylan felt awed by his presence so close to her. He seemed to own the street, the air; he seemed to own her. For the first time she felt very valuable, as if when she was near him, she had substance.

"I'm sixteen," she said.

"A child," Ben snapped. He resented the power Dylan had over him. It was one thing to pick her out and tease himself with the thought that one day he would marry the quiet little girl with serious blue eyes, but what he was seeing now was something quite different. Her eyes had changed; no longer so somber and sad, they were full of promise and yielding. He could feel himself being drawn in.

"Sixteen is not a child," Dylan answered, and once again she did seem just a child.

Ben broke from her hand with relief. He laughed. "I'll talk to you in five years." He began to walk briskly. "In five years we'll see."

Ben and Dylan were married a month later.

"Well, aren't you charming?" Sylvia Solomon said as she opened the door. But while her words were for Dylan, her eyes were on Ben. She stepped back, allowing the two of them in, watching them through catlike eyes.

Then she smiled gaily at Dylan. "I believe I'm not supposed to congratulate the bride, am I? What is it? Best wishes?" Sylvia brushed her powdery cheek against Dylan's by way of a kiss, then moved rapidly to Ben who was hovering in the doorway, his eyes gleaming with pride.

"Ah! The bridegroom." She kissed him on the cheek. "Now it's you I'm supposed to congratulate. She's absolutely marvelous!" Sylvia turned toward the living room. "Sol!" she called. "Sol, come quickly. It's Ben and his lovely new wife."

She took Ben by the arm and confided, "I'm afraid he's already half gone. And don't you go encouraging him to drink any more, you understand? I've asked him a million times, couldn't he just wait until all the guests have arrived before becoming paralytic?"

Sol appeared in the hallway. He was a short bluff man in his early fifties with the remains of gray hair splayed across his pink scalp. He was very drunk.

"Well, I'll be darned," he said as he came toward Ben, one arm outstretched, the other clutching a freshly poured Wild Turkey. He pumped Ben's hand, then slapped him on the back and pinched his cheek for good measure. "So where in the hell is she, for Christ sake?"

Sylvia looked around for Dylan, as if for an object misplaced, but Dylan had shrunk back into the doorway, and it took a while for Sylvia to find her. When she had, she took Dylan's hand in hers.

"Here she is, Sol. Isn't she pretty?"

Sol poked Ben playfully in the ribs. "You old dog." He giggled. He put his arm around Ben's shoulders and led him toward the living room. "Come on. Let me pour you a drink. Then I'll give you the dire warnings we married men are supposed to give young bridegrooms."

"Now, Sol," Sylvia warned. "You leave him alone. He'll find it all out for himself."

Smiling, she held Dylan's hand in hers, and together they followed the men into the living room. Several times Sylvia glanced at Dylan as she led her down the hall. Dylan could feel she was being watched and tried to smile back pleasantly. But the woman was close to her mother's age and a stranger. She had no idea what to say to her; she couldn't even figure out how to start. Dylan wished she had paid more attention when her mother used to take her visiting. What did they talk about? Clothes, she remembered they talked about that, and hairdressers and maids. By the time they entered the living room, Dylan had become panicky. She knew she must talk.

Sylvia seated her in an overstuffed white armchair, Dylan said quickly, "I have a new hairdresser."

Sylvia looked at her oddly. "Do you, dear? Well, it looks very nice. He's done an excellent job. Very becoming."

"It's a she," Dylan answered. Her face flushed, and automatically she looked around for Ben. But he was across the room, standing by the bar, locked in conversation with Sol. Though she couldn't hear what they were saying, she could tell they were talking business.

Sylvia followed her eyes to the men. "Would you care for a drink?" she asked.

"Yes, please." Dylan became aware that her hands were clenched tightly. She opened them, trying to relax, but her fingers were stiff; her whole body felt like it didn't belong to her.

Sylvia was standing over Dylan's chair, waiting. Finally she asked, "What kind of drink would you like? We have everything."

Dylan was confused and embarrassed. "Whatever you're having."

Sylvia laughed. "I doubt that, my dear. I'm on martinis. Why don't I get you a sherry?"

"Yes. Fine. I'll have a sherry."

Dylan felt relieved when Sylvia left for the bar. She watched as Sylvia reached for a glass, then totally forgot what she was doing and began talking to the men. Dylan heard their easy laughter and knew they were talking about her. Embarrassed, she began looking around the living room. She considered getting up and walking around, but she didn't trust her legs, so she sat, a smile frozen on her face, glancing around at the white furniture, white rug, white curtains, white walls.

After a while Sylvia returned with their drinks and sat in the chair next to her, crossing one slim leg over the other, swinging it back and forth nervously. There was a long silence, and as embarrassing as it had been before to be sitting alone in the vast white room, this seemed even worse. Dylan shrank into her chair, almost holding her breath.

Sylvia smiled falsely. "Now I want to know everything about you." She took a large sip of her martini and patted Dylan's hand. "You can't imagine what a surprise it was when I heard that Ben had gotten married. Sol called me from the office and said, 'You'll never guess what our friend Ben has gone and done.' "

She laughed and called over to Sol, "Didn't you, dear?"

"Didn't I what?" Sol answered back. His face was very red and dimpled with good humor.

"Call me from the office to tell me about Ben."

"Damn right I did. This bastard here calls me to talk over the monthly figures, and by the way, he's gotten hitched."

"See, I told you," Sylvia said to Dylan.

Sol added, "And you wouldn't believe me either, would you?"

"It was quite a surprise." Sylvia was smiling gaily, but Dylan caught something in her tone that was not quite so gay, and when she looked up at Sylvia, she saw she was watching Ben strangely.

Sylvia turned back to Dylan. "And now we're a foursome. I can't tell you how glad I am to have another woman around." But she didn't look delighted. "Those two men only discuss business," she continued wearily. "On and on. I tell you, the hours I had to sit there quietly. Yes, and of course provide the food."

She sat up suddenly. "Which reminds me. I'd better check on dinner. I've got a new woman, and I don't have to tell you what that means."

Sylvia stood and began weaving her way toward the kitchen, and Dylan was glad to be alone again. She glanced over at the bar. Sol and Ben were still locked in conversation, heads close together, each with one hand in a trouser pocket, the other clutching a drink. Ben had told her that Sol was one of his closest friends as well as his accountant, but he hadn't mentioned how old he was. She hadn't expected everyone to be so old.

The doorbell rang, and she heard the muffled sounds of Sylvia's answering it. Sol and Ben didn't even notice. Dylan looked down at her hands and found they were clenched again.

Sylvia came into the living room with another couple in tow. "Look who's here, Sol! The Gees."

"Hardly surprising since you invited them." Sol chortled and clasped George's hand heartily. He kissed Beth on the cheek. "What'll you have to drink? The bridegroom's having scotch."

George put out a pudgy hand to Ben. "Oh, that's right! I almost forget. Contrapulations, as the old joke goes."

Beth looked around the living room. "So where's the bride? Don't tell me she's run out on you already, Ben. Though I can't say I'd blame her."

Everyone looked around the room for Dylan, once again reminded that she was there.

Dylan half stood up. "I'm over here."

Beth shook her head at the others. "Look at that. She just gets married and already she's neglected. George waited several weeks before he started neglecting me."

She strode over to Dylan. "Pay no attention to them. They have the manners of a gnat." She put out her hand. "My name's Beth. I'm much too old to be your friend. But I'll try to get you through this evening."

She smiled warmly at Dylan. "I can't think why Ben inflicted us on you so early. He should have sneaked us up on you slowly. Like telling your husband about your earlier indiscretions. Wait long enough, and neither of you will give a damn. But so early? Why, you can't have been married more than two weeks."

"A week today," Dylan answered.

"And you're back in Midland already? Yes, isn't it just like all of them. If I hadn't threatened to back out of marrying George, we wouldn't have even had a week's honeymoon. It would have been two days in the Indiana Dunes."

Dylan giggled. "That's where we went."

Beth shook her head, then looked at Dylan's glass. "What on earth are you drinking? It looks like glue."

"I don't know. Sherry, I think."

Beth grimaced. "Yuck! How would you like a Coca-Cola?"

"Love one, but—" She looked at the others who were still clustered around the bar. "Well, you know."

"Oh, goodness. You can't really care what we think." She took Dylan's glass and leaned to her confidingly. "Look, here's how it will be. The women will all hate you. You're much too young and too pretty. The men will ignore you, except for the occasional pinch. My advice is to have children quickly. At least they won't be able to ignore you. Kids have to pay attention."

For the first time Dylan felt comfortable enough to look at Beth. Close up, Dylan could see she was much younger than the others, tall with jet-black hair pulled back from an assertive face. Her nose was a bit too prominent, her eyes very dark and sure. She was what women often call handsome and men, horsey. She couldn't have been much older than her mid-twenties, but she was dressed like all the other women in a pastel low-cut crepe dress. It did not suit her.

Beth walked away with Dylan's glass and came back carrying a large glass of Coke with plenty of ice.

Dylan smiled at her. She was no longer so nervous. "Do you have children?" she asked as Beth sat down next to her.

"I'm afraid I can't have any." Beth's eyes seemed even larger and blacker. She lit a cigarette, letting the smoke out with a rush.

Dylan blushed. "I'm sorry. I—"

But Beth just laughed. "It's hardly your fault. I found out two years ago, so I'm over the shock. It's funny; that's something you just don't expect. You never wonder, can I have children? You take it for granted."

"You could always adopt."

"Maybe. But I think the urge has passed. And to be perfectly candid, it leaves me much more time for my work."

Dylan was surprised. "You work?" She'd never met a woman who worked before, except maids or shopkeepers, but never a woman like Beth.

"I'm a sculptress."

"Oh, I see. A hobby." Dylan had met women with hobbies.

"Not a hobby. Work. I sell my statues, you see. People buy them. Not that George likes the idea much, but I do quite nicely with them." Again the rush of smoke.

"Ben wouldn't let me work. Not in a million years." The idea made her giggle.

"That's too bad, my dear. You might have liked it very much."

Dylan thought about this. "Yes. Maybe I would have."

Beth looked at Dylan with more interest. "So what do you plan to do with your days?"

"Well, I want to have children."

Beth pulled on a cigarette; her intelligent eyes were sparkling with humor. "It'll take some time, you know."

Dylan smiled. "So I hear. But until then, there's our new house. I'll have to decorate it."

"Ah, really? I'm surprised Ben isn't hiring some dreadful fairy decorator. Well, I must say that is a good start."

Just then Ben came over to the two of them. "What do you mean, not hiring a decorator? I was just talking to Sylvia about using hers. Only the best for the Savages."

Beth stifled a laugh. "Oops!"

But Dylan was turning to Ben. "Oh, Ben, I think I'd rather do the decorating myself. I have some wonderful ideas."

"Of course you'll be doing it yourself. But you'll still need professional advice, where to buy the best kind of wallpaper, that kind of thing."

Dylan looked around the living room miserably. "At least let me find my own decorator."

Ben was surprised. He glanced over at Dylan questioningly, and she seemed to shrink in her chair.

Beth offered, "Perhaps, Ben, she doesn't like what they've done with this room."

"Don't you?" Ben was watching Dylan.

"Well, it *is* kind of white."

Ben laughed. "I guess. But Sylvia says it's the latest thing. Still, I don't suppose it has to be white."

"Everybody's doing it," Beth muttered acidly.

Ben ignored her. "Whatever, we'll talk about it later."

"Yeah," Beth said under her breath. "Like in about fifteen years in the divorce court."

Dylan was trying to catch Ben's eye, but he was avoiding her. He turned and walked back to the bar, leaving Dylan feeling angry and embarrassed.

Beth put her hand on Dylan's shoulder. "Save it till later," she warned. "There'll be plenty of time for that." Then to herself she added, "Oh, boy, will there ever."

TWENTY-FIVE

"Sweet sixteen and never been kissed," Pauline said as she wheeled through the living room of Ben's house, unsteady on her new high heels. She caught sight of herself in one of the mirrored walls and grimaced playfully. It was the act of a child. Then suddenly adult again, she turned back to the crowded room and continued her rounds, laughing and sipping at everyone's champagne. Already she was very drunk.

Elizabeth, who had placed herself in a corner, to be out of the stream of guests, watched Pauline with disapproval and also with sadness. Wincing, she turned to her grandsons nearby, smiling indulgently. And with that smile, she looked almost beautiful.

Elizabeth was fifty-seven years old, and although lines were asserting themselves all over her strong face and her black hair was scored with streaks of white, there was a new elegance to her. For the first time in her life she was taking care of her appearance. Though Elizabeth knew that it pleased Ben for her to be well dressed, as both an act of love and also a reflection of his prosperity, this change was only partly for his benefit, and there was a more compelling reason. Nevertheless, she suspected had she told Ben the real motive behind her changed appearance, he would have wished her back to the original. So she held her tongue, trooping week after week to the hairdressers, suffering their probing fingers, their irritating and ridiculous curlers, their inane gossip, in the vague hope that she would be made attractive. For Elizabeth was lonely. It wasn't that she was unfaithful to Wynn's memory, but it had been so many years since he'd died, so many long cold nights, that finally she was considering remarriage.

The idea had occurred to her while she was getting undressed one evening. She had looked in the mirror and with surprise discovered that she was still, if not young, then not so very old. It was a short journey from this to the obvious remedy of remarriage. Not that Elizabeth was considering this in any particular sense. There were no men in her life except her sons, and had one appeared, she probably would have shied away from him out of a general distrust of anyone not connected to her by blood or, in fact, by her rather long umbilical cord. Nor did her new attitude extend to meeting men. She had few acquaintances and no real friends. She had remained isolated from everyone but her family, and in many ways seemed to consider this a virtue in herself. So she sat at Ben's parties, separate and apart, watching only those connected to her, thinking of no one but them and those who in some way touched their lives. And less than a year later her brief flirtation with the idea was abandoned, or rather it withered on the vine without ever having ripened.

Elizabeth turned back to the room and searched out Pauline. She found her at the bar. Pauline looked up, sensing that she was being watched, then quickly moved into the crowd. But Elizabeth's eyes stayed on her, following her around the room anxiously, unaware of the frown on her face. Or perhaps she wished Pauline to see it.

Pauline was wearing a brightly embroidered white peasant dress.

Her hair was drawn back and curled into thick ringlets, and she looked very much the charming child who was just on the brink of becoming a woman. But Elizabeth suspected she had made more than a few brief forays into that realm. It was not a thought she allowed herself often, but watching her now it was one she could hardly avoid. It was the way Pauline stood when she talked to men, chin tipped up, weight shifted slightly to the side. It was the way she smiled that gave her away.

There was nothing Elizabeth could do about it, or at least there was nothing she could do now. A girl could hardly patch up her virginity like a split seam, nor was there any remedy for loss of virginity of the mind. Once gone, it was irretrievably lost, and Elizabeth suspected there was very little of the innocent about the charming child with the thick glossy sausage curls. At what point Elizabeth had relinquished control she didn't know, but she felt that it had been a great deal earlier and that she herself was very much to blame.

Elizabeth sighed and turned back to her grandsons. She loved watching them. It was like looking back in time, James, with the pinched old man features of a newborn child, Dyer, with his thick serious face and pudgy body. It was rare that Angela let anyone care for Dyer, and Elizabeth was delighted at this brief chance to be alone. Still she could see Angela just across the room, glancing anxiously in her direction, and she knew that the moment would not last much longer.

Dyer was standing on unsteady child feet looking down into James's bassinet with the concentration of a cat watching a fly. He looked around to see if he was being watched, then tentatively put his hand into the bassinet. What he did there Elizabeth didn't know, but it was clear that whatever it was, James didn't like it. He let out a howl that startled the room.

Dyer drew back, stunned by the noise. He began quickly backing away, but his mind was moving too fast for his feet, and with a yell of amazement, he found himself on his bottom. He too started crying.

Elizabeth got up and lifted Dyer into her arms, then took him over to check on James. The damage was minimal. James's face was still bright red and he clawed at the air with his tiny hands and feet, but already the sobs had subsided into hiccups.

Angela's concerned voice came from across the room. "What's the matter?" She rushed excitedly toward Elizabeth.

"Nothing except youth is the matter," Elizabeth answered with a smile.

James was beginning a large bubble, and it wobbled shiny on his lips, while Dyer held loosely to Elizabeth's breast, unsure which way the winds were blowing but prepared for any eventuality. Elizabeth laughed happily and began lowering Dyer to the ground. But Angela was already over to her, arms out to receive her child. As Elizabeth relinquished Dyer, she thought once again how unattractive and bony a woman Angela was.

Though Dyer had finished his own crying some time ago, he started it up again for his mother's benefit. Angela cast an angry look at Elizabeth as she rocked him in her arms and pressed his head against her.

Elizabeth frowned. "Spoil that child you will, if you're not careful."

Angela didn't answer. She continued to rock Dyer gently, but the look of irritation on her face told that she'd heard.

Elizabeth attempted again. "Water a tree too much and the fruit will rot." She knew she was risking an argument and found to her surprise that she wanted one.

Angela looked up from Dyer. "I'm doing just fine, Mother. Thank you."

"Aye. It's not you I worry about. Easy it is to smother a child for women like us."

Dyer was wriggling to get down, but Angela continued to hold him, her anger at Elizabeth making her forget that he was there. "On the other hand, sometimes we can give our children too little supervision."

It was clear from Angela's tone that she was talking about Pauline, and she emphasized the point by glancing around the room in her direction.

Elizabeth sighed, but it was more from anger than sadness. "And what about Evan, then? Or have you a complaint about how he turned out too?"

"I have no complaint about any of your children, Mother. How you choose to run your life is your business."

"And how you choose to run your life is yours?"

"I wasn't saying that," Angela lied. "But essentially, yes."

"Sad it is if we can't learn from our elders. Things passed down are the stronger, for they are rooted to the ground."

Elizabeth knew she sounded sanctimonious, but she didn't care.

Over the years her resentment toward Angela had grown, and while she suspected the purity of her own motives, she also knew in this case she was right.

Dylan was watching the two of them from not far off, a sardonic smile on her face. She knew exactly how the two women felt about one another, and if she were to pick sides it would be her mother-in-law's.

Elizabeth glanced over at Dylan, eyebrows raised in conspiracy. She liked Dylan. Though she had disapproved of their early marriage, and still had grave reservations, she liked her. But always there was a poignancy to her liking, a premonition of trouble ahead. Dylan was a fragile girl; life seemed to be very difficult for her. Dylan never said as much or showed it, but Elizabeth could sense this clearly, and it was the fact that Dylan put on a brave face that worried her most. For while it was Dylan's bravery that Elizabeth responded to, it was her need for it that gave her concern. Once again Elizabeth noted how difficult it was getting older, watching sadly from the sidelines and knowing better, seeing those around you making mistakes, and there was nothing you could do to stop them.

Angela had gone over to Evan and was whispering in his ear, undoubtedly complaining about what she had to suffer at the hands of her mother-in-law. Elizabeth watched them angrily. Well, the hell with both of them! she told herself. But she didn't mean it.

Evan nodded to Angela and lay a reassuring hand on her shoulder, then he made his way across the room. Elizabeth knew what was coming next and braced herself for it.

"May I speak to you a moment, Mother?" Evan asked too politely.

"An appointment you've never needed," Elizabeth answered, trying to keep her tone neutral. She'd decided to play dumb and let Evan bring up the subject. Let him be embarrassed. He deserved it.

Evan guided Elizabeth to a chair and sat next to her on the arm. It was obvious he was having trouble phrasing what he wanted to say. Elizabeth watched him coldly, maliciously pleased but also sad, for it was clear that essentially his loyalties were not torn and that he was only trying to prevent a fight.

"Look, Mother," he began casually, "I know that you and Angela sometimes disagree about how to raise Dyer."

"Good enough my ideas were for you when you were a child."

"That's not the point. Dyer is Angela's child."

"And my grandchild. Much do I care about the man he will be."

"Of course you care. I understand that."

Evan's tone was stirring Elizabeth and she tried to force down the anger. "Making a mistake she is."

Evan stiffened, and though his voice was still pleasant, Elizabeth could hear the tension in it. "I don't agree."

Elizabeth glanced at Evan. Suddenly her irritation vanished and was replaced by concern. She couldn't put her finger on what was different about him, but she was sure something was. For a moment she thought it was just that he had lost weight or was overworked or over-henpecked. But again she ran a mother's eye over his face and decided it was none of those. She feared it was something far worse.

She said softly, "Though strongly I feel, I will stay out of it. For I would not create problems." She put her hand on Evan's arm, but he quickly looked away, and at that moment she knew something important was wrong.

She stroked his hand as she had when he was a child. "It was concern for Dyer, not the lack of it for you, that pushed my tongue. But from now on, not a word will you hear from me." She laughed. "And knowing me as you do, you can imagine how hard a promise that is."

Evan didn't really seem to be paying attention. "Thanks, I appreciate it."

He began to stand, but Elizabeth held his hand. "Please. No need is there to run. Stay a moment with me."

"Okay." Evan sat back down, but Elizabeth could sense his reluctance and this disturbed her even more.

"Something there is that's bothering you."

"Nothing's bothering me," Evan answered. But he wasn't looking at his mother, and she could see just how uncomfortable he was.

"You don't look well," she persisted, though she knew it wasn't that. He looked unhappy; more, he look haunted.

Evan laughed stiffly. "I'm fine. Don't be such a Jewish mother."

"Jewish?" She looked bewildered.

"Oh, never mind. I'm just fine. So you can stop giving me your worried glances." His tone was almost sharp.

"I cannot be shaken free like that. Your mother I am. I know your moods. And though hard it is between mother and son to speak of such things, the need there is and also the desire."

"I told you, there's nothing to speak about. Will you stop making problems where there are none?"

Still Elizabeth held to his hand. "Please. Anger between us is something I do not wish, nor sharp looks or words. But worried I am. And if I cannot speak of it, then the more scared I will become."

Evan turned on Elizabeth. "Scared?" He was smiling falsely, and the tension made his face look skeletal. Evan took his mother's chin in his hand, but his hand felt very cold to her, and it was shaking.

"Honestly, Mother, I assure you that everything is going perfectly. The business is thriving. I have a lovely wife and a wonderful son. What more could a man want out of life?"

Elizabeth answered quickly, "Peace of mind."

"And I have that too. So stop making mountains out of molehills. Okay?"

Without waiting for an answer, he stood and headed back to Angela, as if seeking refuge. Angela saw him coming toward her, and she smiled. It was full of pride and triumph.

Slowly Elizabeth pulled herself up and walked over to the bassinet. James was asleep, one fist clenched to his red wrinkled face. She watched him for a long while, but there was little comfort in the sight of the sleeping child. Underneath the peacefulness, Elizabeth thought she could see traces of his fragility, and she wondered why her family was split in two, one side with too much blood, while the other seemed to be draining itself dry.

"Sweet sixteen and never been kissed," Pauline repeated to Ben. He was standing against the fireplace, downing a scotch, looking around the room with satisfaction. Ben liked giving parties, though Pauline suspected it was not so much because he enjoyed the parties themselves, but because they were his. Ben loved things to be his. He wanted to own people; he wanted to own her. The problem was that once he owned them, he lost interest, and Ben had lost interest in her a long time ago.

Pauline stood on tiptoe and offered her lips to Ben. He stooped, turning his cheek in her direction, but Pauline just giggled and didn't move looking up at him impudently. She reached over and tried to grab Ben's glass, but he held to it tightly.

"Have you been drinking?" he asked brusquely.

"Who, me? Your sweet little virginal sis, drunk?" She laughed, then moved closer to Ben, leaning against the mantelpiece in imitation of him. "So where you been keeping yourself? I haven't seen you in ages."

"I've been busy."

"You're always busy."

A waiter came by with a tray of champagne. Pauline took a glass and drank it off quickly, her eyes on Ben. "I drink a lot," she confided, as she put the empty glass on the mantelpiece. "I'm drunk now."

Ben glared at her. "I don't think you're very cute, Pauline. So cut it out right now."

"Well, aren't we being the big brother? A little late, don't you think?"

Ben sighed. "Come on. No scenes. This is supposed to be a celebration."

"My sweet sixteen party. Big fucking deal."

"Now hold it right there! I don't want to hear that kind of language again."

Pauline stifled a laugh. "Can I talk to you privately, big brother?"

Reluctantly Ben nodded. Pauline took his arm and led him through the room until they had reached the corridor, then she let go of Ben and, holding the wall, propelled herself forward with both hands. It was the action of someone who was very drunk.

When they reached the bathroom, Pauline opened the door and, with a grin, ushered Ben into it. She followed him in, then quickly slammed the door and turned the key in the lock. She put the key down the front of her dress.

Ben leaned against the washbasin, glaring at Pauline. "What is this? A Doris Day movie?"

Pauline merely giggled. She lowered the top of the toilet seat and sat on it. Coyly she arranged her dress around her thighs. It did indeed seem she was playing a part in a movie.

"Confession time!" she announced.

"You *are* drunk, aren't you?"

She stood and slowly moved to Ben. "Yep. Like I told you. Your little sis has been branching out for some time now."

"I think you'd better give me that key. We'll talk about this drinking business some other time."

Pauline drew back playfully. "No. We'll talk about it now. I drink. I smoke. And you know what? I've even slept with a boy. Well, actually several. And they weren't all boys either. You want to hear about it?"

Ben tried to control his voice. "Pauline, I want the key."

"You know where it is, Ben. It's in my bra. Come and get it."

"Stop this!"

"What's the matter? I'll bet you don't get much at home anymore. And Angela has had her kid already, not much going on over there. So why not?"

Ben grabbed Pauline's wrist tightly. Pauline cried out. Her face was bright red, and there were tears of pain in her eyes, but also there seemed to be an enjoyment there, as if she'd been neglected so long that any attention was satisfying.

"You think baby Pauline is stupid?" she hissed. "Well, you're wrong. She's got eyes. She's got ears. And she's damn clever. Smarter than Evan is. Or do you think he suspects? Poor old Evan. He's so thick."

Ben's grip tightened, and Pauline fought against the pain. "Surprised you, huh? Sometimes I even surprise myself. But all I got to do is look at you and Ma, and I'm a little less surprised. After all, I am your sis. Same old lousy genes."

She smiled nastily. "Anyway, here's the deal. As you can tell, I've got a whole lot on this family of mine, and I've got a big mouth. In other words, I can make one heck of a pest of myself. So I've got a proposition for you. I'm sick of school. I'm sick of Ohio. And I'm especially sick of all of you. I propose that you give me an allowance, something relatively generous, and send me far, far away." She smirked. "Let's see. Where? I've got it! How about the south of France? I've read all of Fitzgerald, and it sounds like my kind of place."

Ben was shocked beyond anger. He still held Pauline's wrist, but there was no strength in his grasp. "What's happened to you?" he whispered.

Pauline broke from his hand and leaned against the wall, one hand on her hip, one leg forward. She pulled a cigarette out of her pocket and lit it with a book of matches, watching Ben closely, daring him to move. She released the smoke through her nose in a studied Hollywood manner.

"I've grown up, big brother. Perhaps you were too busy to notice. Anyway, I meant what I said. I can and will embarrass you. Why not? What have I got to lose? But I'll leave you alone if you just send me somewhere nice and warm."

"Never."

Pauline laughed bitterly. "Why? You gonna miss me too much?"

Family Passions 255

"How could you, Pauline?"

Pauline flicked her ashes on the floor and took another deep drag. "How could I what? How could I do this to you? Easy! How could I do this to Mother? Listen, I believe in motherly love about as much as I believe in brotherly love. Like I said, I've got the same genes. And I've learned well. No, sir. It's easy to do. We're a strange family, all right. A bunch of savages. Except Evan, and look what's happening to him. Nope. I'll take care of myself, just like you."

"What I meant was, how can you do this to yourself?"

But Pauline was beyond listening. She walked over to Ben and draped her slim delicate arm across his shoulder, smoke curling around their heads. "When I was a kid I worshiped you. Did you know that?"

"Pauline, please stop. I don't want to hear any more." Ben looked ill.

Pauline put her other arm on his shoulder. The anger was gone from her face, and she looked very young, very frightened. "I thought you were the greatest man who ever lived," she said softly. "When you and Evan started running the Healey Mills, I was so proud of you. God, was I proud. But now—"

She stopped, biting her lip to keep the tears back. She didn't want to be weak in front of Ben; for once she wanted to show him. "You know, I thought one day we'd get married. Of course I was a little confused as to what that meant at the time." She smiled fiercely, and once again her voice was full of innuendo. "But now I know what it means. And I know something else."

She reached up and took Ben's head between her hands. Suddenly her mouth was pressed against his. Ben recoiled, shoving her violently across the bathroom.

"My God, Pauline! You're crazy!"

Pauline laughed loudly, hysterically. She took a drag of her cigarette, but her hand was shaking.

She whispered, "Think about it, Ben. Dylan was my age."

Ben pulled Pauline's cigarette from her fingers and threw it in the washbasin, then he took her by the shoulders and shook her roughly. "You're crazy. You hear me? You're crazy!"

"I may be crazy, but I've really got you going, haven't I?" There were tears of rage in her eyes.

Ben held her by the shoulders and forced his hand down her dress, trying to reach for the key. It was terrifying. He could feel the softness of her breasts under his hand; he could smell her childish perfume, and there was an excitement to her closeness. He recoiled, shaking violently.

Pauline laughed. She caught at his hand and tried to press it back to her breast. Her dress was pulled off one shoulder; her hair had fallen from its combs, and the ringlets were tossed down on her face. She didn't move to straighten herself up; she was well aware of the effect.

Suddenly there was a knock at the door. It was Dylan. "Pauline? Are you in there?"

Pauline giggled. "Hi! How's the party going without me?"

"Very funny, brat. I was getting a little concerned. In fact, everyone's beginning to wonder where you've gone to."

"Just having a little chat with the toilet. Be out in a sec."

Ben whispered to Pauline, "Pull up your dress and straighten your hair."

Pauline smirked. "No."

Dylan called again, "Pauline, are you all right?"

Pauline moved closer to Ben and put her head on his shoulder. "Mmmm," she whispered. "Just fine. In fact, I've never been better."

Ben grabbed Pauline's arm and was about to push her away, but she looked down at her dress in warning.

Ben turned to the wall. What he had just seen in Pauline was terrifying, but what he had seen in himself was even worse. Ben held the wall, trembling. The room seemed very hot, and he was worried he was going to pass out.

Again Dylan knocked on the door. "Pauline. Answer me! Is everything all right?"

Pauline moved up on Ben, turning him around. She looked at him questioningly.

"Don't make trouble for me," he whispered desperately. "Please. I beg of you. Don't."

Pauline raised her eyebrows. "Beg, is it? Now we're getting somewhere."

She called back to Dylan. "Everything's okay, Dylan. Only I just got the curse. Figures it has to happen when I'm wearing white. Would you mind terribly getting me something?"

"Something?" Dylan laughed. "Oh, you mean that kind of something. Sure. What lousy timing."

"Well, as they say, it's better than the alternative."

"Why, you naughty girl," Dylan scolded.

Pauline grinned. "Yeah. Ain't it the truth?"

She listened as Dylan's footsteps faded down the hallway, then reached into her brassiere and retrieved the key. She held it out to Ben. "It isn't finished yet," she teased.

Ben grabbed the key and put it in the lock. With shaking hands he opened the door.

Pauline just laughed. "That's right, brother dear. Run like a rabbit. Run like a hare. But I'll see you later. I promise I will see you later."

But as Pauline stood in the doorway watching Ben retreat, she sensed she was wrong—that she would not see him later, or at least not alone. And she began to cry. Not outwardly; on the surface she kept her tense gaiety as she returned to the crowded living room, but inside of her a desperate scream was building, until her whole body was consumed by it.

BOOK FIVE

WALES
Winter, 1980–81

TWENTY-SIX

Ben saw light, blinding, artificial. It was very painful and he tried to recoil from it. He didn't see Dr. Waring who was shining the light into his eyes, nor did he hear him speaking to Tally or Mrs. Mided. He was aware of nothing but the light. His name, even his own existence was not understood. He was no more than an instinctive, unthinking being who could jerk and shudder away from what was painful. Had there been anything pleasurable, it was unlikely that he would have the awareness to go toward it. That was too sophisticated an action for what had little more consciousness than an amoeba.

"It's a miracle," Dr. Waring said, as he flicked off the light.

"There's that word again," Tally said. But it was only to hide her relief. In fact, she did believe a miracle had occurred.

Mrs. Mided leaned to Tally. "It's lucky we didn't wire the family last night."

Tally didn't answer. She was staring down at Ben, and she was shaking. Finally she asked softly, "Just how much is he aware of?"

Dr. Waring turned to her. "I think right now we should be grateful for life. We'll worry about the shadings later."

"Shadings? It's rather more important than that."

"Not at this point. For now I'm surprised he isn't being carried out of here feet first."

The light had vanished for Ben, but still everything seemed white, and there were shadows that flickered back and forth against the dimness. What those shadows were, he didn't know. Nor did he have the ability to think about them. In the light and dark world he was in, there was no thought.

Tally couldn't stop shaking. "Surely he won't remain like that, will he?"

"I honestly don't know."

"But you must be able to tell if any more damage has been done."

Dr. Waring turned quickly and began packing his bag to avoid Tally. He allowed people two questions to which he had no answer. Any more than that and he became morose. There was just too much that he didn't know, and as he grew older, he could no longer shrug it off; his ignorance plagued him.

Mrs. Mided was watching Ben, head cocked to one side. "Maybe it would be better if he did stay like that."

Dr. Waring shook his head angrily. "Will you two women stop standing over him like crows on a grave?"

He picked up his bag and headed to the door. Mrs. Mided was right behind him.

"Aren't you going to leave us some instructions?"

"Instructions?"

"Well, some kind of medication, for example."

"Wouldn't you say he's had enough of that already?"

Mrs. Mided answered sharply. "That's not what I meant. I was talking about something to counter the effect of the pills he took."

"Perhaps in America they might do that. But here we believe in allowing the body to heal itself."

Mrs. Mided was watching him as a missionary might regard a witch doctor. "How quaint and humorous. But maybe ill-advised. I don't have to remind you Mr. Savage is a very sick man."

He leveled a smile at her. "No, you do not."

Mrs. Mided looked dubious. "Well, you're the doctor."

Ben heard sound though he could not recognize it as speech, but he heard something that kept fading in and out like a worn tape recording, and the shadows were on the move again, crossing the dim light, then disappearing and reappearing elsewhere.

Dr. Waring shook his head and regarded Ben sadly. "Poor man," he said. "I wish you luck. But if you can survive these two women, you can survive anything."

Mrs. Mided bristled. "I'll agree that you haven't exactly seen us at our best. But we're good nurses, and we'll take care of him just fine."

The doctor sighed. "Look, don't pay too much attention to me. I'm an irritable old man. And there's something about this case that's very disturbing. Perhaps if he weren't such a large strong man it might seem less, I don't know, important."

Mrs. Mided intoned, "Every patient is important."

"Oh, good Lord." The doctor groaned. He turned back to Ben. "My dear man. Now I understand your relish for death. They'd have me slitting my throat after an hour." He laughed, but still he looked disturbed, and he left the room very rapidly, slamming the door behind him.

Ben lay watching the flickering shadows and listening to the sound of voices with no understanding, but also no fear. It seemed a strange new experience, as if he were seeing and hearing for the first time in his life, though none of that made any sense to him, for at that point, he didn't even know what life was. But there was a fascination with what was happening in front of him, and he watched and listened with a catlike concentration and delight.

"I don't approve of that Dr. Waring," Mrs. Mided told Tally as she tidied Ben's bed. "Do you think we should call in another doctor?"

"No. I think he's fine. Besides, he's right. We are a couple of old crows."

"Speak for yourself." Mrs. Mided patted at Ben's pillow with more energy than was needed, but she was smiling to herself.

Tally watched her, lost in thought. "I don't know what there is about this case. I really don't. But I agree with Dr. Waring. There is something disturbing about it."

"Not to me."

"Really?" Tally was surprised. "Then I wonder why there is to me."

"Because you've fallen in love with him."

Tally looked at Ben's immobile form on the bed and shivered. "That's ridiculous! What's there to fall in love with?"

"The idea of Mr. Savage, of course."

"But certainly not the man."

"It's always the idea we fall in love with. The man himself is usually a big disappointment. I'm not so old and dried up I can't remember."

Ben could hear the two women laughing. It was a pleasant sound, though he did not relate it to laughter or even to the two shadowy shapes that flickered across his consciousness. But it was a nice sound, just as the light was nice. Slowly he was becoming aware that the light and the sound were separate from him, that they originated outside of him, but he still was not sure what he himself was. Only that he was not the laughter.

* * *

Morning broke in passionate reds and purples. Light poured in the room, and Ben opened his eyes slowly. He recognized the sky. Though he still did not know who he was or what he was doing lying in bed, looking out the window, he did understand that he was a man.

He glanced down at his arms. They were thick strong arms, the arms of a man who had worked. He decided he liked them. He could tell he was a sick man, and though he didn't know what kind of illness he had, he assumed it was grave. Movement was almost impossible for him and very painful. His stomach felt raw; his throat was on fire.

The pain triggered something, and suddenly his mind was filled with memories of picket signs being trampled in a rush to safety and of a choking cloud of tear gas being released into the air. He recognized it as an incident from the past, and also that a great deal had happened since then. He suspected that if he tried hard enough he might be able to reach other memories, perhaps enough to reconstruct the man. But he didn't feel like straining toward them yet. He just wanted to watch.

He turned back to the window and saw the sun rising out of a milky sea of colors. Only the sounds of birds and the scratching of a branch against the windowpane broke the quiet. It felt very peaceful lying there with neither the past nor the future to disturb him. It occurred to him that his moment of peace might be a short one, but he didn't even fight against this. It was as if all his strength to resist had been sapped from him, and he was left merely with surrender.

As time passed, he heard the sound of someone in the room next to his. There was the splash of running water, footsteps, a door banging. Then eventually there was the sharp pungent odor of coffee, coming from downstairs.

It was a wonderful smell, and it triggered hundreds of memories of boyhood and manhood. He did not fight against them; he just allowed the thoughts to play across his mind. They seemed at this point to have no relevance to what he saw out of the window or the smell of coffee or the sounds of morning all around him.

And then slowly with the memories, Ben Savage came back to himself, and he knew exactly who he was and what had happened. In one vivid flash he saw again how he had tried to kill himself. He could feel everything slipping away, and he remembered that he had wanted to scream he'd made a mistake but everything had been moving so rapidly toward darkness that he could not hold on. Horrified, he'd watched as consciousness fell away, knowing that it was too late to turn back. It was too late to do anything but give in.

And yet he hadn't died. He had remained alive, perhaps right back where he'd started, as damaged as before, but alive. And that seemed to mean something very important, though what it meant, he did not know.

Ben heard voices calling to one another, and he recognized them as belonging to his nurses, the two harpies. It brought a smile to his face. He thought of Tally with her stubborn self-righteousness, trying to force him into recovering, as if she could accomplish it with her own strong will. He supposed that once she discovered he was as before, the struggle would be on again.

Rather than making him angry, it amused him. He didn't want to fight against her either; he didn't want to fight against anything ever again.

He was what he was. And he supposed he would find a way to live with it. But he knew that wasn't entirely true. Something very essential had changed, and whatever he became would be new. It was as if Ben Savage had indeed died, and the person who would be born had not yet been formed.

TWENTY-SEVEN

The sky was turbulent with clouds, fast moving, piled one on top of the other. Only little patches of blue showed through, and they were quickly eaten up by clouds as they formed, dissolved, and reformed in eccentric shapes. Everything was in motion. A river cut fluid arcs in the valley. Birds swirled overhead, crying brutally, then falling to the water in search of food. Even the towering ancient menhirs were given life by the quickly moving shadows of the clouds. Only Ben was stationary, a hunched figure, trapped in a wheelchair, the weakness of his near death making him seem even more diminished by the hills.

Tally shivered and turned away. She pulled her muffler around her mouth and huddled against the wind. But she knew it wasn't only the cold that was chilling her; it was the primitive landscape itself. This was one of the secret places. The Welsh kept many of these areas of Druid remains to themselves, protecting them against the trampling feet of tourists with their beer cans, cigarette ends, and constantly probing cameras, as if buried deep in them there was still a residual belief in a brutal religion that was no longer even remembered.

Tally had been living in the area for ten years and had never been there. Oddly it had been Ben, a stranger, who had known about it, pointing it out on a map, making her understand with his halting mechanical speech that he wished to go there.

She found herself wondering why he'd been so insistent about being brought, but that only made her shiver again. She was sorry she had come. The landscape disturbed and frightened her; the sight of Ben, a tiny crooked shape engulfed by the hills, saddened her.

Quickly she moved closer to Ben. Close up he seemed less insignificant and incomplete; close up he became once again a man.

Ben turned his head toward her, but he still seemed deep in thought. "My parents met here," he said finally.

He turned back to the hills and stared out with a look of concentration as if he were trying to discover the two people who'd met there over sixty years ago.

"She was twenty-five. A schoolteacher. He was nineteen. Returning from the mines."

He fell silent, and Tally too found herself searching the hills for the couple who had met years ago. In her mind she could see the darkness of evening, the little troop of coal miners singing as they tramped through the valley toward the welcoming lights of the town.

"She watched from the hills. Picked him out."

Ben's eyes moved rapidly, as if he were seeking the exact spot. Then they stopped. "It was there." His voice was trancelike. "I came from there."

It took Tally a moment to understand, and when she did it disturbed her even more. Ben was actually looking at the place where he'd been conceived. It was unimaginable to her. She had no idea where she'd begun; she was not at all sure she would want to, but one thing she did know, it was nothing like this.

Family Passions

Suddenly a vision of the past stunned her, thigh against thigh, the catching of breath, a cry almost of pain and of something else as well. She almost believed she was seeing the past, though she knew it was only her mind.

"Some place to begin, huh?" Ben's face was guarded, but underneath there was anger.

"I think it's very beautiful," Tally answered. But her mind was still locked into the past. She could see the woman, watching the coal miners as they returned from their long day of work. She could hear the voices echoing in the hills. And in that vision she could imagine how the woman felt, the isolation, the boredom, the terror of being alone. Standing in the hills that evening had changed her life. It had in some way changed the whole progress of life, for from it had come Ben, and from Ben, a son. That one moment had changed everything. She found that very frightening and quite wonderful.

"Not beautiful. Just lonely and desperate." His eyes smoldered. "She was knocked up."

Tally didn't understand her need to defend the past against Ben, but she felt it pushing her. "I saw that picture on your mother's bureau, the one taken on her wedding day. There was love in that picture."

"Love?" Ben laughed strangely. "My father was weak. He did what she wanted."

"It's almost as if you don't want her to have loved him."

"Weak," Ben insisted. There was fear in his eyes, as if he were discovering the weakness in himself.

"Not in the pictures. There was strength to his face. I saw it. And also the love."

Ben didn't answer. He just stared out at the hills. Finally he said, "They didn't even know each other." He paused, gathering his energy. "Just chance."

As Tally watched him, the irritation began to fade and was replaced by sadness. "Why did you want to come here?" she asked him at last.

Ben hesitated, but Tally could feel it wasn't his physical disability that kept him from answering. He was embarrassed. Finally he admitted, "To understand."

"To understand what? Your parents? You lived with them all those years. Surely coming here can't have changed your mind."

"To understand why."

Tally didn't say anything for a long while, then softly she asked, "To understand why you had your accident?"

Ben smiled, but it was clear he did not find it very funny and that it was indeed the reason he had come.

"That is why you wanted to be here, isn't it?"

"Yes, I suppose." He turned away from Tally.

"And have you found any answers?"

He laughed shyly. "No." Then suddenly he grew serious. "I understand nothing."

"Perhaps that's because you've never looked at things freshly. Just as you can't understand those pictures on your mother's bureau; you can't see them as a stranger does."

Ben didn't seem to be listening; he was locked away from Tally, adrift in his own questions. And then his whole face changed, and when he turned back, his eyes were frantic.

"What do I look like?"

"There's a mirror in your room. You've seen yourself."

He looked caged. "But what do I look like?"

"You're a big man. Over six foot two. And—"

Ben cut her off, grimacing impatiently. "I know."

"You have thick gray hair and blue eyes. In fact, you look very much like your mother."

But this too irritated Ben, and he jerked around, opening and closing his hands, making them into loose fists that held only air.

"Don't even know what I look like."

And suddenly Tally understood what he wanted to know. It was something much subtler, much more complex than height or weight or color of hair. He wanted to know how he looked to the world. He had been listening before, and he wanted to see himself freshly, through the eyes of a stranger.

It was something that Tally did not wish to do. He was a patient. She was well aware of any change in his skin color or muscle tone, alert for any nuance that affected his health, but she was unable to look at him as a man, or rather she was frightened to do that, for she could not rid herself of the image of him from before, a hunched little shape against the primitive hills. The pity it evoked was crippling.

She said, "You're a very handsome man."

A childlike delight passed over Ben's face. "Really?"

Tally nodded. "And even though you're in a wheelchair, you seem tall and strong. You seem to be an important man."

Suspicion shadowed Ben's face; his eyes probed hers. He couldn't tell whether she was lying, though he supposed that she was. He had looked in the bedroom mirror many times, and what he'd seen there was terrifying, for alongside the Ben Savage he had always known was an old, crippled man, pale and weak. The two images had alternated, until he was no longer sure which was the real one. But of course he did know. He was an old crippled man, waiting to die. The other man, the strong vital one who had been conceived in these hills, was already dead, and now he was like the menhirs, a gray stone monument without life or purpose, a relic whose meaning no one could even guess.

Ben glanced over at Tally. Her vivid red hair gleamed savagely in the rapidly changing light. Her cheeks were bright from the cold, and the tip of her nose glowed like a child's in the snow. She was so full of life it was painful just to look at her, and she seemed at that moment to exist in another world from him, a world of color and passion, while he, gray and shadowy, only crept at the periphery.

As he sat there in silence, he wondered why he had wanted Tally to bring him there. If he had to come, wouldn't it have been far easier to have viewed this place and the gulf that separated him from it with Mrs. Mided, who like him no longer had a stake in the world?

Yet he was not sure that he was sorry he had done it. Now she would understand what he had become and would demand less from him. But he felt that wasn't the real reason he had wanted her there. He supposed he had wanted her to understand not what he had become, but what he had been. In a way it was a form of bragging. It was as if he were saying, "I once had as much strength and life as these hills. I was conceived in romance and starkness." He chuckled to himself. He really was a very foolish man.

"I'm tired," he said softly. And indeed he did look tired.

Tally kicked off the brake and turned his wheelchair toward the road. As she pushed him back to the car, she tried to understand why he had brought her there, for she was sure that he did have a reason. But in the end she found she didn't understand. All she could be sure of was that bringing her to that place had been an intimacy; he had tried in his own way to form a bond with her.

This surprised Tally, and also it unsettled her, because it demanded something in return. And in that moment of demanding, Ben seemed no longer a crippled patient of hers, but very much the man he had been.

* * *

Tally wheeled Ben into the dining room, keeping her eyes away from the rehabilitation equipment. She stopped the wheelchair in the center of the room and smiled cheerfully, but Ben could tell she was expecting an argument.

"I won't fight you," he said.

"That would make a nice change."

Tally had answered automatically and instantly she was sorry. She glanced over at Ben, but was surprised to find he didn't seem irritated at all; he was amused.

Mrs. Mided opened the door and bustled into the room. "Well, what have we here?" It was clear from her tone she sensed she was intruding and resented it. "Why didn't you tell me we were going to start rehabilitation?"

Tally avoided her eyes. "I didn't want to disturb you. It's quite all right. I'm delighted to take over myself."

"I wouldn't be surprised. That way I get all the dirty work."

Tally saw Ben cringe. She didn't blame him. The indignity of having to submit to being fed and changed was something she couldn't even guess at.

Ben's face was taut. "Sorry I shit."

"Oh, please, don't take offense," Mrs. Mided said hastily.

Tally moved up on her. "How can he help but take offense? Have you any idea what it must be like for him?"

Mrs. Mided retreated into the doorway. "I don't understand what I said that was so terrible."

"You tell her." Ben's eyes were grief-stricken.

Tally turned on Mrs. Mided. "You're treating him as if he were . . ." She couldn't find the word.

Ben turned away. "Thanks a lot."

"I'm treating him as if he were a patient," Mrs. Mided returned. "That's what he is, you know."

"No. You're treating him as if he were a burden, a job, not a human being."

"I'm him?" Ben asked bitterly. "I have a name."

"Yes, Mr. Savage," Mrs. Mided answered. "We all know you have a name."

But Tally was silent. Ben had accused her of being as bad as Mrs. Mided in her own way, and she knew he was right. It was something she'd never admitted to herself, the feeling of superiority to her patients, but Ben was pushing her to recognize it. She looked over at him, but was surprised to find that he was calm and amused again. He was changing; everything was changing. She wasn't sure how or why; all she knew was he was different, and somehow she was being left behind.

Tally held Ben's eyes. "I'm sorry," she said softly. And when she looked back, Mrs. Mided was gone. It was as if a shadow had passed over them. Ben was watching her; he seemed to be asking something of her, almost demanding it. But she didn't know what he was demanding, or perhaps she didn't want to know.

Tally walked behind Ben's wheelchair and pushed him to the parallel bars. "The object is to use these bars to support your body weight. It will help build up your arms. Just like the rubber ball I gave you for your hands."

He smirked. "Threw it away."

Tally pretended not to hear. "Eventually you'll be able to support yourself, then walk the entire length. But for now, just try to stand."

She stopped, waiting for the protest, but Ben was smiling, and his eyes were calm and serious.

"Now try to reach for the bars."

Ben nodded. The bars were just in front of him, within easy reach. Yet already his perceptions had changed, and he knew that for him they were very far away.

Panic took hold of him, and he tried to calm his mind. But there was something keeping him back. It was almost as if he were split in two, with another voice besides his own telling him. "Why bother when failure is so certain? Why try when you will fail?"

Ben blocked out the voice and pushed himself to motion. Slowly his arms began to rise. They felt very heavy, weights that didn't belong to him; still he forced them upward. He could hear Tally saying, "That's very good!" And almost as an echo, the voice inside of him laughed. "You'll never make it. You will fail."

Ben tried to believe he would not fail, that taking hold of the bars was something he could do. He could feel his arms rising in fits and starts, his weak muscles quivering. A dull aching pain began, but there was something good about the pain; it was, at least, some form of life. And then his arms were at the bars, and he rested his hands on top.

Tally was smiling. "Excellent!" She sounded excited. "Now grasp the bars."

Ben tried to take hold of the wood, but his grip was weak; the heaviness of his arms was pulling everything downward, and he could feel himself losing hold. He pressed even harder, refusing the pain, refusing the ridiculing voice, until he felt himself gain a firm grasp, and this time he was smiling with delight and relief.

"Good," Tally said. "That really is good! Now use the bars to lift yourself out of the chair."

Ben concentrated on what he was doing, but he could still hear the voice whining and whimpering inside of him, and now it seemed even louder and more insistent, because taking hold of the bars was one thing but actually lifting himself out of the chair was something totally different. His muscles were like an old man's; the meat was beginning to separate from the bone. He was weak and damaged, and even as he began to press down against the bars and wrench his body from the chair, he knew he would fail.

His whole body clenched. It was a terrible effort, every muscle felt like it was being shredded with pain, yet he hardly moved.

Ben rested for a moment, then again forced himself up. His muscles twitched, and he thought he felt himself rising from the chair, but when he looked down, he saw he had barely moved.

Ben fell back into the chair, defeat pounding through him.

Tally urged, "It doesn't matter if you fail. Just keep trying."

"It matters."

Ben tried again. His aching muscles tightened; everything around him faded, until all he was aware of was the effort. Almost immediately the pain reappeared, building inside of him, beginning to take him over, and he couldn't fight against it; all he could do was give in.

Ben sank back, eyes closed, his hands clenched. Suddenly rage took over. Without even knowing what he was doing, his fist crashed down on the bars. The apparatus buckled, wood splintered, and it broke from the frame.

Ben cried out. He held his hand to his chest as waves of electric pain ran through his arm into his body.

Tally flared. It was almost as if Ben had struck out at her and not the apparatus. "Just what do you think you're doing?" It was the pity and guilt she'd been feeling ever since she'd started this case. She hated it. At that moment, she hated Ben.

Ben was cradling his hand to his chest, gasping for air. He could feel the tears threatening to betray him.

Tally turned away, trying to calm herself, but when she turned back the anger was still there, unreasoning and strong. "That cost you a great deal of money. Though I don't suppose you care about that kind of thing."

She paused, sensing that she was only making things worse but unable to stop herself. "You'll never get anywhere if the moment you can't do something you just bash whatever's handy. Nobody said it was going to be easy. It's going to take a lot of time and work."

"Shut up!" Ben hissed. His voice sounded mechanical, devoid of tone, absurdly comical, and this merely fed the humiliation.

"You can sack me if you like. I really don't care anymore. I'll bet that everyone you've ever had anything to do with was always too scared or beholden to tell you the truth. But I just don't care. You're spoiled and stubborn and petulant, like a three-year-old child. You make things even worse for yourself than they already are."

"Go to hell."

"Quite possibly, I will. But it won't be because of what I'm saying to you. You think you're the only one in the world who's ever been crippled?"

"Yes," Ben answered. "I am. To me."

This stopped Tally. She was silent for a long while. Then she nodded. "Yes. To you."

She walked over to the chair and crouched, until their faces were parallel. "Look, I'm sorry. I know it must be awful for you. Godawful. But don't you see? You have to try. It doesn't matter whether you fail or not. You have this crazy American idea that all that counts is success."

"It is."

"No. It's the trying that's important."

"Too bad the accident didn't happen to you." Ben paused, fighting to control his voice, but the anger was pushing him, and the words flowed out less haltingly. "You'd enjoy the trying. You'd have a real field day."

Tally sighed. "Yes. I suppose it must seem easy for me to say. You're right. I didn't have the accident. And I'm very grateful for that. To say otherwise would be a lie." As she watched him she realized how much he must wish that it had been her instead of him. And how blessed she was that it hadn't.

She tried to keep to the point. "It still doesn't mean that what I'm saying is wrong. I can still be right about your making things worse for yourself. I thought when you didn't fight me before that perhaps you had changed. I thought that you might allow yourself to try."

Ben's eyes were very sad. "So did I."

It was when Ben was like this that Tally found herself most uncertain. She stood up and moved away from him. "It's you who're stopping yourself," she said quietly. "I understand that you're furious. You made me understand just now. But at least try to direct your anger. Hitting that bar took a great deal of strength. And trying to commit suicide? I still can't figure out how you managed that. Use your anger, Ben. Don't let it use you."

"Very beautiful," Ben muttered.

Tally watched him with regret. She no longer felt anger toward Ben or even pity; she felt lost. "If you'd like we can hire someone more experienced at rehabilitation."

"No. I want you."

Tally overrode him. "Perhaps it would be better if I did ring the agency in the morning. I'm sure they'll find someone."

"No!" Ben's voice screeched. "I decide." Then he continued very softly. "I'm still able to decide."

Tally nodded. She walked to the back of Ben's wheelchair. "I think we've had enough for today," she said gently.

From the back Ben seemed so much more diminished, so vulnerable, that it frightened her. Again the pity and guilt returned. She shut them out and kicked off the brake, pushing him out of the room.

"If you don't object, I'd like to take you to my Aunt Edith's for dinner." Her voice was cheerful. "Nothing formal, you understand. I'm not much of a cook. And my aunt is even worse."

It was only later, as Ben sat in his bedroom staring out of the window at the bleak winter rain, that the violent emotions of before began to recede and he was able to think. He wondered what had happened to all the acceptance he had discovered the other morning when he had awakened to find that he was still alive. What had happened to the man who had watched the sun as it rose, who had listened to the sound of the branches scratching against the windowpane and had found that it brought him such joy, such peace, that it was enough? He wondered if it had all been an illusion. The minute he'd tried something difficult, he'd been filled with the same old self-pity and fury, almost torn apart by it, until all he could do was strike out blindly in any direction. It was as if he hadn't changed at all.

Nevertheless, the anger had passed, and once again he was looking out the window, watching the patterns of rain on the glass. The peace had returned too, calming him. He knew that Tally was right about his being stronger when he was angry; even his voice was stronger. He supposed he'd been running on anger all his life, and perhaps that wasn't so bad. It didn't really matter. The passion was a part of him; he couldn't abandon it. And the peace? It seemed to be there for him now also.

Ben was astounded by all these thoughts that were so new to him. He'd never really thought about life before. Until the accident he'd been making exactly the same mistakes he'd always made, reacting to life instinctively without thinking about it. But now he was thinking about it. And it seemed a terrible waste that he was beginning to learn how to live, just when he was going to die.

TWENTY-EIGHT

Tally's Aunt Edith was small and birdlike with wispy dyed red hair curled tightly around her head and fixed in a net. Behind her glasses, her eyes were very blue and alive, almost predatory in their keenness. She had Tally's smile.

"You're the first young man Tally's brought to dinner in years." Edith cast a playful glance at her niece, then smiled at Ben.

Ben was sitting in his wheelchair, looking around the old-lady living room with its doilies and flowered curtains drawn against the snow. Though it was the first social occasion he'd had since the accident, he didn't feel awkward or embarrassed, only happy.

"Young?" he asked, haltingly. "Since when is sixty young?"

"Since I was sixty-one." She laughed. "I'll let you in on a little secret, Mr. Savage. I'm close to seventy-five now. And you look like a boy to me. But of course I am losing my eyesight, thank goodness."

She fixed Ben with her hungry eyes. "You see, nature's very kind. Everything works out so well. Just when you begin to look old and shriveled, you lose your eyesight. And when even that stops softening the blow, you lose your mind. You see how it all works out?"

Tally came up behind Ben with a sherry glass. He nodded and allowed her to bring it to his lips. "You sure haven't lost yours yet," he said.

"Unfortunately I'm one of those fighters who's going to go down knowing full well that they are old and decrepit. I can't tell you how many times I've wished I were the type to nod out by the fire, dreaming about past loves or what kind of pudding I'm going to have for dinner or other pleasant thoughts. It's a shame really. But there it is." She brightened. "And at least I am losing my eyesight."

Tally handed Edith a sherry. "Now, Auntie, there's nothing so terrible about getting old."

"And how would you know?"

"Well, I'm not exactly a girl anymore. I am the wrong side of forty."

"Impossible."

Tally laughed. "That's what I say too. But it's true. After all, I came to live with you over ten years ago. And I wasn't a child then."

Edith thought for a moment. "Well, dear, clearly you must be right. One hardly lies up on their age. Over forty? I hadn't realized. I suppose it's because you don't have any children. One tends to forget about age without any obvious watermarks. Jolly lucky for you too. Even if you do manage to nab a man in the near future, he probably won't expect you to have any children at this stage. Yes, my dear, that's very good. Children are such a nuisance."

Tally was laughing, but Ben could see Edith was embarrassing her and also that she was enjoying being embarrassed.

"And how would you know?" Tally asked still laughing. "You never had any."

"I've been around, my dear. Good Lord, one thing I've learned is that this business of having children is totally overrated, both as an activity and an enterprise."

She smiled playfully. "Can you imagine spending twenty years of your life planning, saving? My God, school fees alone are enough to keep you in servitude for life. And for what? So that your pride and joy, the little darling you devoted all your money and love and time to, can spend the next twenty years on an analyst's couch complaining about how dreadful you were to him?"

Tally was laughing again. It was a surprisingly childish laugh, giggly, hidden behind her hand as if she were ashamed of it.

"Auntie, you're an old cynic," she said. Her face was flushed from the laughter, and she looked very different from the nurse with the cool reserve that sometimes flared into bad temper.

"Not at all. I'm an old realist. Why, the lies we tell ourselves about children! Such as they're a joy and comfort in one's old age. What a load of twaddle! Take me, for example. I never had any children, and am I sad and lonely like everyone warned me? I am not. I'm sitting with my lovely niece and her nice friend, all snug and happy, drinking a sherry."

Tally smiled fondly. "At least you must admit you were lucky your sister had children."

"Yes. Bernice was always a good sister. And you, Tally, were extremely obliging to divorce your husband and find yourself at loose ends."

Ben was surprised. Somehow he hadn't thought of Tally's having had an existence before him. "You were married?"

This seemed to make Tally nervous. She stood quickly and went to refill the sherry glasses. "Twelve years," she answered finally.

"What happened?"

Tally thought for a while. "You know, I'm not really sure. It isn't that I haven't asked myself that question a million times. With various answers. I suppose one of us changed and the other didn't. Or both of us changed. Or perhaps we both didn't change at all, which is worse. All I know is one day we both awakened to discover we were too far apart, and there was no way of getting back."

"The best thing that ever happened to you," Edith said curtly. "A thoroughly unpleasant character was our David. I'm delighted you're rid of him." Then she smiled to banish the seriousness. "Besides, what would have happened to your poor old Auntie Edith if you were still flying all over the world with that silly rich crowd you used to run with?"

Again Ben was startled. He had pictured her married to a nice solid clerk or schoolteacher or even a farmer. Yet he suspected had he looked at her objectively he would have seen a worldliness that did not come from lying in the arms of a farmer or bookkeeper. He knew nothing of this woman who knew so much about him. Nor had she readily revealed anything. He glanced over at Tally. She was looking uncomfortable and exposed, and he wondered why she had brought him there if she hadn't expected exposure. Surely her aunt's little performance wasn't reserved solely for him. She must have known the risk she was taking.

Edith finished off her sherry. Her keen little eyes were sparkling with good humor and the effects of the alcohol.

"Tally, hadn't you better see to dinner?" she suggested. "You can safely leave Mr. Savage with me. I'm too old to be any competition."

"Really, Auntie!" Tally blushed as she left the room.

Edith's eyes lit up. "Of course I'm not too old really." She leaned forward and whispered confidentially, "In fact, I have several boyfriends in the area. I especially like a young farmer down the road. A lovely boy of seventeen who brings me eggs twice a week. But I don't want Tally to know. She might not be so convinced that she ought to be kind to me. And then what would I do? I'd have to have my dinner alone and watch television alone. So I pretend to be old whenever she's around."

Ben laughed. "You do a very good job of it."

"Thank you. It's all done with makeup. Plastic wrinkles, a little shading under the eyes." Edith stopped. Her body contracted; her face was pinched with pain. She seemed almost to shrink in her chair. Then quickly she recovered; her body relaxed, and she was able to manage a smile.

Ben was frightened. "My God! Are you all right?"

Edith tried to recapture the gaiety of before, but she did not look very gay. "Don't worry, my dear. I'm only dying." Then she sighed. "Yes. I'm all right for the moment."

"Shouldn't we get Tally?"

"With all due respects, I don't see what she can do. We all have to die at one time or another."

"She's a nurse."

"And a very good one, Mr. Savage. But even a nurse does not have much influence over death. No. I don't want her to know that anything is wrong. All she'll do is flap and flutter around me and look concerned. I'd much rather things remain as they are. You see, I believe in staying alive until the evidence to the contrary is indisputable."

Family Passions

Ben was watching Edith, but he didn't seem to be seeing her anymore, and Edith could tell his mind was somewhere else. She also knew this was the real reason Tally had brought him.

"We all have to die at one time or another, Mr. Savage," she continued. "Though I must say, the later the better. Meanwhile, I have my sherry and my television, and I have my Tally. We have a good time."

Edith hesitated, waiting for Ben to speak, but he was still deep within himself.

"Tally's told me your doctors think you're dying. Don't believe them. They're all a pack of liars."

Ben pulled himself back to the moment, but it took a great deal of effort. "You believe them for you."

"The doctors? Heavens, no. I never listen to them. It's me. I know. We who are dying can tell it about ourselves. And about others too. Of course, we all lie to one another. When we meet we say, 'My, how well you look,' though we can virtually see our cancers growing or our hearts failing."

She sighed. "You can see life, you know. Well, perhaps not so much see it as feel it. There's a sense. Almost as if one could count the cells dividing. But with us there is nothing. Only decay and stagnation and silence. Nevertheless, we stand on the pavement, lying to one another, pretending we haven't noticed, that we can't smell the death."

Edith leaned forward, fixing Ben with her sharp blue eyes, shifting her glasses and looking through the bifocals. "Oh, no, my dear. Not you. Your cells are dividing like mad, the little devils. I wouldn't be surprised if you didn't even have some children left in you."

She sat back and waved her hand in the air as if banishing the thought. "No, Mr. Savage. Whether you like it or not, you are very much alive. And will be so for a long time, I hope."

Then she looked around impatiently. "Now where is my dinner? That Tally is a lovely girl. But slow. So very slow."

TWENTY-NINE

Midland, Ohio

Dyer lit a cigar and turned his chair toward the window so he could look into the courtyard where the usual ten-foot Christmas tree was twinkling with a hundred lights. Even though it was six thirty in the evening, the remains of a hangover were still on him, and he felt almost poisoned by too much smoking.

He stubbed out his cigar angrily. He'd been smoking and drinking too much recently; the orderly pattern of his life had been shattered, and while he blamed his obsession with Pauline, he knew it was something far deeper. It was as if in discovering that one weakness, all the others were wrenched free also.

Until Pauline, he had kept to a rigidly prescribed path. He had been a well-oiled machine, practical, logical, neither recognizing nor responding to emotions, much less desires. But desire had come to him, and with it the whole crazy, tilting roller-coaster ride of feelings.

There were moments of agonizing jealousy, despair, almost uncontrollable hatred. Not that Dyer had never felt anger in his life. He was a man who could feel anger and apply it when necessary. But that was the point. His anger was a tool, a well-controlled weapon in his arsenal, clean and neat, clearly defined.

What he was feeling now was something entirely different. It wasn't clean and neat at all; it was ragged and swift, spilling over into the rest of his life, twisting into improbable shapes, often masquerading as almost anything but itself.

He'd be walking down the corridor and suddenly old childhood grudges came back, surprising him with their force. Memories long forgotten in the busy rigidity of his life reappeared. And he would think he was angry about them, only to discover that the anger stemmed from something else entirely. Sometimes he wondered if he was going to be able to control it. He had kept everything so tightly restrained that now it seemed a great wave which might at any moment sweep him away.

Most disturbingly, he found himself thinking about his father. Until now, when he remembered Evan, which was as rarely as possible, his feelings had been purposefully foggy. The terror of his suicide had been so overwhelming that he had blocked out the memory, forcing it from his mind each time it appeared. And gradually, as the years went by, thoughts of his father had diminished.

But now Dyer found himself dwelling on him all the time. Surprising thoughts, lacking any coherence, full of intensity. Dyer would be plunged into what seemed like a maudlin pity for the man. Then just as swiftly, he would feel the sharp edges of hatred for his father, and he would despise him for his selfishness, until he was shaking with fury. Eventually the emotion would recede, but he'd know it was lurking there somewhere, waiting to return. And try as he might to block it out, it always did.

Without thinking, Dyer reached into his ashtray and relit his cigar. It was quiet in the offices; the secretaries had all gone home, and only the occasional footsteps of a junior executive broke the silence. Even out in the mill, there was no one around, and the Christmas tree flashed its lights to an empty courtyard and snow-filled sky.

Dyer felt separate and alone as he sat there smoking, gazing out the window. And with the isolation, thoughts about his father returned, creeping in on him gradually, and then the memory he had blocked out for so long, the night his father had died, came back. He had not thought about it for years, but suddenly it was there in the room, with an intensity and clarity as on the night itself. And with it came the memory of something even more terrible. He tried to shrink from remembering, for it seemed a dark hole that would swallow him forever. But the memories were there in the room with him and he could no longer turn away.

Dyer had been twelve years old. He remembered himself as a heavyset, unattractive boy, never really bad at athletics and schoolwork but never really brilliant at them either. While this might have satisfied most boys, Dyer knew the difference and cared. He would have given a great deal to be really good at something. Sometimes he thought he would have even preferred to be bad. Instead he was average, boringly, predictably average.

His cousin, James, on the other hand, had a glib light touch that enchanted his elders and amused the boys his own age. James had been sent away to private school, a good one, where he was doing very badly, but with flights of genius. Dyer was able to take solace in the fact that James only came into his life during summers and holidays. Still, he remembered his homecoming as always being a very painful affair, because every time he looked at James, he was forced to rediscover his own inadequacies.

With all of this, it was also a pleasure when James came home. Dyer liked James, partly because he was amused by him, partly because he didn't have a mean bone in his body, while Dyer seemed to himself an upheaval of sinister thoughts and desires.

It was just before Christmas. James was due to arrive the next day, and Dyer was looking forward to it with the usual mixture of dread and delight. His mother was at a PTA meeting and not expected back for another half hour, and Dyer was upstairs in his bedroom, supposedly slogging through his homework, but in fact reading what had seemed at the time a particularly riveting paperback concealed in his geometry notes.

He heard the shot. Dyer remembered clearly that it hadn't sounded like a shot, just something heavy being dropped. Yet he also remembered that he had suspected what it was.

Dyer had stood up immediately. He did not run from his room; he just stayed where he was for a long time. His heart was beating very rapidly, and he was scared. Then slowly he crept out the door and down the stairs, heading straight for the kitchen. Once he reached it, though, he didn't enter; he just stopped at the threshold, looking around.

There was blood everywhere, splattered on the walls, the floor, the furniture, a brilliant spray and once in a while, a thick blob, like a child's painting. It was the first thing he saw; it was the thing he remembered most vividly.

For a long while he didn't notice his father, so mesmerized was he by the unintentional art. Yet there was the feeling that he was only delaying the inevitable, and when he lowered his eyes, he knew exactly what he would see.

And then he did see him, and it was terrible. His father's twisted body lay under a spray of himself, looking almost like the forlorn remnants of a hedgehog beaten into the road. There was an expression of animal incomprehension on his partial face, as if all humanity had been lost in that one second of unearthly surprise.

Dyer remembered clearly that he hadn't screamed. He'd been riveted by the twisted shape, his mind struggling with the idea, taking it in haltingly, though from the first he had known what he was seeing.

Finally he became aware that there were several pieces of paper propped against a bowl of plastic fruit his mother kept on the breakfast table. Dyer had walked slowly to the note. And already he was asking himself the question: Hadn't his father known that it would be he who found him?

The note was several pages long, obviously worked on for some time, then copied out meticulously. It was addressed to no one, and the top of the paper was headed: I have wronged. What followed was a detailed listing of Evan's sins, both real and imagined, against various people and institutions. In it Evan told of his various misdeeds in business, his part in forcing out both Dylan's and Angela's fathers, and buried within, a vague reference to his suspicion about Dyer's parentage. This last was too sophisticated and veiled for Dyer to understand, though he could feel the importance of it while missing the sense.

But above all, as Dyer stood there in the kitchen, carefully reading through this plea for forgiveness and understanding, he kept wondering, Hadn't his father known that it would be he who would find him?

When he was finished, he carefully put the note back on the table, then ran out of the kitchen and into the hallway to wait for his mother. He still hadn't screamed or cried; he was completely cold and reasonable. Except, he remembered, he couldn't stop shaking.

It was not until later that night that he did cry, and by then it was too late. It was as if the emotion had passed him by. As he lay in bed at Ben and Dylan's house, looking at the shadows of James's toys, all he could keep thinking were strange irrelevant thoughts like, What would this do to Christmas? Would he still get presents? He tried to remember past Christmases, frantically calling back every detail. Even then he'd suspected this was crazy. Yet he couldn't stop.

After a while he became aware of voices coming from downstairs. Quietly he got out of bed and crept to the door, opening it slowly and standing in the threshold, blinking at the light.

There were several voices. His mother's was not one of them, and he reasoned the doctor had given her something to make her sleep, but he heard his grandmother, his Uncle Ben, Aunt Dylan, and even his Aunt Pauline. He could tell there was sorrow in their voices, and there was something else there too, something close to anger.

Dyer moved across the hallway to the banister. He could see them all, hunched around the table, captured in the light of a chandelier.

Pauline was talking. Her voice was sharp, yet tinged with fear. "They say suicide is a form of revenge."

Ben was clearly disgusted and very tired. "For Christ sake, Pauline, why don't you shut up for once? Haven't you got any decency?"

Pauline smiled nastily. "Indeed I have. As a matter of fact, I have a great deal more than any of you who will weep and beat your breasts and totally miss the point."

"And just what is the point?" Ben asked wearily.

"Have you read the note?"

Elizabeth snapped. "The note we have all read. No need there is to repeat it." She looked ravaged. Her thick hands were clenched in her lap, and she sat very straight in her chair, as if this were the only thing keeping her together.

Dylan touched her mother-in-law's arm fondly. Her voice was hushed. "What I don't understand is, why did he feel so guilty? I've seen the haunted look on Evan's face. I'm sure every one of us has. But of all the people who didn't need to feel guilty—"

Pauline jumped in. "Are you sure what you were seeing was guilt?"

Ben turned on her. "And what does our resident shrink think it was then?"

"Fury."

"Brilliant, Pauline! You're an absolute genius. Now I'll ask you the same question you just asked me: Did you read the note? Did you understand what it said? Christ." He shook his head and reached for the scotch bottle, then stopped himself. "For Christ sake, I don't know what he was talking about. All those terrible things he'd done? I don't know what he was talking about."

"Well, I do."

"Oh, shut up, Pauline."

Dylan shot Ben a warning look. "Maybe we should give Pauline a chance to speak."

"Why? All that comes out of that big mouth of hers is crap!"

Elizabeth went rigid. "Enough it is right there! Withered I am by sorrow at the death of my son. It is not for the living to make things worse."

Ben apologized. "I'm sorry, Ma." And this time he did reach for the scotch bottle. "Maybe we'd all better go to bed."

Pauline took the bottle from Ben and poured herself a drink.

Nobody even tried to stop her. "Not till I have my say," she answered angrily. "Last week, all the way back to Midland on the plane, I kept asking myself: *Why do I come here for Christmas?*"

Elizabeth answered, "Your family we are. You cannot deny your blood."

"Family? Like hell, family. I dropped out over seven years ago, and I haven't regretted it for a minute."

Dylan was watching her. "Yet you still come back."

"Yes. And maybe it's because I knew at some point I'd be able to say the things I'm about to say. Or rather that Evan has said for me, if any of you had the sense to know it. Maybe, in a way, I've been waiting for this."

Ben downed his scotch. "All right, Pauline. Since you seem so damned determined. Speak and be done with it. I've got a hell of a lot to do in the morning. Plus there's the business to run."

Dylan muttered. "Jesus, Ben."

But Ben was shaking; his face was white, and there were traces of fear in it. It was a face filled with sadness, but also with guilt. And though he was trying to hide it, he wasn't doing a very good job of it.

"Thanks for your permission, Ben," Pauline said. "I think I will continue. Because I think Evan hated us all. I think he wrote that note to make us feel guilty. Not that he knew it, mind. Evan turned everything in on himself rather than own up to what he was really feeling."

"And what was that?" Ben sneered.

Pauline's eyes narrowed. "Hate, Ben. He hated us."

A shiver passed over Elizabeth. "Enough, Pauline. Your brother it is you're speaking against."

There were tears of rage in Pauline's eyes. "Hate, mother. Can't you see we caused his death? And I for one feel terrible about it. I could see what was going on. Even in my short visits. I could see what hell Evan was going through. But what did I do? I made it worse. I pushed him—" She stopped.

Dylan was watching her. "Pushed him to what?"

Pauline shook her head but didn't answer. For a moment it looked as if she were about to cry, then the emotion hardened into anger and she turned on her mother. "And you, my dear mourning mother. Don't you feel it? Were you guiltless? You must have seen his agony and just ignored it."

Elizabeth was silent for a long while. "Years ago," she said softly. "And many times there were that I tried to speak to him of it. And yet once—" She stopped, then continued falteringly. "Last week it was that he came by my house. And nothing out of the ordinary did he say." Elizabeth stared straight ahead, as if seeing it all again. "And I felt grateful," she whispered. "I felt grateful not to hear."

Again Dylan touched her mother-in-law fondly. "I think we all saw it but were too involved in ourselves to do anything."

"It was not for you," Elizabeth answered. "He was my son."

Ben's face was very white. "Go on, Pauline. Continue. Because we all know it's me who you really blame."

Pauline smiled cruelly. "You see what I mean? See what suicide does? It makes us all feel responsible. And that's what it's intended to do. People who just die can be forgotten. But not a man who commits suicide. We will feel Evan's hand on our shoulder always. We will see his finger wagging at us in our dreams. We all have become his murderers, and instinctively that's what he wanted. Which, my dears, is no act of love."

Pauline paused and swallowed her drink greedily. When she continued, her voice was killing. "Even Angela. She's asleep now. But if I were her, I'd never be able to sleep again. Her love smothered Evan. She ruled his life. She took his pride from him."

"Hogwash."

"Would you prefer me to add he suspected she betrayed him?"

"Silence, child!"

"Mums the word, Mom."

Ben was glaring at Pauline. "Now on to me, right? I assume you're about to tell me all the terrible guilts Evan put on himself were my doing."

"I'm about to tell you how much he despised you."

Dylan was stunned. "Why, Pauline, Evan loved Ben."

"He *pretended* to love Ben. He probably even convinced himself, poor guy. But never mind any of that. Because whatever Ben did to him, he's gotten his own back. Ben will feel forever that it was he who caused his death. And he'll think we feel that way about him too. He'll have to live with that until he dies. Some adoring, huh? A real brotherly act."

Elizabeth's face was cracked with lines. "No more will I hear, Pauline."

"No, Ma. Just this once I'm going to have my say. Then I'll never bring it up again."

She finished off her drink and poured another. Her eyes were full of defiance. "The odd part of the note, and in fact the whole suicide, is why did Evan do it when there was a chance that Dyer would be the one to find him?" She paused, and there was a long silence.

Finally Ben spoke; his voice was very weak. "Well, you might as well tell us that too, since you seem so determined."

"I think we all have to agree it was on purpose."

"Not necessarily," Dylan answered, but it was clear that the same thought had occurred to her. "Perhaps he thought that Dyer was already asleep. After all, Angela was due back soon. It was logical to think that Angela would be the one to find him."

Elizabeth was shaking her head. "Not in his right mind he was. Not thinking at all."

"And yet," Pauline said. "And yet. After all, isn't the most logical assumption that Dyer would hear the shot and come running down to find him? Which is exactly what happened. A pretty terrible thing to do, don't you think? And the note? Also a charming touch to warm his poor little son's heart."

Ben was clearly stunned and repulsed. "You mean to say you think he hated Dyer so much he wanted to damage him forever?"

"No. I don't think that. No matter what his suspicions, I don't believe Evan was a cruel man. He loved Dyer."

"Then why?" Elizabeth asked. Her voice sounded ghostly.

Pauline too looked haunted. She whispered, "I don't know, Ma. Maybe it was a message to him. Maybe this all was intended for Dyer."

"A message?" Ben's voice was sneering. "What the hell kind of message is that?" Then he thought for a moment. "And even if you're right, what could it mean?"

Pauline stared at him. "I don't think Evan knew it. It was something totally unconscious. But I believe somehow he wanted Dyer to hate you as he did. I think he wanted revenge."

Ben began to tremble, and Pauline turned away from him, looking out into the hallway, as if she were trying to escape.

Suddenly she stood, pointing to the top of the stairs. "Look up there. It's Dyer!"

Their terror-stricken faces turned to the landing and saw Dyer staring down at them.

It was Ben who rushed upstairs, took Dyer in his arms, and carried him back to the bedroom. Dyer remembered that Ben sat on the edge of the bed, his head in his hands, waiting for him to fall asleep. In all the years, neither of them had ever mentioned that night. Dyer supposed Ben had come to the conclusion that he was too young to have understood any of what he had heard.

But Dyer had understood some of it, and he'd had to face the fact that his father did know what would happen and had wanted it.

Every night after that he would lie in bed, trying to contact the ghost of his father. Mornings he'd wake up, dream-twisted sheets all around him, and his first thought would be that his father had not come and told him what was required. Yet always there was the feeling that if he tried hard enough he would know. But that would be total annihilation. So he would turn from it, instinctively preferring the agonizing questions to the terrifying answers. For he was a young boy; he was scared, and not understanding meant survival.

At least with his mother, he understood what she wanted, and with an almost religious fervor, he tried to transform himself into what she desired. He became to Angela not just her son and husband, but her reason for living. Constantly he was tortured that she, like his father, might commit suicide. He watched in agony as his mother shriveled before his eyes, growing thinner and paler, as if life was being drained from her. In her empty staring eyes he could see the questions: *Why am I alive? Why am I not dead like my husband?* And he strove unceasingly to offer up an answer, though he was always aware it was an inadequate one, hoping that if he worked very hard, it might be enough to keep her with him.

Eventually Dyer stopped waiting for his father to explain; slowly the sight of his twisted body receded, and only his mother's pinched face remained for him.

But tonight as Dyer stared out at the twinkling lights of the Christmas tree in the courtyard of Midwestern, it was the memory of his father that impressed itself on his mind. And for the first time in years, he wondered again if his father had been sending him a message, and if so, what it was.

Then suddenly it was there, as if he'd always known, and he suspected that indeed he had. Now he could see plainly that his father's suicide was not an act of hatred directed against him. Though Dyer might have supplied the reason, it was directed at Ben, the man he suspected had betrayed him, the man who had showed him his own inadequacy.

Was it true? Was he Ben's son, not Evan's? Dyer closed his eyes

Family Passions

and, without knowing what he was doing, rocked himself back and forth in his chair. There was no real proof. Certainly he looked like Ben, but he looked like his grandmother too. But deep inside he could feel that he had always suspected it. There had been the note, too sophisticated perhaps for the boy to understand but not the man; there had been the looks and whispers. Was it true?

A violent tremor passed through Dyer, and he shook his head to rid himself of the thought, trying to block out the question, no longer searching for the answer. Still, one truth remained. His father had suspected it. It was that which had driven him to suicide. That was what the message meant.

Still, Dyer could not understand why his father had entrusted this message to him. Had he really done it because in some upside-down way he had hoped Dyer would avenge him?

As Dyer sat staring at the blinking lights, even the answer to this seemed clear, and he knew why his father had had to kill himself to deliver this message, why he had seen no other way out. Alive, Evan's legacy had been less than when he was dead. By his death he was trying to give Dyer a purpose. Just as Dyer had supplied a reason for his mother to live, so Evan had hoped to supply a reason for Dyer. He'd just been too stupid to see it.

Dyer turned away from the window, then quickly picked up the telephone and placed a call to Tokyo.

It was not until the next day that Hamayoshi returned his call. "Ah, Mr. Savage!" Hamayoshi sounded as if he'd just swallowed a mouse. "I was beginning to give up on you."

Dyer picked up a cigar that was smoldering in his ashtray and leaned back in his chair. "I was just wondering when you'd be back in the states. I think we should have some further discussions."

"Quite honestly, I don't plan on returning for some time." He paused then added pleasantly, "But I don't see why we can't have these discussions on the telephone."

Dyer laughed. "I think what we have to talk about is too big to be reduced to a few phone calls, don't you?"

"No, Mr. Savage. I have discussed far larger transactions in much less, shall we say, formal surroundings." He giggled. "Let's face it. Midwestern Steel is not exactly the biggest project I have on my plate."

Dyer stiffened. He tapped his cigar nervously against the ashtray. "But nonetheless it's a project you're eager to see completed."

Hamayoshi laughed. "You're quite right. Thank you for pulling me up short. I would like very much to reach agreement on a deal. Nevertheless, I still believe we can cover the essentials over the phone. The details can be ironed out later. In person, if you wish."

Dyer didn't answer, and Hamayoshi took this for a yes. "Good," he said happily. "Now, I see no reason to mince words between us. We are both practical men. And we both know the bottom line. What I was thinking of was two million, beyond the value of the stock of course. Deposited with our friends the clockmakers."

"If I were you, I'd put that kind of thinking right out of my mind." Dyer sounded very angry.

"Oh, please, Mr. Savage. It was just, as you say, an opening bid."

"Well, Mr. Hamayoshi. It was, as you say, a nowhere bid."

"And you suggest?"

"One hundred million."

"That is ridiculous!"

Dyer smiled, then stuck his cigar in his mouth. "Oh, please, Mr. Hamayoshi. It was, as you say, just an opening bid."

Hamayoshi was silent for a while. "Yes, yes, of course. We both have the same fault. We underestimate the opposition."

"Come on. You don't believe that for a minute."

Hamayoshi giggled. "Quite. Let's get down to cases. Now as we both know, the price should lie in the area of ten to fifty million."

"That's a hell of a large area."

"But a nice area, don't you agree? Now during this conversation we can explore this area, hacking and chiseling at each other's price. Or we cannot waste each other's time and immediately repair to the middle. Which, if you'll excuse my saying, we would have arrived at anyway."

Dyer was becoming angry again. Of course, Hamayoshi was right; that was exactly where they would end up, a dollar more or less, but he resented being told it. He sat for some time, staring at the lit end of his cigar and the thin veil of smoke rising from it.

Finally Dyer said, "When?"

"It shouldn't take long to get that kind of money together. Almost as soon as you wish."

"It's not the money I'm talking about. When will you be taking over the company?"

"Ah, I'd rather not be tied down to a date just yet, if you don't mind." Hamayoshi paused, then continued casually. "By the way, how is your stock situation sorting itself out?"

"You should know. It's obvious you've got your ways of finding out what's going on around here."

"They tell me everything remains the same."

"They tell you right."

"How amazing. For once I get completely accurate information. You can't imagine how difficult it is for me to separate the truth from the twaddle. But anyway that is not your problem." He hesitated. "So you do not control more than your own stock?"

"Mr. Hamayoshi, as we decided in our last conversation, that means nothing. The other stock is as good as in my hands."

"That was before we mentioned figures. At this point, 'as good as' is not the same as 'is.' "

Dyer began tapping his cigar impatiently on the ashtray again. He didn't answer.

"Mr. Savage? Are you still there?" Hamayoshi asked. He didn't sound very worried.

"I'm here."

"But you're not pleased with the way the discussion is going. I understand. I am like you. The effort and time is spent making up one's mind. Once that is accomplished the details always seem to take too long. Let us start again. I agree with you. The stock is as good as in your own hands. I think we both understand that to mean both yours and your cousin's. But I would like it all tied up before the money is transferred. I don't think that's unreasonable, do you?"

"No," Dyer answered stiffly. "That is not unreasonable."

"Good. Very good. Then we both agree that thirty million is a fair sum, and that until you have the stock or at least the voting proxy in your hands, this amount will not be deposited."

"Yep."

Dyer leaned back in his chair. Now that the dirty work was over, he was eager to be done with the call. Hamayoshi was right. The energy went into the making of a decision. Once that was done, the rest was tedious. But also he knew he was eager to forget what had passed between them. He felt as if he were being surrounded by dark shadows. What he was doing was wrong; he knew it, and it scared him, and the sooner he was finished with the call, the sooner he could block it from his mind. Later, of course, when he implemented the agreement, he would have to be reminded of it, but for now all he wanted was a stiff drink and some fresh air.

"Oh, one other thing, Mr. Savage." Hamayoshi's voice had grown very delicate. "What are you doing about Anti-Cor?"

Dyer was surprised. "Nothing seems to escape your spies."

"I like to be kept informed."

"Then you should know nothing is happening with it. There's a skeleton staff; some work is being done, but it was Ben's baby. I'm just letting it wither."

"It's a good process."

"Then I'm afraid that's where you're not well informed. Anti-Cor is not cost effective. I'd cancel all research if I weren't worried it might cause a fuss."

"That would be a mistake."

"Look, Mr. Hamayoshi, there's a difference between us. You're a negotiator. I know the business inside out. Anti-Cor is too expensive to use in appliances. Given a miracle, it might break even in automobiles. About the only place where there's a chance of making it pay is defense. And certainly after what we decided today, that is not an area Midwestern would want to become involved in."

Hamayoshi didn't answer, and Dyer laughed. "The Justice Department wouldn't look too kindly on a Japanese-owned steel company bidding on a defense contract, eh?"

"My consortium is not purely Japanese, you know. We have a multinational flavor to us."

"Doesn't matter. Still applies."

There was a pause before Hamayoshi replied. His voice was very soft but very firm. "Nevertheless, we would like to see research on Anti-Cor stepped up. In fact, we'd like to see it given top priority."

Dyer was working on his cigar again, angrily turning it in his teeth. With each passing minute, the darkness seemed to spread more completely over him. He shivered. "Are you telling me that without Anti-Cor there's no deal?"

"I'm telling you nothing. I'm suggesting you start up Anti-Cor again."

"Against my better judgment?"

"Sometimes a person can be too close to see the implications."

Dyer was silent. He had stopped chewing on his cigar, but he held it tightly between clenched teeth. Not a muscle moved, and he stared into space. He was thinking. Then slowly he came to life.

Family Passions

"Exactly what implications are you talking about, Mr. Hamayoshi?"

"I don't know that it's important."

"Don't you? Well, I do. Let's run through this together, shall we? Now, as I said before, the only chance of making Anti-Cor cost effective is in the area of defense." Dyer's voice became very hard, and there were the beginnings of fear in it. "Just what kind of game are you playing? What exactly are you planning?"

Hamayoshi laughed. "Not another attack on Pearl Harbor, if that's what you're imagining."

"You know perfectly well that's not it."

"Then what are you imagining, Mr. Savage?"

"A little free-lance business. Libya, Iran, the IRA, those nut cases in Italy. You name it."

"You have quite an imagination."

Dyer whispered, "Just exactly who are you?"

"You've checked my credentials."

"Yes. I have. You are, as you say, a consortium with a multinational flavor. And I know about groups like yours. They sell to the highest bidder. They have no allegiances."

"And what are your allegiances, Mr. Savage?"

Dyer recoiled. Suddenly he could see how far he had gone, and he wanted to run from it in terror. "I think I'm just beginning to find out. You can forget your deal."

Hamayoshi giggled. "And this phone conversation? What shall I do about it?"

There was something in Hamayoshi's tone that stopped Dyer. "What do you mean?" he asked anxiously.

"Well, certainly it must have occurred to you that I was recording it."

Dyer closed his eyes tightly. In the corners he could feel tears burning.

"Surely the idea must have crossed your mind. Well, anyway, Mr. Savage. It has been recorded."

"Yes," Dyer said slowly. "But your recording means nothing if I back out. And I do back out now, Mr. Hamayoshi."

"There's still the issue of your company. I hardly think if they hear this they'll find you were acting in a manner befitting the future president of Midwestern Steel."

Dyer opened his eyes. He could feel the tears slip down his cheeks and he was shaking. "Don't forget your part of the conversation was recorded too."

"Quite," Hamayoshi answered evenly. "If this conversation were ever revealed, it would not be very favorable for me either. But there's an essential difference between us. I'm Japanese. Remember? We're the ones who produced the kamikaze. Indeed, there is no question that as an individual I would be ruined. But my consortium would not. And that means a great deal to me. As for you, your loyalties lie purely with yourself. Though this disclosure would not destroy Midwestern it would ruin you, both with your family and with your company, and that would be the only thing that would matter."

Dyer was silent. The tears had slid down his face, disappearing into his shirt collar, and there were no more. But his hands felt cold, and he still was shaking.

Hamayoshi sounded calm. "Everything will straighten itself out as soon as your stock situation is resolved. Truly, don't let the other part worry you. You made your decision the moment you picked up the phone to call me. All else is commentary."

THIRTY

It was with a feeling of dread that James climbed the stairs to Elizabeth's house. Never before had she called him at the office and asked him to come over. So far as he knew, she never telephoned anyone in the family, just allowing them to stop by naturally. But his grandmother had telephoned him, deliberately, even though she was sure to see him at Christmas dinner the next day, and he knew that whatever had prompted the call must be very important.

Elizabeth answered the door immediately. Clearly she'd been waiting for him to come, standing near the threshold, anxiously glancing at the old discarded wristwatch of Ben's she wore strapped around her thick graceless wrist.

"Kind it is that you came so soon," she said as she opened the door.

James's concerned eyes ran over her. "Are you okay?"

"Aye. Well enough for an old woman." She led James to the living room. "A drink I won't offer. For enough there is of that already from what I hear."

Then she stopped, angry at herself. "Fool! The wrong way have I started. In my mind, ever since I rang, I have rehearsed our conversation. But hardly are you through the door, and already I am wrong. And for that I am truly sorry."

Her eyes were imploring. "Please, sit you down, and don't leave me."

James couldn't hide his reluctance, and perhaps he didn't want to, but he took a seat and waited until his grandmother had made herself comfortable. As she lowered herself into a chair, James noticed how feeble she had grown since the last time he'd seen her. But this was only a passing thought; mostly he was scared. Now he knew why she had called him, and why she had been waiting at the door so anxiously. He pulled out a cigarette, but he didn't feel much like smoking, and he just held the lighter in his hand, feeling its cold smoothness.

Elizabeth laced her broad fingers in her lap and stared down at them, determined to start slowly. "An old woman I am," she said finally. "And not well acquainted with the world as it is. Nor, truth be known, have I ever been. My world it is what's immediately around me. And never has there been the time or inclination for much else. This I tell you so you will forgive my bluntness and my stupidity while still listening to my words. Aye, for though limited my experience, much there is that I understand about life."

James broke in. "Grandmother, I know what you're going to say."

"No one knows what the other will say, till it is said. I'm sorry, James. But a talk is necessary, if for no other reason than my own relief."

She stopped, rubbing her face roughly with her thick wrinkled hands. Clearly she did not know how to proceed and was suffering. Then finally she asked, "What will become of us when Ben dies?"

James had never seen his grandmother out of control before, and it scared him, made him feel cast adrift. He'd always counted on her as the one permanent thing in his life. His mother gone, his father never really there for him, his grandmother had been the rock he'd moored to as a young boy. And though he rarely visited or thought all that much about her, still to this day she was his foundation. But now, seeing her so unsure and afraid made him aware that she was just a very old woman who soon would die.

He blocked out the thought. "Things will go on just as they do today. Dad's been away over three months, and everything's going well."

"Is it, then?"

James asked quickly, "Do you have any reason to suspect it isn't? Has something happened?"

"No. But rapid you are to jump to doubt. And that merely increases my concern."

"Don't worry, Grandma, I won't let anything happen to Midwestern." James looked down at his lighter. Its shiny surface was smeared with fingerprints. "Look, I'll tell you something that I wasn't planning on mentioning. Dyer and I had a talk recently, and I reminded him that I hold a large amount of Midwestern stock. I've forced him to give me a greater say in the running of the company."

"And he accepted this?"

"Yes, he did," James answered surely, and for a minute he almost convinced himself. But when he glanced over at his grandmother, he saw that she was frowning. "You don't believe it?"

"It I believe. He is another story entirely."

James was surprised. Whatever his grandmother's feelings about members of the family, no matter how obvious, she was careful not to say anything, as if in giving her anxieties word, she gave them reality. But now she was staring at him pointedly, and it was clear what she was thinking.

"Well, whether he meant it or not, he has no other choice. He needs my support."

Elizabeth was staring at him. "And I need yours. A child you are no longer, and yet still you act the part. You do not work hard. You do not care. This I have always known. But now it must stop. The drinking, the spending money. All of it must stop, and you must take over. There is only you to guard us now. The family has need of you."

"No, Grandmother. Not me." His voice was almost pleading. More than anything he wanted to tell her that he was weak and malleable, that he could only form a resolve, not act on it. He wanted to explain he'd thought for one brief moment in Dyer's office he had finally found strength. Yet how long had he held to it? He'd never explained himself to anyone except his own reflection as he stood looking into the mirror in the morning, when the excesses of the night before were plainly imprinted.

James remembered his cigarette and lit it. But he didn't put the lighter away; he kept it in his hand, turning it over and over. Then suddenly he was talking, without thinking, but just talking in the vague hope that someone would listen and perhaps excuse him or perhaps intervene. "I don't know, Grandma," he said sadly. "It's as if there is this inherent weakness in me, a fault that's been there since birth, certainly since I was very young. There are times when I feel everything strengthening, and I try to convince myself that it isn't there or at least that it's begun to heal. But that's never for long. God help me, it's always there."

"Then you must fight it."

James laughed sadly. "You think I don't try? Jesus, I've turned myself inside out from trying." He gripped tightly to the lighter, as if it could save him. "Grandma, I don't know how. Just tell me how."

"I think you already know the answer to that."

He nodded and turned away, looking around the room desperately, as if for somewhere to hide. Then finally he said softly, "I saw my mother."

Elizabeth sat up. "Dylan? You've seen Dylan? How is she?"

"I think I like her."

Elizabeth smiled fondly. "Aye. Always I liked her too."

"She asked after you."

Elizabeth nodded. "Aye. Dylan. Aye."

"She thinks a great deal of you."

Elizabeth looked at him. "Why did you go there?"

"That's the same question she kept asking me."

"And your answer?"

He shrugged. "Search me, Grandma. I wish I knew why I do half the things I do."

Elizabeth didn't say anything for a while. She was still staring at James, shaking her head slowly, sadly. Then suddenly she blurted out, "You must give him up."

It was as if James had been slapped across the face. Though he knew his grandmother suspected his life-style, he assumed it was something she kept from her thoughts, protecting both herself and James. He had been somewhat prepared for her lecture about his drinking and spending, but he had not expected her to touch on this.

James sat motionless. He didn't answer her; he couldn't answer her.

Elizabeth sighed. "Aye. Well, thank you at least for not lying. Little there is that escapes this town's attention. And even I, cut off as I am, hear things that I do not wish to know." Then her face became very sad, very pensive. She leaned to James and put her large hand on his knee.

James turned away from her. He felt as if he were being stretched apart. Every muscle in his body ached. Finally he turned back. "Must we talk about this?"

"We must."

"Oh, Christ." This was said with no anger, only a weariness.

Elizabeth nodded slowly. "Why? This is something I just don't understand. Why?"

"Don't look to me to explain it to you. Oh, I can give you all kinds of glib psychological explanations. But none of them seem true, or at least wholly true."

Elizabeth closed her eyes. "Are you at least happy, then?"

"Oh, God. Sometimes I hate it."

"Then why, James?"

"I don't know." He was imploring. "Don't you see? I just don't know."

"I must understand. I have to find an explanation. What is it that this man has which cannot be found in a woman?"

"Grandma, listen to me. It doesn't have to do with it being a man. That's the whole damn confusing part. I chose this kind of life, but I could have chosen any number of others. Maybe I picked it because I knew it would hurt everyone the most. Look, it's not just a physical thing for me. Otherwise I'd be in one of those nice stable little relationships with no danger and all safety. And you might not like it, but you'd lump it. But it isn't like that for me. It could have been B girls or whips and chains or types like Boris. And that's the point. The problem is not what I am, but *why* I am."

Elizabeth nodded to herself, trying to understand. Finally she asked sadly, "Then why are you, James?"

James just shook his head. He was crumpled into his chair, his eyes begging her to stop.

"I can't not ask you, James. Though sorry I am, still I must try to see."

"What difference can it make?"

"I believe in you."

"Please don't. Please give up on me."

Elizabeth shook her head. "Even should I wish to and know you well, I do not. I never could do that."

"Jesus, Grandma, I'm not worth it. Not one of us is. Forget for a while that we're your family. Look at us callously, coldly, without the veil of love, though God only knows how you could love us, but I know that you do. I'm a weak man, that's all I am. With the curse of seeing clearly who I am. And Dyer? Look at him. A man with strength but no humanity. And Pauline? Bitter, angry, destructive. Or Uncle Evan? Or even Ben? It's as if with each generation the strain has weakened. The only lucky thing in this whole sad tale is that it seems it will stop here. Because from what I can tell neither Dyer nor I will have children. And that is a gift from the gods."

Elizabeth was horrified. "No! This you must not say."

"Why? Because it's true? Use your eyes, Grandma. Look at us. Do you know what my mother said? She said you were worth more than any of us. And it's true. We aren't worth your concern or your love. We're withered and decadent and spilling our seeds on infertile ground. And I must say for everyone concerned, that's about the best news since the destruction of Sodom and Gomorrah."

"Stop it, James! Kill me you will with your words, for they slaughter all that I live for. Never have I believed in God and salvation and the afterlife. The only reason I have ever been able to find is the family. Without it is . . ."

"Chaos?"

"Aye. Without it is death."

James's face was very white. "Don't put your trust in me. I'll only let you down."

"The easy way out you take."

"Don't believe it. Sometimes I think it's far harder to be weak." He paused, becoming angry at himself. "Of course it isn't. That's just another of the lies I tell myself, another aspect of the fault in me. But I can't help it. None of us can."

"You could be strong. You do not try."

"Grandmother, sometimes you can be a very hard and judgmental woman."

Elizabeth sighed; it seemed to come from deep inside her. "I'm dying," she whispered.

James was silent, and she wondered if he had heard her. "For some time have I known, though I did not wish to speak of it. No one have I told until now."

Still James didn't answer, but there were tears in his eyes, and she could tell that he had understood and was beyond words.

"Of course, no surprise there is. An old woman I am. And old women do die."

James whispered, "Is it certain?"

"Cancer."

He took in breath. "Yes. Of course. Have they told you how long?"

"Aye. Enough time there is to finish up. Which is what I intend to do."

"You think you can just take the family, give a stiff shake, fold us up and pack us away neatly?"

"I can try."

James watched her sadly. "You really believe people can change."

"I must."

James nodded. "I understand." He stood stiffly.

Elizabeth looked panicky. "Is that all you can say?"

"That's all I can promise," he answered. "There's a great deal I can say. But none of it means much anymore, does it?"

"I cannot die with fear for my family in my heart."

"Grandma, you're asking me to change years of weakness for an ideal I don't even believe in."

"Do you believe in me?"

He knew what was coming next. "In other words you're asking me to change for you?"

"If truly there is the belief that I'm worth it."

"Good Lord, you're as sly and as cunning as they come."

Elizabeth smiled solemnly. "Then do it for my slyness. Or anything you like. But for God's sake do it. So little time there is, and so much to be done."

James was motionless, then he nodded and quickly left. But once he was outside, he paused, looking back at the old Victorian house, and he was crying.

"I want you out of here!" James strode across the living room to the guest closet.

Boris looked up, surprised. He was in the kitchen, breaking eggs into a large aluminum bowl. He had decorated the whole room with mistletoe, and a large sprig of it hung from the doorway, blocking his view. Still, he could see James in the other room, reaching to the top shelf of the closet, taking down one of his suitcases. He unzipped it and threw it open onto the leather couch.

Boris said nothing and went back to his eggs. But a moment later he put the bowl down and walked to the threshold.

"All right. You might as well tell me why you're angry."

"I'm not angry," James answered tightly.

"Funny. You sure could have fooled me." Boris stayed in the doorway, frightened to come out into the living room.

"Look, I just want you out. But I'm not angry at you."

"Really? Then who are you angry at?"

"I guess I'm just angry at myself."

"As usual." Boris watched James with understanding.

James sank into a chair, his head in his hands. "Oh, God, Boris, I suppose you deserve an explanation. But it's all so long and complicated, and in the end, the answer is the same. You'll have to leave."

"I see." But Boris didn't move. He glanced toward the kitchen counter at the bowl of eggs and little pile of grated cheese. "I bought the store out of mistletoe. I thought it would make you laugh. I . . ." He didn't continue. He walked into the living room and sat in a chair. "You're right," he said softly. "I do deserve some sort of explanation. At least so I know what I did wrong for the next time. You know?" Again his voice drifted off.

"It isn't anything you've done. Can't you get that through your head?"

"I'd be delighted to. If only you'd give me a chance."

"Oh, Christ."

Boris said stiffly, "Do you mind if I have a drink before I pack? This is not exactly a pleasurable experience."

James waved his hand toward the bar. Boris got up, poured two brandies, and brought one over. James took the glass without saying a word, and Boris retreated to the center of the room.

"It's not fair, you know? It's just not fair. If two people spend time together, there are certain things they have the right to know. Even in our crazy society, there are certain rights."

James nodded. "That's just the point. It's the society I'm rejecting. Not you."

"A fine distinction," Boris said, his composure returning. "I am part of the society. Therefore you are rejecting me."

"Look, I'm not in the mood to argue semantics."

"Well, what is it that bothers you about it? Things have changed. It's not as if this were a totally unusual situation anymore. Far from it. Even in stodgy old Midland."

"It's not that. Jesus, it's not any of that."

"Well, what is it, the drinking, the drugs? We don't have to do that. Lots of people don't. I don't care. I don't need it."

"You don't exactly discourage it either though, do you?"

"Look, James, I'm not your mother. I don't tie you up and force you into the Empire Club every night."

"I know. I know. But I just keep thinking it has to stop somewhere, and this is a start. It's like a symbol to me."

"To you? Or to your family? That's what it is, isn't it? It's your family who told you to get rid of me."

James didn't answer.

"For Christ sake, speak to me, James. I deserve it, damn you!"

"All right. Let's say it's partly my family."

"But surely they all must have suspected for years. Who said something? Dyer?"

"No. Not Dyer."

"Certainly not your Aunt Pauline. She hardly has the right to talk. Who was it, your mother? You said you went to see your mother, but you didn't talk about what happened. Was it she?"

James laughed bitterly. "Hardly."

Boris nodded. He was pacing now, and he looked nervous, but not nearly so frightened. "Then it was your grandmother, wasn't it?"

James didn't answer.

"Look, we can overcome that. If you find it too hard, we can move away. San Francisco, Los Angeles, New York. You name it."

James flared. "What the hell are you talking about? I work here. Remember Midwestern Steel?"

"But you don't have to, do you?"

"Of course I have to." James was becoming very angry.

"Come on, James. You're not exactly a poor man. I know you draw a nice salary and all that, but I'm sure other arrangements could be made."

James glared. "What arrangements?"

"You could sell your stock. I'm sure you have a good chunk of it.

Family Passions 303

And I wouldn't be surprised if you stood to inherit a great deal more. Your cousin, Dyer, might be interested in buying it, for example. Arrangements could be made.''

James shook his head. "You just don't get it, do you?"

Boris was pacing again. He felt tight and scared, and he couldn't look at James. "I most certainly do get it. Don't give me any bullshit about loving dear old Midwestern Steel. I'll tell you what you love and it has nothing to do with oxygen furnaces or hot rolling mills. It has to do with living life, not that deathtrap of a business you drag yourself into every day. You know what you look like at the office? You look like you're in pain. The first thing you do every evening is have two drinks just to clear the office out of your mind and return to the land of the living. You should see your face every evening like I do. Then you wouldn't hand me any more garbage about Midwestern Steel. If you're looking around for a reason for your drinking and drugs, look there. Take my advice, get out now, while you still have your soul."

James looked crushed. "I have obligations."

"To whom? Your grandmother?" He laughed angrily. "Do you tell her how to live her life? Would you go into her house and order her to do something that would kill her?"

"Working at Midwestern is hardly killing me."

"Really? Are you sure it isn't?"

"Well, then so is the other."

"What? The life we're leading?"

He walked over to James and crouched by his chair, unsure whether to touch him. "I told you before; we don't have to do it. You want to move away? I'll do it. You want to become some ordinary little middle-class couple? I'll do it. The question is, do you hate me along with the life we're leading?"

James looked at him. "You know I don't hate you."

"Good. At least we've got that much straight. Next question. Do you still love me?"

James's voice was pleading. "Don't you see, that's not the point."

"Of course it's the point."

"I have an obligation to my family."

"And don't they have an obligation to you in return? Sure, it's easy for your grandmother to tell you to give up the only thing that makes you happy, but what does she offer you in exchange?"

"You're twisting things, don't you see?"

"All I see is that I care for you, and I care what becomes of you.

And it seems like I'm the only one around here who does. All your grandmother cares about is the family name."

Boris sensed he had gone too far and quickly added, "Look, fine. That's what's important to her, and I respect her for it. But what's important to you? Can you honestly say you give a good god damn whether the name of Savage continues through the ages?"

"I don't know."

Boris stood up. "Okay. Fine. Then I think it's about time you tried to figure it out. I think it's about time you decided what is important to you. Not your blessed father or grandmother or cousin or anybody else who wants to tell you what to do."

James smiled ironically. "And that includes you?"

Boris returned his smile. "Well, of course, you might allow a passing thought to me." Then he grew serious. "No, listen, I'm giving you good advice. Think about it. Who makes you happy? Them or me? I guess in the end it comes down to that, you know. Making a choice between us."

"It's all so damn complicated. It seemed so clear before, but now it's so . . . I just don't know what to do." James rubbed his head with his hand, but he looked less distraught and unsure.

"Okay, then let me tell you what to do. First you finish your brandy. Then we'll both get up and go into the kitchen, and you'll start chopping the onions, while I butter the soufflé dish. And then I'll make a good vinaigrette. And you'll wash the lettuce. And I won't bring the subject up again. And you'll sleep on it. Then when you're ready, we can talk again. Okay?"

James was silent; he didn't even move.

Boris stood over him. "Now listen to me, James. You don't have to come to a decision right this minute. It can wait. Everything can wait." He smiled. "Except the soufflé."

James finished off his brandy and sat staring at his empty glass. Then he looked at Boris. "Okay. Like you said. Everything can wait."

Boris took his glass from him, and James wearily pulled himself from his chair and walked with him to the bar.

THIRTY-ONE

Wales

Tally slipped on her nightgown and opened the shutters. Cold damp air rushed into the room chilling her, but she didn't move from the window. She almost welcomed the discomfort as at least some kind of feeling.

A cold white moon was high in the sky, leaving icy streaks of light on the hills, making the snow on the trees glitter. It was beautiful out there, but empty and cold and dead. There was, she supposed, beauty in death.

Next door she could hear the sounds of Ben moving his wheelchair around his room. He was able to get around by himself now, but it was slow painful work and unbelievably frustrating. He was even able to walk by holding the parallel bars, though that was unbearably difficult for him and beyond tiring. Still, he forced himself to do it. His angry defiance was astounding to Tally, and frightening too, very frightening.

Tally shivered and put her arms around herself, but she didn't leave the window. She stood transfixed, looking out at the silvery landscape and thinking about the man she heard moving on the other side of the wall.

His voice was becoming stronger, his words more sure, full of tone and color. It was a miracle to watch, and he too recognized it. Yet, oddly, he'd insisted that no word of his progress be sent home. Did he hope somewhere in his unexpressed dreams that his recovery might be so complete that one day he could return and surprise everyone? Was it possible he believed he might resume his former life? It was exactly the kind of arrogance she would expect from him, and she found herself growing irritated at it. At the same time it was impossible to believe that he was going to die. He seemed so much alive, as if in coming close to death he had finally conquered it.

Tally laughed at herself. That was just the kind of ridiculous emotional thought she might have had when she was younger. Years ago she had run from all that, recoiling from life as from a searing flame. She'd made a conscious choice to live in a smooth peaceful round of the expected, and she knew if she had to make the decision today, she'd make the same one. Nevertheless, standing in the darkness on Christmas Eve, hearing Ben in the room next door, Tally's quiet was disturbed, and the peaceful life she had chosen seemed empty and lonely.

Her mind went to David, her ex-husband, who one day became a stranger though she'd known him better than anyone. The memory of their angry silences came back, the deadening aloneness as they both sat at the breakfast table, each encased in his own world, the clinking of china and cutlery growing louder and louder as they became two separate beings, living in parallel worlds, with nothing in common. She could see David, standing in the bathroom, a towel wrapped around him, scowling into the mirror as he surveyed his face, obsessively searching for any mark that might reveal the passing years. More and more as he could see age creeping up on him, he became terrified. Yet he seemed only able to exorcise his terror by multiplying it, by chasing after increasingly younger people, by pursuing his endless round of parties and his romances with something close to a frenzy.

It had been a terrible time for Tally, one she had never fully recovered from. All the same, looking out at the cold moon, she remembered it with a certain amount of envy. While she had felt sad then, at least she'd had her sadness; at least she'd had something. Now she had nothing.

Ben was still moving around next door. She heard the water running, and imagined him struggling to pull himself to his sink, clutching at the bowl with his strong hands and splashing water onto his face with his awkward shaky movements.

Once again she wondered what he could be thinking as day after day he pushed himself to recover. It was inconceivable that he actually believed he would be well enough to return to Midland yet something in her believed in it too.

Oddly she found herself resenting it. She had seen that kind of thing before in nurses and social workers, family and friends, the anger when someone regained his independence, the inability to give up the superior position. And yet she suspected in this case, it was something more.

The sound of water stopped, and she could hear Ben pushing his wheelchair out of the bathroom and into his room. She turned from the window and quickly got into bed. She didn't want to stay on this job anymore; it was too risky and scary. She supposed it was Ben's defiance, the fight that he was putting up that disturbed her, and also his tranquility, as if in the struggle he were finding a kind of peace. As she watched him, she became unsettled, sometimes even frightened. There was the feeling he might engulf her.

Tally pulled the covers tightly around herself and lay in the darkness. She heard Ben in his room, transferring himself to his bed. And as she listened, she wondered if it was only Ben who was damaged, or what she herself had become.

When Tally entered Edith's neat little-old-lady bedroom with its fussy wallpaper and matching curtains, Dr. Waring and the district nurse were already there. Dr. Waring looked up and nodded to her, but there was none of the usual irony in his glance. Tally was his patient's niece, and his brusque manner was never shown to relatives. The nurse was a woman Tally had met many times, but she too seemed changed. She hardly looked at Tally, as if frightened she might be asked a question she didn't want to answer. Nevertheless, her slow plodding movements gave her away. Everything about her said there was no need to waste energy; the outcome was inevitable.

Edith lay motionless, but as Tally pulled up a chair to the bed, she opened her eyes. Her lids were very heavy and rimmed with scarlet. It was with great difficulty she was able to focus.

Slowly she reached out her hand to Tally. Taking her aunt's fragile hand in hers, feeling the parchment skin so frail and cold, Tally could see how very ill she was and that she was going to die. Already life seemed to be leaving her, shrinking from her extremities to her center.

It seemed impossible to Tally that she hadn't noticed before how thin her aunt had grown. Rapidly in succession she saw all the incidents she had ignored, the signs she had shut out in her desperate attempt not to see what she supposed she'd known all along.

Tears came to Tally's eyes, and she fought against them. She didn't want to break down now. Still, the sadness remained, threatening to overwhelm her, and behind it, terror, childish and unreasoning. She didn't want her aunt to die. She loved her; she needed her. Edith was her last tie to the world, and without her, Tally would be totally alone.

Edith smiled thinly and whispered. "Merry Christmas." Her lips were trembling, and her eyes were very watery and full of pain. Every movement seemed to cost her a good deal.

Tally stroked her aunt's hand. "I'm so sorry I wasn't here for you."

Edith's eyes sparkled. "Darling, with all due respect, your being here would not have made any difference."

"At least you wouldn't have been alone."

Edith laughed, but it was hollow, as lifeless as her hand. "I'm afraid I'll have to become used to that. Unfortunately you won't be able to come with me. Not that I wouldn't be happy for the company—" She stopped. Her breath was coming quick and shallow.

"Don't try to talk, Auntie."

Again the hollow laugh. "What should I keep my voice for?" But she had grown weaker, and she paused, closing her eyes, looking inward. "I wonder if they have television where I'm going."

She opened her eyes and looked at the ceiling. There were tears at the corners, and slowly they slipped down the sides of her face. "I expect they do, you know. Of course there's no guarantee which way I'm going, is there? I haven't always been a very nice woman." She paused, thinking, then tried to look happy. "Ah, well, the last great mystery. It's really rather exciting." Her voice trailed off, and she closed her eyes again.

Tally didn't say anything. She was aware that Dr. Waring and the nurse were leaving the room; she could hear the sound of their footsteps on the creaking floorboards as they went down the stairs. There was a clock ticking not far off, and Tally realized it was her own wristwatch. The room was that silent.

Eventually Edith opened her eyes, but she didn't seem to be seeing anything. "How's Ben?" she asked.

"He's fine. He's using the parallel bars now. He wants to try two canes. It's ridiculous, of course. But who knows. He might be able to do it."

"He will. He's a tough customer." Edith fell silent, gathering her energy, then she turned to Tally, and this time it was clear she was seeing her. "You'll take care of him for me?"

"Naturally. It's my job."

"That is not what I meant and you know it." Edith cringed. For a moment she seemed to collapse inward with pain, then slowly she recovered. Tally could see what an act of will it must have been for her to talk, and how important it must be to her. She felt the chill inside her crack; tears threatened to break through, and she clutched her aunt's hand tighter, as if trying to force life back into her.

Edith's voice was thin. "I regret leaving you alone like this."

Tally looked away. "Now, Auntie, you aren't going anywhere, so please stop talking that way."

"We never lied to one another before. Let's not start now." Her eyes were demanding. "He's a good man, Tally. Better than he even knows. You see, he's just a young soul, and young souls are like that. They haven't been on earth before, and it's all rather confusing and complicated to them. It's up to us old souls to show them the way." She smiled weakly. "On the other hand, young souls can be the most fun. As long as they're shown."

Tally was crying now; she didn't answer.

"Promise me that you'll try."

Tally nodded. She could feel the pressure going from Edith's hand, and she wanted to scream, but she couldn't. She couldn't even look at her aunt; she knew if she looked at her there would be no control.

"I'm tired," Edith said. "Strange. That's all it is. I'm just very very tired."

Again Edith closed her eyes. Tally sat holding Edith's hand. And sometime in those few minutes of silence, Edith crossed from life into death.

THIRTY-TWO

David Tanchan had been driving all night. In fact, he'd been driving the better part of two days, and he felt exhausted and angry and unsure why he'd even made the trip. He lit a cigarette, decided he didn't want it, then made himself smoke it out of irritation. He turned on the car radio and swung through the garble of French and German until he found BBC 3. But even on the classical station they were just talking, and talk was the last thing he wanted to hear.

David switched off the radio and stared out at the gray mist that held the countryside like a gloved fist. For a moment he was tempted to turn back. He certainly wasn't very optimistic about receiving any comfort from Tally. She'd left him before, and it seemed unlikely she'd changed her mind in the intervening years. Yet there he was, driving for days, like a salmon fighting upstream. He told himself he had nowhere else to go, and the terrible part was he knew it was true.

The exit was just ahead. Again he considered turning back, but he knew he wouldn't do it, out of cowardice or perhaps the opposite.

Seeing the gray lonely countryside he was passing, he tried to imagine Tally living there, her only company farmers, retired clergymen, and shopkeepers. The thought was ridiculous, yet he also knew that it wasn't. She was obviously in hiding, and being somewhat acquainted with that need himself, he understood. He was even able to see his own part in driving her to it, and while he wasn't exactly pleased about that, he wasn't entirely sorry either. At least it seemed a link between them.

David consulted a slip of paper on the dashboard, then turned off the main road. The house was just ahead. Even in the gray Welsh light, he could see it was a pretty house, large, rambling, of weathered stone, set back a good distance from the road. Traces of snow clung to the shadowy places, and there was smoke rising from the stone chimney into the early-evening sky. The lights were on and the curtains drawn. He could not see inside.

He'd had a great deal of trouble tracing Tally to the nursing agency and even more trouble in persuading them to tell him where she was, so he had set off considering the possibility that his information had been incorrect. But as he slowed the car and came to a halt at the front gates, he sensed that he hadn't been misinformed and that Tally was inside.

David turned off the motor and lit another cigarette. This one he wanted. Snow was falling all around him now, and chill damp air seeped into the car, penetrating his clothes.

In the house a light went on upstairs, and the silhouette of a middle-aged woman walked through the room. David surprised himself by being relieved that Tally's patient was not a man. He laughed at his childishness, but still the relief remained.

He sat there for a long while, smoking and watching the evening darkness closing in, thoughts bouncing up and back in his mind anxiously. And after a while he made up his mind to go in, as he'd known he would.

It was Tally who opened the door to him. She seemed to draw back. "David!"

David smiled sarcastically. "You might at least pretend delight."

Tally composed herself. "You're wrong. I *am* delighted."

"Then you might at least allow me through the door."

Tally laughed and stepped back to let David in. "You must understand I'm somewhat surprised."

"Really? I don't know why. It's only been ten years." He walked past her. "You needn't bother telling me how well I look. I look terrible."

Then he stopped. His face was sad. "But you look wonderful. My God, you really do look wonderful."

She blushed. "Even after all these years?" She was trying for sarcasm, but her eyes were serious.

Then suddenly Ben's voice boomed from the living room, and the mood was broken. "Who's at the door?"

Tally giggled, almost girlishly. "It's for me, Ben. My husband."

"Ex-husband to be precise," David answered loudly for the benefit of the man in the other room. To Tally he just raised his eyebrows.

"I'd hardly say that jealousy is the appropriate emotion at this point."

"Not jealousy. Only curiosity."

"Even curiosity might be considered a presumption."

Tally laughed and began leading him to the living room, but when she glanced back, she saw that David wasn't smiling, and he really did not look very well. He was thinner than before, and his tall elegant body had taken on a joylessness that saddened her. His face was still youthful, his blond hair only traced with gray, but everything about him told that he was ten years older. There was a frost of disappointment.

She stopped just short of the living room. "Why did you come?" she asked softly.

David took a while to answer. "I really don't know."

Tally could tell this wasn't true, and that he'd come in some way hoping for her to save him, though from what or whom she didn't know.

Tally entered the living room. Though Ben had been in his wheelchair, a blanket over his legs when she left, now he was sitting in one of the chairs. Tally could see the wheelchair where he'd pushed it into the corner of the room. The blanket she could not see at all.

Ben put out his hand and said heartily, "My name's Ben Savage." But his eyes were searching David's to discover whether his voice gave him away.

If it did, David gave no hint of it. He took Ben's hand and shook it. "I'm David Tanchan."

"Have a seat," Ben boomed. He was desperately trying to give the impression of robust health, though even he could tell he was going too far with it. He glanced over at Tally to see if she'd noticed, but she wasn't looking at Ben. She was watching David.

David smiled shyly. "I really wouldn't mind a drink."

"I can't say that I would either." Tally walked to the bar and began pouring.

Ben noted she didn't have to ask David what he drank, but then she wouldn't have to. Irritated, he turned his gaze on David. "Tally didn't tell me you were coming."

"Tally didn't know. Did you, Tally?"

"How true."

She flashed David a smile that he answered with one of his own, and in those two smiles was a whole dialogue. It doesn't matter how many years have passed; once people have lived together, the silent messages are in place, and each knew what the other was thinking.

Tally handed the drinks around. But when she tried to help Ben with his glass, there was something about the way he looked at her that told he didn't want her aid.

David was sitting well back in his chair, relaxed, comfortable. "I know this may sound crude to ask. But after all, I am part of the family, so to speak."

Tally frowned at David, though there was no real rancor in it. "So to speak."

David hesitated, but it was more for effect than out of embarrassment. "As I was saying, this may sound like I'm prying. But in what capacity is Tally here?"

"She's my nurse."

"Quite. I see."

Again Tally giggled, and Ben felt himself becoming angry. He turned on David and asked with pointed politeness, "So, tell me, Mr. Tanchan, what do you do?"

"Do?" But it was clear from David's face that he understood the question.

"For a living, I mean." Again Ben's tone was very polite, but there was a challenge in it, barely hidden.

It was a challenge that David understood. It amused him, but also it brought up all the old unpleasant feelings of uselessness and waste. "I write," he answered. "Occasionally and badly."

"But profitably?"

David raised his eyebrows. "I get by."

"Anything I might have heard of?" Ben's voice was tight.

"Quite possibly. But all that is very boring." David seemed to relax even more; there was a casual ease to him, as if he were in his own home. "And what do you do, Mr. Savage?"

"I own a steel company."

"Really? Any one I might have heard of?" David did not attempt to hide his sarcasm.

"I doubt it. It's American."

"Interesting," David said with no interest. He turned back to Tally. "You really do look well, you know. In fact, better than ever."

This seemed to embarrass Tally. She glanced down at the floor, and when she looked up, her color was still high. "How is everyone?"

David took a while to answer. "The same. Boringly, depressingly the same. Everything and everyone is just as you left it." He laughed. "I'm beginning to get the feeling that once you're past a certain age, nothing changes. As if you only get one or two choices early on, and all the rest follows."

He glanced up and saw Tally's eyes on him. Then he became animated. "Actually if you think about it, even those choices could be preordained by your parents' choices or your grandparents', all the way back. Good Lord, your whole life could have been decided upon by some gorilla eating bananas in the trees."

He stopped and smiled at Tally. Again there was the look of familiarity between them.

"Right," he continued. "The old gang. Let's see. Oh, yes. The Bensons have two children now, twins, Brian and Martin. Wretched scrawny little things. And their parents hate them greatly. As do we all."

Tally laughed. "Well, it serves them right. God, I remember

how they used to torture themselves and us about not being able to have children. She was always sending him in to have tests. Or was he always sending her?"

"He was sending her. Don't you remember, she went into the hospital to have her tubes blown."

Tally giggled. "Of course! Trudy's tubes. How could I forget them?"

"Now, now, we were all very concerned about Trudy's tubes. We spent a great deal of time and energy on them."

"But I thought the operation was a failure. Don't you remember? All the temperature taking and charts and nothing happened."

"Ah, yes. But unfortunately they found one of those new fertility drugs. Still, I suppose it could have been worse. They could have had quints."

Tally was excited. "And who else?"

"Remember the baron?"

"Some baron. All I remember was he claimed to be a grand national chess champion and he was a lousy player."

"Still is, I suppose. But it seems he really was a baron. Not only that but a rich one. His father died serveral years back, and he inherited rather a lot of money."

Tally roared with laughter. "You're joking! I'll have to write to him. He owes me twenty pounds."

"Forget it. Once he got the money, he turned us all off. Seems we weren't lofty enough company for him anymore."

"Or perhaps he didn't want to pay me back my twenty quid." Tally fell silent. She was watching David, and she looked very serious. "And how are you really?"

David waved the question away and took another sip of his drink, but his eyes told her that he was not doing very well and that he'd come there as a last resort.

Ben was watching the two of them, understanding very little of what was passing between them, but resenting their closeness and all it implied.

"I hope you'll be staying to dinner," he said coldly.

Ben's voice seemed to surprise the two of them; they had forgotten that he was there. It took a long while for Tally to echo the invitation.

"Yes. Please do stay," she said finally. "There's always plenty. We have a cook in from the village. And she's used to large families."

"Is she the woman I saw upstairs by the window?"

"No. That's Mrs. Mided. She's another nurse."

David glanced over at Ben, and it was clear from his gaze that the fact that Ben needed two nurses was not lost on him.

Ben turned away. He was still holding his scotch, untasted. He hadn't even tried to drink it, afraid he might make a fool of himself, and he was sure David had noticed this too. The shame was astounding. At that moment he wished he was as before, an inhuman relic locked into a stony existence, rather than the half-man that he was now. He glanced over at Tally, wondering if she was aware of what he was thinking. But Tally was watching David, her mind on the past.

Finally she said softly, "Auntie died last week."

"I'm so sorry." David reached over and touched her hand. "I know you were very fond of her." His hand remained on hers, and he looked into her eyes before he took it away.

"Edith was a wonderful woman," Ben added, though he knew neither of them was listening.

And suddenly he felt very tired. He hated sitting there, trapped between the two of them, an immovable rock in the flow of the conversation. He wanted to go to his room and sleep before dinner; in truth he would have been happy to sleep right through it. But he knew if he left now, there would be the demeaning transfer back to his wheelchair, and he refused to do that in front of David.

Yet the time would have to come. Even if he didn't take a rest, he would have to get himself to the table. Mrs. Mided would bustle in with her unfeeling nursey manner, and she would fuss and bother, and he would become once again an invalid. It had to happen sooner or later. Why not now, at his own convenience?

But Ben couldn't do it. All he could do was sit, rigidly clutching his drink, listening to the ebb and flow of a conversation that didn't include him.

All this passed, but Tally didn't notice. Her eyes were on David.

And then Mrs. Mided did enter the room, all fluttery and efficient. "Now, Mr. Savage," she scolded loudly. "We've totally forgotten our nap before dinner."

She found his wheelchair in the corner and pushed it over to him. Ben submitted as Mrs. Mided helped him to his chair and wheeled him from the room, but he refused to go to bed, and sat by the window, staring out. Though he could hear Tally asking about friends from the past, he wasn't trying to listen anymore. His mind was blank and his heart was hard, as stony as his body had once been.

Tally was sitting at her dressing table, looking into the mirror, when David knocked softly at the door. She wasn't surprised. She'd known all through dinner and the long evening he would come to her room. She supposed she even knew what he'd say, though she couldn't begin to imagine how she felt about it.

It had been Ben who had suggested that David spend the night. The invitation had been given with little enthusiasm, and David had accepted it with little gratitude. But from the beginning, Tally had expected the invitation and also the acceptance, and she didn't know how she felt about that either.

David hesitated in the doorway, smiling tentatively, as if frightened to come in. It was an act, of course, and Tally had seen it many times before, but also she knew that it was real. He was carrying a bottle of scotch in one hand and two glasses in the other. During their marriage they had drunk a lot of scotch together. It had started out as a ritual and ended as a refuge.

"Tell your patient I'll replace this." David was still smiling sheepishly as he walked in. He sat on the edge of the bed.

Tally retreated to her dressing table. "My patient has a name."

David laughed. "And what a name! Savage. But I suppose in his time, he must have been."

Tally stiffened. "That wasn't very nice."

"You're right. I'm sorry." David poured two scotches and handed one to Tally. He looked upset. "Sometimes I really don't like myself much."

"Very often you don't."

"Yes. I'm an incredibly shallow man." He lifted his glass to the wall. "Please accept my apologies, Mr. Savage. We all have our disabilities. I as much as you." He downed it quickly.

"You drink too much."

"Still." He poured himself another glass but he just placed it on the floor. "You do look wonderful. I think I've told you that before."

"You mentioned it. Yes."

There was a silence, David staring at the floor, Tally looking out the window at the black night.

Finally David said softly, "I finally figured out why I came." He smiled at her, but his face felt like a mask, awkward and tight.

Tally watched him with sadness. She could see from his expression how hard it must have been for him to take those few steps to her room and that he was now regretting it.

"Why are you looking at me like that?" David asked irritably. He hated himself for sitting at the edge of her bed like a scared child seeking refuge from the night monsters in the warm, lighted room of his parents.

He picked up his drink and swallowed half of it. "It isn't making it any easier for me having you watch me like that."

He paused, smiling at his awkwardness, and with the smile, he seemed to relax. "Oh, Christ, I suppose what I mean is, please make it easier for me. But it doesn't get any easier, does it? Funny. In the end you're really no different than when you were an adolescent. I've been a grown up for twenty-five years now. And the most ridiculous part is I don't think I've learned a thing. Certainly my manners are better. I'm more polished, and I don't get quite so nervous when I have to telephone a woman. At least I don't have to write my little speech on a slip of paper."

He took a sip of his drink, then he leaned back on the bed. He no longer looked so tired and strained; everything was easier about him. "I say, have I ever told you that's what I did when I called you that first time? 'Hello,' I said, reading it right off the paper. 'This is David Tanchan. I was wondering what you were doing Saturday night.'"

"And what did I answer?"

"Ah! You were busy. But I was prepared for that. I had an alternative night written on my crib sheet. Nevertheless, it did lack a certain spontaneity. And if you'd been busy then too, I would have been stuck. Christ, I used to hate that whole performance. Well, I still do really. As I said, inside I'm no different. I haven't changed at all, the same insecurities and fears, the same doubts and questions, and I hate it, Tally." He stiffened. "I suppose I really hate myself."

"And anyone who dares to love you."

His eyes lit up. "God, you are clever. You really are something." And then the sadness was over him again. "Of course you always were."

He took a sip of his drink and avoided her eyes. "I still talk too much, don't I?"

"Only when you're nervous."

"Yes. Only when I'm nervous." He took refuge in his drink, then continued softly. "You know, there never was anyone else."

Tally went rigid. "Oh, really? Well, you did an excellent job of pretending."

"They meant nothing."

"To whom?" Tally could feel all the old resentment rising inside her, and the ten years had not diminished it. She couldn't even look at David. "Do you have any idea how it was with everyone saying things, of course carefully veiled, every time they met me? Do you know the agony of all those nights when you had to see an old friend or publisher or whatever excuse your furtive little brain could come up with? And I knew. God, how I knew. But, oh, no, they didn't mean anything to you. That was your problem. Nothing and no one meant anything to you."

"You did."

"So you say now."

"Then perhaps I have changed."

David was still holding his glass, but he didn't feel much like drinking anymore. He placed it back on the floor next to him. "I've been thinking of moving to the south of France, Le Lavandou, a nice town, quiet off season, so I can write."

"Alone?"

"Aha, you see, she still cares."

"And she still hasn't received an answer." Then she stopped. For in truth the bitterness came more from habit than from feeling. Impossible as it seemed, she had forgiven him long ago. Or perhaps even that had dried up in her. "I'm sorry," she said softly. "You don't have to bother answering. It doesn't really matter."

David held her eyes. "No. Not alone. I can't stand to be alone anymore. Not even for a few minutes."

"Ever."

"Okay, ever. It's too noisy when I'm alone. All those voices in my head, going on and on at me. 'Why did you do that? Why don't you do this?' At least when someone else is talking it's quiet." He hesitated, gathering courage. "And you, Tally? Are you alone?"

"Yes. Not that I say that with any particular pride."

"And the man in the other room?"

"Ben?"

"Whoever. What about him? I've seen the way he looks at you. And, I might add, there's something about the way you look at him. Don't tell me you're just here in a business capacity. Or what I mean is, please tell me that's what it is."

Tally laughed. It seemed impossible that David could imagine she was interested in Ben. And yet something inside her wondered if she wasn't.

It took a while for her to answer. "If you're asking whether I've slept with him, no, I haven't. If you're asking whether I was tempted—then I don't know. Perhaps I was."

David glanced away. "Good old honest Tally."

"You always could depend on me for that."

"I always could depend on you for a lot of things." David went very quiet. He looked around the room, at the furniture, the floor, anywhere but at Tally. "Perhaps I should have written a crib sheet," he murmured.

Then suddenly he sat up, as if forcing himself to action before thinking crippled him forever. He put his hand out to Tally. "I love you. I always have. Even during our worst, I loved you."

Tally looked at David's hand reaching out to her. She looked at it with neither anger nor love, and yet she could not turn away. In it she saw the hand of a child, full of uncertainty, but also full of trust. There was a death in that outstretched hand, and yet, at least, there was life in that trust.

"I need you," David said. "I need you desperately. Please take me back."

Tally didn't move. As she looked at David's hand reaching out to her, she felt the weight of her loneliness. Her aunt was dead. She had no one to love or care for now, except a long string of patients stretching far out into the horizon of old age. She thought of Mrs. Mided, sitting stiff-backed in her chair, flicking cigarette ashes into a tiny ashtray as she stared into space. She wondered if eventually she wouldn't become like her. It was possible. Without giving love you dried up. You could survive without being loved, but you couldn't survive without giving it.

It would be so easy to reach out to him. He needed her, and she supposed she needed him too. Yes, she needed something, another voice in the darkness.

She stared at him, but still she hesitated. If she reached out, it was a closing off of all options, a death; yet she wondered if that wasn't what she craved most. Recently life had been startling her into an awakening that was sharp and painful, for what good was awakening if it was only to loneliness and emptiness?

She felt tears come to her eyes; her whole body was trembling, but slowly she forced herself to reach out her hand toward his.

Suddenly there was a knock at the door. It swung open, and Ben was standing there, his weight supported on two canes, his face very white. He glared at David.

"Get out of here!" he demanded. "This is my house, and I want you out now!"

Tally was only partially irritated; mostly she was numb. "Ben, please. There's no reason to be angry."

Ben didn't dare move from the doorway. It had taken all his energy just to get himself down the hall. "My name is Mr. Savage, if you don't mind. I am still your employer."

"Well, then, act like one. You asked David to spend the night, not I."

"I changed my mind." Ben knew he was making a fool of himself, but he couldn't stop.

David shot a look at Tally, one of those old ones they had shared when someone was acting particularly disagreeable and entertaining.

"So sorry, mate," he answered. "I'd like to oblige you. But it is rather late to be finding a hotel."

"I don't give a shit, mate. You can sleep in the ditch for all I care. I want you out now!"

Tally laughed nervously. "Ben, this is silly."

Ben turned on her. "Fine. Then I'll be silly. If you want to screw around, it's your business. But you're not doing it under my roof. This is my house, and I won't have that kind of crap going on here. You understand?"

David watched him with amused detachment. "You're jealous. No one has been jealous of me in years. What an ego boost."

Tally turned on him. "Shut up, David!"

David laughed, and this made Ben even angrier. "Why, you smug bastard! I ought to beat the shit out of you!"

"You shut up too, Ben. This has gone far enough. I don't think it's very funny anymore."

"I do," David said. But it was clear that he was beginning to find it not very funny.

Tally ignored him. "Now, Ben, why should you suddenly care that David is spending the night?"

Ben looked away. Everything was becoming confused. He didn't know why he was there; he couldn't understand what he was feeling or why he had just said what he had.

"I don't know," he answered faintly.

Tally relaxed. "Well, I promise you that David will be gone in the morning. Is that all right?"

"No. That is not all right. I don't want him here."

Then all at once sanity returned to Ben. He looked down at himself, standing in the doorway in his dressing gown, his weight barely supported on two canes, and he realized how foolish he must seem to the two of them who were healthy and whole. Tally's cheeks were shining with health; even David had lost the tired sadness of before, and his elegant frame seemed so alive and vital. Suddenly Ben felt very childish and frightened.

"Okay, okay, so I'm jealous. I'm making a fool of myself, and I know it. Stay wherever the damn hell you want to. I don't care anymore."

Humiliated, Ben turned himself around, clutching his canes, then he started down the corridor to his bedroom. He couldn't bear to look at the two of them any longer.

"Are you still awake?"

Ben rolled over and saw Tally standing over him in the darkness. He turned back to the wall without answering, hoping that she would leave.

Tally remained where she was. "Ben, please, I want to talk to you."

"I'm sorry," he said finally. "Forget everything I said before. I'm a ridiculous old man, and I made a fool of myself. If you could just pretend like it never happened, I'd be grateful." He sounded shattered.

"I don't think you made a fool of yourself."

"Oh, sure! Look, nurse, you're off duty now. So you don't have to be kind to me."

"You could go off duty too, you know." She sat at the edge of his bed. "Besides, I won't forget what you said before, because I think you meant it."

"Like hell, I did. You can do as you please."

"Ben, please, let's not fight."

Tally's tone surprised Ben. He rolled over and looked at her. The light from the open doorway caught her hair, but her face was in shadows, and he wasn't sure what her expression was.

"Where is David now?"

"I sent him to bed."

"And he went willingly?"

"Perhaps less than willingly. But he went." She hesitated, then pushed herself to continue. "Was what you said before true? Were you jealous?"

Ben was annoyed. "How could I be jealous? I'm a sixty-year-old man, crippled, dying."

"You aren't dying. You must know that by now."

"Fine. Sixty years old and crippled is enough."

"You are recovering."

"I know. I'm a god damn miracle, huh?"

"Yes. You are."

He sighed. "Look, Tally, it's as if I'm split in two. There's the Ben Savage of before and then there's the Ben Savage of now. And sometimes I forget which one I am. That's what you just saw. I forgot. But the old Ben Savage is dead. Eventually I'll get it into my head exactly who I am."

"And when you do recover?"

"You don't for one minute think I will?"

"I don't for one minute think you won't."

This stunned Ben. "You really mean that?"

"Let me put it this way. As your nurse I think there's a small chance that you might. But as a person who's begun to know you, I'm sure you will. You told me before that it was hard for you to see yourself as you are, but I don't think you know who you are."

He was confused. Everything in his mind seemed to be breaking apart, and he didn't know how to reform the pieces. "And you do? Okay, then, who am I?"

"Don't you see? I'm not sure either. I know you too well. It's hard for me to judge anymore." She sounded confused. "All I know is I don't see you like you said."

"An old cripple. Go on, say it."

"But I don't think of you like that."

"Then how do you think of me?" He sounded tired and pushed too far.

"I think of you as a man."

Ben drew in breath. It was an instinctive reaction, and he was immediately ashamed of it. Yet the words kept going through his mind, and he realized they were the only ones he wanted to hear. He could feel the tears inside of him, and he tensed to stop them. But he wanted to cry, in gratitude; he had never felt so grateful for anything in his whole life.

Then a moment later doubt took over, and he was turning away from her. "You just feel sorry for me."

"I hate to disappoint you. But that's exactly what I don't feel." Without thinking she put her hand on his. "I haven't felt anything even resembling pity for some time." She stopped, quickly withdrawing her hand.

Ben watched her. She seemed to be so unsure, almost frightened. "Is something wrong?" he asked.

She turned away self-consciously.

"Have I offended you?"

Tally sat up very straight. "That's all I really wanted to say. I hope you didn't misunderstand."

She seemed as if she were about to get up, but she didn't. And Ben lay in the darkness, watching her face that was hidden in the shadows, uncertain what she was thinking, or if she was even thinking of him at all.

"I was jealous before," he admitted. "I know I had no right, but I was."

Still, Tally didn't leave, though Ben sensed that she wanted to. He'd never seen her so torn, and it stunned him; it was pushing him to say things he didn't want to say. Ben rolled back to the wall, hoping that Tally would slip out of the room before it was too late and he made a fool of himself again.

The quiet weighed on him; he couldn't even hear her breathing, but he could sense her there, very close to him, and he realized he didn't want her to go at all. He was trapped, unable to go forward, unwilling to go back. All he could do was lie there in silence, staring at the darkness.

Then he became aware of a shifting of weight off the bed, and he knew Tally was going. Suddenly he became panicky. He didn't want her to leave. He felt like she would take everything with her when she went, even the air; he felt almost as if he would die.

Ben turned back, but Tally was already going, and he wanted to hold her there, though he didn't know how.

Ben's voice was haunted. "I guess I'm starting to care for you. I hadn't realized it. Or at least I wouldn't let myself realize it. If that embarrasses you, I'm sorry. I promise I won't let it get in the way.

It's just I wanted to tell you that. And how much I appreciate what you said before."

"You sound grateful," Tally said angrily.

"I am."

"For what? What in God's name are you grateful for? Don't you understand anything?"

It took awhile for Ben to answer. "I'm beginning to think not."

"Don't you see? I don't want your gratitude. Or your promises not to let things get in the way." She stopped, desperately wanting to leave, yet wanting to stay also.

Only a moment before it had all seemed so clear. She had reached out to David and been prepared to take him on forever, knowing perfectly well the sacrifices and the gains. And yet now nothing seemed clear; everything was turning inside out, and she found herself speaking as she had not meant to, driven on not by reason but by something very hungry and powerful.

"I think I care for you too," she said softly. "I suppose I'm fascinated by you. I don't understand any of it, but I do know that I don't want your gratitude, as if you got a gold star from the teacher, and one day when you've recuperated and gone back to the real world, you'll remember me fondly. Can't you understand? I'm a woman. You were surprised that I regarded you as a man, but you can't even see I'm a woman."

"That was never in question."

Tally didn't answer; she hadn't even really heard what he said. The terror gripped her; the risk she was taking seemed at that moment too great, too overwhelming. Yet she couldn't move; she felt trapped. And then finally Tally broke from it and turned to leave. "I'm sorry if I awakened you. I'd better let you sleep."

Ben whispered urgently. "Please don't go. Please don't." Ben couldn't continue. If Tally rejected him now, as he knew she would, she could damage him forever. Yet at the same time, there was the feeling that this was his last chance, that without her he would be damaged also. Ben couldn't move. He was caught between the two fears, until he sensed he might break apart.

"I have no right to ask you this," he said at last. "I just have no right."

Again he paused, the fear of rejection torturing him into silence. But as the quiet grew, so did the fear of losing everything. "I want you to stay with me," he said softly. He could hear Tally take in breath, and his fear grew. Once more he saw himself as a foolish old man.

Family Passions 325

It took awhile for Tally to speak. She sounded frightened. "Are you sure?"

"Sure that I want you to stay? Oh, yes. I'm very sure of that." He laughed sadly. "But there's nothing else I can be sure of."

He stopped, mortified, yet knowing if he hadn't said this the humiliation could be so much worse.

Tally felt Ben's fear. Suddenly she understood just how much he must have at stake, and all concern about herself vanished. "I'm sorry," she said. "I put you in a terrible position. I only just saw it."

Ben smiled ruefully. "I guess the nicest thing you ever said is that it hadn't occurred to you."

Tally sank to the bed next to Ben. All thought had ceased and she was no longer torn, for the decision had been made. "Please forgive me."

Ben reached out tentatively and touched Tally's neck. The softness of it stunned him. He had forgotten how it felt to touch a woman, or else he hadn't allowed himself to remember, but her skin felt so delicate, so incredibly alive and real that he was astounded by it.

Slowly his hand moved to her shoulder, and that too seemed a miracle. He could feel the passion beginning in him, a hollow aching that grew in his center. He couldn't speak; he could hardly breathe. He slipped his hand under her sweater and moved to the gentle swelling of her breast. He could hear the sound of her breathing so close to him. The warm woman smell of her body made everything inside him stir. Her body seemed to yield to him, and suddenly the doubt and fear disappeared. He was no longer trying to understand, he was no longer even thinking. He was only a man.

THIRTY-THREE

Midland, Ohio 1981

Every morning when Dyer walked through the corridors of Midwestern he made sure that he strode very rapidly, barking orders in a loud staccato voice. It created an atmosphere among his employees, almost a hysteria, so that when his footsteps had long faded and he was well away, involved in his own daily routine, the echo of him remained, acting as a whip to their backs. It was almost as effective as placing his desk in each one of their offices and sitting over them like a schoolmaster.

Dyer did not realize that this was very much like his grandfather, Nicholas Healey. Dyer remembered little about his grandfather, only a vague memory of a broken and embittered man, smelling of stale tobacco and sour milk, staring out the window of an old-age home at a scrawny palm tree. By the time Dyer was grown up, Nicholas Healey was dead, ironically never living to see the child he had so despised turn into a man not at all dissimilar to him. Probably Angela was the only one who recognized the likeness, and perhaps it was this that fed her obsessive love of her son.

But while Dyer may have in many ways resembled the other branch of the family, it was only his connection to the Savages that counted. And today, as he strode down the corridor, his secretary, Carrie, struggling to keep up with him, his mind was devoted to them.

As he passed Boris Tanderoff's office, he jiggled the doorknob and said, "Come into my office and bring the latest issue of *Steel Today*."

He didn't wait to see if he'd been heard but continued to his office. He knew Carrie would follow up.

Just as Dyer was lighting a cigar and taking his first sip of coffee,

Boris was shown into his office. Under his arm he was carrying a large stack of trade journals.

"I brought some extra copies with me, in case you needed them."

Dyer was pretending to be scanning a letter, but in fact he was watching Boris from under lowered eyelids. He waited until Boris was seated, then put the letter on the desk and took a puff of his cigar. "How's it going?" He leaned back and allowed the smoke to pour from his mouth.

"We ran two full-page ads. I think they looked fairly impressive, despite a lousy reproduction—"

Dyer interrupted. "Not *Steel Today!*"

"But you said—" Boris smiled slyly. "I see."

Boris did not continue, but sat staring. Boris could see Dyer was becoming anxious and that gave him a feeling of power. Dyer wanted something from him, something he couldn't get on his own, and as small and unimportant as Boris might be, it made him the most consequential man in that room at the moment.

He said at last, "Things are going very well."

Dyer puffed irritably on his cigar. "What the hell does that mean?"

"Do you mind if I smoke too?"

"I don't give a damn if you burn. I asked you a question."

Boris lit a cigarette and answered with studied calmness. "You asked me to play whore to your little cousin. And that's exactly what I'm doing. We screwed three times last night. Would you like the details?"

Dyer went rigid, his face flushed with anger.

Boris smiled fiercely. "I may not have a lot of pride. But I do have some. And if you treat me like a whore, that's exactly what I'll act like. And if you treat me with respect, you'll get that back too."

There was a struggle in Dyer's face, then it went blank. "I didn't mean to insult you."

Boris grinned. "I accept your apology. Now tell me precisely what you want to know."

Dyer didn't answer. He just stared resentfully at the end of his cigar. He'd been pushed too far.

Boris smoked in silence for a while, then relented. His tone was slightly condescending. "We've been seeing a great deal of one another. He's even bought me a new wardrobe." He touched the lapels of his suit jacket and smirked. "What do you think?"

"I don't know much about clothes."

"But we do, eh? Yes, well, we do. We like beautiful things. No crime in that, is there?"

"None I know of."

"Good. I'm glad I have your approval. Yes, as I told you before, things are going very well."

Dyer was embarrassed. "And he feels about you?"

"Head over heels. The man is absolutely fascinated with me. All I have to do is flutter my eyelashes and he's—"

"Enough!"

Boris laughed. "Now, don't get all delicate with me. After all, it's the same for us. In fact, I'd say it's a lot less disgusting than a man who's incapable of loving anything, male, female, or even dog."

Dyer knew this was directed at him, but he wasn't insulted. People like Boris didn't command enough respect to insult him. "And he relies on you?"

"I think he'd be desperately upset if I left him."

"Yes, certainly. I'm sure he would. But what I mean is, does he listen to you? Do you have any influence over him?"

Boris leaned back in his chair and watched Dyer. He could tell how impatient he was for his answer. He smiled and took in smoke, letting it drift from his mouth. "He'd drag his balls through broken glass for me."

"Good." Dyer stuck his cigar in his mouth and picked up a piece of correspondence. "That's all I wanted to know."

Boris didn't move. "Your grandmother's been working on him. She wants him to get rid of me, stop spending so much money, drinking, you know."

He paused, smirking. "If you ask me, she wants him to star taking his rightful place around here. Who knows? Maybe ever challenge you."

Dyer muttered, "Yeah, that'll be the day."

"Were you aware your grandmother has cancer?"

Dyer shivered. He didn't answer, but it was clear that he was not

"I'm sorry to be the one to break it to you," Boris continued "But she told James by way of trying to get him to toughen up, suppose."

Dyer tried to shake off the sadness, but beneath it was somethin far worse, almost a panic. He didn't want his grandmother to die He loved her. He craved her love, but even more, he needed th feeling that at least he loved someone. Without her was an emptiness, a dark terrifying hole with no salvation.

He fought against the darkness. "And did it work?" he asked sharply.

Boris smiled. "For about an hour. I told James I thought we ought to go away somewhere together." Boris eyed Dyer slyly. "I suggested he sell his stock first." He saw Dyer stiffen and this made him laugh. "To you, actually."

"I didn't tell you to do that. What the damn hell made you think I wanted you to do that?" Dyer felt the darkness all around him now, and he wanted to strike out against it, but he knew that in the end, it would win.

"Oh, come on, I never believed that phony explanation you gave me about just wanting me to keep tabs on your cousin. I always knew what you were after. I pretended to believe you; I let you underestimate me because I thought it would be to my advantage to wait until my bargaining power was better. And now the time has come. Yes, there James was, all afraid and unsure, and I thought to myself, *What better time to speak of stock selling and such?*"

Dyer didn't say anything for a long while, his face a mask. "And will he?" he asked finally.

"He hasn't decided yet. But the truth is I don't want him to. Not until you and I straighten a few things out."

"What things?"

Boris took a deep drag of his cigarette and blew the smoke out dragonlike. "Well, first of all I wanted to hear you admit that you really were after his stock."

Dyer was no longer fighting the darkness; he allowed it to creep over him softly. He watched Boris stone-faced, but he didn't seem to be irritated anymore; he seemed somewhat amused. "I want his stock."

"Then I want rather a lot of money."

"Which you'll get from James. When he sells."

"Wrong. Which I'll get from you."

Dyer's eyes narrowed. "Don't try to play both ends against the middle with me."

"Wouldn't dream of it, darling. You're not my type."

"And don't give me any of your fag humor. You got enough money from me to become James's friend."

"Which I did. Right? No. What you wanted from me was much more. And much more is very expensive."

Dyer watched him through a veil of smoke. "And who says you can deliver?"

"You must have thought so."

Dyer flicked his cigar nervously. "You're really enjoying this, aren't you?"

Boris suddenly became very intense. "Damn right I am! Hey, I'm just a little immigrant turd from the backwaters of Calumet City. I never had a big house or car. I never belonged to a country club. I didn't grow up with any of the things you took for granted. But I watched your type for years, gliding by me in limousines, your hair all slicked down, your clothes all neat and clean."

Boris lit another cigarette and took in the smoke with pleasure. "And here's the thing. With all of that, you need me. Now, that's enjoyable. Perhaps even more enjoyable than the money." He laughed. "Well, maybe that's going a little over the top. But it's fun. Yeah, I like it fine."

"Delighted you're getting your kicks, Boris. Tell me, did you have any particular sum in mind?"

"I've been toying with the idea of a percent of the asking price. Say five percent?"

Dyer just laughed.

Boris smoked calmly; his eyes sparkled. The two men remained as they were for some time, then Dyer picked up a letter from his desk and glanced through it. Suddenly he looked up. "You're fired. From both jobs. You'll get your final check through the mail."

Boris didn't move. "From both jobs, eh? That wouldn't be very wise. I could tell James what you were up to. I don't think that would be to your benefit."

Dyer answered sharply. "Nor yours either, smart boy. You tell him, and you end up with nothing. Both from me and from him."

"I know. You see, we need one another. If I don't cooperate with you, I'm out in the cold. And if you don't cooperate with me, you get nothing. That's why waiting before this discussion seemed like such a good idea, making a sort of mutual dependency grow. We have too much on each other to sever our relationship." He was smirking again. "Well, now, where do we go from here?"

Dyer worked on his cigar. "It's called finding a common ground."

Boris nodded. All his enjoyment was back. "In other words,

two and a half percent, deposited with the Swiss and automatically transferred on completion."

Dyer too was smiling. "In other words, one half of one percent, deposited with the Swiss. Take it, and count yourself lucky. Then get the hell out of here, before I puke."

THIRTY-FOUR

All the way from the airport, Dylan had debated what she would call Elizabeth when she saw her, but in the end she called her "Mother" instinctively, naturally, as if twenty years hadn't passed.

Elizabeth didn't answer. She just stood at the threshold, her sharp eyes running over her daughter-in-law's features, as if in that one glance she could discover everything.

A moment later the two women embraced, though neither of them knew who initiated it, and Dylan started to cry. She tried to pull away, embarrassed, but Elizabeth's arms held her tightly.

"No need there is to feel shame at tears," she said soothingly. "It is that which makes us human."

Elizabeth could feel Dylan relaxing in her arms, and she held her tenderly, as if she were her own child. Though Elizabeth too was carried away with sorrow, she couldn't cry. She supposed all the tears had been frozen out of her in the harsh winters in Wales, when fatherless, her mother dying, she had sat at the edge of her bed, arms clasped around her, and realized there wasn't another human being in the world who cared about her. All the tears had gone out of her then, and they had only returned twice, on the docks of New York and when Wynn had died. But the emotion had never deserted her, only the weeping, and she stood cradling Dylan in her arms, feeling that she was perhaps the only woman in the world who had ever understood her.

Finally Elizabeth pulled herself together and held Dylan at arm's length. "Good it is to see you. Far better than I would have guessed. I knew that James had gone to you." She smiled, and there was an honesty in that smile reserved for very few people, perhaps only Ben. "And I expected you. I knew you would come."

Dylan smiled back. "I'll bet you did too."

Elizabeth gazed at her warmly, then began moving toward the living room. As she walked, Dylan realized how frail Elizabeth had become, and she turned her eyes away in defense. But the house that had once been so familiar held little comfort. Every piece of furniture was a memory; even the sound of the floorboards and the pungent smell of furniture polish stirred the past.

As they walked by the kitchen, Elizabeth asked, "Are you hungry, child?"

It was a voice from long ago, and Dylan smiled in response to it. "No, thanks, Mother. I ate on the plane."

"Then you've only just come?"

"I called you from the airport."

Elizabeth smiled. "A good woman you always were. Thank you for coming to me first."

"I wanted to."

"Even better that is."

Elizabeth held onto the furniture as she made her way to a chair. Dylan watched sadly but did not offer to help. Even with twenty years separating them, she knew instinctively it was something her mother-in-law would not want.

Elizabeth seated herself with great difficulty, then smiled faintly, trying to cover. "Are you staying for long?"

Dylan too sat down and instantly realized it was the chair she always used to sit in. "I really don't know," she answered.

"As long as there is need."

"I guess we'll see." Dylan hesitated. "I smoke now. Do you mind?"

"Hard it is to see how smoke can harm an old woman like me. Nor will I lecture you it's bad for your health, for that I'm sure you know. Your own affair it is." She frowned. "So much there is that's everyone's own affair." Then she smiled mischievously. "Far easier it would be if everyone just listened to me."

Dylan giggled. "I always used to say you'd have made an excellent queen."

The two women laughed together. There was a warmth and understanding in that laugh; there was a history.

"I have missed you," Elizabeth said sadly. "Not till this day did I know how much. When you left Ben—"

Family Passions

"I don't think we have to discuss that." Dylan lit her cigarette; her hand was shaking.

"Nay. We must. Lest it become a barrier between us. There is nothing so terrible in my heart that you need be frightened of my words."

"Or that I haven't thought myself."

"Always the trouble that was, my dear. Always you spent too much time in the dark corners of your mind, suspecting things that were far worse than what was true."

Dylan looked away from Elizabeth, but she could feel the old woman's eyes on her, and she sensed that they were kind eyes and that indeed she had less to fear from Elizabeth than from her own imagination.

Elizabeth sighed. "Hard it was to come here. Don't think I don't understand. Not a word have we spoken in twenty years, no contact, no sign. Though well you knew how Ben felt. And so there was the fear it applied to me."

She grew thoughtful. "But different were my feelings. And different my thoughts. It was right for Ben to be angry with you. And I understood it, and backed him. I too felt anger and confusion and betrayal. But think you I could not see his part in the failure? His shortcomings? Of one thing I am sure. He loved you. He really did love you. And you hurt him by your leaving as ever a person has hurt another. But wrong does not rest solely on one side, it spreads through lives touching everyone and everything. And Ben wronged you. He treated you as his property. And I watched, my heart in my mouth, as he let everything fall apart."

"What is past is past," Dylan said. "I was a child, and though Ben was so much older than I, he was too."

Elizabeth smiled. "Always he was a child. It was his charm."

"Yes. It was charming. But he left a lot of damage along the way."

"Aye. Often in those days I thought to give warning to him, perhaps even to force him to grow up. But never could I do it. I loved him for it. In that, I expect the wrong spreads to me. For I allowed him to see the world as he wished to see it."

"When he saw it at all. Mostly he just reacted to it. Giving what he wanted, taking what he wanted." Dylan stopped, afraid she had gone too far.

But Elizabeth just shook her head, her eyes alight with memories.

"Like a child, grabbing at life. And never there was the understanding of why people resented what he took."

"Or what he gave."

"Aye. The largest part that was. The resentment at what he gave. For always it was what he wanted to give. Always it was what suited him. And that which people wanted to give in return, he spurned. So strong was the need to control."

Dylan was amazed. "I never realized."

"That I understood Ben? That I saw him as a man?"

Dylan nodded.

"Then there I was wrong too. For alone you must have felt with no one to turn to, no one on your side. And I, out of loyalty to Ben, could never come to you. Perhaps a mistake there is in that. Will you forgive me, then?"

"I'd hardly say there was anything to forgive. You did what you felt was right. Besides, there's no way of telling if it would have made a difference. And even if it had, whether you would have hurt Ben more than you helped me."

Elizabeth looked relieved. "As you said, what is past is past. And now we have well and truly buried it. Though glad I would be to see even one of those days, hard as they were, rather than what is today."

Her voice faltered. "The feeling there is that I have failed, Dylan. That everything I believed in, everything I worked for, is dying. Nor can I do anything but watch and mourn."

Elizabeth looked desperate. "I have told James. And well it is that I tell you. I'm dying. For some time have I known. And perhaps it is best."

There were tears in Dylan's eyes. "No. You don't mean that. You don't want to die."

"Aye. I don't. But I wish I meant it." Elizabeth bit her lip, then continued passionately. "Oh, when will I have finish with life? For clear it is that life has had finish with me."

The blood had drained from Dylan's face. "You're sure then?"

"Oh, aye. I'm sure."

Dylan was shivering, and her voice was very small. "Soon?" She dropped her cigarette onto the carpet and picked it up with shaking fingers.

Elizabeth nodded. "Sometimes the feeling there is that death is so close all it would take is to let down my guard and allow it to fall over me. But this I cannot do. Oh, Dylan, tired I am. Tired and fed up. For it does not seem as time goes by, that things make themselves better. Only worse and more of the same. And tiresome it becomes as it whirls around again. And you say to yourself, 'Aye. But I've been this way before, and I know how it all comes out. It's a path I've traveled so often, with nothing but pain and sorrow at its end. Why then must I start it all over?' "

She became angry at herself. "But stop. No more of that must I speak. For to old age belongs this weariness. No use have the young to hear of it. This discovery must they make on their own."

Dylan suddenly looked old. "I've felt that way many times."

"Have you? Aye. I feel you have. Sorry I am of that. For you should not know of such things yet."

Dylan smiled sadly. "I'll do my best to change, Mother."

Elizabeth returned her smile. "An interfering old woman I am. And melancholy too. But cheered I am by the sight of you. And the feeling there is, now that you're here, all will come to right." Elizabeth became silent, pensive, but her mind was no longer on the past, it was on the future. "He's living with someone, you know. And much of the problem that is. A bad lot that 'un is. Selfish and proud."

Dylan was surprised. "You've met him?"

"No. But as good as that. Believe me, well do I know that I am an old woman with little understanding of where the world is going or why it would wish to go that way in the first place. But this 'un is bad. Seen him I have. If only from a car window. But there is much that can be told from looking. And when you're my age, there's time enough for it."

Elizabeth paused, but Dylan could see how much she needed to tell this story, how hard it must have been to keep it to herself.

"Handsome he is. Dressed well too. Though nothing do I know of the latest fashion. Yet can you tell by the expense of the cut and the way a man holds himself in it."

"And that's what you have against him?"

"No, child. Hush. Though a liar I'd be if I didn't admit that angry I am it's from James's pocket the means comes. Yet I ask myself, how different is it to a woman? Would there be the resentment if for a wife they were bought?"

"And would there be?"

Elizabeth sighed. "Old I am, and truly I don't understand. But I am trying, with all my might. And I believe it is more than the fact that it's a man, rather that it is *this* man. For I've seen him, Dylan.

And what I have seen I'll never forget. Two weeks ago it was. I had hired a car to take me to the cemetery to visit Wynn. All changed down Primrose Hill way it is since you've left. With dozens of small shops selling God knows what."

"Boutiques?"

"Aye. Boutiques," she repeated disdainfully. "But something they are to look at as you go by and the people who parade in front of them. Like market day when I was a girl, though to me far less exciting. Oh, Dylan, bored they all looked. Both the men and the women, walking arm in arm, with faces like they'd rather be anywhere, even the devil's own home, than where they are. And one such couple I saw. Or at least, I should say, one of them looked bored. And as I watched him out the window, I thought what a million pities it is to have so much, yet get so little pleasure."

She stopped and sighed deeply. "Then it was that I noticed the other's face. It was not boredom that I read there, but pain and sorrow, an agony reserved for the gravesite. Dylan, it was James. Our James. Now nothing do I know about this man of his, nor ever do I wish to. For the whole of the story was on James's face."

Dylan was very pale. "Poor James," she whispered. "How he must hate himself."

"And well he might. For he makes himself hateful."

"That kind of attitude isn't going to help."

"Aye. But it is not in me to be otherwise. I spoke to him of it. I talked of my death and the family and the obligation."

"And he didn't listen?"

"Oh, listen he did. He fairly quivered with listening. But he did nothing."

"Which probably only makes him feel worse and causes him to need what little he gets from someone like that man even more."

Elizabeth shrugged. "Beyond me all that is. Which is why I've pinned my hopes on you."

"You're putting a lot of faith in me for some unknown reason. I don't see what I can do."

"You can stop James."

Dylan laughed. "Stop James? From what? From being homosexual? I doubt I could do that. I'm not sure I even want to."

"No." Elizabeth shook her head. "You purposely do not understand. Stop James from being weak. Give him strength."

"Mother, I'd say I'm the last person who could do that. I'm hardly in a position to pass judgment. Besides, as you yourself said, people will please themselves, and there's little anyone else can do about it."

"Forget what I said before. For I was feeling sorry for myself and old and used up. But having you here like this, being able for the first time since Ben to talk of what I feel, has made me younger. And I have changed my mind."

Elizabeth clapped her hands together. The blood returned to her face and indeed she did look younger. "Talk to him, Dylan."

"I can't see what difference that will make."

"His mother you are."

"It's a little late, don't you think? He's a grown man."

"James? Not a day has he grown since you left him. A child he was then. A child he is now."

"Like Ben."

"Aye. Like Ben in that. And perhaps much more. But it is up to you to discover. It is up to you to try. Love him, Dylan. Love him enough to fight for him. Far easier it is to be kind and compliant, to let a person go, thinking to yourself that this is a sign of love. It is not, of course. Just the easy way out. Loving it is to stand up and be strong. Loving it is to fight."

"I don't know that I have the strength."

"The strength there is. All it takes is to find it. And strangely it comes, from odd places and times. Have you guilt, child? Think you ever on the fact that you left him as a boy?"

"I live with it every day."

"Then from there is it you will draw the strength."

"Jesus Christ, what the hell is going on?" Tom Lindsay asked as he walked into Dyer's office. He looked agitated.

Dyer picked up the phone and asked Carrie to hold all calls, then he tilted his chair back and watched Tom with impassive eyes. "I gather you're talking about my memo on Anti-Cor."

"You're damn right I am."

Dyer's tone was very reasonable, but there was a tightness to his voice. "You should be delighted. It's your department. More money, more staff. It's top priority."

"Yeah, but the question is why."

Dyer still stared at him evenly, but there was anger burning just beneath the surface. And underneath that there seemed to be something pretty close to fear. Tom could sense all this, though he could not have given it words. All he knew was suddenly his irritation was replaced by suspicion.

"I demand to know why," he said harshly.

"I've done some rethinking, and now I feel Anti-Cor is good for Midwestern."

Tom didn't say anything. He just stood watching.

Finally Dyer broke the silence. "You find something particularly sinister about that?"

"I think something is up. Yes." Tom paused, thinking. "I don't know. I really don't. You haven't given me a reason for this sudden change of heart. There must be a reason, a real, practical, down-to-earth reason."

Dyer was unmoved. "Like?"

Tom remained silent. He didn't have any proof that Dyer was doing something wrong; he wasn't even sure that he was. And yet the feeling was there, nagging at him.

Dyer's tone was friendly and calm. "Look, Tom. I don't know why it is, but every time something vaguely related to me comes up, I get the feeling you have doubts. Do you know what I mean?" Dyer's face was veiled in smoke, which rose like steam.

"I don't know. It's just . . ." Tom fell silent.

"It's just I'm not Ben?"

Tom ignored this. "It's just there's a rotten smell around here, Dyer."

Dyer's eyes were glittering. "Such as?"

"Such as James and that phony baloney assistant of his. You've got him under your thumb."

"What does that mean?"

"I don't know. Don't you understand? There's just this feeling that something is going on; something is changing. Then there's that four point nine percent of the stock business."

Dyer recoiled. "How the hell do you know about that?"

"A little birdy told me."

Dyer fought to control himself, and when he spoke, his voice was more reasonable. "I assume it was a little Mason Josephs bird. Well, fine. It's true. Obviously someone has it in their head to try to gain control of Midwestern. They won't, of course, but that's exactly why I need to have my hands firmly on the reins. Now, doesn't that make more sense than any hazy ideas that something evil is going on here?" There was silence.

Dyer sighed deeply. "You always suspect the worst of me, Tom. Don't you see that? And here, once again, when I do something you think is actually good for you, you immediately jump to sinister conclusions."

Tom didn't answer. Perhaps Dyer was right; perhaps it was a personal grudge against the man that was motivating him. He'd seen that kind of thing in himself before. Yet he couldn't help feeling that this was different; something was going on. He watched Dyer's face, as if he could discover the answer in his features.

"So what is it?" Dyer asked after a while. "Are you thinking of quitting? Is that it?"

"I *should* quit. That'd set Anti-Cor back a good deal. That'd stop you."

Dyer laughed with annoyance. "Stop me from what, Tom? Don't you see how crazy this all is? Look: I need you. Anti-Cor is big. So what's the problem?"

Tom felt the urge to leave so overwhelmingly that he had to force himself not to bolt from his chair and run as far away from Midwestern Steel and Dyer Savage as possible. But what if he was right and there was something going on? Who would there be to prevent it? It was a ridiculous thought, of course, because there would be nothing he could do. Yet in the end he was all there was. Though he knew he would lose, he couldn't allow himself to give up without even trying. He owed it to Ben. He owed it to the past.

"No. I'm not quitting, Dyer," Tom answered finally. His tall thin body had suddenly become rigid, his eyes hard. "I'm staying right where I am, and I'll be watching you, lad. I'll be watching you closely."

Then he left the room without another word, while Dyer sat behind his desk, smoke drifting around his head in soft blue clouds.

THIRTY-FIVE

Pauline poured a drink, then walked to her dressing table and turned on the lights. Her face was captured in the mirror, every line and imperfection unmasked. She sat down and began inspecting herself clinically, as an architect might the topography of a building site. Then suddenly she began to cry. Grief swept over her swiftly, descending as a heavy blow, and she bent her head onto her arms, feeling the waves of it passing over her.

"I hate you," she whispered. "God, how I hate you."

Blindly she reached out for her drink and fed it to herself like an invalid. Then once again her head fell to her arms and she was crying again.

After a while she sat up. Her face was ravaged now, purple lines under her eyes; her skin looked parched.

"You ugly bitch," she said to her image in the mirror. "You're hateful and cruel and you deserve to be ugly."

Pauline's hands went over her puffy face, nails digging in at her cheeks. There was a terrible urge to disfigure herself, to make her face as damaged as she felt. Then she stopped, looking around wildly. She considered going to the medicine cabinet and downing all her sleeping pills. But she didn't move. She just sat at the dressing table, sipping her drink, feeling the numbness begin to creep through her body. And after a while she looked back in the mirror and assessed the damage.

It was six o'clock, and Dyer was due to arrive in an hour. Undoubtedly her face would still be swollen, but the red marks of her nails would disappear. If she didn't cry again, she could probably hide what had happened under makeup. But she knew she would cry again. She could feel the tears just under the surface, threatening to break through, and she doubted she'd be able to hold them back.

Pauline rarely had black moods, but when she did they were always like this, descending upon her suddenly, heavily, and lasting for a long time. She never knew when one of these moods would surprise her; she never knew its cause, but she suspected this one had been hanging over her for days, perhaps even weeks.

Pauline laughed out loud, raised her glass, and toasted her image in the mirror. The truth was this black mood had been threatening to come on for far longer than days or weeks or even months. This mood had been the work of a lifetime.

It was the guilt, of course, the guilt that she had suppressed for so many years, until both it and the incident that had caused it had faded. Yet the impact had suffused her whole life, coloring her actions and words, building to these sudden black moods when she would be cast back violently to the moment when it had all begun.

It had been just after her sixteenth birthday, and Evan had planned to take her to dinner to celebrate. The two of them had never spent much time alone. She remembered that the invitation had been extended in an awkward, almost courtly manner, and when she'd met him at the office after work, it'd been clear this was something he'd been looking forward to.

He'd offered her a drink to make her feel grown-up, ginger ale with a slight dash of bourbon. And all the while she'd sat there, sipping her drink and listening to Evan talk, she'd been aware that Ben was just down the hall in his office. She'd worried that he didn't know she was there; she'd worried that he did know and was staying away on purpose. The pain had grown, stunning her with its force, until all she could think of was running down the hall and pushing her way into his office. But she hadn't run down the hall; she'd just sat there, sipping her drink and half listening to Evan's attempts to make this a special occasion.

Finally they'd finished their drinks, and the two of them had walked out into the night with its drape of silt and burning steel. Pauline had spoken loudly as they'd walked, hoping that her voice would carry across the courtyard to Ben's office, though she'd known there was nothing she could do anymore; it had all been done on the night of her party.

Evan had taken her to the dining room of the Park Lane Hotel. And she'd hated him that night; she'd hated him, and she'd led him to it. Slowly but surely she'd orchestrated the whole thing, watching as his face grew pale, his back rigid. She'd done it, knowing that he of all people didn't deserve it and that she wasn't really angry at him at all. But her fury had been burning so brightly, she hadn't known who or what she was angry at. In fact, she hadn't fully known she was angry. All she'd been aware of was a storm inside of her, pushing her onward.

She'd watched Evan, almost stalked him, waiting for the right moment. Then she had struck, without provocation.

The main course had come, and she'd sat playing with her fried potatoes, as if deep in thought. And when she'd begun, it had been haltingly, as if she regretted every word.

"What do you do when you hear a rumor, and you know it isn't true, but there's nothing you can do to stop it?"

Evan had smiled at her. It had been a kind, paternal smile. Pauline hadn't really known her brother very well, but always he'd been gentle, almost fatherly to her, so unlike Ben.

"I always ignore rumors," he'd answered softly.

"But sometimes you can't ignore them. Sometimes they get under your skin."

"Which is exactly the intention. That's why I ignore them."

Pauline had nodded, but it had been obvious from her expression that his answer had not satisfied her.

He'd put his hand on her arm. "Do you want to tell me about it?"

The kinder he'd been, the more the resentment had grown. "No," she'd answered. But she'd known he would not accept this, nor had she wanted him to.

"Maybe you'd better tell me."

Pauline had seen a look of misgiving pass over his face, as if he were having a premonition of what she was about to say. But though he'd been fearful, gentleness had won out. "Come on," he'd urged. "You can talk to me."

Pauline had stammered. "Well, it's just that I know it isn't true, but there are people talking, you know, and they're saying things about Dyer."

Evan had gone stiff. He'd hardly seemed to be breathing. "What could they find to gossip about in a little boy?"

Again Pauline hadn't answered. She'd played with her potatoes, her eyes on Evan. Though she'd been sure she wasn't telling him anything he didn't know, she'd been equally sure the telling would damage him. For a moment she'd wanted to turn back, to stop the words before they came out, but at the same time the fury had been there, tearing at her, pushing her forward.

"Come on, Pauline. You've started something. You might as well finish it." Evan hadn't sounded angry; he'd sounded scared.

"It's only that they say things about Dyer looking more like Ben than you, and. . . . Do you know what I mean?"

It had taken a long while for Evan to answer. "I know what you mean."

"And I'm not sure what to say to them."

"Who is them?"

"People."

He'd looked ill. "A lot of people?"

Pauline had stared at her plate. "It's only that I know what they're saying isn't true, but—" She'd stopped.

"You realize it isn't true?"

It had been clear that Evan was trying to sound convincing, but he hadn't been able to do a very good job of it. It was the way he'd sat, and his eyes, haunting, haunted. His steak had become cold, and he'd no longer even attempted to eat it.

"Of course I know it isn't true," Pauline had answered vehemently. "But when they talk like that, I don't know what to say."

"It's very simple. Ben and I are brothers. We're from the same family. There are always differences and similarities in the way people look in families."

That time he had sounded more convincing. His body had relaxed; the color had begun to return to his face.

That had only seemed to feed her rage. Again she'd tried to stop herself, but there had been nothing she could do; the anger had twisted and turned inside her like a snake.

"Yes," she'd said slowly. "But even personality differences?"

"Even personality differences."

"So why do people say things like that?"

"Mischief, cruelty, you name it."

Pauline had not looked sure. "Then why do I feel so . . ."

"Uncertain?" Evan's face had begun growing pale again. He had been fighting very hard to keep himself together.

She'd taken his hand in hers. "Oh, Evan, I shouldn't be saying this to you. I'm upsetting you, I can see."

Evan had tried for a smile. "Of course you aren't. Don't you think I've heard the rumors? But I ignore them. I know what's true."

Pauline had hesitated, and then there had been a torrent of words. "I guess it's just that it took so long for Angela to become pregnant, and everyone knew she was trying, and then finally she was pregnant, but the baby didn't look like you at all; he looked like Ben. And everyone knows how close the two of you are, and I suppose it's just a logical assumption."

"Stop it!" Evan had grabbed Pauline's arm, his nails cutting into her flesh.

Pauline had cried out, "You're hurting me!"

Evan hadn't seemed to have heard her. It had been as if everything inside of him was collapsing, and he was being crushed under the weight of it. But slowly he had loosened his grip, and Pauline had been able to remove her hand.

She'd looked around. Several people at the other tables were watching them. "I'm getting you mad," she'd said. "I didn't mean to upset you like this. After all, you'd know if there was a problem. Don't they say the husband is always the first to know? Or is it the last? Well, anyway, I'm sure you'd know if there was anything funny going on. You'd see it in her eyes, right? Angela isn't the type who's a good liar."

"She loves me," Evan'd said, but it had been more to himself than Pauline. He'd hardly even seemed aware that she was there. It'd been as if a fight were going on inside of him. Pauline had seen his muscles clenching, holding his body back. His lips had been pressed tightly together, trembling, and she hadn't been able to look at his eyes.

As she'd watched him, the full impact of what she had done hit her. She'd wanted to hurt Evan; she'd wanted to make him suffer, but once she'd accomplished it, all she'd wanted to do was take it back.

Pauline had clutched at Evan's arm, trying to rouse him. "Evan, I'm sorry. I really am."

Evan hadn't answered.

"I didn't mean any of what I was saying. I really didn't." Pauline had become scared. She'd known she had gone too far, and she'd feared she wouldn't be able to stop it anymore. "Evan, I didn't say anything so terrible it should make you that upset. Honest."

She'd watched Evan as he sat rigidly staring, and her desperation had hardened. After all, she hadn't really said anything more than what he'd probably heard a million times. She couldn't help it if he obviously suspected it was true.

She'd turned back to her dinner and begun eating quickly, but with little relish, and for the rest of the evening she'd avoided his eyes. She had kept telling herself, over and over, that she hadn't

Family Passions   345

meant any harm, that she'd told him nothing he hadn't already known. And in a few days the incident had begun to fade for her.

Except it hadn't faded. It had sat somewhere deep inside her, waiting to come out, poisoning her system, spreading guilt and resentment through her and forcing her to exact punishment on herself.

The doorbell startled Pauline, and she was surprised to find herself seated at her dressing table. She'd been that buried in the past.

She glanced in the mirror. Her face was shining eerily in the fluorescent lights; her eyes were no longer so red, but there was an unattractive puffiness to them that showed she'd been crying. She debated whether to let Dyer see her like this, then decided she would. Perhaps she'd even cause a scene.

Dyer was leaning against the door, jabbing at the bell insistently, and already he was becoming edgy at the thought that Pauline was not where he wanted her.

Pauline opened the door and, without saying a word, turned away from him and walked back into the living room.

"You took long enough," Dyer said as he pushed in and headed for the bar. "I won't ask whether you want a drink. You always do."

Pauline watched him hulking over the whiskey bottles and felt the anger moving inside of her. It was a hard knot at the back of her throat that was throbbing and swelling. While she feared it, she welcomed it too, for always afterward there was passion, terrible and swift, all-consuming. She could feel the excitement just under the surface, filled with danger.

Dyer left her drink on the bar and walked to the couch. It was only then that he noticed she was still wearing a dressing gown and that her eyes were swollen.

Pauline glared at him. "What's the matter? Aren't I dressed right for the occasion?"

Dyer didn't answer. He was looking down at his drink pensively; he could tell he was going to need it.

Pauline's voice was insinuating. "After all, I am your aunt. Aunts don't always have to look elegant for their nephews, do they?"

Dyer just shrugged. Pauline was trying to push him, and he wanted to stop her, but he didn't know how. So he sipped his drink in silence, avoiding her eyes, unaware that this only fed her anger, unaware that anything he did would provoke her.

Pauline stood in the center of the room, staring at him fiercely. She could not understand what drove her on, tormenting her until she lashed out brutally, tearing at people's minds like a wild animal. As always it was impossible for her to think when she was angry; it was only afterward that she'd be able to gather any meaning from her actions, and by that time it would be too late to change things. Perhaps that was why she did it.

As Dyer watched Pauline, it occurred to him that he should leave and avoid what he could sense was going to be a fight. But he didn't leave; he didn't even move.

Pauline was still standing in the center of the room, as if even sitting with him was a concession she was not willing to make. "You said you had some business to discuss," she said curtly. "What is it?"

"I'm not sure that now is the time. Why don't we hold it till later?"

"Ah, but there may not be a later. One never knows."

Dyer refused to be drawn in. "If you don't mind, I'll take the chance."

"Suit yourself. You always do."

Still, Dyer remained where he was, and he couldn't understand why he was doing exactly the opposite of what he knew was right. Then slowly he became aware that he too wanted an explosion. It was a call to something in his center, very dark and deep. It had been years since he felt that part of him being touched, and he fought to regain the icy hardness that was usually his.

"So what's up, Pauline?" he asked harshly. "It's obvious something is, and you're just dying to let me have it."

"Why, little nephew, how perceptive we're becoming. You really astound me."

She paused, waiting for him to answer. Then, seeing that he would not, she continued. "Actually, I've been thinking about the past. In fact, your father. But I don't suppose you remember all that much about him."

"I remember." Dyer gulped down his drink and went for another. His body felt powerful and wild.

Pauline laughed. It was a strange, choked-off laugh, full of fury. "But you're not anxious to talk about it, are you?"

"Not particularly."

"So what was the business you came on? You can tell Auntie Pauline, your partner in crime."

"Like I said before. Let's talk about it some other time."

Pauline snapped her fingers. "Right you are, Dyer! Anything you want, Dyer! What shall we talk about then? I know! Let's talk about the weather. It's cold, isn't it? They say this is the coldest January since 1956. Well, I knew there had to be something outstanding about this month."

She paused, becoming conscious that she was waving her arms around, as if working herself up to something.

Then she continued softly. "Actually I was thinking about how I killed your father."

While Dyer wanted a fight, this was not a battleground he would have chosen. "It wasn't you who killed him; he killed himself," he answered sharply.

"I knew your perceptiveness couldn't last. Don't you know your father only finished the job? We killed him."

Dyer laughed coldly. "Now it's *we*?"

"Yes, yes," she said impatiently. "Me and Ben and my mother and Angela. And of course you."

"I did nothing to my father."

"Oh, I know. Poor little child of twelve. What could such a young boy do to harm his father?"

"Look, Pauline, I don't want to continue this discussion."

"Would you rather talk about business?"

"I'd rather talk about neither, thank you. In fact, I'd rather leave."

"You know where the door is."

Dyer rose and walked to the door.

Pauline smiled nastily. "Of course if you do, you can't have control over my stock. I'll vote against you on every motion. Whatever you want, I'll take the other side."

He sneered. "Don't be ridiculous!"

"Why, Dyer, you know you can count on me to be exactly that. Ridiculous is my middle name."

"All right, then, that's what you'll do." It was as if he were talking to a child.

"Oh, come on. You don't expect me to believe you don't care. I know you do. In fact, I'd be willing to bet that's one of the reasons you came here."

She walked over to Dyer, baiting him. "Just one, of course. But an important one."

She was watching him for his reaction, measuring how much she was getting to him and enjoying it. "As a matter of fact, I'd say you're planning something right at this moment. Now would be the time your turbulent little brain would be coming up with a scheme. Something important, little nephew?"

Dyer's eyes were very cold. "Maybe."

"Aha! So what is it, then?"

"Why should it make a difference, since you plan to stop me?"

"I plan to . . ." Pauline hesitated, calculating the changes on his face. "To tell you the truth, I don't know what I plan at the moment."

She took a sip of her drink, then played the ice around in her glass as she was playing Dyer. "It all depends on how I feel. Which all depends on how you treat me." She frowned petulantly. "And right now, I want you to talk to me."

She tried for a teasing little-girl look, but her face was still in red blotches where she had scratched at it, and the puffiness around her eyes only emphasized their cold anger. It was a ravaged face that looked up at Dyer, and he shivered at the sight of it.

Then suddenly everything about Pauline changed, and she looked as if she were about to cry. "Please sit down, Dyer. I really do need to talk to you." She sighed. "I get like this sometimes, and if I have no one to talk to, it eats me up inside."

Dyer nodded and reluctantly went back to his seat. Her quick changes of mood were confusing him, and he didn't notice she was smiling again.

"And when I get like this, the only thing I can do is find someone. You know what I mean, don't you, Dyer? And you wouldn't want me to do that."

Pauline began closing in on Dyer, and he could feel exactly what she was doing, but he couldn't stop her, and he couldn't stop himself.

"I don't give a damn," he said.

"I'll bet." She grabbed his arm, but he threw her hand off. "Oh, come on now, Dyer. Don't be mad at me. I'm feeling sad and lonely, and I do want you to stay and talk to me."

"What do you want to talk about?"

Again there was the petulant little-girl frown. "I told you before."

Dyer shook his head. "I don't want to discuss business."

"Well, that's a first! Okay. Then let's talk about your father, my brother. Let's talk about Evan."

"What exactly is it you want to say? We wouldn't want anyone to accuse you of discretion."

Pauline's eyes narrowed, and she looked like a ravaged cat. "I want to talk about his death. And how you killed him."

"Would you like to tell me how, in that tiny disturbed brain of yours, you figure that I killed him?"

"You were. That was enough."

Pauline began walking around the room unsteadily. Her tight angry face glowed ghostly in the pink light. "Haven't you ever suspected it was because of you he committed suicide? Of course you have. Just a little bit?"

Dyer didn't answer. Anger was growing, and he could feel his body being taken over; the power of it was mesmerizing.

Pauline was breathing heavily. "You must have thought about that, once, twice, maybe many times before. Even old cold fish Dyer."

Dyer gazed at Pauline. Not a muscle in his body was moving; his lower lip was slack, and he looked moronic, devoid of thought, devoid even of feeling.

Pauline laughed. "Well, maybe not. Sometimes I wonder if it isn't a gross exaggeration on my part to assume you are even alive. Maybe you are just a machine like everyone says."

She looked at Dyer, and it was then she sensed the danger. But again she laughed, misjudging it, or perhaps it was this she'd been waiting for.

Her voice was deadly. "No wonder I can't come with you. It's just like fucking a machine. A real wham-bam-thank-you-ma'am experience. You come in here to get your engine adjusted. Oil the old valves and wheels, huh? No wonder I'm bored out of my mind."

Dyer exploded into motion. He grabbed Pauline by the arm, slashing her across the face with his hand.

Pauline screamed. She tried to pull away, but Dyer was holding her too firmly, pinning her to him. His eyes were no longer blank and empty; they were like an animal's.

Dyer could hear Pauline scream, but it seemed to come from a great distance. The taunting smile was gone from her lips, but he could still see it in his mind, and again he struck her across the face. Her flesh felt soft and yielding under his fist, and this only compounded the anger. Her scream excited him.

Pauline tried to wrench from his grasp, but his powerful hand was clamped to her arm, and she could merely jerk crazily from side to side.

"My God! Stop it!" she yelled.

But Dyer only wanted to feel her flesh under his hand, and he struck her again, leaving a bright red weal across her mouth.

Pauline gasped. "Please, God. Please, please, stop," she whimpered.

She was crying now, violent sobs, and her face was streaked with red marks.

Slowly Dyer became aware of what he was doing. He pulled back, releasing Pauline's arm and letting out a muffled cry of his own.

Pauline clutched at her face with her hands, weeping softly, and yet she was aware of everything that was going on around her, and there was a feeling of quietness inside her, almost a kind of satisfaction.

Dyer backed to the couch and fell into it. He knew he should be feeling some kind of remorse, but he didn't feel sorry for what he had done, he felt suddenly relaxed, peaceful.

Pauline watched him for a long while, then she walked over to the bar and poured them both fresh drinks. She handed one to Dyer and sat on the couch next to him. They sipped their drinks slowly, neither of them saying anything. But they were watching one another, and there was something pretty close to understanding in their gaze.

Finally Pauline said softly, "I've never come with anyone. Funny, isn't it? Unbelievable really. But I never have. It's not that I don't get excited. It's only that suddenly something clicks off. Right in the middle, I seize up. Just like a motor. It used to drive me crazy. Absolutely crazy. Which only made things worse. Now I'm used to it."

Dyer nodded, but it was clear that he wasn't really listening. He was staring at his drink, the calmness blunting all guilt and shame. He wished he could stay like this forever, just allowing the thoughts to wash over him without their having the ability to really touch him.

Finally he looked over at Pauline. She was watching him with tired sad eyes. It was such a familiar face, one from his childhood, one he'd seen tilted up at him in the animal excitement of sex. And yet she had said that she never came with him.

He no longer felt angry at her for that; he felt only a kinship. In his own way he had never come with a woman; at least it had never been like they said it was. Pauline was right. To him it had always been about as meaningful as having his engine tuned.

"I'm sorry for everything I said before." Pauline was staring down at her hands, and indeed she did look sorry. "Do you hate me now?"

"Is that what you want?"

Pauline shrugged. "I did. I wanted you to despise me. I think I even wanted you to hit me like that."

Dyer sighed and stretched back against the couch, feeling the warm waves of relaxation washing over him.

He replied after a while, "You didn't say anything that wasn't true. You can't apologize for fact."

He shivered, suddenly seeming to come back to life. "Don't kid yourself. I've thought very often it was my fault my father killed himself."

"No, Dyer. I didn't mean that. I was just trying to get at you. I was just trying to blot out the truth." She looked at him, and there were tears in her eyes. "It was me. I told him about certain rumors, about my suspicions. I went out to dinner with him, and I told him right after my sweet sixteen party." She laughed sadly. "Some sweet sixteen I was."

"You were only a child."

"A very old, very nasty child."

Dyer shook his head. "He wouldn't have believed you."

"He believed me, all right. I doubt that I was the first to tell him. But God, Dyer, what if I was the last!" She was staring at him, terrified.

"It was years later. Don't you see it wasn't you?"

"I baited him. I pushed him." Pauline was bent over, crying into her hands, covering her face with them.

Then she became aware that Dyer was standing over her. He knelt to her, and when she looked into his eyes she saw tears.

"It wasn't you," he said gently. He took her in his arms.

Pauline succumbed to him; his strong muscular chest shielded her; his arms surrounded her. Tenderly he cradled her, and she allowed his body to engulf her.

She was only vaguely aware of his voice, soft and soothing, repeating in her ear, "It wasn't you, Pauline. It was him. It's what we both know. It was Ben."

BOOK SIX

Spring, 1981

THIRTY-SIX

The sun was cold white, yet there was warmth from it. Ben was on his knees in the newly turned earth. He put down his spade, removed his gardening gloves, and took a clump of soil in his hands, crumbling it between his fingers. It was very cold; crystals of ice still gleamed in it, and Ben was reminded of something that had happened a long time ago, though he couldn't remember what.

He turned back to the ground and began digging again. His body was aching, but he'd become used to it. At first he'd had to tell himself that each pain brought him closer to recovery; now it was merely an annoyance. Increasingly he was growing stronger, and though he still limped and his speech was slightly slurred, the disabilities that had tortured him before were essentially gone.

He dug deep in the earth; sweat was pouring off him and his hands felt numb from the cold. It was an uncomfortable feeling, but very alive, and as he stooped to the frosty ground, he remembered the memory it evoked. It was the burial of his father and the shiny crystallized earth they had thrown on his coffin. And with this memory came many others of his father, and he was stirred by images of him, hunching close to the fire, sipping his tea and fighting the cold wind on his way to work. Once again he could hear his terrible coughing, and he remembered how that night Evan had said there had been much magic in the man. If there had been, Ben had never seen it. But he was beginning to realize there were many things he hadn't seen. Perhaps there had been magic in Evan too, though once again Ben had never recognized it. He'd loved him; he'd cared deeply about him, but he hadn't respected him.

Ben dug his spade in deeply, hurling the soil across the ground with his strength. Even today he could not think of Evan without being overcome by emotion. With each memory, sadness and guilt came rolling in on him. Even an insignificant incident from their childhood seemed suffused with his death, for though his suicide had taken only a second to perform, it had become his whole life. Yet alongside the guilt and sadness, Ben also felt angry at Evan. It was something he'd never admitted to himself until that moment. Still, if what Pauline had said was true and Evan's death was a stroke of hate, a way of paying him back forever, it was something he didn't deserve.

Ben stopped digging. But hadn't he himself attempted suicide? He wondered if he too had been trying to pay someone back, and if so, who. He thought for a while but could come to no conclusion. What he remembered was that life had seemed too unbearable to be lived; he had felt damaged; he had felt half a man, and if anger and revenge had been mixed in there, it had been only part of the reason. Perhaps Evan had felt the same, damaged, half a man, and if he had blamed someone for it, that was not important; it was the pain of inadequacy that moved his hand. Evan's face reappeared to Ben, and the anger faded, leaving only sadness and a feeling of profound kinship.

Ben glanced back at the house. He thought he saw the kitchen curtains move and wondered if Tally was behind them, watching him. He suspected that she was. Often he discovered her watching him, though when he asked her, she rarely admitted it. He laughed fondly. It was something he understood well; he was a proud man himself, and while caring came hard to proud people, admitting it came even harder.

A moment later the kitchen door opened and Tally came out, carrying two cups of tea. Ben pretended not to notice and continued digging the earth, but he was smiling now.

Tally stood for a while, watching him, then she sat on the ground and held out his cup. "I didn't think I'd be able to persuade you to take a break, so I brought the break to you."

Ben put down the spade and gloves and sat next to Tally. "Who'd believe I'd be drinking tea? In America only old ladies and sick kids drink the stuff."

He took the steaming cup and smiled. Then as he stared out at the faintly green budding trees, a dreamy calm came over him, and it took a long time for him to speak. "I wonder when you stop feeling so damn lucky."

Tally touched his hand and smiled. "Maybe you never do."

Ben thought about this, then shook his head sadly. "No. It goes. Number-one rule of life. Everything goes. Both good and bad."

Tally asked, "Even love?"

Family Passions   357

He looked down at her. "I don't know. I wonder about that too. But I just don't know. Even with all my supposed experience."

Tally smiled. "The less said about that the better."

"Aha, the jealous type, eh?"

Tally was embarrassed. "No. Not at all. I don't like jealous people."

But Ben was grinning. "You can't fool me. At least for a moment you were jealous."

Tally was turned away. "I can't fool you, can I?" she asked softly.

"Does that upset you?"

"A little. But I think I like it too. It scares me though. It puts me off balance. But maybe that's the part of it I like. Do you know what I mean?"

Ben nodded. "Yeah, I know."

"I suppose that I always seem so competent and in control, as if I understand everything. But of course no one really knows what I'm thinking inside. I suppose until now, I didn't want them to."

Ben watched her fondly. At that moment she looked so young, so vulnerable, he wanted to protect her from everything; he wanted to protect her from herself. "I don't know that I understand you either, Tally. But I am trying."

"Well, at least you have glimpses of me. And when you do, I'm no longer in control. It makes me feel like a child, and that's frightening and real and . . ." She broke off, then finally continued sadly. "But if you're right, that feeling will go too."

Ben watched her for a while, then whispered softly, "I don't want you to go. I've never said that before. But please don't go away."

Tally's face was turned from Ben. "I'm not going anywhere."

Ben took her chin and turned her to him. "Please," he said softly.

"And you? Are you going away?"

"Never!"

Tally laughed but there was a soft sorrow in it. "Remember your number-one rule of life. Everything goes. Both good and bad."

" Well, this good thing doesn't."

Tally turned back to the house, and Ben could see she was unsettled. Then slowly she turned back to him. "Are you sure you're not staying here because you're just running away?"

"From what?"

"You haven't let anyone know you're recovering. Why?"

The mood was broken. Ben sat up, his eyes seemed very far away. "They don't matter anymore. I'm a different person."

"But not even your mother?"

"I will tell her. She's the only one who I want to know."

"Nevertheless, you haven't. Why? Are you afraid she'll tell you to come back?"

"I'm a big boy now. My mother can't tell me where to go."

"But she could pressure you."

Ben smiled fondly. "Could and would. You should see her when she wants something. There's nothing she won't try, begging, wheedling, flattering. Nothing. She talks about the obligation to the family, to life, and implied, of course, to her. God, I can just see her doing it. And it works too. I'm the only person in the world it doesn't work with. That's probably because I can see all her moves. I guess we're too much alike." He suddenly became serious. "But for all that, I think she'd understand."

"And if she didn't?"

"I put in sixty years for her dream. Enough. I can be pretty stubborn too, in case you haven't noticed."

He turned to Tally, smiling, but she didn't smile back. She persisted. "And you're sure you're not just waiting until you're completely recovered, then you'll go back and leave me behind?"

"I am completely recovered, in case you haven't noticed." He grinned. "Or is that by way of complaint?" He put his arms around Tally. "Any complaints, huh?"

She smiled up at him. "Oh, God, Ben," she whispered. "None. No complaints at all. I just don't want to lose you. I don't want you ever to go."

Tears came suddenly, and, ashamed, she tried to brush them from her cheeks. But Ben held her in his arms tightly, then he wiped the tears from her face with his hand.

"I'm not going anywhere without you, Tally. I promise. I'm going to be with you forever."

Mrs. Mided closed her bedroom door and motioned for Tally to take a seat. She herself didn't sit but walked to her bureau. She looked very serious. Picking up a letter, she held it in her small veined hand, then she pulled on her glasses. Still, she remained at her bureau, as if unsure what to do.

Family Passions 359

Finally she said, "This letter came today addressed to me. I thought you'd want to see it first. Then I think we should give it to Ben."

She nodded to herself, then walked over to Tally and handed her the letter.

Mrs. Mided turned away; she didn't want to watch Tally's face as she read it, but when she turned back, Tally was still looking at the letter, though Mrs. Mided felt sure she had finished it some time ago.

Tally looked up. "Who is Angela Savage?"

"Ben's sister-in-law. I met her when I met his mother."

"All the letter says is that Mrs. Savage will not be writing for a while and that Angela Savage will be doing it for her. Ben told us to answer letters by saying that his condition's the same. I don't see why this one is any different."

"Because between the lines it implies something's wrong with Mrs. Savage."

Tally stood and moved to the window. She pulled the curtain aside and looked out. Ben was working in the garden. He looked very small against the green-brown hills, like an animal scampering in the newly grown grass.

She sighed. "Perhaps." She turned back. "But it could just be that she has the flu."

"Mrs. Savage is eighty-six years old."

"And Ben says as strong as an ox."

"Even oxen die. I think I have to give Ben the letter."

Tally shook her head. "And I think we should telephone first and find out before we worry Ben. After all, he hasn't completely recovered yet."

"Hasn't he?"

Tally folded the letter. "I don't want to worry him, unless we have reason to."

She handed the letter back. Mrs. Mided took it, but she did not put it away; she just held it in her hand. "I'm not sure who it is you don't want to worry, him or you."

Tally looked back out the window. Ben was patting at the earth, making little rows. He stopped and glanced up at the house. He must have seen the curtain move because he waved.

Mrs. Mided was staring at Tally. "That's the question, isn't it? Who are you trying to protect?" She took off her glasses and rubbed her eyes with the back of her hand, then she put the letter on top of the bureau. "What if Mrs. Savage is very sick?"

Tally became irritated. "I told you before. I think we should ring first and find out."

"And I asked you, who are you shielding by that? You know darn well, even if she isn't really sick now, it'll have to happen sometime. You're going to have to know. You can't protect him forever."

"Of course I can't. But not just yet. He needs time."

"He needs time or *it* needs time?" Mrs. Mided was watching her.

Tally walked to the bureau and fingered the letter, but it was more to avoid Mrs. Mided's eyes than anything else. "I don't know what you mean."

"Don't you? Look, Tally, I understand you're worried. Goodness, I'd have to hold myself back from just tearing the letter up and throwing it away. But don't you see? There's no more time for it to grow stronger between the two of you. Angela Savage has made sure of that."

"All I'm suggesting is that we telephone first and find out. If his mother is ill, I'll tell him. Believe me, I wouldn't hold back a thing like that."

"And if she isn't ill?"

Tally just shrugged. She was still staring down at the letter. Mrs. Mided walked to her and put her small bony hand on her arm. "You aren't planning on telling him then, are you?"

"There would be nothing to tell."

"It's just what needs to be found out about his mother's health needs to be found out by him."

Tally shook her head, but she didn't answer.

Mrs. Mided continued. "It's not your place to decide whether he gets the letter or not, or whether he calls Midland or not. That's really what you're worried about, isn't it? You're scared once he calls, he'll want to go back."

Tally's voice was very soft. "Yes."

"You can't keep love alive on lies."

"It wouldn't be a lie."

"It won't be the truth either if you don't give him that letter and let him make his own decision about Midland." She watched Tally sympathetically. "Look, I'm a great one for oversimplifying things, but this is one choice that's clear. Hide that letter, and you'll kill your love."

"Even if nothing is wrong, and he doesn't find out?"

"Yes. Because you'll know what you did. And you'll never feel free with him. It'll always stand between you."

She stroked Tally's hand gently. "Besides, you still won't have the answer to your question, will you? You still won't know if he'll leave you. But you'll always be on the lookout for it. And that'll kill your love as sure as anything."

"I've never been to Venice," Ben said, as he walked around the bedroom undressing for bed. He seemed very excited, guarding a secret. "Not even on business. But I saw a movie that took place there once, and it really looked like something."

Tally sat on the edge of the bed, legs crossed, like a little girl. "Yes, it is lovely."

Ben was disappointed. "Then you've been there. Damn!"

He opened his drawer, pulled out two tickets, and threw them on the bed. "I was hoping to surprise you."

Tally jumped off the bed and grabbed up the tickets, excited. "Where did you get these?"

"I have my ways. Actually I sent Mrs. Mided on the mission. She can be very discreet, you know."

Tally smiled. "Yes, I know."

But there was a numbness behind that smile, and Ben could see it. He walked over to her surprised and disturbed. "Hey, we don't have to go to Venice. We can go anywhere in the world you want. You name it: Africa, Asia, the North Pole. Hell, I could even buy a piece of the Pole if you wanted it. I'm a very rich man, with nothing better to do than spend it on you."

He took her in his arms, but her body felt distant, unreachable. "Look, we don't have to go anywhere, if that's what's bothering you. We can just stay here, the two of us. Or even the three of us if you want Mrs. Mided to stay. She's not such a bad old girl once you get to know her."

Ben held Tally in his arms, but she felt more fragile than usual. He thought he felt a shiver go through her, and he tried to tilt her head up toward him, but he could sense her resistance.

"Have I done something wrong?" he asked. "You might as well tell me now. I hate all the rigamarole of trying to extract it from you."

"No. You've done nothing wrong."

Ben waited for more, his frustration mounting. "Well, what's up? I can feel something is."

Tally nodded. "How right you were, Mrs. Mided. It's happening already." She smiled stiffly at Ben. "I almost made a terrible mistake, that's all."

She sighed and went to her purse, fumbling in it for the letter, then she handed it to Ben. "It came this morning."

Ben took the letter and read it slowly, then his face crumpled. "Jesus Christ."

"I'm sorry."

He was lost in thought for a moment, then he asked, "You think there might be something wrong with my mother, don't you? But doesn't it make sense that if there were really something wrong, they'd phone not write?"

"That's why I almost didn't give you the letter. I didn't want to upset you needlessly. I wanted to telephone first."

Ben stiffened. "I'm hardly an invalid anymore. I can place the call by myself now."

Tally turned away, embarrassed. "I'm sorry."

"You don't really think I'm not able to handle my own affairs? Or is there something I don't know? Am I really sicker than you told me?"

Tally turned back. "No, of course not, Ben. Don't you see? It isn't that there's something wrong with you, or even that I want to keep you an invalid or anything like that." She paused, unable to speak. Then finally she forced herself to continue. "It's that I was frightened."

"What's there to be frightened of?"

"Mrs. Mided says I'm worried that if you ring America, you'll want to go back and leave me."

Ben laughed. "That's ridiculous. You don't think there's another woman in Midland and that once I see her, I'll never think of you again?"

"Maybe."

"Tally, look at me." He waited until she had turned to him. "There is no one else. I promise. The only other woman I ever cared about was Dylan. And that was a long long time ago. Another life." He laughed. "Sure, I was no missionary when it came to women. Not by a long shot. But they never touched me. Not really. No other woman has done that but you."

Family Passions

"I suppose it's not so much a woman I'm worried about. It's your business. It's steel. You said that touched you."

Ben laughed. "Not in quite the same way."

"But you told me your business consumed you; there was no room for anyone else."

He took her in his arms and held her. "And I also told you I've changed."

"And then there's your mother and your family and . . ."

Ben was holding her tightly to him, and he was laughing. "Do you honestly think a cold ingot or my name over the gates or a bunch of no-good leeches can compare with what I have right here today?"

Her voice was pleading. "I don't know."

"Then you can't think much of what we have, can you?"

Tally held close to Ben, relieved. But slowly she became aware his body was growing tense, and when she looked at him, he was glancing at his watch.

"What time is it in Ohio now?"

Tally didn't look at him. "Five o'clock in the evening, I think."

"Tom doesn't get home until seven or seven thirty. I'll call then. I'd rather speak to Tom than Angela."

"You're not going to call your mother?"

"I don't want to shock her. It's better to call Tom."

"I see." Tally pulled away and she didn't say anymore. She supposed that could be the reason he didn't call his mother, but she suspected it was not. And she began to wonder if she was the only one who was frightened of his family's influence, or if Ben had a fear of his own.

Ben sat in the darkened living room, holding tightly to the telephone receiver. He could barely contain himself; he was shaking with laughter, but also there were tears in his eyes. "So, what's new, Tom?" he asked excitedly.

Tom's voice was tentative. "Ben?"

"How ya been?"

Tom couldn't speak for a moment. "Please, whoever this is, don't tease me like this. It isn't funny. Okay?"

"This is no joke, Tom. It's me."

"Ben? I can't believe it. Ben?" He laughed, scared. "Will you listen to me? I sound like a broken record. Jesus, Ben. How are you?"

"Never been better, you old dog."

"I can't believe this. I just can't believe it!"

"I gotta use a cane, you know? Damn thing makes me look old."

There was a long pause, then, "I'm sorry, Ben. But I just can't talk for a moment."

Ben could hear the tears in Tom's voice and it touched him. Finally he asked, "How is my mother, Tom?"

"Jesus, Ben. I'm not sure. Sick. But I don't know how bad. Still, you know Elizabeth. She's as strong as an ox. She'll probably outlive us all." He laughed, but it was forced, and almost immediately he grew serious. "I don't know what's the matter with her. Shit, no one tells me anything anymore. It's like a god damn secret society around here."

"What do you mean?"

"Never mind. I'll find out about your mother for you."

"Tom, what did you mean about it being a secret society? What's going on over there?"

"Ben, Jesus, that damn nephew of yours." He sighed. "But forget it. You're better. That's all that matters."

"My damn nephew what?"

"I don't know." He stopped. "Christ, you floored me so much I almost forgot to tell you; I've got a foothold on Anti-Cor. We're using a variation on the black box with a partial vacuum."

Ben smiled. "You see? I knew you'd find a way. Well, congratulations!"

"Yeah, it's great." But Tom didn't sound very pleased about it.

Ben pressed. "Tom, what the Christ is going on? Tell me."

"See here, Ben. I have no proof."

"Proof of what? Come on, damn it! I'm fine now. And I want to know."

"Are you really fine, lad?"

Ben laughed. "You should only know how fine."

"Then come back. Come back now. The stockholders' meeting is in less than a month."

Ben didn't answer. He looked out the window at the night sky. The moon was riding the crest of a bank of clouds, bathing the surrounding hills in silver light.

After a while he said, "I'm sorry, Tom. But the only thing that's going to bring me back is if something's wrong with Mother. And even then it'll only be temporarily. I've had it with Midwestern. I've had it with business and the family and the whole blasted thing. I've found out that there's more in the world. I've found a woman."

"Yeah, okay." Tom sounded anxious and disappointed.

Ben was silent, thinking, then he said, "I just can't leave now. Remember, you always used to tell me there was more to life than steel? Well, you were right."

"Yeah, sure, lad. I understand."

Ben hesitated, then asked softly, "What's Dyer up to?"

Tom sounded relieved. "I can't be sure, lad. But I think, just think, that Dyer might be planning to sell the company out from underneath us."

"Dyer? I don't believe it. He loves steel."

"He hates you."

Ben thought about that. Again he glanced out the window, but the moon had disappeared behind the clouds, and all he saw was darkness. "To whom?"

"I can't be sure. Look, I don't even know if he is planning that. It's only a hunch."

Ben cut him off. "Never mind. I'll bet I know to whom. But look, even if he tried something like that, he wouldn't get away with it. He can't sell Midwestern himself, and the board would never approve it."

"When you were here? Sure. But now everyone's scattered. Jesus, no one knows what he's doing anymore."

"I've got to think. Give me a moment to think." Ben was telling this more to himself than Tom. Then finally he said, "Okay. I get you. But listen, don't tell anyone about talking to me until I say so. Okay?"

"You bet!" Tom sounded happy. "Ben, I'm so glad for you. I guess I'm happy for us all."

Ben hung up, but he remained at the window, looking out at the black night and the faint silhouette of hills in the distance, and when he turned back, he saw Tally standing in the doorway, and he knew she'd been there for some time.

"It would only be for a few weeks," he said quickly. "There's just some things I've got to straighten out. Then I'll be back."

But Ben's voice sounded false even to himself. Already he could feel his heart pounding with excitement, and in his mind, he could see the gray steel being fired to red.

Tally didn't move. "Of course, you'll be back before I know it."

She smiled and waited as he walked to her. But she was looking away from him, her body tight and guarded, and inside of her everything was beginning to wither.

THIRTY-SEVEN

Ohio

It was seven thirty in the morning, and Dyer was already seated behind his desk, drinking instant coffee and reading *The Wall Street Journal*. He threw the paper down angrily. The financial news was not good, though this could hardly come as a shock; the *Journal* had been reading like an obituary column for too long to surprise anyone anymore. Midwestern, along with almost every other company in America, was suffering from the recession. A sick economy strangling off a terminal business. It was a new world, a world of plastics and reinforced concrete, and there wasn't any part of the industry that hadn't been completely altered. Even the making of steel was changing. The days of producing from ore were almost gone. Mostly they were using scrap, and there was more than enough of that around. It was hardly a healthy sign.

Dyer sat hunched over his coffee, sipping it slowly, warming his hands on the cup. He was tired of reading how bad business was; he was tired of watching the stock market bouncing around like a rubber ball in response. It was a bad time to be doing business in America; it was an even worse time to be starting one up.

Dyer knew all too well the importance of timing in life; he also knew that men rarely had a say in their own. Very soon he would have to be thinking of starting a new business, and hard times or not, he would have to be ready.

The question, of course, was what would he be investing in. And while the prospect of answering this question was frightening, it was exciting too. Here he was, a grown man, able to ask himself something usually reserved for children. What did he want to be when he grew up?

Indeed, what did he want to be? At twenty-one he hadn't had much of a choice. Certainly he could have bypassed the family business, though the pressure would have been enormous. Nevertheless, he could have opted for staying at the university and completing a law degree or becoming a stockbroker or commodities dealer. There were options. Of course then it had seemed as if he had no choice, and in fact he suspected he would have been no happier had he been brokering a carload of pylons or pleading a case at the bar.

This time though, things were different. Now besides the obvious experience he had gained, he would also have considerable cash backing.

With this thought, the reality of how he would be getting the money came back to him. Dyer tried to shut out the thought; it was better to concentrate on the end just ahead, shining brightly, seductively. As for the means, there was nothing he could do about it.

Yet his mind returned, and he could never keep it away for long. Dyer had never done anything immoral in his life, aside from a few furtive fixed tickets, that kind of thing, but this was clearly immoral, and every time he thought about it, the perspiration started to flow and his heart clenched like a fist to his chest. He thought of his grandmother. While what he was doing wouldn't harm her on any realistic level, on all the other levels Dyer would be hurting her terribly. For he would be killing the dream.

Again he tried to block out the thought. He reminded himself that it would be like starting a new life; everything would change; maybe *he* would change. Slowly his excitement returned.

Dyer continued to sip his coffee, staring into space and allowing his mind to wander over the possibilities. It was a tranquil moment, but it didn't last long. Suddenly he became aware of a great deal of noise coming from the reception area. He glanced at his watch. It was only eight A.M. Carrie never put in an appearance before eight thirty, but he supposed it could be James or Tom or one of the juniors who had a key. He was about to get up from his desk and warn them to be quiet, when his office door was pushed open. After that, movement was impossible.

Ben stood in the doorway. His face was flushed with anger, but he was smiling too. It was not a pleasant smile.

Dyer couldn't move; he couldn't even speak. He just sat there, slack-jawed, staring; he looked almost Neanderthal.

Ben laughed at him. "Glad to see me?"

He made his way into the room, trying to rely on his cane as little as possible, but he was tired and shaking and very excited, and at that moment he needed his cane more than ever.

Dyer didn't move. It was as if everything had shattered, and he was unable to reform the pieces into anything coherent.

Ben stopped at his desk, putting his broad hands on the top of it, leaning toward Dyer. "Are you enjoying the office?" he asked sharply. "Not a bad one, eh? Plenty of room to squirm around in. Good view of the mill you're trying to take away from me."

Ben fell silent. His legs were beginning to shake; his heart was pounding heavily, and he was worried that he might fall. Finally he smiled angrily. "Only problem is, the office could use a good cleaning. There's a lot of garbage that needs taking out. Like that big hunk of trash behind my desk. Then we'll get rid of all the muck and mire that was collecting around it. Japanese muck and mire, for example."

Ben moved over to a chair, trying to regain his composure. There was a moment of intense sorrow, then, suddenly, he thought of Wales. He could see the little gray farmhouse and Roman church outside his window. The clarity of it stunned him. He could see Tally running toward him, the sunlight sparkling her hair into brilliant copper. From the moment he had boarded the plane, Wales had begun to recede for him, and he had been instantly consumed by Midwestern. But now the memory of what he had left only a few hours before was back, and he couldn't shake it.

Dyer watched Ben in silence. The shock was lessening for him, and slowly his mind was beginning to grasp the fact that he was seeing Ben. There'd been a moment when he'd been tempted to invent excuses, to come up with lies, but he doubted that would have done any good. And even if they would have, Dyer was no longer capable. It was Ben standing there, alive and well, ready to claim back everything as his and leave Dyer with nothing.

Dyer's voice was vicious. "The accident left you with a speech impediment, did you know that?"

Ben recoiled. The sunlight and the church and the glowing of Tally's hair disappeared, and he was left only with his anger. His voice was sharp. "Are you going to get out from behind my desk on your own? Or am I going to have to call the garbage collectors to carry you out?"

Dyer merely smiled. His mind was becoming clearer now. What exactly did Ben's coming back mean? Certainly it meant a fight. From what Ben had said before it was clear he suspected something about Hamayoshi, though where he could have gotten that information, Dyer couldn't imagine. One thing was evident; he wouldn't be able to get any proof. Hamayoshi would have been careful about that. So there would be a fight, but if he kept his head, the outcome would be the same. Midwestern had changed. He was close to getting Pauline's and James's vote now. If they stuck, and he bet they would, Dyer had control of a majority of the family stock, and he also had the secret 4.9 percent voting with him.

Dyer got up from behind the desk. "Here you are, Ben. It's all yours." He smiled fiercely. "Or at least temporarily. But of course you don't know that yet. Never mind. You'll find it out soon enough from James and Pauline." He paused, allowing Ben to take this in. "So why don't you just limp on over to your desk. It won't be for long."

Dyer's mention of James and Pauline startled Ben. Almost immediately he was able to hide his shock and also his fear, but Dyer had seen it, and Ben knew that he had. Ben pulled himself from his chair unsteadily, holding tightly to the arm. He was frightened he might fall.

"I want you out of my office and out of Midwestern entirely."

Dyer laughed. "Sorry, Ben. You may be able to throw me out of your office. But you can't throw me out of Midwestern."

"Yet."

Dyer pulled out a cigar, lit it, and blew out the smoke calmly. "That remains to be seen."

Ben hesitated. He couldn't be sure that Dyer was telling the truth about James and Pauline, but he suspected that he was. Ben tried to calm himself by thinking whatever had happened was in the past. Now that he was back, Dyer could not be so certain. Dyer was still smoking confidently, but Ben could see the tension pulling at the sides of his mouth, and he sensed that Dyer was worrying about that too.

Ben reminded Dyer. "There's a stockholders' meeting in less than a month. Then we'll see."

Dyer shrugged. "Yep. It should be very interesting. All the savages scurrying around the carcass."

"It'll be your carcass."

"Don't be sure. After all, there's no loyalty among savages. We just hunt around for fresh meat."

"I'm too old and tough to be eaten."

Dyer smirked. "You were bankrupting the company before your accident. Don't think everyone doesn't know that." He took in smoke and released it in a cloud. "And look at you now. You aren't quite the same as you were."

Dyer began to pace the office. His body was full of intense energy, his movements were slow and strong. He knew Ben was watching him carefully and understood what he was trying to imply. "After all," he continued, "I'm young. In fact, you could say I'm in my prime."

He strode to the door and stopped there, looking back at Ben. "So I'll see you at the stockholders' meeting with all the rest of the savages. Then we'll see who's on the menu."

"First call Tokyo."

Dyer feigned confusion. "Now, why would I want to do that?"

Ben imitated him. "Why, I haven't the faintest idea. But how about dialing, and seeing if the two of us can't figure out a reason together."

"It's your office. You make the calls."

Dyer reached for the doorknob, and Ben yelled, "Stay here!"

Dyer turned back angrily, but he didn't leave. He just stood at the door, glaring at Ben.

Ben let go of the chair and made his way to the door. Dyer watched him coldly. He was no longer frightened; Ben was just a man, a flawed, imperfect man, and with every step, he could see that plainly.

Ben stopped at Dyer and grabbed hold of his arm. He held him tightly, watching his eyes, challenging him to strike out. But under Ben's anger, there was something else feeding his fury, for this was a violence that only could come from tenderness betrayed.

Finally Ben spoke. He still held to Dyer's arm, but his voice sounded shattered. "I gave you everything. I brought you into this company. I trained you. I pushed you forward over my own son."

"Like hell! You did what was best for Midwestern. Business is business, isn't that what you always say? Besides, it was my right. Midwestern belonged to my father too. Remember?"

"It was your right to enter the company, but I didn't have to do anything for you. That was not your right. That was my gift."

Ben stopped. His breath was coming quickly now; his bad leg felt twisted and burning. While he had always been aware that Dyer was his son, he had never felt it so strongly before. But now, as he stood locked to Dyer, he was aware that this was his son and that he was being betrayed by him. It was as if part of him was being torn, ripped and bleeding, from his center.

It took him a long while to speak; his eyes were intensely sad. "You were glad about what happened to me, weren't you? You wanted me out, once and for all."

"I always wanted you out, from that very first day you brought me in here and allowed me the privilege of hauling ass at the hot rolling mill. Was I glad about what happened to you? Yeah, I think I was. Hell, we're being honest, maybe for the first time. I wanted you dead, Ben, dead. Not that I would have done anything about it. I haven't killed yet. Too bad you can't say the same."

Ben recoiled. "What the hell is that supposed to mean?"

"My father, your brother. Remember him?"

"Your father committed suicide."

"Yes. I recollect that. But why?"

"It's something I ask myself all the time."

Dyer turned away, puffing at his cigar, trying to display a calmness he didn't feel. The fury of all the years was rising, and he knew now that he would say everything.

"I'll tell you something, Ben. I did better than ask myself; I asked *him*. When I was a kid, every night before I went to sleep I used to ask him. But of course we know the answer to that question, don't we? After all, he left a note."

"It was rambling and full of self-pity and . . ."

"Go on, Ben. You're about to say full of lies, aren't you? Well, go on. Tell me that the whole part about his suspicions isn't the truth." He paused, then continued sharply. "You see, Ben, I remember the note."

"Why haven't you asked your mother? Confront her with it?"

"You know I can't do that. You know what her life is like now. She goes nowhere, sees no one. She does nothing but mourn for my father."

"She loved him very much. In many ways he saved her life."

"And he loved her. Only problem was, he had this brother with a big cock and an even bigger mouth."

Ben was silent for a long while, and when finally he did speak, his voice was very soft and tortured with shame. "Your mother went to the doctor secretly for a checkup. He said she was fertile. It was then we began to suspect that it might be Evan."

"Oh, Jesus!" Dyer was rocked back, his eyes wide and shocked. Though Ben had told him nothing he hadn't really know, the confirmation shook him with a terrible force.

Ben sighed and looked away. He wasn't sure his legs would hold him up anymore, but he was afraid to move to a chair. He felt dizzy.

"Go on," Dyer urged angrily. "Tell me. I want you to tell me it all."

Ben's lips were trembling, and he couldn't control them. All he kept seeing was Evan's face before him, growing thinner, more careworn, and the terrible image of his twisted body. Ben cringed. Then finally he forced the words out, but it was more as if he were talking to himself than to Dyer. It was more as if he were talking to Evan.

"It was your mother's idea. We thought we'd be able to keep it from your father. But he suspected." Ben shook his head. "No. Not just suspected, he knew. But please believe me, we didn't mean to harm him. We thought we were doing right. It was out of love for Evan, not the opposite. My God, we certainly didn't mean to destroy him."

Dyer felt very cold and he was shivering. "But you did destroy him. You were always being better than him. You even fucked his wife better."

Ben's voice was choked off. "I'm so sorry . . ."

"For whom? For me? Forget it. I'll survive. And I'll fight you. You'd be better off feeling sorry for yourself. I have an excellent chance of winning."

Ben turned away from Dyer. He couldn't bear to look at him anymore. "Under it all, you are my son."

"No, Ben, I'm no more your son than James is. An accident of birth. That's all it is, and that's all you ever acted like it was too. You may have given us that one twisted little sperm. But that's it. Not all that much to do with making a man."

Dyer walked to the door, but he didn't open it, though he didn't bother looking back at Ben. "I was serious about winning. I will."

"You'll tear this family apart if you do."

This time Dyer did turn back. His face was very white, and his eyes glittered from it feverishly. "And so will you, Ben."

He took a few steps toward Ben, then stopped. "Don't you see? Haven't you always known? It's between us. Just like out in the jungle. A fight to the finish. Even if we both bring each other down."

This time Dyer did leave, slamming the door behind him. Ben stood motionless, listening to his angry footsteps as he passed through the reception area and out into the steel yard.

THIRTY-EIGHT

Ben closed Elizabeth's door and walked down the stairs. He stood in the corridor for a long while, unsure whether to go into the living room. He could hear the nurses bustling around upstairs, and he thought he heard the sound of his mother's voice, high-pitched and frightened. But he knew that whatever she was saying had no relation to Ben or to today. It was addressed to the strange inner world she was inhabiting, the world of her past colliding with the blank wall of her future.

He shivered. The smell of antiseptic from his mother's room was still in his nostrils, and his own illness was too recent for him not to remember; it would be a long time before it left him. So much illness and death. It seemed as if that was all he'd seen recently. Perhaps it would be better if after all he didn't go into the living room and just left the house for the pungent cool of evening.

Still, he hesitated in the corridor. His mother lying in the bed, gray and lifeless, bore no relation to the vital woman he remembered. If she were still there, she would be in her living room, where everything would be as it was.

Ben walked down the hallway and into the vast dim room, and the moment he entered, he could see nothing had changed. The furniture was still arranged as it had been from the first day they moved in. He remembered the day so clearly, the excitement of new smells, the irritation of packing cases, and then, at last, the calm of evening when everything was in place, the movers gone, and they'd sat in the living room, looking around and trying to integrate the strangeness as home.

His mother's nurse told him that she'd collapsed in this room and was found several hours later by the cleaning woman. But any signs of the disturbance she might have made were now cleared away, and the room looked as it always had, shadowy and tidy.

As he stood there he could imagine his mother reaching for a glass on the sidetable, adjusting a cushion as she sat. Then, suddenly, what might have happened, the pain, the dizziness, the turning of furniture and her falling. He saw her unable to move, screaming for help, and he felt the terrible wait she must have had until someone did come. The nurse said his mother had been all right when they'd found her; it was only later, after she was safe, that she'd become delirious. Possibly the effort of keeping herself alert had been too great, the terror of lying there alone and unaided, too shattering.

Ben tried to shake off the image, but it kept coming back to him. If only he'd been there, perhaps he could have prevented it. At least he could have tried. But he knew in fact there was very little he could have done, and the thought came as a relief, but also as a heavy emptiness. Just as there had been nothing his mother could do for him, so she too was alone, a twisted piece of driftwood tossed in the dark ocean.

As Ben stood in the living room, ghosts of his mother all around, he heard the doorbell ring. One of the nurses opened the door, and there was the sound of footsteps, then a voice he hadn't heard in twenty years.

Dylan paused in the doorway, uncertain whether to enter. "Ben! How are you?"

She looked so different that Ben didn't answer; he just stared at her. He supposed when he thought of Dylan, which was rarely, it was as the little girl he had married, not the woman she became. But as she began walking toward him, she seemed once more, very much Dylan, and somehow that was even more startling.

Ben shook hands with her. It was an awkward gesture, and neither of them could look at the other.

Finally he said, "Tom told me you were in town."

Dylan grinned nervously. "Me too. I figured we'd bump into each other. But I certainly didn't think we'd do it so soon. Or in such tragic circumstances." She paused and this time she was

Family Passions 375

looking at him sadly. "I'm so sorry, Ben. This must be terrible for you."

Ben nodded. "And you too. You always were fond of my mother."

"Yes. We got to spend some time together before . . ." She felt herself begin to give way to emotion and stopped. She remembered too well how much Ben hated that.

Ben turned away from her, and he sounded irritable. "I haven't seen James yet, you know? Carrie told me he called in sick today. But I think he found out I was back and was scared to come in."

Dylan shrugged, then she went to the chair she always sat in. Ben too took his place, and a smile passed over his face; he seemed to understand.

Dylan smiled back. "The more things change, huh?" She lit a cigarette. "Why didn't you tell anyone you were getting well?"

"Why didn't James come in to see me?"

Dylan hesitated. "I wish I could explain James to you. I wish I could explain him to me. Or to himself, for that matter. All I do know is it wasn't from want of emotion. I suspect it was from quite the opposite."

"That makes no sense."

"Oh, Ben, the ironies of life have always escaped you."

Ben threw up his hands. "Great! Here's where we launch into one of your little lectures and you throw around a bunch of words I don't understand." He stopped himself. "Jesus Christ. Twenty years and I slide right back into the old arguments like it was yesterday. I'm sorry."

The apology surprised Dylan, and she looked at Ben, really seeing him for the first time since she'd come into the room. Indeed, it was clear twenty years had passed, and he looked a great deal older. Undoubtedly part of that was due to time, part of it was a result of the accident. Still, he was a handsome man, tall and proud. But there was something different about him too. It was a softer face that was across from her, less sure, more human. At that moment she decided she liked his face very much.

Ben was watching her too. "You look very well, Dylan."

"Older."

"Sure. But it looks good on you. You seem more . . ." He searched for the word.

"Solid?" she offered.

"It's as good a word as any. Yes. Solid. Comfortable."

Dylan smiled shyly. "I am a little, though not nearly as much as they promise. I thought at fifty you were supposed to be full of self-possession and control. But it ain't like that, is it? Still, it's a far cry from being twenty, thank God. I wouldn't go through that whole performance again for a million dollars."

"I would."

"Yes. That was the difference between us. There was too large of an age gap. I was always too old for you."

Ben laughed. "Well, you'll be glad to know I've aged some since you knew me." Then he looked suddenly serious. "I guess I've done some thinking. There was certainly enough time for it." He tried to wave the seriousness away, but it stayed over him.

Dylan was staring at him. "You know, I think I like you. Can you beat that? After all those years of anger and resentment, I come home to find you aren't such a bad guy after all."

Ben was taken aback. "Why is it you always say exactly what you're thinking?"

"Not enough brains to be duplicitous, I guess. I'm sorry if I've offended you."

"You didn't. I'm the same way. Someone told me that's a very American trait." He was still watching Dylan, but it was clear that his mind was far away.

"American? I don't think so. Maybe it's a family trait. Your mother's like that, and she isn't American."

"Mother? Jesus, Dylan, she's the biggest liar on two legs. It's just that she mixes up truths and half-truths so much you can't tell the difference."

"Maybe. But at least she never knows she's doing it. She believes every word she says."

Ben smiled sadly. "Yeah, doesn't she ever. Christ, Dylan, it's not just that she's my mother, but she's a hell of a woman. She really is."

Dylan nodded but didn't answer. She felt tears come to her eyes, and when she looked at Ben, she could see them there for him too.

There was a silence, but it was no longer from awkwardness; it was from sorrow and the comfort of sharing it with someone who understood.

Finally Dylan said, "I wonder if she knows you're here."

"I'm sure some of her does. The important part knows."

Dylan glanced up at Ben. It was as if she were seeing a new person in the frame of the old, and she was surprised and slightly off balance.

Family Passions 377

Ben found himself growing annoyed at her gaze. It broke the comfort and sorrow, and he turned away, saying coldly, "I've fallen in love, Dylan."

Dylan flushed. "Apropos of what?"

"I'm just telling you, that's all. Her name is Tally. She's a nurse."

"In Wales?"

Ben nodded. He knew he had said this to hurt Dylan, though he didn't know why. Then after a while he asked, "Why did you leave me, Dylan? I never really knew why."

"You never wanted to know. You wanted to fix blame. And that you couldn't do. Don't think I wasn't aware of what you suspected was the reason. You thought I left you for a woman, didn't you?"

"You went to live with Beth. It was a natural conclusion."

"Was it? You know, I don't think it was a natural conclusion at all."

"But, I notice, you haven't ruled it out."

She shrugged and lit another cigarette. Her hands were shaking.

Finally Ben said, "I'm sorry. I don't know why I'm going after you like this. I guess I'm just looking for someone to blame. I want someone else to take responsibility for what happened to our marriage and James and everything. It would be so much easier if I could only find a reason besides myself. But it was me, wasn't it?"

"Oh, I had my part in it too. But, yeah, so did you."

Ben nodded. "What went wrong? Why did you leave me?"

Dylan laughed sadly. "I left you because you didn't give a damn about me. I was just one of your possessions, a little more expensive, a little less important than, say, our house."

"You know that wasn't true."

"You never talked to me. You never confided in me. It was always Evan or Tom or the boys at the mill."

"Or my mother?"

Dylan nodded. "Yes. I guess I even got to the point of resenting her."

"It wasn't because I didn't love you."

Dylan sighed. "I guess there are different kinds of love. But I felt as if I had no place in your life. And I certainly had no place in my own either. And even James. You know, Ben, I could talk to him and play with him till I was blue in the face, but one word from you and the sun came out for him. I was so lonely."

"And all the while, you were the most important person in the world to me."

She smiled ironically. "In retrospect."

He thought about this. "I really messed up, didn't I?"

"Yeah, you really did. Oh, well, it's over now."

"Still, it's a damn shame, that's all. And I'm very, very sorry."

"Darn you," Dylan said softly. "There you go being likable again. It was really so much easier over the years being bitter. Why do you have to confuse me by being nice?"

Ben grinned. "You aren't helping by being so charming either."

She blushed and looked away. It took her a while to speak, and then her voice was very soft and tentative. "It was never like that between Beth and me. We were just close friends, like sisters. But it wasn't like that."

"You didn't have to tell me. My question was out of line."

Dylan took a long drag on her cigarette and watched him evenly. "That's okay. I want to be friends. And if that means we're going to have to get all that old stuff out of the way, well, then let's do it."

Ben found this funny. "Friends? I don't know that you and I can manage that. There was always so much more and so much less between us."

She reached over and touched his arm. "I've spent the last twenty years thinking about the so much less. But you're right, there was so much more too." She realized she was touching him and broke off, getting out of her seat and moving away, embarrassed.

Ben too felt uncomfortable. All those years, Dylan had been merely a source of pain for him, but suddenly he remembered there had been moments of joy. Dylan was a different woman from the one he'd chosen to remember. Certainly the woman standing in the living room was. "The past colliding with the present," he said ou loud, though he was speaking to himself.

Dylan, however, didn't seem to have heard. "There's anothe reason for us to be friends now," she said.

"You mean James?" Suddenly he looked very tired. "Jesus Dylan. I just don't get it. I guess I'm to blame there too. yell at him. I'm impatient. I don't mean to be, but it's as if he look around to find the very thing I can't take. And God help me, th minute I see him I explode. Then afterward I feel so ashamed. Bu the next time, it happens all over again, and I seem to have n control over it. Why the hell didn't he come in today? I'm his father for Christ sake."

Dylan laughed. "That's why he didn't come in. You know, Ben, I don't think you have the slightest idea who James is. And maybe that's why he doesn't know either."

"And you do?"

"No. But I'm damn well going to find out. And you should too."

"You really think we can save James?"

"No. Only he can do that. All we can do is believe in him. Not push him into a mold and be furious when he doesn't fit. Not expect him to fail or be weak. Just let him be who he is and believe in him. It may not be the answer. But it's not a bad start."

There was a noise in the corridor, but Ben wasn't aware of it. He was staring at Dylan, trying to understand.

A moment later the door opened and James walked in. "Well, well, well. Will you look at this? Happy families."

He walked over to Ben and put out his hand. He was smiling falsely and his mouth was very tense and dry. "Glad to see you looking so well, Dad," he said.

Dylan shot Ben a warning look, but he ignored it. "And I'm glad to see you've recuperated from your illness."

James just shrugged. He went to the bar and poured himself a double. "You know you might have told us that you were recovering instead of pulling this Lazarus act. The least you could have done was tell Grandma."

Ben exploded. "Where in the hell were you today?"

"Sick day, Dad. Even the Savages get them. Of course in my case every day is sick day, right?"

Dylan stood. "I think I'd better leave."

James flared. "Yes. Go right ahead and leave. You're good at that." Then he stopped himself. "I'm sorry, Mother. I didn't mean to say that. I'm not angry at you."

Dylan glanced over at Ben. Though his face was turned away, she could sense the anger in it; his neck was very red and stiff. "Would you like me to stay?"

This was addressed to both of them, but it was James who answered. "I guess it would be better if you did go. I'd like to talk to Dad alone."

Dylan quickly collected her handbag and left, but neither of the men spoke until long after she had gone. James just stood watching his father. He could see traces of his illness etched into his face; he had heard the slight slurring of speech and noticed the cane. Yet oddly he was surprised not by how much his father had changed, but by how much he had remained the same. The man sitting across from him was still very much his father.

"Why didn't you tell me?" James asked at last. "I thought you were dying."

"Hoped is more like it."

James took a gulp of his drink and sat down. He didn't answer.

"If you were so damned concerned about me, why didn't you come into the office? Was it because of your little conspiracy with Dyer?" He waited for a denial from James, but there was none. Then he muttered, "Oh, never mind, it doesn't make any difference."

"That's why I didn't come in. Because it doesn't make a difference. It never did. That was our problem."

Ben glared at James in silence, then he said, "I kicked Dyer out."

"So I hear."

"And you could be next."

"To tell you the truth, I don't give a damn."

"You never did. And that was your problem."

James shrugged. Suddenly he felt himself relaxing. The thought of leaving Midwestern forever seemed not a punishment but a release. The pain of not being good enough had grown through the years, and instead of becoming inured to it, he had become inured to himself. Though leaving had not been something he could manage on his own, he hadn't been able to bear staying either. So he'd remained, locked in his conflict, becoming more extravagantly slipshod at work, more disagreeable to his father, drinking more, sleeping less, hoping that someone, anyone, would make the decision for him. And now his father had.

"I'll be out first thing in the morning," he answered evenly.

But this did not seem to please Ben. "Not until you tell me about the Jap deal Dyer was cooking up."

"I know nothing about any Jap deal, as you so handsomely put it I wasn't made privy to what Dyer was plotting. Nor did I care. He just wasn't you. That was enough."

"They say he bribed you with some fancy new title."

"Go on, what else do they say? That he bribed me with some fancy new assistant? Well, maybe. But at least it showed I had some value to him. At least he thought me worthy of bribing."

He paused and stared into his glass, then he continued sadly. "But you know what? I would have gladly sold him out for a smile from you. And I suppose Dyer wouldn't have done whatever the hell it is that you think he's done, if you'd have given a damn about him either. You hated us both. Always."

Ben was stunned. "You're wrong. All I wanted was the best for you. Maybe I went about it in the wrong way. But if there was a problem, it was that I loved you too much."

"Bullshit, Dad. At least admit it now. You hated us because we're young. That's the one thing you can't deprive us of. It's our turn now, and you know it."

Ben was slumped in his chair, watching James sadly.

James began to laugh, but it was a strange laugh, close to a cry, then all at once his face changed, and he looked like a little boy. "Didn't you realize I loved you? I would have done anything to please you. Even if it meant hurting myself."

Ben shook his head. "I never knew."

"You never wanted to know."

James broke off and went for another drink, then continued sharply. "But all that is over now, Dad. You see, I just don't care anymore. I don't want your love. I don't want your approval. I don't even want your god damn job. All I want is to never see you again."

Ben rose. "Please, listen to me. Don't go, son. Let's try again. I want to understand."

But James just shook his head. "Forget it, Dad. You're thirty years too late."

He slammed his glass down and walked to the door. He paused, looking back at his father. He could see the expression on his face, the look of a man who had been betrayed. But James didn't care. He was no longer angry or even sad; he felt released. He left a moment after that.

Ben sank back into his chair, watching after him with fury but also with loss. He was trying to think about the velvet-green hills of Wales, but his mind was stuck in the room and Midwestern, and after a while he got up and walked back into the corridor. He paused at the stairs, looking up at his mother's room. He could no longer hear her speaking to herself. It was very quiet.

As he stood there, he wondered what she would tell him to do, but he knew in the end she would tell him to fight. It was what she had always asked of him in the past; it would be what she demanded of him now. Yet in all those years she had never told him how; it was only the fighting she'd taught him, not the method, and he felt very lost as he walked out of her house and back onto the evening streets.

Ben's house had been kept as it always was, by Elizabeth's determination and the rest of the family's general apathy. For months maids and cleaning women had dusted furniture, scrubbed floors, and polished silver for the mice and spiders who had become the only permanent residents.

Ben pulled his car into the circular driveway and shut off the motor. He didn't get out but just sat there, watching evening shadows falling all around and the lawns turning pink under the last rays of the dying sun.

It looked very beautiful to him, more so perhaps because of the distance of time and all that had happened to him in between. During those months in Wales, he had hardly thought of his house, and when he had, the images of it had been oddly frightening, almost sinister, as if something awaited him there that would overpower him. But now as he sat in the car, watching the light slip from his house, it looked to him as it had in the past, splendid, impressive, more a symbol than anything else.

Through the garage window, Ben caught sight of Henry, reaching to one of the shelves, picking up a wrench, then ducking down quickly as he tinkered with one of the cars, putting it in perfect running order for no one.

Ben had met Henry over twenty years ago, when he was a shoeshine boy in downtown Midland with a ready smile and patter. Ben had hired him on a whim and had seen Henry through several wives and children. Of course, Henry had seen Ben through quite a few changes of his own.

Henry's head bobbed up again, but this time it stayed at the window, staring at the driveway. Clearly he was wondering what the car was doing there and why the driver wasn't getting out. Ben chuckled to himself. He supposed Henry would become curious, then suspicious, and eventually he would come out of the garage to investigate. Ben could imagine Henry's expression when he realized who it was. At first he'd be shocked, then genuinely pleased to see him. The thought came as a stab to his heart, for he felt at that moment that Henry might be the only one who was pleased.

Ben continued to sit in the car, watching Henry, but in his mind he kept going over what had happened, trying to twist it into some kind of shape he could understand. He replayed the arguments he'd had with James and Dyer, investigating them for things unsaid or underlying meanings that would prove to him that what he had heard was not true. For if it were the truth, it destroyed not only his future but his past. So he sifted through the conversations, searching for clues that told him that his sons still loved him, and even in their hate he found evidence of the opposite emotion.

Again Henry's head disappeared from the window, and this time he came out of the garage, wiping his greasy hands on an equally greasy towel. He moved slowly toward the car, squinting into it, and now there was no longer suspicion on his face. Henry stopped at the edge of the driveway, shaking his head. He looked very shocked, but underneath he seemed to understand, as if his expression were lagging behind his brain.

Ben rolled down the window. "Sorry I gave you such a surprise."

The tall black man didn't answer for a long while. He just kept shaking his head, and in his eyes there were tears. Again it struck Ben that the only person who seemed happy to see him was the one least connected to him.

"Why didn't you tell us, Mr. Ben? We thought you were dying."

He seemed genuinely upset, and Ben couldn't look at him.

"If only you'd told us," Henry repeated. "We could have organized some kind of reception. Not that we haven't kept things up. Your mother's seen to that but . . ."

Ben opened the car door, and Henry grabbed the handle and helped him out.

Henry said softly, "I hear Mrs. Savage is sick. Is that true?"

Ben nodded, but still he avoided Henry's eyes.

"Real bad?"

"I'm afraid so." Ben took his cane out of the car and made his way to the front door.

Henry followed just behind him. "That's a hell of a thing to come home to, Mr. Ben. I'm sorry to hear it."

Ben reached into his pocket, then realized he didn't have a front door key. He rang the bell. "Yeah," he repeated softly. "It's a hell of a thing to come home to."

THIRTY-NINE

Pauline walked into the Park Lane dining room and pretended to scan the faces of the diners for Ben though she'd spotted him the moment she'd come in. Ben watched as she feigned recognizing him, then walked over to the table. As always, he was surprised by how young she looked and also how sad.

She stopped in front of him and waited until he had stood to kiss her cheek.

"My, my, such an affectionate display," she said, as she moved to the other side of the table. Again she waited, allowing Ben to pull out her chair for her. It was a studied attitude. She could have been meeting a friend for lunch, not a good friend, but an acquaintance with whom she had only the past in common.

"You look very well, Ben. I'm so pleased for you."

Ben took his seat and smiled at her guardedly. "It's great to see you too, Pauline."

"Really?" She motioned to the waiter to bring her a drink. "You've caused quite a stir, you know. All of Midland is abuzz. I'll say this for you, you sure know how to pull off a resurrection." She smiled nastily. "Oh, well, you always were convinced you were the second coming."

Ben ignored her sarcasm. "I've been to see Mother," he said.

She received her drink and swallowed half of it before speaking. "How is she, talking or silent? Personally I prefer her in the silent stage, don't you?"

"Not now, Pauline. Not when it's her."

"Hey, Ben, who knows? Could be it runs in the family. Maybe she'll pull off a resurrection job too. After all, we're on a streak now."

Ben watched her sadly. "Don't you feel anything?"

"Don't you worry, Ben. I feel. I feel too much."

"Mostly bitterness. That's the emotion I've seen most since you were a kid."

Pauline tried to pretend that this hadn't hurt her. "And you, Ben? I can't say that I've seen a grand display of the finer emotions from you either. Or at least ones that weren't designed to get you what you wanted."

"Which means?"

Pauline hailed the waiter and ordered another drink. When she turned back to Ben, she no longer looked so upset. "Several people at the other tables are watching us. I love being the object of crass gossip, don't you?"

Ben persisted. "I want to know what you meant before."

Pauline smiled calmly. "I'm talking about stocks and voting and a certain meeting in the not so distant future. I'm talking about my five percent, and why you asked me to dinner."

"I won't lie to you; I'd like you to back me. But that isn't why I asked you to dinner."

"You'd like me to back you? No, Ben. You'd like to have steak for dinner or another drink or perhaps you'd like to get laid. But you *need* me to back you. *Need*, Ben. Something quite apart from like."

"Shall we order?" Ben asked coldly.

"Oh, I've offended you. Have I been crude talking about business matters on such a pleasant social occasion? You will forgive me, won't you? I can be so gauche sometimes."

Ben sighed. "You'll never change."

"Mmmm. Isn't it reassuring? The Rockies may crumble. Gibraltar may tumble. But some things never change. Yes, let's order."

Pauline looked at the menu. "I think I'd like meat tonight. Something nice and bloody like steak."

She fell silent and studied the menu, then she looked up suddenly. "I've been seeing a lot of Dyer recently."

Ben wasn't listening. "That's nice."

"No, I mean, really seeing Dyer."

Ben looked up, watching her face, trying to make sure he had understood.

Pauline smirked. "That's right, Ben. You got me. Hey, look, any port in a storm, eh? Especially a home port. I like to keep things in the family, as you might perhaps remember."

Ben shivered. "I remember."

Pauline watched him for a while, then slowly her face began to change and there were tears in her eyes. She turned away, trying to hide them, but her voice sounded very sad, almost frightened. "I lost you that day, didn't I? Not that I ever had you, but I lost you."

Ben was touched by the sorrow in her face. "You frightened me, Pauline."

"I repulsed you. Go on, say it."

"No. It was more complicated than that. You scared me, both for you and . . ." He paused, then forced himself to continue. "And I guess for me too."

"You mean there was a moment you were tempted?"

Ben looked away. "Yes, I suppose I was."

Pauline sighed deeply. "It's as if I'm doomed to repeat that night over and over in my head. And I guess in reality too. That was why Dyer, huh? God, I am a sicko, Ben. Sometimes it even surprises me how nuts I am." She looked at him as if begging for something.

Ben watched her with sympathy. "Do you think you can stop?"

"Stop what? Dyer? No, Ben. It's gone a little too far for that."

"You mean to tell me you love him?"

She laughed. "Jesus, Ben. You haven't a clue about life. It's absolutely amazing to me that we came from the same background, the same planet even. You haven't an inkling how I'm feeling."

"I guess I never did."

Pauline felt the tears well up again, and she knew that Ben could see them too. He turned to call the waiter, and they placed their orders, each trying to avoid the other's eyes. But after they were finished, they still found themselves sitting alone together and the mood was as before.

Pauline played with her drink. "Do you think I'm crazy, Ben?"

He touched her hand. "No, of course I don't."

Pauline pulled away. "I am, you know. I've had shock treatments. Did you hear about that?"

Ben shook his head sadly.

"Well, I did, and you know what that means. It means I'm crazy."

"No, Pauline. It means nothing of the kind." He forced a smile. "They say if you think you're crazy, then you aren't. Crazy people always think they're sane."

Pauline shook her head. "You don't understand at all. Oh, well, never mind. I don't understand either. So let's drop it."

"I feel as if I've disappointed you."

"Get in line. Everything and everyone disappoints me. Especially myself." She paused, thinking. "You know when I was a kid they said I had real potential in school?"

"I remember. The teachers used to call Mother in and tell her you could do anything in the world you chose. And do it brilliantly."

"Yes. Unfortunately I chose to ruin my life. But I must say I certainly did it brilliantly."

"If you feel that way, then change. It's not too late."

"Oh, Ben, sometimes you can be so wonderfully naive, almost childlike. I don't have time to change. Nor do I want to. It's like this: I look around and see all the smug little people going about their smug little lives. And there isn't one of them I envy, Ben. I may not like myself much, but I'm the best of the bunch. So I'm not about to change and become a humdrum housewife or good auntie or dutiful daughter or any of the other things expected of me. I will continue to drink too much and take pills and have my naughty little nights. Because as lousy as my life may be, I couldn't bear the other way." She paused and then whispered, "I couldn't bear to be you."

Ben said nothing, and soon their dinners arrived. They ate in silence, each looking at the other as little as possible. And after a while Ben broke the silence.

"What are you going to do, Pauline?"

"About what? Dyer? About my life?" She smiled cruelly. "Or about my stocks?"

"About any of it. About your life."

She sat back and watched him cagily. "I've seen Dylan, you know. She looks wonderful."

Ben stopped eating. "I've seen her too."

"So what are you going to do about her?" The sadness was gone now, and Pauline could feel the anger building again. It was a much better feeling, and she smiled in response to it.

"I don't know what you're getting at. There's nothing to do about it."

"Oh, come on, Ben. She wants you back."

"Don't be ridiculous. That was over twenty years ago. A lot has happened since then."

"Like that woman in Wales?"

Ben drew back, surprised, and Pauline laughed gaily. "I may not be in Midland often or long. But I like to keep abreast. Tom implied that you were involved with someone. Fast work, Ben. Trust you to find solace in your time of need. So what is it? Real love? Or just a convenient fling? Or what?"

"Pauline, I'd rather not discuss my personal life."

"Aha! And now you have the answer to your question. I'd rather not discuss my personal life either."

Ben thought about this. "You're right. I didn't mean to pry. I can't play big brother with you. I never could."

"Well, well, well, aren't we being reasonable. Let's just keep this a pleasant little reunion. No more of the old struggles and power plays." She took a large gulp of her drink and watched him. "If I didn't know better, I'd think you'd changed. Of course, I *do* know you better. And you're no different than the day you left here. You're no different than you ever were."

"What the hell do you want out of me?"

Pauline seemed to be enjoying this. "The truth for once."

"You've always gotten the truth from me."

"Like hell! And don't play the injured party with me. It's not your style. Now, this little reunion of ours was called for a very good reason. And all the mincing words in the world can't obscure the facts. You want my vote, plain and simple."

"The fact is, even if I didn't need it, I would have had dinner with you. You're my sister. And that's true too."

"You always were a lousy liar, Ben. Always. Now look. Let's talk turkey. Because I'm getting bored as hell sitting here, and I'm ready to leave. Now, do you want my vote or not?"

Ben looked at Pauline. Her face was taut and angry, and she no longer looked young to him but very old and ugly. Looking at her made the ache he'd been feeling since he'd come back to Midland even stronger.

"Yes," he answered after a while. "I do need it."

Pauline sat back satisfied. "Isn't it nice? Everyone wants and needs poor old Pauline."

She leaned forward, her long nails working at a thread in the tablecloth, her mouth parted. "The question is, what does poor old Pauline need and want? Or rather, who? And the answer is so terribly clear. You see, I may not be very stable or even very nice. But one thing I know and that's which side my bread is buttered on. And whatever the moral implications and whatever the future or lack of it, at least for one moment Dyer needed me, not my vote but *me*. Now, you might be surprised by this, because it's something totally lacking in you. But I'm a very loyal little creature. I'm sticking with Dyer."

She stood abruptly, shoving her chair away from the table. Then without another word, she turned and walked out, leaving Ben alone among the cheerful clatter of diners.

FORTY

Ben couldn't remember a time when driving through the gates of Midwestern didn't give him at least a momentary thrill. There was always something to catch his eye, the glittering fire of a furnace, a massive mountain of taconite, a steelman striding across the courtyard. Always in the past the sounds and brilliance had stunned him anew. But the day before, driving through the gates of Midwestern after all those months, had been unlike any other time in his life. He'd felt as if he were coming home after a hundred-year banishment. Well before the gates, the power of his longing struck him and remained with him long after he was seated behind his desk.

This morning, though, driving into Midwestern was totally different. Gone was the excitement and the expectation, gone was the pride. There was a terrible collapsed feeling in the center of him. The only time he'd ever experienced anything like it was after his accident. There was the loss, the emptiness, and above all the sheer terror. Now once again he was feeling it. He was losing his family; he was losing Midwestern.

Once inside the gates, the feeling did not recede but grew. He thought of his mother, dying upstairs in her bedroom. He was losing her fight.

Ben pulled into his parking space, turned off the engine, and watched the long-legged secretaries in their light spring coats greeting one another, holding their hair down against the gusting warm wind. Young men in business suits, carrying briefcases, shook hands and eyed the girls as they walked to the doors. Everyone seemed happy. Ben supposed they all had their problems—unpaid bills, nagging spouses, sad loves—but that morning all of them seemed to be pausing on the stairs, looking around at the new spring flowers, feeling the soft breeze against their faces, and thinking that it was truly good to be alive.

Ordinarily this might have given Ben pleasure. This morning it seemed only to increase his pain, and at that moment he hated the joyful smiling faces that streamed toward his offices, hated and envied them.

He climbed out of the car, forgetting his cane. Then he remembered it, and there was a surge of fury. He wanted to bang it against the car and break it in two; he wanted to hurt something; he wanted to strike back at a world that was striking out at him. Instead he took out his cane and briefcase, slammed the car door, then slowly limped toward the offices.

The minute Carrie saw him, she poured his coffee. She too had that smiling spring look, and Ben had to control himself not to be irritated at her. He supposed more than anything he wanted to be alone. He didn't want his telephone to be ringing or his mail to be spread out on his desk. He didn't want to go through the long list of appointments with its haggling and cute remarks. He just wanted to sit alone in his darkened office and think.

Ben waited as Carrie placed his coffee before him and began puttering around his office, watering his plants, straightening the things on his desk; he wished that she would go. But once she had left, the despair only seemed to grow. On the walls of his office were framed photographs tracing the history of Midwestern Steel right back to 1888 when Nicholas Healey's father had founded it. At that time it was no more than a rolling mill, without even a railroad track. Slowly buildings were added, facilities modernized, and it was all to be seen in the photographs, like a family album. The last picture was one Ben was especially proud of: It was an aerial shot of Midwestern Steel where the mill seemed to sprawl to the horizon like a great city.

Ben turned away. He couldn't bear to look at the pictures. But on the other wall there were more pictures, framed newspaper clippings, family portraits, even a snapshot of Ben shaking hands with President Eisenhower and a signed portrait of John F. Kennedy. They too seemed a reproach.

Ben pulled himself from his desk and went to the door. "No calls for a while, please, Carrie."

She looked back, surprised and concerned. "Are you all right, Mr. Savage? Is there anything—"

"I'm fine." Ben closed the door on Carrie's last words, but he could still hear the unasked questions, the sound of telephones ringing, the clacking of typewriters, a day beginning in a business over which he was losing control.

He walked back to his desk and sat in his chair, feeling the sadness building inside of him. For those few months in Wales, he had convinced himself he didn't care, but now that he was back, he realized he did care, very much. Perhaps Tally had been right when she'd told him he was hiding, because now that he was back, Midwestern Steel did seem important again, and losing it felt like a death. Even greater than his obligation to Midwestern or the family or the dream, there was the terrible feeling of desertion. Midwestern was the one thing he'd created in his life, and it was his own family who was out to destroy it.

Ben slammed his fist on the desk. He was being told that he had no place in the world, and the worst part was there was a certain justice to it. Hadn't he come very close to renouncing everything himself? Suddenly the peace he had found in Wales seemed a betrayal. To be alive meant to work, and working meant existence. A man needed to have something to show after every day, but what did he have to show from Wales? Except love. Yes, he remembered he'd had love. But now he knew that wasn't enough.

Slowly everything began to make sense. Caring about people only brought disappointment and loss, and in the end you were left with nothing. It was Midwestern Steel that was important; it was the dream that had a permanent meaning. And for that he had to win.

Somehow this made Ben feel better. He remembered his coffee sitting untasted on the desk and began to drink it. It was cold, but strong and bitter; he felt it reviving him, and as he sat quietly, feeling his energy returning, he began to think things out logically.

There were three weeks before the stockholders' meeting; hardly an age. Still, there was time to do something, perhaps even show his family they were wrong. Their mistake was they had underestimated him; they had shown him their hands too early, and now he had time.

Ben drank the coffee greedily, feeling the adrenaline kicking in and his energy rising. What he needed was a coup, something that would turn the tide and indicate a change. Given that, he would be able to turn it into a stampede. People were predictable. When times were bad they preferred to keep the status quo or return to the past. Whatever they did, they did not look to a thirty-four-year-old boy to lead them; they wanted a man of experience. Ben had to find some way to prove it.

It was less than an hour later, as Ben was once again taking phone calls and yelling orders, that he saw the opportunity. When Carrie announced that Senator Morrison's office was on the phone, his first reaction was to tell her to pretend he wasn't in. But he didn't say that. Instead he asked her to keep him on hold. Oddly it only occurred to him gradually that he was considering the possibility Morrison might still be open to giving Midwestern a government contract.

He stalled, doodling across a memo pad, making rows of boxes in firm broad strokes. There was no question that a big government contract would be just the thing to start a stampede back to him. The problem was Morrison had already let him know how he could get that contract, and that was something Ben was not prepared to do.

He continued to scrawl his firm heavy lines across the paper. It was a terrible choice, one he didn't want to make. Stay clean and he lost everything, or dirty his hands and he could keep it all.

Ben put down his pen, but still he didn't do anything. He could see the lights on his telephone, ten lines and all of them flashing. It was the sign of an important man, and in the end he had to believe that mattered. He had spent sixty years believing it, and now it seemed impossible he'd had doubts. If he picked up the phone it would betray everything he stood for, but if he didn't, wouldn't that be a betrayal too? And at least this one would be only temporary. He would never have to do it again. All he needed was this one chance; after that everything would go back to normal.

Before he could change his mind, he punched the button on his telephone. He was smiling tightly, his body alert and tense. He could not give up his business now. Later there would be time to grow old, but he couldn't do it now.

FORTY-ONE

Dyer was rarely in his apartment during the daylight hours. Usually he would come in after dark, fix a drink, take out a casserole the maid had left in the oven and eat, watching the television. After that he'd go to bed. Mornings he would dress automatically, without looking around, his mind on the day ahead. But he had been home for three days in a row now, and as he looked around his apartment it seemed alien to him and also very small. He felt trapped by it.

The phone startled him, and it was a while before he answered, but the moment he put the receiver to his ear, he forced himself to become alert. The call came from far away; there was that sound to it, almost as if the voice were under the water.

Hamayoshi giggled. "It seems you weren't lying about your uncle not being gravely ill. It's a case of sometimes we know more than we know."

Dyer tensed. "How did you hear about that? Did he call you?"

"Relax, Mr. Savage. No, he didn't call me. Though I wouldn't be surprised if he didn't suspect a great deal. I heard of his return through what you assured me is my very reliable grapevine." He paused. "Of course, this changes things rather a lot."

"In what way?" Dyer was trying to sound calm, but he was off balance, and he was sure Hamayoshi could hear it.

"Well, first of all, I have the greatest respect for your uncle. He is a very wily man. Second of all, it also makes a difference psychologically. As we discussed that first time, Mr. Ben Savage *is* Midwestern Steel. It's as if his face is stamped on every ingot that comes out of your mill. Of course I don't need to tell you any of that."

Dyer's voice was brittle. "The point is, what do you plan to do about it?"

Hamayoshi ignored his question. "Third of all, and you may not be aware of this, Mr. Ben Savage has been in contact with a certain senator in Washington."

Dyer didn't answer, and Hamayoshi laughed. "Ah, so you were not aware of it. But you grasp the implications, I can tell. Yes, I assume he did his arithmetic and saw that if he didn't do something drastic he could be holding the short end of the fifty-five percent stick. And that's assuming he doesn't know about my four point nine percent. If he does, I can imagine he's extremely upset."

"Maybe he does know."

"I doubt it. We have all been extremely cautious."

"Except me."

"Mr. Savage, we learn by making mistakes. I'm very sorry about that taping incident, but it was necessary. And you, at any rate, have gained a valuable lesson from it. But anyway, now is not the time for self-recrimination. We must discuss what to do."

"In other words, you're not backing down?"

"For a moment you hoped, eh? Yes, that would suit you just fine. You have most of the votes now. If I backed down, you wouldn't have to worry about your earlier indiscretion. And on top of that you'd have that tasty little tidbit about Senator Morrison. It would be a good position to be in, but unfortunately, Mr. Savage, you are not in it. No, I don't plan on dealing myself out yet. It's just become interesting."

Again he giggled, then his voice grew very businesslike. "Now as I said, Mr. Ben Savage has the psychological advantage, and if he gets the government contract, that will certainly work in his favor. After all, your cousin and aunt are free agents. I don't have tape recordings against them. And let's face it, just one whiff of defeat and they'll desert. For all their talk about hating Ben Savage, they'll run like rats from—"

Dyer interrupted. His voice was strangled. "What do you want from me?"

"Why, Mr. Savage, I want you to stop him, of course. I can assure you it won't be all that hard. By calling Senator Morrison he played right into our hands. If the Justice Department ever got wind of that, they'd clamp down on Mr. Ben Savage so fast he wouldn't know what hit him."

"If the Justice Department ever got wind of you they'd clamp down on Mr. Dyer Savage so fast he wouldn't know what hit him. Remember our little discussion on Anti-Cor and its possible uses?"

"Indeed I do remember. And I also remember that I was having it with you. But you see, the Justice Department won't hear of me. What they will hear of is Senator Morrison. And they will hear of him from you. In actuality, your uncle's return is a blessing in disguise. Everything remains the same, only better."

Dyer exploded. "You expect me to go to the Justice Department and turn in my own family?"

"Yes. That's exactly what I expect. Nor do I think my expectations will be disappointed. After all, everything remains the same, if you get my meaning. My threat still holds. Let's face it, Mr. Savage. You and I have gone too far together. Even if you wished to pull out, you couldn't. After all, though not a penny has changed hands and you might avoid jail, I doubt you'd be left with much of the brilliant future you're so keen on." His voice became brutal. "You would be totally ruined. No family. No job."

He laughed softly, like a pigeon cooing. "So you see, it's you or him. Now, there hardly seems to be much of a choice when it's put like that, does there?"

FORTY-TWO

When Tom walked into Ben's office for their evening drink, Ben was on the phone. He shot Tom an apologetic look that said he was trying to wind up the call, and Tom went over to the bar to pour himself a drink. He didn't mind waiting. It had been only a few days since Ben's return, but already everything seemed as it had been, and Tom counted himself lucky just to be in Ben's office watching him hunched over his phone. It was a sight that reached back through the years.

Evening light tipped through the window, haloing the room in a pink and yellow glow. Tom took a sip of his drink and felt his insides warming. He doubted he had ever felt so content in his life.

A moment later Ben hung up and said in mock anger, "Hey, you bastard, where the hell's my drink?"

Tom laughed. "Sorry, but it's going to take me a while to get back into the routine."

He poured a large scotch, feeling the reassurance of the familiar. It was only as he handed Ben his drink that Tom caught sight of a sadness in Ben's face.

"What's bothering you, lad?" he asked as he sat on the couch opposite.

Ben sighed. "Just missing some things, I guess."

Tom smiled. "Things or people?"

"Yeah, people." Ben was embarrassed.

"Have you called her?"

"No. There's nothing really to say. The only thing she'd want to hear is that I'm coming home. And I can't say that yet."

"Home, is it? So now Wales is home. I guess it's the old saying, home is where the heart is." He laughed happily. "Well, at least wait until after the stockholders' meeting. Okay? Just clean up the mess."

Ben interrupted. "Dyer has the votes."

"Now, don't you be too sure of that, lad. In the end they'll all come around. James, Pauline, and don't forget the rest of the stockholders. You think in a choice between you and Dyer, they'd pick him?"

"Dyer says I'm old and they'll see it. Dyer says I have a speech impediment and a limp and they'll see that too."

"Let them. When the chips are down, they'll back you."

"Maybe." Ben turned to the window. The sun had set, and the clear flames of the furnace licked at the darkness. There was no one walking around; even the sound of the railroad was stilled. Midwestern was running short shifts, and there seemed to be a pall over the mill.

Ben turned back. "I think four point nine percent of our stock is in the hands of the Japanese. And if I'm right, I know the head guy. A real character if I ever met one. I've got a feeling he may have got to Dyer. That's what this whole reversal on Anti-Cor means."

"I told you something was going on. So they have some stock? Jesus! Well, what do we do about it?"

"Nothing. I have no proof. And I'm not likely to get any either. Knowing them, they'll have covered their tracks too well."

Ben's despairing tone unsettled Tom. "But if you bring it up at the stockholders' meeting . . ."

"It'd blow everything apart. No proof. Just a bunch of hunches Dyer'd make me look like a jackass." Ben shrugged and stared at his drink, then downed it. He put the empty glass on his desk decisively, but he didn't move. Finally he said, "So don't tell me the rest of the stockholders will be behind me."

"Four point nine is only a small percentage. There's always the rest."

"Who'll stand on the sidelines, waiting until they smell the winner. I'm beginning to believe you're the only one I can trust." Ben was looking at Tom; his eyes were almost pleading.

Tom tried for a smile. "Well, you always said you liked a good fight. Here's your chance."

"Yep. Great fight. Win and I tear this family apart. Lose and Dyer tears this family apart. Either way we lose."

Tom nodded and hid in his drink. He wouldn't have liked to be in Ben's position. "But remember this, lad. If you have to lose, it's better to do it by winning."

Ben jumped on this. "If only I could be sure of winning though. But it looks like just the opposite is going to happen. It looks like Dyer is going to win and sell out to the Japanese."

Tom was becoming upset. "Then we won't let him win."

"Yeah, we won't let him win."

Though Ben's tone was discouraged, there was something else in it too, something almost deliberate about the way he was acting, as if he'd planned out this conversation and was leading Tom to the questions and responses he wanted.

Ben took down his drink in silence. He was watching Tom now; the sadness of before was gone and replaced by determination. "I just can't let him win."

Tom didn't answer for a long while. He couldn't shake the feeling that he was being led somewhere. "We'll do our best," he answered carefully.

"The problem is, what if our best isn't good enough?"

Ben leaned back in his chair; his face was creased with concern, but he was avoiding Tom's eyes. Then suddenly he sat forward. "Look, here's the way I see it. I have to prove that I'm still in control, that I can hack it. Then, maybe, I'll get the votes. I can't expect to be the head of the family if I don't act like it."

Tom felt a chill go through him. "I don't understand what you mean."

Ben sensed the misgiving in Tom's voice. "I mean simply that I need a coup."

Tom stiffened. "What's going on, Ben?"

"I'm just stating facts."

"Are you? Or are you obscuring them? If you're trying to play with me, lad, you'd better stop and come out with what you want right now. I'll not be led around by the nose like this."

Ben retrenched. "I'm sorry, Tom. Look, what I really want to know is how close are we on Anti-Cor?"

"I told you on the phone. Soon."

"Yes. But how soon?"

"Why?"

Ben looked away. "It could be the break I'm looking for."

"Why?"

"You know as well as I do, a discovery looks good on the record."

Tom persisted. "Why?"

"Why, why, why," Ben said irritably. "Because it means more contracts, that's why. What the hell reason did we start on it for?"

"Which contracts?"

Ben was becoming very angry. He gulped half of his drink and stared at the glass. "Come on, Tom. It's pointless to play dumb. We both know what kind of contracts."

Tom stared at Ben, hoping to discover something in his face that would tell him he'd misjudged the situation. But everything about Ben told him he was right. It came as a blow, yet even worse, it came as no surprise.

Tom's face was very pale; his lips were trembling. "How stupid do you think I am? That stockholders' meeting is in just over two weeks, and I haven't got the cost down low enough on Anti-Cor. How the hell could you put in a bid and win a contract before the meeting?"

"I believe you will do it soon."

"So you put in a phony bid? Without any facts and figures you bid low just on the chance that I do it? Bullshit! You know damn well that if you did that and made a miscalculation, you'd be ruining yourself and Midwestern in one stroke."

"That's the chance I have to take."

"Is it, lad?"

Ben stood and walked from behind his desk. He looked edgy and tired; his leg seemed even stiffer than usual. "I don't know what you're getting at."

"Oh, yes, you do. You aren't bidding low. That isn't the plan at all." Tom's voice cracked; he was close to tears. "I won't allow you to do this, Ben."

Ben sat next to Tom. He hunched forward, rubbing his forehead with his hands, and when he stopped and looked at Tom, his eyes were very frightened. "I just can't afford to play this one straight. I could lose the company."

Tom put his hand on Ben's shoulder. "It isn't worth it. Nothing is. Do you know how long you could go to jail for something like that? Do you know how long all of us could go to jail?"

Ben didn't answer. Tom had never seen him like that. "You have to promise me you won't go through with it."

"I'll lose Midwestern if I promise that."

"You'll lose Midwestern if you don't. What the hell does it all mean if it's based on corruption?"

"I love this company."

"So do I. And I love you. I want you to promise me that you'll forget any idea of a bribe."

Ben lied. "It's too late for that."

Tom shivered. "Then just withdraw the bid. Without it the bribe means nothing."

Ben stood and moved over to the window. The sky was black now, and the flames seemed to pierce it. Tom walked to Ben, putting his hand on his shoulder, waiting until he had turned around and their eyes had met.

"What's happening to you, Ben?" he asked sadly. "What are you becoming? If you do this, it won't make any difference if you win over Dyer. You'll both be exactly the same."

Ben glanced away, trying to avoid the disappointment in Tom's eyes. "Is that what you think of me?"

Tom's voice was firm. "I want you to promise to drop the bid. I want your solemn promise on this."

Ben continued to look away. Finally he sighed. "All right, you win. I promise."

But Tom could tell he was lying. He waited, hoping that Ben would turn back, but he didn't; he just stared out the window at the black sky.

Tom inched away from him. "So you think I'm a fool now too!"

"I said I promise you!"

"No, Ben. You're telling yourself it's expedient; you need me to set everything up. Then I'll be in so deep, I'll have to go along with you. But I stop here."

Tom's eyes played over the office, and in those few seconds it was as if every hour of their lifetime together died. He began to walk to the door. "You can find someone else to help you take Midwestern apart. I'm finished."

Ben was right after him. "Don't you understand? I'm doing this for Midwestern."

"You're doing it for yourself. And I won't be a party to it."

"Tom, we've been together all these years, through everything, the good and the bad, and you've always stuck by me. You can't forget all those years. I want you to stand by me now."

"Need me to stand by you is more like it. How will it look at the stockholders' meeting if I've resigned? Dyer will make a big deal out of that, won't he? That's what you're scared of. Well, let me tell you something. It'll look like exactly what it is."

Tom regarded him coldly, as if he were a stranger. But still he hadn't left, and Ben took heart.

"Tom, you know as well as I do, sometimes you have to look at things objectively. Sometimes you have no other choice but to."

Tom wrenched the door open with disgust. "Forget it, Ben. Now you're even beginning to lie to yourself."

A moment later he was gone, striding out of the office and into the night. Ben turned from the door and watched out the window as the thin old man disappeared into the blackness.

FORTY-THREE

Ben sat in a taxi, a briefcase on his lap. He'd allowed himself only one scotch, not enough to dull his senses, just enough to take the edge off of his feelings. But it hadn't helped much; he still felt as if he were about to cry. From the moment he had taken that call from Senator Morrison his whole life had changed, and though he might tell himself that it was only a short detour, he feared it wasn't true.

Ben looked out the window, but he couldn't concentrate on what he was seeing. His mind stuck stubbornly to what he was doing, and nothing could erase it for long. He had been told to arrange for the money to be drawn from several different accounts, but still he had agonized that this might appear suspicious. Now as he sat in the taxi, the money in the briefcase on his lap, he wondered if it truly might appear suspicious, or if it weren't just the remnants of morality that had been bent so far it threatened to snap. It seemed impossible to him that the man who had found a simple peace and contentment in merely watching the sun rising or the sound of branch scratching at a window could be doing something like this.

Ben had caught sight of himself in a mirror as he stuffed the bills into his briefcase. He had seen his frightened furtive eyes like those of a deer caught in the headlights of a car. He'd turned away immediately, but still the image of himself remained.

After that he'd sat on the edge of his bed, waiting for the call, clutching his briefcase, and it had all seemed so sordid and melodramatic, like a back-street abortion in the fifties. He hadn't realized it then, but he'd still had a chance to back down. At the time he had thought of nothing; he'd just sat on the bed, staring, and then the call had come, and he'd been told an address, and events had seemed to take him over. But now, as he sat in the taxi gazing out at the dark repetitive streets, he realized he'd had a choice then.

And suddenly he realized he still had a chance to back down now. All he would have to do was tell the driver to turn around before any real damage had been done.

There was a moment of intense relief, a crazy euphoria. If they called him later, he could tell them he had changed his mind. Certainly Midwestern would lose the contract, but in the end would it really make all that much of a difference? He had lost control over Midwestern already; Tom's going would tell everybody that. Even a business coup like he planned would probably not change the way things were headed now. Nothing would. All this would be was an unnecessary corruption.

Ben leaned forward in his seat, watching the lights of the city gleaming insistently in the black night. It would be so easy. Just tell the driver to turn around, and it would be over.

But Ben didn't say anything; he didn't move. He just watched as the city lights flashed by the window, holding tightly to his briefcase, stunned and stonelike.

And gradually he realized he wouldn't be able to stop. Even though this corruption might not save him, he had to try. At least if he went down, he would go down fighting. The alternative was to lose totally, and Ben had never faced a partial loss; he knew he couldn't survive a complete failure. He'd been right to fear coming back to Midland; once back, all the rest had been inevitable.

Ben clenched his fists angrily; his mouth felt very dry. Still he sat quietly in the taxi as it rushed toward his appointment.

A few minutes later the taxi stopped in front of a modern apartment building in a quiet residential neighborhood. It took Ben awhile to realize they were at their destination. He supposed he had expected a rat-infested tenement with a bare light bulb, not the substantial middle-class building he was seeing.

He paid the driver, then got out and walked to the entrance, slowly, haltingly, though he knew there was no longer any question of his stopping. He supposed there never had been.

As he stood outside the door, looking at the list of tenants' names alongside the buzzers, he realized they hadn't given him any further instructions, not even an apartment number. He scanned the names, but not one of them seemed familiar.

The taxi pulled away, and Ben looked around, unsure what to do. The street was one of the new ones that had sprung up ten years earlier in the economic boom. It was the kind favored by young up-and-coming junior executives' wives, supermarket managers, dress shop owners, just rows of similar apartment blocks, lines of parked Pontiacs and Chevrolets, no traffic, no pedestrians. In most of the windows there was the flickering light of television; the sound of a Barbra Streisand record came from a window across the street.

Again Ben looked at the names on the buzzers, running through them with no expectation. And suddenly he became frightened. He was standing in a strange neighborhood with $150,000 in a briefcase; he didn't even know whom he was meeting. At that moment there seemed to be only one explanation; he was being set up for something. He knew nothing of the people he was dealing with, except that what they were doing was illegal, so surely they wouldn't be averse to doing something worse.

Ben felt trapped and alone. The street seemed darker than before, with only little pools of light around the lampposts.

Suddenly a buzzer sounded. The front door clicked, and the lock sprang open. Ben didn't move. He stood, staring at the door, as the buzzer sounded insistently. Eventually he realized the decision had already been made, and he opened the door and walked into the lobby. Almost immediately the buzzer stopped; the lock clicked closed behind him.

It was very quiet inside but well lighted and modern, with an elevator and several potted plants. There were apartments beyond the lobby, but all the doors were closed, and no one was in sight. The only sign of life was the sound of a television from farther down the hall.

The gears of the elevator began to work; there was a grinding as it stopped at one of the floors. Ben could hear the doors open, then after a moment, close. The elevator began moving down.

Ben walked to the elevator, tensely clutching his briefcase. It was close to a minute before it stopped at the lobby, but when the doors opened, there was no one inside. The doors closed again, and the elevator began moving.

The sound of the television stopped, and there was total quiet. Ben looked around, confused and fearful, but everything seemed completely normal. It was just the lobby of a middle-class building, decently furnished, well kept to a point, at least enough to keep the building inspectors away.

He saw one of the doors beyond the lobby open. He waited for something to happen, but no one came out, and he could feel the panic rising inside of him. He wanted to run.

All at once a man's voice came from behind the partially opened door. "Thank you very much. You can leave your package in the lobby."

It was a well-educated voice, the voice of a man who belonged in that building, and perhaps it was that which startled Ben most.

It took awhile for him to answer. "I think there must be some mistake."

"There's no mistake. Just leave it in the lobby. Everything will be taken care of."

Ben looked around anxiously. "You don't even know who I am."

There was a soft laugh. "Nor do I want to." This was said very quietly.

"You want me to leave it right here?"

But there was no answer. Ben stood where he was for a long while, unsure what to do, then finally he leaned the briefcase against the wall.

"I'm leaving it next to the elevator."

Again there was no answer. Ben stood motionless, waiting. He heard the elevator begin its grinding again. "Did you hear what I said?"

"Yes, thank you."

The apartment door closed, and there was silence except for the sound of the elevator stopping on another floor.

Ben turned and walked to the front door. When he reached it, he glanced back, but still nothing had happened. It occurred to him that he could easily be under surveillance by the police. He half expected to hear a shrill whistle and see the streak of blue uniforms as they rushed out to grab him.

There was a grinding sound, and Ben whirled around, his heart pounding wildly. But it was only the elevator stopping at the lobby again. The door opened and there was no one inside. Ben guessed it was probably broken.

The fear was becoming a knot of pain inside of him; his heart was clenched and tight. He stayed where he was only a moment longer, then he moved to the front door, jerked it open, and rushed out.

It was only when he had walked for several minutes that the panic began to recede. Just ahead was a main street. There was a taxi cruising, but he didn't hail it; he just continued to move rapidly through the night. His heart was still pounding heavily, but his head was becoming clear. He wondered if he had made a mistake leaving the briefcase in the lobby. It could so easily have been the wrong address or the wrong apartment. How did he know it wasn't just somebody expecting a delivery of liquor or groceries, not a briefcase stuffed with cash?

Ben stopped. Briefly he considered going back to check, but he knew there was nothing he could do now. Even if the people were honest enough not to pocket the money and bring it to the police, Ben could hardly claim it. He had left $150,000 in the lobby of a totally respectable building, without knowing, without even seeing who received it. It was sheer madness.

Ben began walking again, turning corners without any awareness of where he was going. In the end he doubted that it had been a mistake, not the way the voice had said that it was better they didn't see one another. That hardly seemed a likely response to a delivery of groceries.

This thought calmed Ben a little, but the tension remained, and underneath it there was something pretty close to anger. The problem was, everything had been so pedestrian, so matter of fact. What Ben expected, he didn't know. He supposed he'd expected something like on a television show or Watergate, with disreputable men and sleazy back-alley drops, code words and veiled threats. But this could have been a postman dropping off mail, a messenger delivering some mundane papers. It was clean and neat and over with in under three minutes, and that was the part that jarred him most. His decision to give a bribe had, in so many ways, been the most important in his life. In one stroke he had turned from everything he believed in, corrupting himself totally, and he'd anticipated that he would have to suffer for it in some way. Instead he was back out on the street at only a quarter to nine in the evening, unpunished, unhumiliated. In fact, completely untouched by the whole affair.

With surprise, he found that he had circled back to the apartment building. Fearfully he walked to the front door and cupped his hands against the glass so he could see in. The lobby was still empty, but the briefcase was gone.

He stood, looking into the deserted lobby for a long while, then slowly he turned away, walked back to the main street, and hailed a taxi.

There were few cocktail lounges left in Midland, but this was one of them. Ben supposed that today most young people went to discotheques, while their parents cowered at home, afraid of the night streets. Ben himself hadn't been to a cocktail lounge since he was in his twenties and feeling the first flush of affluence. It had been an in-between time for him, when he was too rich for the bars he used to frequent and not quite rich enough for the private golf clubs and at-home parties of the truly upper class. It wasn't even as if he'd enjoyed them that much, but as he'd ridden in the taxi, the flashing of a cocktail glass with its little neon bubbles had called to him, and the idea of the lounge's clean, nondescript, motellike atmosphere appealed to him as being unrelated to his life.

He sat down in an imitation red velvet booth at the back and ordered a double scotch from a tall, bleached-blond waitress with long legs and a plastic smile. She was wearing a uniform that was early Playboy bunny, a bit frayed at the edges from repeated cleanings, though, Ben noticed, not repeated enough. Everything about the place was a bit worn and frayed at the edges, even the customers, but he guessed in a way that was what he wanted.

Ben drank rapidly, eager for the numbness to kick in, and he ordered another before he was even finished with the first. Instinctively he reached for his briefcase, then remembered he had already turned it over.

Ben drank his scotch, trying not to think about what he had just done, but it lay there on his mind, covering everything, and it wasn't until he was halfway through the third drink that it began to leave.

"Ben? Ben Savage?"

Ben looked up. She was tall and blonde and very attractive, with just a trace of a southern accent, enough to seem light and cheerful without sounding stupid. Her face seemed slightly familiar, and Ben fought against the drinks and his thoughts to remember where he'd met her before.

She merely laughed. "That's all right. I don't go in for hurt feelings. I only met you once. At your sixtieth birthday party. And we were both much the worse for wear."

Ben remembered she was the woman he had taken upstairs that night. They had fallen on the floor together, the sounds of the party reverberating all around them. And it had been quick, almost brutal, and very exciting. He tried to recall if she was someone's wife. He could not.

Ben stood. "Jesus, I'm sorry. I was a million miles away. Of course I remember you."

She smiled. "Of course I remember you, Melanie."

He returned her smile. "Of course I remember you, Melanie. Please sit down."

She slid into the booth with that soft southern gracefulness, then lacing her fingers together, she rested her hands on the table. The waitress came over and took her order resentfully. Ben supposed Melanie was a woman who was often resented, and she wouldn't know why.

She leaned to him. "I heard about your accident, Ben. Actually I read it in the newspaper. And I was terribly sorry. Not that I got to know you well." She paused, embarrassed. "Anyway, I'm so glad to see that you've recovered. You must be very happy to be home again."

Ben tried for a smile, but he couldn't manage much of one, so he nodded and took a sip of his drink.

She watched him. "Am I disturbing you?"

"Just a bad day, that's all."

"I can leave if you want me to." She gazed at him frankly, but everything about her seemed to say she doubted she'd be asked to leave.

"No. Stay. I hate to drink alone. Just give me a moment to unwind."

Someone put money in the jukebox, and a 1950s tune blasted from it.

"Here?" She laughed, and it was as calm and soothing as her smile.

It made Ben laugh too. "Yeah, I guess this isn't the greatest place in the world to relax."

He watched Melanie steadily, and for the first time seemed to be really seeing her. Clearly she wasn't the kind of woman who hung

Family Passions 407

around in cocktail lounges or, in fact, hung around anywhere at all. She wasn't the kind of woman who needed to.

"Why are you here?" he asked gently.

She looked suddenly sad. "Probably the same reason as you. I didn't feel much like seeing anyone I knew."

"Yeah, well, we sure messed that one up. The first person we see is someone we know."

She laughed. "That's all right. We don't really know one another. After all, you didn't even remember my name."

They sat in silence for a while, regarding one another, then she finished her drink and put it on the table.

Ben put his hand on her slim arm. "You're right. This isn't much of a place to unwind. Why don't we go back to my house? It's much quieter. And on the whole the service is a lot better."

She grinned. "But sir, we've only just met."

Ben threw some money on the table. "Then allow me to introduce myself. My name's Ben Savage."

She stood up and extended her hand. "Glad to meet you, Ben. My name's Melanie."

Ben pulled on his trousers quickly. His bad leg felt unbearably stiff and painful; he was worried it might buckle under him. He couldn't look at Melanie. He knew if he looked at her, the humiliation might overwhelm him. From the moment he'd opened the door to his house, he'd known that he didn't really want her. He should have made up some excuse, given her taxi fare and sent her off, right there and then. But he suspected that underneath all the excuses, it had been more than a lack of desire for her that was plaguing him; it had been a lack of desire for himself. He had betrayed his company and his family; now he was even betraying Tally. It was as if he was pushing himself to tear down everything he'd ever built up in his life. And he hated himself for it.

Ben pulled on his shirt, still not looking at Melanie, hoping that she would take the hint and leave. But she didn't leave. She lay across the bed, smoking a cigarette, the covers draped around her so that only her head and arms were showing. After a while she stubbed out her cigarette, but still she stayed, lying on the bed and staring up at the ceiling.

She rolled over and leaned on her elbow. "It's probably only natural with everything you've been through."

He wanted to tell her that it had never happened before, even at the worst times in his life. Then he wanted to throw her out. Instead he dressed himself, carefully, as if he were on his way out, though it was only two in the morning. He caught himself going for his tie and stopped.

"Ben, why don't you come back to bed?"

Melanie's voice was very soft and gentle, but behind the kindness, he could hear the slight superiority. It was a studied tone, the sort one might use with a child.

He stood at the mirror, combing his hair, trying to avoid looking at himself, especially his eyes. He couldn't bear to look at his eyes.

"Would you mind if I asked you to leave?"

"Not at all," Melanie answered, but she sounded like she minded very much.

She paused a moment, then got out of bed and went for her clothes. Ben could see her in the mirror; her smooth tanned skin glowed in the dim light. She really was extremely attractive. He supposed that was why she was moving around the room undressed, to prove that she was attractive and that the fault was in him.

Ben closed his eyes. He hated her at that moment; he hardly even knew her, but he hated her with the vehemence reserved only for people very close to him. She slipped her arms into her blouse but left it unbuttoned, so that her breasts were partially exposed, and she moved slowly, sensuously, touching her body as she pulled on her skirt. Every gesture seemed a reproach.

Then still half-dressed, she walked behind Ben and put her arms around him. "Are you sure you wouldn't like to try again? We have most of the night left."

Ben froze. The humiliation was overwhelming; her touch was repugnant. He pulled away. "Leave me alone. Please. Just get out."

Melanie recoiled, more from his tone than anything else. Quickly she fumbled for her nylons and put them on. "You son of a bitch," she said.

Ben turned to the wall, hoping that when he turned back, she would be gone. But time passed, and she was still there, standing in the room, her blouse only partially buttoned, her boots lying next to her, pigeon-toed on the floor.

Ben turned away again, but when he turned back, she was still there.

Family Passions 409

It seemed as if she were going to be there forever, standing in the middle of his bedroom, watching him with smug, accusing eyes.

He tried to control his voice. "I asked you to leave."

Melanie started to cry. "You're treating me like a whore. I'm not a whore, god damn you!"

Ben didn't answer, and Melanie gathered her boots, trying to pull them on. She began to cry again, and the emotion made her awkward. She struggled with her boots, getting angrier and angrier as she lost her balance.

"It's not my fault." Her voice was choked off.

Ben answered wearily. "Just get out. Please. Before I throw you out."

"Don't you dare!"

Suddenly Ben flared. He grabbed her coat and handbag off the chair and thrust them into her arms. Then he started nudging her toward the door.

Melanie whirled around and struck Ben across the face. "You bastard!" she screamed.

For a moment it looked like Ben was going to hit her back. His face was bright red with rage and there were tears in his eyes.

"Just typical," Melanie said. She went for the door, clutching her coat. "Blame the woman, because the man can't get it up."

Ben whispered, "Please get out. Please, please, just leave."

"Hey, don't worry. There's nothing here that interests me."

She slammed the door shut, but Ben had turned back to the wall, and he hardly noticed that she was gone.

FORTY-FOUR

"Dad, do you mind if I talk to you a minute?"

It was ten thirty in the morning, and though Ben answered the door dressed, it was clear he had fallen asleep in his clothes from the night before. He looked very crumpled and weary.

As Ben stepped back for James, he tried to force himself to wake up, but he couldn't. He felt hung over from the drinks and the emotion of the night before. He supposed he had a headache, but at that point it was difficult to find any part of his body that didn't hurt, and inside he felt worse; inside he felt torn apart.

"You look pretty rough," James said. "Would it be better if I came back later?"

Ben shook his head and flopped onto the couch. He couldn't get any words out at the moment; he wasn't even curious why James had come. He felt only empty and lost.

James looked around at the living room; dirty ashtrays and liquor glasses covered the coffee table; cushions were strewn on the floor. "Where is everyone?" he asked, picking up a cushion and tossing it back onto a chair.

Ben answered vaguely. "Day off, I guess. Yeah, Sunday. Day off."

James sat in a chair and watched his father. He had expected to be greeted with anger or at least coldness. He knew in his father's eyes he deserved it, and was surprised and confused by this reaction. He suspected it was more than a hangover. Through the years he'd seen his father nursing many hangovers, but it had never been like this.

It was Ben who spoke first. His voice was very weak and beyond sadness. "I don't know why you came here, James. I don't know that I want to. But if you came to gloat, go right ahead. I just don't care anymore."

"I didn't come for that."

"It doesn't matter."

Ben slumped forward, rubbing his forehead with his hands. Finally he said softly, "You were right and I was wrong. I suppose you've heard about Tom leaving. I was banking on Anti-Cor." He laughed bitterly. "Yeah, banking on it. Without it I've probably lost. I've lost my company, my family, and the worst part is, I've even lost myself. Well, the hell with it. To hell with all of it. I just don't give a damn anymore."

Ben stood and began to move aimlessly around the room. "I'll fight, of course. I suppose for no better reason than I don't know what else to do. But in the end, I'll lose."

"Listen to me, Dad. I didn't come here for this." James hesitated, and when he finally did continue, he sounded pushed too far. "Look, I wanted to tell you that I'll back you. I thought I was such a big man, so tough, so independent. But I couldn't go through with it. You're my father. Nothing can change that. No, that's not what I mean. I don't *want* to change it. With all the anger and bitterness and everything, I love you. I always will. I guess it took a complete breach to make me see it."

A tremor went through Ben. "Oh, God," he whispered. It was barely audible, no more than a sigh. But other than that he was silent, stonelike; it was as if he hadn't heard James at all.

James watched his father, trying to understand what he was feeling, but he had never been able to read his father's thoughts, remained a stranger to him, as always.

James turned away. What he had hoped for, he didn't know, but whatever it was, he was once again disappointed. And then after a while he turned back, and though Ben hadn't moved, James was stunned to discover there were tears in his eyes.

Finally Ben shook his head. "No, James, don't do it. Don't back me. Even with your vote I'll probably lose. Take my advice, do what you planned. It's what's best for you."

"That depends on what you think of as being best for me."

But Ben wasn't listening. "No, please, do as I say. It's not that I don't appreciate this." He paused and his voice cracked. "I don't suppose I even have the right to expect you to understand what this means to me. But I also know what it'll mean to you."

James laughed. "What? Dyer won't like me anymore? I won't have a job at Midwestern? What exactly will it mean? On the other hand, if I desert you now, what will it say about me?"

Ben watched James for a moment, then quickly turned away, ashamed. "Don't you understand? There's a very good chance I won't win."

"You gave me a first-rate education, Dad. I can add."

Ben said softly, "I don't get you."

"Nope. You never did. The sad thing is, neither did I. At least till now. I guess part of the problem is that we both look for the worst in people. We're always wary for the angle, even in ourselves. We judge harshly, then get angry at each other when we're judged in the same way. It's a strange and terrible family we've made. But it's a family nonetheless. And we're all we've got."

James waited for his father to answer, but he didn't. He just stood in the center of the room, looking away in silence, and James wondered anew if this was because of too much emotion or too little.

He sighed. "Look, Dad, I know I've been a lousy son. And I won't lie: There's every likelihood I'll remain so. But that's the way it is, and I guess you're going to have to take me as I am. And you haven't been so hot as a father either. But I'm going to have to put up with that too. Because we're all we've got. And that's enough. It has to be."

Ben hadn't moved, but his eyes were still filled with tears, and he could feel himself trembling. More than anything he wanted to take James in his arms and hold him. In truth, he wanted to be held. But the two men had never touched one another since James was very young; even then it had been only rarely, and he couldn't break through their self-imposed isolation.

James too seemed unsure what to do, then in order to do something, he took out a cigarette and lit it. He looked up at his father, remembering how ill he was. "I'm sorry. Is my smoke bothering you?"

Ben shook his head; his face looked stricken. Once again James saw how upset he was and how hard he was trying to keep himself together.

Ben's voice was weak. "Would you mind if I had a drink? Maybe hair of the dog will help."

"Coffee would be better. Want me to make some?"

Neither of the two men could look at one another; neither knew what to say.

"Yeah, coffee would be great," Ben answered quietly. He sat back down on the couch, thinking, then suddenly he asked, "You still like baseball? There's a Reds game on at noon."

James was in the kitchen, searching the cupboards for a coffeepot. "We could order up some sandwiches from Norman's and watch it."

Ben smiled. "Great. It'll be like old times."

"Yeah, just like old times," James repeated, though he knew there had never been old times, and only now there was a chance that they might begin to build them.

FORTY-FIVE

Dyer had taken the early-morning shuttle to Washington, and all during the plane ride and later in the rented car his mind had revolved quickly, but his resolve hadn't wavered. He had begun to believe that even without Hamayoshi's pressure, he would have made the same choice. It was him against Ben now. He could bring Ben down. There was the ammunition, and he knew exactly how to use it. He supposed it had always been that way, as if his whole life had been leading him to this moment, only now he knew it.

It was close to noon when Dyer pulled up in front of the Justice Department. He found a parking space several blocks away, then quickly got out of the car and walked back to the building. He hesitated for a moment at the steps leading up to it then took them rapidly, in twos, like a child. And all the while his mind was filled with the intense excitement of bringing everything crashing around him.

It was only when he reached the top of the stairs that he paused and looked out at the street. It was a cold day in Washington; icy breezes surprised the cherry blossoms, showering them to the ground. Dyer's breath poured in a white cloud from his mouth, and he could feel his skin shrinking from the cold; it felt sensitive and tight.

Dyer turned back to the building, but still he stayed where he was, staring sightlessly into the sterile corridors beyond the doors. Suddenly memories, sharp and vivid, surprised his mind, piling on top of one another in no apparent shape or order. The strongest were of his father, how he had turned gray and wasted, how he had fallen victim to fits of crying and depression. He could see his mother, sullen, stolid, growing even more silent as things became worse. And he remembered himself, lying in bed in the darkness, understanding little but sensing everything. Above all he remembered the feeling that his father had brought shame on the family, and that behind it there was an even greater shame, one his family would not outlive.

The shame was clear now, of course. Though he'd repressed the knowledge, he supposed it was something he'd always known. He'd felt it in his genes, in every cell of his body, and though he'd rebelled against the thought, he couldn't escape it.

Several minutes passed, but still Dyer stayed, staring into the building, his jacket flapping in the chill wind. And slowly as he stood there, his resolve began to waver, and what had seemed clear only a few minutes before now became confused. He remembered his father just before he died, his crazy anxiety attacks, his bouts of weeping. He hardly seemed a man worth plotting an act of revenge for; he hardly seemed capable of ruling Dyer's life. He had simply been a man, weak and kind, caring and scared and a million other things, but only a man. Just as Ben was; just as he himself was. Did a man have the right to reach beyond the grave?

Though Dyer didn't know if Evan's note had truly been a plea for vengeance, now he saw that the decision to implement it rested solely with him. It was for him to decide what this act would do to his life, what betraying the family would mean to him. Up until then he'd only been reacting off of people: Evan, Ben, his grandmother. Never before had he so clearly wondered what would it mean to him.

And that was the point. While Evan had raised him and for that Dyer owed him a gread deal, he did not owe him his soul. That was Dyer's own.

He could destroy Ben and with him Midwestern Steel. But by destroying Midwestern, he would take down the only thing the Savages had ever done that meant anything. It was what his family had created in life, a feeble monument perhaps, but a monument nonetheless. Destroy Midwestern and he would in that one gesture make purposeless his grandmother's lonely vigil on the hill, his grandfather's frightened but determined flight to America, his own mother's stand against her father and all her pain of childbirth. Nothing that had been done would have any meaning. The long years of work Evan and Ben had put in to build Midwestern, the plans, the dreams, the hopes they had shared. None of it would exist anymore. Could he take responsibility for that?

It was as if Dyer was awakening from a dream. Already he had turned away from the doors and was looking back down the stairs. He could not go in. It surprised him he'd ever thought he could.

Family Passions

Suddenly Dyer felt the cold, and he quickly descended the stairs, holding his jacket tightly closed against the wind. He knew now that he would fight Ben, using all his youth and energy and power to try to bring him down. It would be a fight to the finish, and Dyer had every reason to believe he would win it. But he would fight Ben in the right way; he would not destroy Midwestern in the process. He no longer could go that far. The question of course was what Hamayoshi would do now. His threat still remained; he could still expose Dyer. But by doing that he would also be exposing himself and his consortium. After that, even Hamayoshi had admitted, the consortium could not continue with plans to take over Midwestern. All Hamayoshi would be gaining if he went ahead was bringing them both down for nothing. Hamayoshi's whole plan hinged on Dyer caring more about himself and his future than anything else, and ironically, now that he no longer did, there was a very good chance he would be safe.

Not that Hamayoshi would take this lying down. Dyer expected he would threaten him. He knew he was running the risk that out of anger Hamayoshi might perform the kamikaze act he'd promised and expose what Dyer had said, both to his family and Midwestern Steel. Dyer thought about this but came to no conclusion. In the end he didn't know what Hamayoshi would do. Only one thing was clear, and that was that he would at least understand; Dyer couldn't destroy what his ancestors had built.

Dyer climbed back into the car and started it up. He felt tired, almost spent, but also he felt relieved. He smiled to himself as he swung the car into traffic and promised himself a drink as soon as he got to the airport, not because he needed one, but because he deserved one. It had been a hell of a day.

FORTY-SIX

Though Elizabeth was dressed and seated in a chair when Ben came in, he could see how ill she was. Her skin was gray and lifeless; there was a dullness to her eyes, as if there were no depth or sparkle to them, and he knew in that moment, this was only a temporary respite. From the way that she greeted him, he could see she knew it too.

Elizabeth's eyes were filled with tears. Ben had never seen his mother cry, and it touched him even more than her brittle thinness and wasted color. He leaned to her, gathering her gently in his arms, holding her carefully, for she felt as delicate as a dried flower, and he was worried she might break in his arms.

"Oh, God," she murmured, putting her head on his shoulder. "Oh, God, to have spared you."

Her body trembled from emotion, and Ben was terrified holding her; it was like cradling a dying bird. He could feel himself begin to cry and he fought against it; that would only make them both even more frightened.

Ben loosened his hold, though he didn't move away. His mother was looking at him sadly, but her eyes no longer looked so flat and lifeless; they were glinting with tears and also the joy of seeing him. At that moment she looked very much as she had.

She sniffled several times, then slowly became more composed. She smiled ironically. "Fooled me you did that time, Ben Savage. For I believed in my heart you were gone."

Ben tried to smile back, but it was a rueful smile and his voice was very hushed. "Look who's talking."

She sighed. "Aye. Maybe. That remains to be seen."

Ben tried to ignore the sadness in her voice. "Well, you always said I was full of surprises."

"But never of the pleasant variety."

"And this one is pleasant?"

"Passably, as if you don't know. Though cruel it was of you to scare me like that."

"I'll try not to do it again."

"Please." Elizabeth took the sight of him in, greedily running her eyes over his tall strong body. Once again she began to cry, but almost immediately she stopped herself. This was no time for tears.

"Well, sit you down, Ben. No need there is to prove how well you are, for already I have seen it with a mother's eyes."

Ben pulled a chair close to Elizabeth, and she reached her arm out to him. It seemed very fragile, so unlike the broad, strong, mannish arms of the woman he remembered. Only her hands remained untouched; they were still muscular and wrinkled with a rough, weathered skin. They were good hands; they were his hands.

Elizabeth put her hand in his, then quickly withdrew it, for it was quivering slightly, like a dying leaf in the wind, and she didn't want him to notice.

She said quickly, "Tell me then, all that has passed."

"Right now I'm more concerned about how you are."

"No need there is to discuss it, for living it has been quite enough for me."

Ben refused to be put off. "Please. I want to know how you feel."

"Is it lies you've come for, Ben Savage?"

"No, the truth. That's all I've always wanted."

Elizabeth raised her eyebrows. "Not quite accurate is that. But never mind. I feel as tired and used up as a dish towel after three days in the mangle. Older than Moses and as weak as an infant. Other than that, as well as can be expected." Then catching the look of concern on her son's face, she stopped. "Better than that do I feel, Ben. Though not as before. And anyway, there is a wariness about it all, for I fear it will not last. But please let's not speak of illness any longer, either mine or yours. Thankful I am that we have this moment together. For how many times did I think during those long months just past that I would give anything I owned to have you sitting here beside me as you are? And lo, I do."

She grew suddenly tense, and her eyes probed his. "Have you eaten anything, Ben?"

He smiled. "I had breakfast. I'm not hungry."

"Oh, aye? I know your breakfast, a glass of orange juice and a gallon of coffee. All of you young 'uns are the same. Know you well, a body cannot work properly without its fuel." She waved her finger at him. "Now listen carefully. I'll not have this in my house. Go directly to the door and call down for something substantial."

"Really, Mother, I'm not—"

"Do not contradict me. Go right this minute. Quick sharp!"

Ben shook his head, smiling, then got up and went to the door. He called down, "Could somebody bring me some coffee?"

"And toast!" Elizabeth growled.

"And toast," Ben added.

When he turned back, Elizabeth looked satisfied.

"Quite the lady I've become, as you can see. I have whole troops of staff at my beck and call." A sigh shook her frail body and her eyes looked very sad.

Ben sat down next to Elizabeth, but he was avoiding her eyes. He understood exactly how she felt about other people doing things for her, and he didn't want to think about all it implied.

They sat in silence for a long while, until the coffee and toast had come. After she had watched him eating it for some time, she asked softly, "What are we to do, Ben?"

"About what?"

"About Midwestern, of course. Know you any other subject that occupies my mind as it does?"

"I don't think we have to discuss that right now."

"When if not now? Six feet under will be a far less pleasant spot to carry on this discussion."

"Stop it, Mother."

"Aye. If only I could. But control over death is something I don't have. And since we've been allowed this brief moment together with so much on our minds, then speak of it we must."

Ben nodded, but said nothing, and Elizabeth could read the fear in his face, and see how much he wanted to spare her from all that had passed.

Finally she said, "Dyer came to me yesterday."

Ben was surprised. "He was here yesterday?"

"Straight from Washington, D.C., he came, and then over to me. He sat by my bed, talking and talking, though he was not aware I understood every word. And perhaps it was this that made me as I am today. Perhaps it was he who woke me from my dream."

She paused, looking at Ben pensively. "Ben, he went to the Justice Department to report you." She saw him startle and added quickly, "But he did not go in."

It took a long while for Ben to speak. "Are you sure he didn't?"

Family Passions 419

"Aye. This he told me as he sat by my bed, and he was not in the mood to lie. Nor did he know I could hear him, so he told me all." She gripped Ben's arm. "Oh, Ben. Terrible things he confessed. He told me he had made a deal."

"What kind of a deal?"

"With the Japanese." She sighed, then forced herself to continue. "Also he told me he knows he's your son."

Ben looked away, but she clutched tightly to his arm. "Think you I didn't suspect? Nor that Angela could resist telling me? No, a surprise it was not. Not even to him. Though at first it caused him to hate you even more. But understanding came quickly upon it, for always the hatred was partially envy, and finally he realized all that he'd inherited was well and truly his."

"James is my son."

"Both of them are."

"Come on, Mother. You know you don't trust Dyer. You yourself have doubts about him."

"The truth that is. I will not deny it. Still, Dyer did not report you, and there is something in that."

Ben didn't seem convinced. "If you think for a minute that Dyer isn't going to oppose me at the stockholders' meeting, you're crazy."

Elizabeth answered impatiently. "You've not been listening. Never did I say he will not oppose you. That he will do with all of his strength. But now he will do it the right way."

"He won't win."

"No guarantees there are who will remain."

"James came and promised to back me."

"For that I am glad, nor does it surprise me. But that is only part of the tale. Dyer is young and strong. Think you truly this will pass unnoticed by the rest?"

Ben flushed angrily. "I'm not an old man."

Elizabeth watched the tension in his face grow. "Nor are you young either."

"I can win."

"Can you, then? How? By being corrupt. Know you well that Dyer told me everything. Why it was that he went to the Justice Department. What you and that senator were planning. No, nothing did he spare me, thinking I could not understand. It was as if he were speaking to himself with me as mediator. But an understanding there was of all that he said. Aye, and all the things unsaid too."

Ben stood abruptly and walked away. He didn't look at his

mother; he couldn't look at her. Then finally he said softly, "I had no other choice. What did you want me to do? Give up Midwestern?"

"If necessary."

Ben began pacing. Tension was rushing through his body, and he needed to move to relieve it. "Come on, Mother. I can't believe you mean that. You don't know what I came back to find."

"I was here."

"Dyer was trying to sell the company out from under us all. I had to do something."

"Not that."

"Then what? What would you have done? Just given in?"

"No, nor that. I would have fought him with everything in me. Except my soul."

"And if you had lost?"

"I would have let him have Midwestern and saved myself."

Ben was moving quickly around the room, fighting the anger. "No. I don't believe that. Not after all that talk about the dream. Jesus, for years that's all we ever heard, the dream, the dream. What was the dream about, if it wasn't Midwestern?"

Elizabeth was glaring at the wall. "And think you I meant this by the dream?"

Ben stopped and looked at his mother evenly. "Listen, Mother, once you buy in, you buy in all the way. If you count Midwestern as the most important thing in your life, then you have to be prepared to defend it at all costs."

Elizabeth turned to him. She looked very tired and old. "Then perhaps the fault was in the dream." She paused for a moment, and when she began to speak again, her voice was weak. "Hard it is to remember how I felt before I lay dying. Aye, for then perhaps I might have counseled otherwise. All I know is how I feel now. And now the world looks different to me, though every detail of it remains the same. So many questions go through my mind. New questions or at least newly put. And I do not know the answers to these questions, only I know the asking."

She put her hand out to Ben. Her eyes were pleading. "Sit you down, son. Please. For by moving around the room as you are, there is the fear at every moment you will leave."

Ben turned and went back to his seat. Elizabeth took his hand in hers and held it for a long while, feeling his warmth moving through her body. Then she sighed. "Never have I felt old before, Ben. Always I've felt as if I were pretending." She broke off for a moment. "Never have I been so unsure of life. Never has it seemed so confusing."

She looked at Ben with very frightened eyes. "I do not know what it all means, and there is the truth. Always I thought I understood. I was able to plan and hope and dream and know so clearly that what I believed in was right. But last night as I lay in the darkness, I thought of the past. Over and over the memories came, with more detail on each repetition but also with more confusion. Until finally I realized I did not know what had happened all those years ago. Only I knew what I wished. Again I saw that time on the docks, but this time differently. I kept going through the memory, sifting it for truth, until I did not know what was real. Was it I who talked to your da of the dream, or he to me, or did it all come to me later? Nor could I even be sure there had been a great white ship, or if I'd seen it in a dream. I lay there, trying to recall the truth, and telling myself no difference did it make, for it was real enough in my mind. But, Ben, a difference it does make. Those details are important. For otherwise there is no such thing as truth, but millions of truths, one for every person walking the earth and many for each of them too. And that is chaos."

She stopped, and there was fear in her eyes, as if she could see the chaos closing all around her. But then forcing herself back to calmness, she continued slowly. "And much confused did I fall asleep, and sick at heart. For never had the question 'What does it all mean?' have no answer. But last night it seemed like that. And when I awoke, still the question was there, and my brain was whirling, for never was it made for such thoughts. Only simple and crude it is, fashioned by a brutal hand, able to grasp hold of an idea and stick like a bulldog, but little more. And now crumbling were the ideas even as I held them, and at that I did not know what to do.

"And then it was that I saw plainly before me what was there all along. The dream cannot live in steel structures or names or empty ideals, but only in people. And I feared I'd wronged those I loved most by my sureness of what was right. Think you I never realized what coming to America might do to your father? Well, I did think of it. But nothing there was that could stop me, not even that. Yet only now have I seen the wickedness in it. And only now do I wonder: What have we become that is so great and noble, that I drove both myself and others to the sea?"

She tried to stand but found that she couldn't. Feebly she reached out her hand. "My son, perhaps the fault lay in the dream."

"I never thought I'd hear you say that, Mother."

"I never thought I'd die before."

Ben stood up, walked to Elizabeth, and took her broad hand in his. He was fighting to understand. "What are you asking me to do?"

"Their turn it is, Ben. It is for us to give it to them."

Ben was stunned. "You're asking me to step down in favor of Dyer?"

"In favor of Dyer and James."

"Never."

"Just think about it."

"There's nothing to think about. Dyer and James would ruin Midwestern in less than a week."

"This you cannot guess. Perhaps they will grow if given the soil."

Ben shook his head. "It's too much of a risk."

"The greater risk it is for your soul."

Ben stroked her hand. He no longer felt angry; he felt very lonely. "Mother, look, I know what I'm doing is wrong, but it will only be for a short while. That's all I need. After that everything will be as it was."

"Will it?"

Ben answered with conviction. "Yes. Of course it will."

"No, Ben. So sure of this you cannot be. For often I have seen fruit which has rotted starts with a blemish so small that in the beginning it is impossible to see. Yet at that very moment, the heart is being eaten alive."

"That's still no reason to chop down the whole tree."

Ben took his mother's face in his hand and tilted it up to him. "Look at me, Mother. Do you see an evil man?"

Elizabeth's eyes filled with tears. "No, Ben, of course I do not."

"Then understand: I cannot give up Midwestern just like that. I can't tear it up by its roots and leave it to die."

Elizabeth thought about this for a while, then patted his hand lovingly. "Aye, son. Aye. Tired I am and old and sick of this world. So unsure I am which course is right. Perhaps the truth under it all is everything has its season. And an old woman's wisdom is a young man's chains."

Yet she continued to look disturbed, and after a moment she added, "Still I must ask you to think of what I said. Understand clearly the choices and pick your path wisely. But know in your heart, whichever you chose, I will always back you."

FORTY-SEVEN

Midwestern Steel's annual stockholders' meeting was always held in the ballroom of the Park Lane Hotel. It was an immense room with ornate molding, imitation frescoes, phony gilt-framed mirrors and rather good chandeliers, Ohio's idea of Louis XIV. The floor was of highly polished wood, laid at a time when labor was plentiful, supplies cheap, and there was still a reverence for the past. The room had a magnificence of a sort, and for that reason Ben chose to hold their first meeting there. He saw it as a kind of revenge against Nicholas Healey and Leon Wittiker and all of their class who used it for their parties. After that it became something of a tradition.

There were a great many traditions during the Midwestern stockholders' meeting. There was always a short, informal cocktail hour before it started, held in an adjacent room. There were always the buttons passed out by two Midwestern secretaries sitting behind a long green table at the entrance. There were always the bound annual reports, though quickly leather covers gave way to plastic.

Inside the ballroom, in front of the two ranks of folding chairs, a long table was set up for the board of directors. At each place was a pad of paper, sharpened pencils, bound annual reports—these still in leather—and a water glass. Several microphones were placed along the table and throughout the room.

Even the order of entering had become something of a tradition, with several of the junior executives arriving first, passing among the stockholders during their drinking hour. James, as the closest the Savages had to an outside man, was the first member of the family who came, and he would talk to the stockholders, jollying the women, nodding with the businessmen.

Fifteen minutes before the meeting was due to begin, the ballroom doors would be thrown open, and everyone would drift toward the meeting. It was only then that the rest of the family would arrive.

Last was always Ben, who would stride in exactly on time, just before the double doors were closed.

The meeting would be kicked off with a short welcoming speech by James, then a report from Tom, followed by one from Dyer, and finally a longer, tougher one from Ben. There would be some voting, then everyone would go home, and the cleaning staff would move in, trashing the papers and discarded buttons, picking cigar butts out of the sand.

It was the same every year, reassuring to some, boring to others. Only Ben seemed to regard each meeting afresh, as if he had no idea what was coming next, glancing around the ballroom at the upturned faces eagerly, with profound excitement.

James lit a cigarette, took a deep breath, then walked into the room of stockholders for the thirteenth time in his life. He thought about the number thirteen for a moment, then smiled at himself; he wasn't sure which eventuality was the unlucky one; they all seemed equally grim.

Martin Gordon, president of the Washington Savings and Loan, was talking to Mason Josephs, and it was with them that James started. He grabbed a glass of champagne, though he wouldn't be drinking it, and joined in the conversation. James always felt out of place with the cigar-smoking, handkerchief-in-the-pocket group, and while he did his best not to show it, he suspected that they knew. Nevertheless, he laughed and kidded with the men, talking about golf scores and business. He knew how to play the game.

A half hour later, the double doors to the ballroom were opened and several of the old ladies rushed in. Fussily they took seats close to the front, commenting loudly that there ought to be a nonsmoking section, as they placed their hangbags in the precise spot where everyone would trip over them.

James walked into the ballroom, maneuvering around the handbags, speaking to several of the old ladies, smiling and laughing with the men, but his eyes were on the double doors, as he waited anxiously for the rest of the family. As soon as one other member entered, he could excuse himself and move to the front table, and though he was hardly looking forward to the meeting ahead, at least it would mean that he was one step closer to getting it over with. So he watched the doors, chattering absentmindedly, and the minute he spotted Pauline, he moved to the front.

Pauline was wearing a navy suit that was nicely tailored but not overly fashionable. As always, she seemed to be playing a role, but

Family Passions

this one was as a member of the board, and she was playing it well. Pauline took her place at the table, gracefully lacing her fingers in front of her, and gazed out at the gathering crowd with a concentrated expression.

But when James kissed her on the cheek, he noticed her eyes were sparkling with malicious pleasure. "Well, won't this be fun?" she said happily.

James didn't smile. "I can hardly wait."

"Now, James, you have to see it in the proper light. Can't you just feel the excitement? We're Midland's greatest theatrical company. And we're opening in a new production, entitled 'Get the President.' "

"Subtitled 'Before He Gets You.' "

Pauline shook her head. "Naw, I don't think that'll play. Ben's not about to get anybody."

"We'll see."

Pauline was surprised. "Don't you think Dyer is going to win?"

"Let me put it this way. No matter what happens, no one is going to win."

Pauline clapped her hands together with delight. "How very pleasant. I hadn't thought about it that way. But I like it. Yes, the last act could be positively spellbinding, Shakespearean really."

James looked away. He didn't feel much like laughing. Oddly he was beginning to realize how much he cared about the outcome. Even Dyer's losing seemed to mean something to him. He truly believed no one could win.

Pauline was watching him. "Good Lord, don't tell me you're losing your sense of humor! You were the only one I could rely on to care as little as I."

"You do realize, this little final act, as you call it, could end with all of us losing control of Midwestern Steel?"

She mugged. "I know. Isn't it too simply dreadful? I haven't had a wink of sleep over it."

It was at that minute, that Boris entered the room, quietly, almost stealthfully, and he took a seat in the back. Pauline spotted him immediately and watched James, trying to see if he had noticed. From the look on his face, she gathered that he had.

"Well, well, well. And to what do we owe this unexpected pleasure?" she asked.

"I don't know." James was turned away from Pauline, but she could tell he was upset.

"Is the wedding off, then?"

"Cute, Pauline."

"Oh, God, a divorce in the family. How shocking."

James was still turned away. "Look, if you have to know, and I'm sure you do, I stopped seeing Boris last week. He was manipulating me and the company. No big surprise, I guess. Not even to me. It just took a lot of thinking to admit it."

"Then why is he here?"

James shook his head. "He no longer works for Midwestern. I asked Dad to fire him."

"And did he?"

"So far as I know, he did." He thought. "Yes, I'm sure he did."

"Well, maybe he's one of our shareholders."

James nodded slowly. "Or maybe he's *representing* one of our shareholders."

Pauline was about to ask what he meant, but she looked out at the quickly gathering crowd and noticed Dylan entering. Dylan had not come to a stockholders' meeting in twenty years, and she glanced shyly around the room as if frightened of being noticed. Then she seemed to pull herself together, and she walked over to the table.

Pauline leaned to James. "Oh, goody! Even the extras are putting in an appearance. This is fun!"

Pauline rose and kissed Dylan on both cheeks. "Darling, I had no idea you'd be here."

Dylan was looking at James. "Neither did I."

"James and I were just discussing how upsetting all of this is."

"I'm sure you were."

Dylan took James's hand and held it tightly for a moment. She whispered, "Your grandmother's on her way up. She insisted on coming."

James looked worried. "In her condition? That can't be wise."

"I tried telling her."

James laughed sadly. "I can just imagine. It's like telling a baby not to be born."

Elizabeth entered in a wheelchair pushed by one of her nurses. Even from far away James could see her face was caked with makeup, badly applied. Obviously she was trying to hide how ill she was, but the clownish makeup only seemed to emphasize it. It was terrible to watch her as she struggled for her usual ironic smile, trying to pretend that she wasn't frightened for herself as well as her family. And yet James found there was something wonderful about it too.

She was pushed to the table, and Pauline went over and kissed her cheek. James followed, but when he stooped and kissed her, her skin was cold and smooth like marble, and he hated the feel of it under his lips.

"How are you, Grandma?" he asked.

She waved the question away with her hand. "Tom it was who brought me. He came after all." She sounded relieved.

"Even Mother's here."

"Aye, I know." She looked at James. "Scared I am, James, for I have presentiments."

"Yeah," he answered softly. "I'm scared too."

Elizabeth seemed surprised. "Are you, then? That at least is a good sign, for when there is caring enough for fear, there is also enough for hope."

She gazed at James fondly, then patted his hand, but a moment later she was glancing at her wristwatch nervously. "Where are Dyer and Ben?"

Pauline leaned to them. "They're probably still out sharpening their claws on a tree."

Tom held Angela's arm as they came through the double doors. Angela paused briefly, looking around the room, and though her tight little face was stern, almost cold, there was a gleam of triumph in her eyes. Tom took her over to the table and waited until she had paid her respects to Elizabeth. Then after making sure she was comfortably seated, he walked to his seat next to James.

James extended his hand. "I'm glad you're here."

"So am I," Tom answered. He shook hands with James, but his eyes were on the double doors, and it was clear he was waiting only for Ben.

James looked out into the room. The stockholders were all seated, talking to one another. The sound of two hundred voices mixed and grew louder. Only the old ladies sat silently, hands folded on their laps, like good little children waiting for the teacher.

Dyer stopped at the doors and gazed at the group of people in the room. He could see his family at the front table and was pleased that no one had spotted him yet. It was an exciting feeling, standing at the entrance, an outsider in a scene where soon he would be playing a leading role. He wondered if any of Hamayoshi's men were there; he supposed someone would have to vote the stock. Then he noticed Boris sitting in the back of the room, and it took only a second for him to understand. Again he reassured himself that there was nothing Hamayoshi could do. Certainly he could bring Dyer down, but in the end, nothing would be gained by it. It would be a risk with no possible gain, and though Hamayoshi might be a man who liked to gamble, he wouldn't throw both the stakes and the cards away for nothing. Still, Dyer didn't completely believe that. It was a question without answer, until later, and by then it would be too late.

Elizabeth caught sight of Dyer, just as he decided to enter. He walked briskly, surely, though he was carrying a large stack of papers under his arm and it must have been awkward. He was neither smiling nor frowning; his face was almost totally blank. Elizabeth could tell he was prepared for a fight, and wondered how much he was willing to risk to win. She tried to remember that he'd turned back from the Justice Department, but she was also aware that was when he'd thought he would win. What would he do if he saw he was going to lose?

Dyer leaned to her and kissed her on the cheek. She took his hand in hers and gazed into his eyes. But she didn't understand what she saw there; she never had.

Dyer took his seat and began going through the papers he'd brought in, shuffling them back and forth efficiently, keeping his eyes on the sheets as they fell under his hands. Elizabeth watched him intently. He wasn't really looking at what he was doing; his businesslike manner was covering something.

Time passed. James glanced at his watch anxiously, and he could see that several of the others were doing the same. He tried to catch Dyer's eye to ask him where Ben was, but Dyer was looking at what he was doing, seemingly unaware that Ben was late.

Elizabeth too was watching Dyer, and it was to her that James addressed his silent question. Elizabeth understood and shrugged her shoulders. Her eyes were frightened.

Only Pauline seemed to be smiling. She leaned toward James. "So where's the big cheese?"

James shrugged, and this time Dyer did look up. He seemed very nervous now. There was a film of perspiration on his face. He glanced at his watch and muttered under his breath, "Jesus Christ!"

Angela tapped her son's arm and said too loudly, "Do you think something's happened to him?"

Pauline overheard. "Goodness, I hope not. What a disappointment that would be."

"Silence, child!" Elizabeth's voice was sharp, but her eyes were on the door, and even she didn't seem to care what Pauline was saying. She was worried for Ben.

Dyer looked back down at his papers, but now it was clear he was aware of the doors and the fact that Ben had not walked through them.

Then once again he glanced at his watch, and this time he leaned across Ben's empty chair and whispered to James, "He's over five minutes late, for Christ sake."

James whispered back. "What should we do? Should we start without him?"

"Shit, I don't know."

They both looked out at the stockholders. Several of them were trying to catch their eyes. Mason Josephs was even gesturing to them.

James leaned back to Dyer. "Maybe we'd better begin and pray he slips in before the reports." He paused and then continued softly, "God, I hope nothing happened to him."

Dyer nodded and said soberly, "Me too. I want to beat the pants off of him, but I don't want something to be really wrong." He thought about this. "Funny, isn't it?"

"Yeah, it is strange. The whole damn world is strange. I'll tell you one thing, this business of growing up isn't like I thought it would be."

Dyer agreed. "Yep. I sure didn't expect it to be so complicated."

James laughed. "That's odd. And I didn't expect it to be so simple."

The two men smiled at one another with understanding. Then James stood and walked to the microphone.

FORTY-EIGHT

Tally sat at the foot of the old man's bed, one eye on her patient, the other on her knitting. She dropped a stitch, swore silently, then picked it up. After a moment she laid her knitting down on her lap, but almost immediately her mind began to wander. She forced herself to stop. If only she could control her thoughts she'd be fine; if only she could make sure she didn't think.

Tally pulled back the curtain and looked out the window. It was late afternoon, and all up and down the streets of Maesteg, women were rushing their shopping home for tea. It was sunny and warm outside; the windowboxes were bright with daffodils and tulips, and there was the smell of lilacs in the air. Tally watched what was going on below with surprise. It was easy to forget spring when you were a nurse. Always you were moving from one darkened room to another, the smell of antiseptic and illness in the air. She shook off the bleak mood and picked up her knitting. No, it was definitely better when she didn't think.

The old man stirred and muttered a few words. Tally got up and moved to him quickly, but by the time she reached the bed, he was asleep again. The thing to do was numb yourself. If you didn't think about the past or the future, if you just plodded forward, slowly, mulelike, eventually the pain would recede; the emptiness would take over, and then you would be all right.

Tally sat down in her chair and picked up her knitting, allowing the rhythmic sameness of her movements to take her over. It was quiet; there was only the sound of her needles and, from farther off, a grandfather clock, ticking irrevocably. They were soothing sounds, and slowly the long emptiness enclosed her. It was only when she felt a tear moving down her cheek that she realized she was crying.

She heard the front door open downstairs and guessed it was the next-door neighbor coming to make them tea.

"Mrs. Kite," she called. "Is that you?"

Again the old man stirred, but it was only a movement in his sleep. Tally heard the old woman's footsteps in the house and called again. "Mrs. Kite, I'll have my tea in here, please!"

Tally waited patiently, counting stitches, consulting her pattern, then beginning to knit again. In a few minutes Mrs. Kite would bring in the tea, asking after the old man's health, making a few jokes to him though she knew he no longer could understand, then she'd sit with Tally, cheerfully talking about the weather or what she'd bought for dinner. After a while she'd leave. Finally the night nurse would come, and Tally would go back to her aunt's house, though it wasn't her aunt's house anymore. It was hers, and there would be dinner, then bed. And the next morning she'd wake up, hurrying to her patient and her knitting. Tally had received a letter from Mrs. Mided the week before, and from what Tally could gather, her life too was the same. On and on.

There was a knock on the bedroom door, and Tally put down her knitting with a sigh. "Not a moment too soon, Mrs. Kite," she said with relief. "I could use a cup of tea."

"It isn't Mrs. Kite."

It took a moment for Tally to understand. Then suddenly she stood, dropping her knitting. The yarn caught on her foot and everything pulled off the needles as she ran to the door. But Tally didn't notice; she was crying and laughing. Her auburn hair had pulled from her combs and spilled over her shoulders.

Ben took her into his arms and held her. He couldn't speak; all he could do was hold her closely, and inside he too could feel himself crying, though the tears were from joy and redemption.

MAX

BY HOWARD FAST

At twelve, he plunged into the raucous streets of New York's Lower East Side to support his mother and her five other children. At twenty, street-smart, driven to succeed, his dream of a Hollywood empire swept him from a nightmare world of easy sex and hard percentages to a fantasy world of dream merchants, tycoons—and bitter truths. $3.95

At your local bookstore or use this handy coupon for ordering:

Dell	DELL BOOKS MAX 16106-1 • $3.95 B010A
	P.O. BOX 1000, PINE BROOK, N.J. 07058-1000

Please send me the above title. I am enclosing $ _____ (please add 75c per copy to cover postage and handling). Send check or money order—no cash or C.O.D.'s. Please allow up to 8 weeks for shipment.

Mr./Mrs./Miss _____

Address _____

City _____ State/Zip _____